Also by William Gray

SHARES

William Gray

SIMON & SCHUSTER

New York   London   Toronto   Sydney   Tokyo   Singapore

SIMON & SCHUSTER
Rockefeller Center
1230 Avenue of the Americas
New York, NY 10020

SIMON & SCHUSTER and colophon are registered trademarks
of Simon & Schuster Inc.

Designed by Elina D. Nudelman

Manufactured in the United States of America

10 9 8 7 6 5 4 3 2 1

Library of Congress Cataloging-in-Publication Data
Gray, A. W. (Albert William)
        Shares / A.W. Gray
            p. cm.
            1. Phillips, Bino (Fictitious character)—Fiction. I. Title.
    PS3557.R2914S53 1996
        813'.54—dc20   95-9618 CIP
    ISBN 0-684-81096-4

ACKNOWLEDGMENTS

Folks contribute. If they don't, a writer's out in the cold.

Michael Korda and Chuck Adams edited this book. They cut, and then cut the cuts, and both reader and writer are better off for their efforts.

Dominick Abel's my agent, the guy responsible for selling my manuscripts. Without him no one would have seen my work save for my wife, kids, and four cocker spaniels.

Sergeant Benny Newsome of the California Highway Patrol gave me earthquake information. He was on duty that fateful day, and I don't envy him for it.

Officials of the Dallas Theater Center gave me a tour, and so did the staff at Hockaday School. While I made use of these tours in physical descriptions, fictional employees of the Theater Center, and of the fictional girls' school depicted herein, are by no means based on actual persons, living or dead.

As always, my beloved wife, Martha, kept my nose to the grindstone. Without her, I doubt I would have finished.

All of the above, and many others, enhanced the quality of the book. Any shortcomings you note are the author's fault and his alone.

For Gregory William Gray

Littlest Injun
Not the leastest by a longshot

Part I

PLANNING

"And when you saw these people, what were they doing?"

"Just standin' around at first. Then they drew in close together an' went to whisperin'."

"Could you hear what they were saying?"

"Oh, no, sir. They was bein' real quiet an' hush-hush about everything."

"Their manner was, they didn't want anyone to know what they were discussing?"

"I'd say so, sir. Wasn't nothin' about the way they were standin', or the way they were lookin' around, exactly. But I could tell them people was up to no good."

—from trial transcript,
State of Texas v. Gilbert Wayne Arrington
and Ronnie Louis Ward

1

"We've got, as I see it," Randolph Money said, "four shares. Here, I'll show you." He stood and leaned over the table, reaching to the unoccupied place setting for the silverware: a bread knife, a salad and a dinner fork, one spoon. "The guy doing it, that's one." He laid the knife in front of his plate with the blade pointing away from him, then paralleled the dinner fork six inches to the right of the knife. "And that's two," he said. "The second share, that's, what we'll call our holder. The guy keeping the merchandise. Then there's"—now lining up the spoon, a handbreadth more to the right—"the planner, that's me"—finally plunking down the salad fork—"and our outside connect. A deal I've made. Guy we've got to have."

Darla Bern poked lettuce and one piece of green pepper into her mouth, lifted her napkin from her bare thigh and patted her lips, then sipped ice water from a goblet. "Are you leaving me out?" She wore dark, purple-rimmed L.A. Eyeworks with the emblem etched into the right lens. "I'm no guy, in case you didn't notice."

"Figure of speech, babe," Money said, leaning back with his chin propped on his lightly clenched fist. "Anybody can see that." He was in his fifties, stomach hanging over his charcoal gray swimming trunks, matching shirt unbuttoned and draped around his hips.

"I'm not into feminism," Darla said. "I just want an understanding who we're talking about. The main problem I've got is with the first share. I thought we were talking two people doing it."

"At least you've been paying attention." Money raised one finger, making a point. "And why doesn't it surprise me that's the share you're interested in? Hold on." He reached over and relieved Basil Gershwin's place setting of its spoon.

Basil's mouth opened partway, revealing masticated ham. "How'm I going to eat my dessert?"

Money placed Basil's spoon alongside the knife, arranging the two utensils so that their handles touched. He sat back. "There. As I see it now, two people doing it." He had skinny white legs and wore leather sandals, one foot forward, the other under his chair and resting on its toes.

"You're putting them close together," Darla said, "to show it's still just one share, right?" A white bandanna held her shoulder-length auburn hair in place. A towel was draped around her shoulders, revealing taut bare midriff, a strip of purple bikini across her chest. Her voice was a husky Lauren Bacall alto, melting-pot accent straight from Southern Cal.

Money smiled. He had wide-gapped teeth with silver fillings. "That's the way it is. We're talking Share Number One as you. You get somebody else, babe, what you pay them is between the two of you, as I see it." Slightly nasal New York manner of rolling his syllables, wavy gray hair parted on the right, combed straight back from his forehead.

"I thought you said an even split," Basil Gershwin said. He stabbed the ham in place with his fork, sawed with his knife, then poked the severed bite into his mouth left-handed with the prongs pointing down.

"I did, but there are limits," Money said. "Everybody's got their own share to worry about. Like running a hot-dog stand or anything else. You take in a half million and blow six hundred thou, hey, don't come running to me about it. For my part I'm dealing with three people, you two plus the outside connect. Everybody's got the same share regardless. What you spend out of yours—well, hey." He spread his hands, palms up.

"I can't spend shit right now," Basil said. "I got no money." A white San Diego Marina cap squashed down his hair, tufts protruding over the tops of his ears. His baggy flowered bathing trunks were Fab Five style, down to his knees.

"We've talked about that," Money said. "I'm fronting you traveling money. Nobody but me in a bind up front, okay? It's just, once the profits are in, yours are yours and mine are mine. How we account for our money is our business. And turn that fork over."

Basil froze with a bite an inch from his mouth. "Huh?"

Money snatched Basil's fork, turned up the prongs with a hunk of ham impaled. He carefully placed the handle in Basil's right hand, curling the thumb and forefinger around, Miss Manners fashion. "That way," Money said.

Bushy eyebrows moved closer together. "The fuck you doing?" Basil was shirtless, curly hairs around meaty brown nipples. His arms were thick, as were his calves and ankles

Darla spread her fingers across her forehead, shading her eyes. She looked toward the pool, her expression like, Oh God.

Money said to Basil, "I'm not getting on you about your manners just for the hell of it."

"The fuck's wrong with the way I eat?" Basil looked at his fork, now with the handle balanced on his curled middle digit.

"What we don't want, what none of us want, is for anybody to remember us. It's a posh neighborhood where we're going to be operating, at least as uptown as this place." Money gestured around at waiters hustling to and fro from the poolside bar, at women in French-cut one-piece suits, men in boxer trunks and even one guy on a chaise longue wearing bikini briefs. The sign beyond the low brick wall read, "Newporter Inn Club." Visible on the horizon, catamaran and schooner sails puffed out in the Southern California breeze. A man wearing spotless white deck pants came out of the hotel, checked his watch, then went back inside. "What you want to do," Money said, "is dress and act so ɔu're part of the scenery. Your clothes are an easy knockoff, that nat. And believe me, you go to these places eating as if you're from Dogpatch, shoveling it in, these waiters will remember you. You've got to blend in."

"I can do all that if I have to," Basil said. "But this is just us."

"Meaning, we're not due any respect?" Money pointed a manicured finger toward Darla, who raised one foot up onto her chair, a tanned knee pointing up.

"You need to get in the habit," Money said. "This isn't any West L.A. down here, my friend. Newport Beach people notice a person, his eating habits. It'll be the same in Texas. How do you stand with the parole people?"

Basil laid down his fork and folded his arms. "Same as you, I guess. We got out the same day."

"Yes, but I've never had to report to anybody. Just mail in a form every month giving my whereabouts. Seems I remember you had to check in with a parole officer every week. If we're going to be traveling, you can't report to anybody. We don't need the parole officer out looking for you, as I see it."

"That not reporting, I figured that for a snitch deal. Guys that cooperated." Basil had a wide humped nose, broken several times. His nostrils flared.

Money thoughtfully took a bite of crisply fried calamari and chased it with a sip of Perrier. "Tell you what. Let's keep things in perspective and you off the defensive. Nobody's knocking you. And I'm certainly no informant, a lot of men, coast to coast, still working in the banking business can testify to that. But you've got no idea why you and I might be different as far as the Parole Board's concerned? I don't have any history of violence, reported to Pleasanton directly off the street to do my time. Same as our actress friend." Darla smiled acknowledgment and struck a

Jacqueline Onassis pose, the refined lady lunching poolside at the upscale hotel and yacht club.

"You, on the other hand," Money said to Basil, "graduated *up* to Pleasanton through the system. You did time where? Marion, Illinois, toughest joint in the country. Then on to Leavenworth, right? So you were a good boy in those places, and as a reward they let you finish your time in a camp. That's the difference. Let's face it, my friend. You are one violent guy. Which is exactly what we need with what we're planning to do here, as I see it. But gives you problems the rest of us don't have. Such as, how close are they watching you?"

"I don't report no more," Basil said. "Same as you. I mail in a form every month."

"Now, that's some progress. Your parole is finished when?"

Basil raised his fork to his mouth, prongs down, half the impaled bite hanging by a rind of fat. He paused, switched hands and turned the prongs up. Darla nodded approval. Basil looked proud of himself. "Two thousand eight," he said. "Done ten inside, been on the street six. Total of thirty years." He poked the ham in his mouth and chewed with his mouth closed, watching Darla from the corner of his eye.

"Fourteen more to go," Money said. "But they're not keeping tabs on you?"

"Nah. They don't know shit about what I'm doing." Basil peered at the lined-up silverware. "While we're on it, I got a question."

Money smiled board-of-directors fashion. "Of course. This is our last little get-together, we need to iron things out."

"You're saying four shares, right?"

Money watched him.

Basil frowned. "Well, that part's okay, but . . . I'm the holder guy, right?"

"Yeah, the one keeping the merchandise in cold storage. You've got a better name for it, let me have it."

"So how come," Basil said, "I need you to help me out?"

"We talked about that. You'd go nuts in isolation day and night. You need to go downtown, take in a movie or something. So I'll spell you with the baby-sitting."

"Yeah, okay. But that means I'm supposed to give you part of my money?"

"That goes without saying, babe. I mean, we're talking simple economics here. You use me, you pay me, as I see it. You want to use somebody else, as long as it's someone we can check out . . . hey, you'd have to pay them same as you would me. What, you want me to help you out for free?"

"So you're going to get one full share," Basil said, fingering the spoon, "and I got to pay you on top of that? Sounds like horseshit to me, pal."

"It would be the same if I had to get, say, Darla here, to help me with the planning. I'd have to split with her."

"Yeah, but you already got the fucking thing planned."

"Basil. Basil, Basil. Let's don't get bogged down in bullshit here, not at this meeting. We're here to discuss the big picture. The little things you and I will hash out in private. Keep focused on our overall goal, babes."

Darla blinked and leaned forward. "Which is what for us and what for you?"

"Same identical thing." Money smirked and waved a hand as if batting mosquitoes. "I just believe in being real. What, you want me to pretend everyone's some kind of team player? I'm not, you're not. This is a me-first world, babes.

"Look around you," Money said. "Right now, three days after New Year's, we're basking in eighty degrees. The forecast for the playoff game in Buffalo is something like four below, minus thirty windchill. That's where I come from, people freezing their asses off and pretending they like it. Where would you like to be the rest of your lives? Aside from one delectable piece of ass, I've left nothing in Buffalo, babes, and you think there's not plenty more of that in California? Now cut this personal crap. Hey, think six months ahead. You want to, cutes, you can produce your own picture and be a star. Basil wants, he can be king of the Eighth Street rummies, I care? The point is, after this we can do what we want. Now, if there's anything else that's important . . . nothing irrelevant, now."

Darla tossed her napkin onto her plate and pushed her half-eaten salad toward the center of the table. "I've got a little picky to talk about," she said. Basil pulled the remnants of her meal over alongside his own cured ham and scalloped potatoes.

Money intertwined his fingers behind his head. "We've already okayed the guy you're using, cutes. So what else is on your mind?"

She grimaced slightly at the expression "cutes." She removed her sunglasses and used one corner of her towel to clean the lenses. Darla's eyes were ice blue, lashes long, the barest trace of shadow on her lids. "It's about this fringe person." Her shoulders were the color of light rum.

Money's gaze roamed over the silverware. "Oh? The outside connect, right? Why am I not surprised you're wondering about that?"

"We don't know who this is or what they're supposed to be doing."

Money folded his arms. "Yeah, okay. I'll buy that."

"I mean, all this organizing and joint decisions you're talking don't seem to go both ways. I've been in this from the start, so how come we've got this new somebody-or-other involved?"

"You had a germ of an idea, babe," Money said, "that I've turned into a plan. Just because you happened to be in a coed prison with a guy doesn't mean you're inspired. I won't tell who the outside connect is, but I will tell you why we've got to have him. That's going to have to satisfy you, as I see it."

Darla looked at her lap. "It's still something I brought you."

"I'm not running that down. But in any organization there's got to be a leader, and certain things, for security reasons, only that guy can know about." Money pointed a finger. "And while we're talking whose idea was what, let's don't forget my connections in this, coincidental though they may be. So happens you had a thing in prison with a guy that's suddenly got something to do with people I know way off in Dallas, Texas. Small world, and thank the lucky stars for that."

"Still my original thought."

"So it was, cutes, I'll concede. If you're looking for someone to play one-up with you, you've got the wrong guy."

Basil swallowed a bite of potato. "How we know this fringe asshole ain't something you're making up, so's you can get another share?"

"You don't. You won't. Like everything else I do, I've studied this proposition from A to Z, which is the main reason I'm living in Newport Beach and you're up on Eighth Street with half the world's wino population."

Basil scowled and laid down his fork.

"If that hurts your feelings," Money said, "it does. Feelings don't matter in an organization. Now listen up. Anything like what we're planning, if the people go along and pay up, don't come dragging in the FBI, we're home free. Under those conditions any jackass can do a kidnapping, right?"

Darla and Basil exchanged a look.

"But suppose they do call in the feds," Money said. "What's the main problem with that?"

"They're going to arrest your ass," Basil said. "What are we, stupid?"

"That's a good question, babe. Come on, think. Why does it screw up the deal when the FBI comes in?"

"Because," Darla said, "you can't get the money delivered without them seeing whoever picks it up."

Money pointed a finger at her. "Now that's worth an 'A.' I've studied cases. Big one, down in Georgia and Florida, two people buried a girl in a box, gave her food and air to last a few days, had the money delivered out on a pier. Absolutely impossible for them to get the money without being seen, right? Once the girl's family called in the feds, the jig was up. That's what's going with our fringe guy. A fail-safe, so that even with the bloodhounds on the trail we can get paid. The odds are three to one that our people will call in the law, so we've got to get ready for the worst."

"How're you planning to do this?" Darla said. "Like, we're just supposed to trust you, right?"

Money showed a hard-nosed, my-way-or-the-highway look. "That's what you've got to do, babes. And I'm not just playing *I've Got a Secret* here. The entire operation depends on the outside connect being just my deal. I know who it is. Nobody else can."

Basil finished off the potatoes, pushed his plate away, and started in on the salad. "I better not find out the fringe guy is you, trying to fuck us out of more money."

Money blinked. "I don't know what you'd do about it if you did find that out. But you won't. It's a real guy."

"Who's just going to grab the money and sprout wings," Darla said. "Vanish or something?"

Money had a sip of Perrier and didn't answer.

"We're putting a lot on the line," she said, "not to know any more. They've done away with parole since we got out, you know. Beginning nineteen eighty-seven, you get twenty years federal you do it all. No more coed prisons, either. A girl could get randy."

"I've said all I'm going to about the outside connect," Money said. "Now. You two in, or you two out?"

Darla looked off. Basil chewed lettuce.

"That's better," Money said. "Anything else? We won't be meeting down here again."

Darla put on her sunglasses. "I'm not sure I go along with the bit about waiting till April."

Money scratched his chin. "No way can we get set up any sooner. You've got to move down there, get a place to live . . ."

"Which will take until the end of the month," she said.

"Besides which, cutes, there's the weather. Spring's nice in Texas. I'm never doing anything again where I'm freezing my ass. The rest of the winter's going to be a bitch. Springtime, that's when we're moving. So. We know all the dates and times, what each of us is charged with doing, right? Be sure on this. We won't have any more contact until the whistle blows. Darla, this guy you're using. He's not going to go nuts on us, right?"

Darla played with the purple strip between her breasts. "I can handle him."

"And the Theater Center guy down in Dallas? Come on, Darla, you're talking about trusting me, what about me trusting you? This is a guy I know nothing about."

"I've never met him either, but I've got ways to know about him. He's a man," Darla said.

"Which in your case should be enough said, right? So okay, I'm not worried about that particular guy, I've got all the confidence in you. It's another male person I'm concerned with."

Darla looked at him.

"It's delicate, babe," Money said.

Darla raised a hand like, So what? "You're talking about Frank."

"Painful as it may be to you, we've got to talk about Frank."

"So what's to talk about? He's another guy."

Basil continued to eat, his gaze alternating between Money and Darla like a tennis fan's.

Money ran his fingers through his hair, looked at his knees, then back up. "I judge people, and I'm pretty good at it. I got the impression, you and Frank, he was more than just another guy. This is something we've got to talk about. Every successful deal I ever saw, somebody's getting screwed. That's Frank's role in this, the one getting screwed. If you're going to have a problem with that, we need to know now."

Darla's ice-blue gaze was suddenly hostile. She put her L.A. Eyeworks on. "You think I'm carrying a torch or something? It was just a little thing. I've had things before. I've had things since. 'Stand by Your Man' isn't my favorite song."

Money studied her, the classic jaw, athletic body arched in an all-business attitude. Finally, Money said, "Emotions are what mess things up, Darla."

"I've got no emotion," Darla said. "And if I did, it wouldn't be for him. Frank's just a means to an end in this."

"You're sure of that."

She looked away like, Why are we talking about this?

"So I'm taking you at your word," Money said, grinning around. "And that's all we've got to talk about, as I see it."

As the stout lady approached the counter, Frank White made the following assessment: rocky road, two scoops, marshmallow topping. Whipped cream, nuts and a cherry, the works. He touched his white paper hat. "Help you?" Frank said.

She slid onto a stool, stone-faced. "Mr. White?"

He immediately altered his assessment to: Federal government. "Yes, ma'am."

She hefted a big brown shoulder bag onto her thigh, lifted the flap, and handed him a business card. He held the card between his thumb and forefinger and squinted. Marjorie Rapp, United States Parole and Probation Officer. He dropped his hand, said, "Yes, ma'am," a second time, then motioned to the two teenagers down the way who were clamoring for service. Frank raised his voice. "Be with you in a minute."

Marjorie Rapp was thirties, with short brown hair and a faint mustache on her upper lip. She wore no makeup; brown eyes with grainy lids. "I'm your new person, Mr. White."

Frank wiped his hands on his apron. "Yes, ma'am. What happened to the other guy?"

"Mr. Berger?"

"I suppose. In two years I've reported to three different people."

"Mr. Berger took a job in the private sector."

"Yeah, I remember he was talking about some security service. Listen, you care for a cone? Cup or something?" Frank gestured at the drums of vanilla, cookies 'n' cream, chocolate decadence, all labeled with little white pasteboard signs and fronted by a display window.

She clutched her purse. "Only if I pay."

"Certainly, certainly. Hey, I wouldn't want you to think . . ."

She scanned the rows of two-gallon containers, concentrating briefly on the sherbets. "Fudge ripple, then."

One of the teenagers shouted, "Hey, we're in a hurry."

Frank smiled apology at Ms. Rapp. "You mind?" he said.

"Not at all." Brief and brusque, impersonal. "You don't seem to have that much business."

"We've just opened up for the day. Plus it's winter. Things'll pick up once it warms up." He raised a finger. "Be just a second, ma'am."

He went down the way, retrieving a scoop from milky water, grinning, showing jutting cheekbones and a shock of brown hair poking out from underneath his hat. "Hi, kids."

The boys wore loose jeans and Doc Marten boots. Their hair was dreaded, a couple of freakers. Gangbangers, Frank thought, way out of place in the Loew's Anatole lobby, amber skylight forty stories above, balconied rooms ascending on all four sides. One kid said, "How much is a cone?"

Frank continued to smile. "Scoop, buck-eighty you want it in a cup. Cone's fifty cents more. Two scoops, three dollars."

One boy, a skinny blond wearing a black Oakland Raiders jacket, wrinkled his nose. "Shit, mister, you're trying to fuck us."

Frank's grin felt frozen on his lips. Pisswilly, he thought, gearing up to start something. "It's Häagen-Dazs," Frank said. "Gourmet ice cream."

The other kid was even blonder than the first, bleached hair greased and stroked up into points. He wore a black T with the letters "F.U.C.T." emblazoned across the front. He nudged his buddy. "How 'bout if we pissed in them containers, man? You think the price'd go down?"

Frank cut his gaze to his left, where Marjorie Rapp watched intently. Visible beyond her was the entrance to the high-style French restaurant, jacketed waiters hustling to and fro with lunches hidden under chrome half-spheres. Frank bent close to the counter. "Look, can you guys cut me some slack? That lady down there . . ."

The boy in the Raiders jacket wore a skater cut, sides shaved with a Number One guard, hair sprouting long on top and drooping down over his ears. "She somebody you're fucking?"

Frank's smile faded. "No. No, she's not. Cup a buck-eighty. Cone two-thirty. Which do you want?"

Skinny licked his lips. "Maybe we just take it, huh?"

Frank wondered how this pair had made it into the lobby, security guards posted at every door. "You don't take it. If you get it, you pay for it."

"Hmm. How 'bout if we hassle your lady friend?" The kid wore one gold earring, left lobe.

"I don't think you'd like that much," Frank said. "She's not my lady friend. She's—"

"Maybe your sister then. Got a—"

"—my parole officer."

"—big ass. Huh?" The boy looked down the way, eyes widening.

"And the way they handle punks like you in the joint," Frank said, "is bend them over and take turns. What they do on the street is shoot the little bastards." He brandished the scoop. "Cup, buck-eighty. Cone, fifty cents more. What's your pleasure, gentlemen?"

The boys exchanged glances, all the toughness fading, confused now. Finally the skinny one said, "Two-scoop cup, sir. We can split that, can't we?"

• • •

Frank carried the sugar cone stuffed with fudge ripple down to Marjorie Rapp. He'd scooped a little extra, not that Rapp would notice. She took a small lick, watching the teenagers over her shoulder, the two kids at a small round table sharing a cup with two plastic spoons. "Friends of yours?" she said.

Frank bunched up his apron, drying his hands. "First time I ever saw them."

"You're sure of that."

"They're high school kids, ma'am. I'm thirty-five."

"You have to watch your associates," she said. "My experience is, it's one of the most important things. Running around with felons is grounds for reincarceration."

He clenched his jaws, nearly losing it, forcing his tone to be mild and matter-of-fact as he said, "I know about associates, but I have to sell ice cream to anybody that comes up. It's the job."

Her eyes narrowed. "And I suppose you don't ever see any of your old penitentiary friends. Do tell."

"I've seen exactly one, in all the time I've been out. I didn't do my time in Texas is one reason I never see anybody. A guy named Wilbur Dale came by here one day and had a shake. I talked to him maybe five minutes, total, and he was a customer. I know the rules, ma'am."

Her tongue flicked out, scraping a ribbon of dark chocolate cream into her mouth. "Working in major hotels is a problem. A lot of drug trafficking going on. Wasn't there a bust here recently?"

"I read about it in the paper," Frank said, "same as everybody else. One of the upper floors, around one in the morning. I'm off at four P.M."

"Did Mr. Berger approve this employment?" Her mouth tightened suspiciously.

Frank picked a cup up from the counter, fished in a drawer, dropped more plastic spoons into the cup, and replaced it near the register. "No, actually it was . . . Miss Cree, I think. Three parole officers ago—sometimes I get confused."

"We transfer a lot," Ms. Rapp said. "Get promotions."

"Good for the officer," Frank said, "but makes it sort of tough on the parolee. You get used to one officer's likes and dislikes . . ."

She looked across the lobby, at two chicly dressed women window-shopping at New York Duds. "This hotel environment is the major problem I have."

"I try to stay clear of the riff-raff, ma'am."

She smirked. "Is that what you call having one of your prison friends drop by for ice cream?"

Frank bent down, pretending to check the Freon pressure while expelling air through his nose. He straightened up. "I didn't invite Wilbur Dale by, ma'am. He just showed up. While he was eating his ice cream he did ask a lot of questions about where I was living and what I was doing. I might've told him too much—I'll plead guilty to that—but I was trying not to be rude. I've never seen him since."

"That doesn't mean you won't."

"If I do I'll give him the brush-off."

A rivulet of chocolate ran down the side of her cone; she snatched a napkin and wiped the runny stuff away. "I was reading your file, Mr. White. What reason did you give for transferring here from California?"

"Well, it wasn't really a transfer. You should look again. I'm from Dallas, but I was doing time in California, at Pleasanton."

"That far from home?" Showing her surprise, just a hint of wind leaving her sails as she realized that she wasn't entirely up to date on this guy.

"Yes, ma'am," Frank said. "Federal regs are, they parole you to your sentencing district. This was mine."

Her tone assumed a snappish edge. "I know the rules, Mr. White. What kind of drugs were your specialty?"

He looked at her.

"Your crime," she said. "Was it cocaine or something worse?"

Frank swabbed the counter with a damp towel. "I've never

been involved in drugs in my life, Ms. Rapp. You must have been reading someone else's file."

"I don't make that kind of mistake."

"Well, someone's made a mistake. I was in law enforcement." He laid a handful of napkins in front of her, the melting ice cream now dribbling onto her fingers.

"Oh? Maybe we should update."

"That would be nice," Frank said.

She wiped her fingers as Frank drew her a cup of water from the spigot. "Were you local or federal?" she said.

"Dallas Police Department. That's why they shipped me to Pleasanton. The Bureau of Prisons sends cops they convict of something as far from home as possible, to keep them from running into people they busted on the job. It's for protection purposes."

She soaked a napkin in water and finished cleaning her hand, then licked melt from around the cone's edges and bit off a mouthful of fudge ripple and sugar crust. "This is messy. I'm familiar with BOP rules, too. So you were a policeman. Bribes, or . . . ?"

"I never took any bribe."

"Maybe I should read up, then."

"Maybe you should. It would save a lot of trouble."

"Well, was your crime job related?"

Frank tugged at his ear. "Yes, ma'am, if you want to call it a crime. I shot a guy."

"It's something they're cracking down on," Ms. Rapp said. "Trigger-happy cops."

"I wasn't particularly happy. The guy was sort of trying to stab me."

She licked ice cream and watched him.

"He was black," Frank said.

"Oh. A racial crime."

"I don't notice a man's race when he's coming at me with a

pig-sticker, ma'am. But that's what they made of it. The guy's father was on the city council, and there were a lot of demonstrations. Internal Affairs cleared me, but then the feds stepped in."

"They have to," she said. "A lot of whitewashing goes on."

Frank averted his gaze. "If it was a crime, I've paid my debt. Embarrassed my family . . ."

"Your debt isn't paid," she said, "until your parole is finished."

"I know all that, ma'am. I'm working and doing what's expected of me."

"What about your wife? Is she employed?"

Frank did a double take. "I've never been married."

"Your file says . . ."

"That's what I'm trying to clear up, Ms. Rapp. Evidently when they shipped my file from California some mistakes crept in. Suddenly I'm a married drug dealer instead of a single cop. Every parole officer I've had since then, they were going to straighten out the record. But so far no one has."

"So you're not married. Involved?"

"In my job."

"No women?"

Frank wondered why this was any of the Parole Commission's business. "There's one girl I've been seeing."

"I frown on cohabitation, Mr. White. A lot of problems there. Your woman, she's not into drugs?"

"We don't live together, and she teaches school. And I don't know if I'd call her my woman. We only met a couple of months ago."

"A teacher. That's a plus."

"She lives at the school," Frank said, "as dorm mother. Counselor, or whatever. Riverbend School for Girls."

"Ooo, that's sort of an uppity place."

"It's expensive. A lot of rich people's kids."

"Is she a Christian woman?" Ms. Rapp smiled, a line of chocolate above her upper lip.

Frank wondered if that was a good description of Meg—a Christian woman. He'd never thought about it. "She's Presbyterian," he finally said, and then added, "We worship together." He supposed it was worship, tuning in occasionally on a church service telecast while changing channels, lying around on Sunday morning.

"That should be good for you," Ms. Rapp said.

"It seems to help."

"I think we may have a foundation here that I can work with. Without you changing jobs."

"I sure do hope so," Frank said. "And see if you can do something about correcting my records, will you? I think that'll go a long way toward helping me get rehabilitated."

She arched an eyebrow. "And you're sure this one person is the only one you knew in prison, that you've had contact with?"

"Wilbur Dale?" Frank pretended to think. "Yes, ma'am, he's the only one. If I see anyone else I knew in California, I'll let you know."

"See that you do," Ms. Rapp said.

When the big quake hit, Gerald Hodge rode tall in the saddle. *Eeee-hah.*

He lifted his ass high to drive it home, the woman writhing beneath him with her head turned to one side, eyes shut tight, graying hair spread out over the pillow, biting her lip to hold back her screams. She loves it, Gerald thought. Shit, they all do. Then all at once the vibrations began, low at first, building to a crescendo. *Rum*-ble. RUM-ble. BOOM.

Gerald froze in mid-stroke. The bedposts rattled and rocked. The floor and ceiling wrenched in opposite directions. The walls quivered. Glassware tinkled. Jesus H. Christ, Gerald thought. A torrent of water drenched the sliding glass doors on his left. *The pool*, Gerald thought, *the fucking water is sloshing out of the pool.* The woman clamped her legs around his waist. "Come on, baby," she moaned. "Come on, come *on.*" Plaster rained down on Gerald's back.

He gripped her inner thighs and tried to pry her legs apart. She squeezed him even tighter. He gritted his teeth. "Quake. *Quake, goddammit.*"

She squealed and threw her arms around his neck, pumping faster and faster with her hips. "Quick. Oh yes, baby, quick, quick, quick . . ."

Gerald let go of her thighs and wrestled with her forearms. *She's fucking strangling me,* he thought, *oh Jesus Christ, I'm going to die right here. Old superstud is headed for the big clusterfuck up yonder. Jesus Christ, I'm going to . . .*

The room tilted. The bed bucked and squeaked. The intertwined couple pitched sideways, hit the carpet rolling, and bounced across the floor to slam into the base of the sliding doors. Gerald stared out through the glass. Seen in a shower of moonlight, the carport buckled. The concrete split. With a squeal of bending metal, the woman's Mercedes lurched, then tumbled trunk-over-hood-ornament down the incline to vanish in the blackness of Topanga Canyon. More plaster fell. *To hell with this,* Gerald thought. He turned over, yanked the woman on top, and used her body as a shield.

The quake subsided as quickly as it had come. The tilted room was still as death. Dust hung in the air. Gerald inhaled. He sneezed.

The woman's eyelids fluttered. A grain of mascara dribbled onto her cheek. She looked toward the pool, rolling waves now subsiding, untangled herself from him and rose on her haunches. "What happened, Boots?" Then, more shrilly, "What *happened*, Boots?"

He looked at her, skinny thighs and drooping boobs, the gray in her hair illuminated by a slant of lunar brilliance. "Earthquake," he said. "You never seen an earthquake before?"

She raised her hand to cracked lips. "Earthquake?"

He struggled to his feet, canting himself against the tilt of the floor. His clothes had fallen against the wall. He walked side-hop, pulled on his red silk briefs, and picked up his hand-tooled leather boots. His Stetson was upside down on the carpet. He jammed the hat on his head. "Right. Earthquake. Right."

She sniffled. "My house, Boots. My *house.*"

Gerald thought, *Boots your ass.* In the distance an air-raid siren whined. "You think your house is fucked," Gerald said, "you should've seen your car." He shrugged into his oversized western shirt, flowered quilting at the shoulders, and closed the snaps one at a time.

She looked through the glass toward the shattered carport. "My car. My *car* . . ."

He found his loose, boot-cut jeans, planted his rump on the corner of the bed to slide his legs in. Then he yanked on his boots and pulled his pants legs down. "Your car."

Her mouth twisted in anguish. "What are you *doing?*"

He stood, flipped on the bed lamp and looked in the mirror. *What a bod*, Gerald thought, *tapered waist, thighs to make women drool.* "Getting dressed," he said. "What's it look like I'm doing? I got an appointment." He turned sideways, watching his reflection as he humped his pelvis forward. *Weight in fucking gold*, Gerald thought.

"You're not *leaving me.*" A tear rolled down her cheek.

He gently closed his eyes. Jesus, he guessed it would be hard on her, him going. *Tough shit*, Gerald thought. "Got to," he said.

"But when will I see you again?" Turning to him, cupping her veined breasts, fifty-five if she was a day, thinking the floppy boobs were a turn-on to him, trying to sex him up.

"Rest of the month you can come by the club. February I got an audition down at Chippendale's." He dusted plaster from his hands. "If the club ain't fallen down. Fuck me, is this something, or what?" He dug a pouch from his back pocket and snorted a palmful of Mexican brown. The woman's image blurred, then cleared.

She pouted, standing, her belly pooching out. "I was going to cook us breakfast." Seeing him watching, sucking in her stomach and raising up on her toes.

He listed a step to his left, then steadied himself with a hand on the dresser. "Doubt your stove's working." The bed lamp extinguished. "There goes the power. Poof, huh?" he said. Liking the darkness better, so's he didn't have to see this pitiful old broad.

She stepped toward him in the semilight. "Don't leave me, Boots."

Her vanity chair was on its side, her purse on the floor, contents spilling out. He grabbed the soft leather flap and hoisted the purse up, fishing around inside. "Tell you what, being as how I'm not sticking around for breakfast, I'm knocking a hundred off your tab." He dug out a wad of bills. "Only three hundred you owe me, okay? Bargain days." He dropped the purse and stumped toward the kitchen, elevated heels bunching his calf muscles. "I'm taking some beer," he said.

She followed him, leaning forward, fighting her way uphill. "Is it just the money?"

He opened the refrigerator, gravity taking hold and slamming the door into the kitchen wall. He found a six-pack of Silver Bullets and pried out one can.

She reached the doorway, grasping the jambs on both sides. "It is, isn't it?"

He popped the ring tab and glugged. "Hmm?"

"The money."

"Well, what do you think it is? Shit, look at you." He dangled the torn carton from his fingertips.

Tears welled in her eyes. She sobbed.

"Don't start fucking crying," he said. "Look, you want a good humping, you come to the right place. It's what you're paying for. It's what I keep myself looking like this for. You're expecting a friend, go someplace else. I got too many women to take care of, be hanging around with one."

Three hours and two ass-kicking aftershocks later, southeast bound on the Hollywood Freeway, Gerald slammed the lever into PARK. He climbed down from his midnight blue Ford Bronco and tilted his Stetson back, looking behind him at five lanes of bumper-to-bumper stock-still Caddys, Mercedeses, beat-up Fords and Chevys, a guy with skinny arms on his right driving a

Jag. As far as Gerald could see, people riding their horns, cussing, shooting the finger; traffic backed up all the way, Gerald figured, to the ocean and then some. Same in the opposite direction, the downtown L.A. skyline towering over an endless row of cars, no movement in the traffic, Gerald thinking, Jesus, maybe everybody'll just sit here till they starve to fucking death.

He'd been doing just fine, zipping along at a steady fifty-five on the Ventura, figuring to be in his apartment five-thirty, six o'clock, when he'd come to the big cloverleaf where the Ventura and San Diego freeways joined, autos bottlenecked coming from the south on the San Diego, Jesus, five-fifteen in the morning, what did all these fucking people think they were doing? Deejay on 96.5, only C&W station in Los Angeles worth listening to, explained it this way: the Santa Monica Freeway had collapsed, diverting all traffic north to the Ventura, there to hook onto the Hollywood to proceed downtown.

What's this collapsed, Gerald had thought, *you mean the freeway just* . . . ? He pictured the scene, the ground cracking open and swallowing the whole fucking road, moles the size of elephants eating people, dragging them down into the bowels of the earth. He'd grabbed his cellular then and punched in the station's listener hotline number, which he did every so often to correct some asshole who'd called in misinformation about Patsy Cline's birthplace or something. Seventeen consecutive times he'd gotten the busy signal, *bawwk, bawwnk*, as he moved foot by foot down the Ventura to the Hollywood, forest-covered mountains on his left, the Hollywood sign on the hillside hazy in smog, the dropoff on his right showing low-slung office buildings, the round Capitol Records structure near Sunset Boulevard.

He'd kept his cool, smiling left and right at pissed-off horn honkers, watching a couple in a Mazda, the girl draped all over the man, the guy wiggling around behind the steering wheel like maybe getting a hand job in the middle of the freeway. Now, less than a hundred yards short of his Normandie Avenue exit, stopped dead still, Gerald standing alongside his Bronco with his hat tilted back. The Bronco was in the wrong lane, two spaces over from the righthand shoulder, Skinny-in-the-Jag directly beside him, and between Skinny and the shoulder a woman in a Suburban packed with snaggle-toothed kids. Gerald halfway expected another aftershock, pictured the whole fucking freeway as it twisted snake fashion, autos flying left and right and banging into the railings.

He went around the nose of the Jag and past the Suburban to eyeball the shoulder, satisfying himself that there was room between the curb and rail for the Bronco to drive the hundred yards to the Normandie exit, piece of cake, no sweat. Then he retraced his steps and moved alongside the Jag, Skinny cutting his gaze and then looking quickly away, ignoring the crazy cowboy wandering around on the Hollywood Freeway expecting a handout, selling flowers or something.

Gerald knocked on the window, the guy inside wearing a cloth vest and no shirt, goatee on a pointed chin, ignoring someone five feet away rapping on the glass. One thing Gerald couldn't stand, people ignoring him. He braced his hands on the roof and shoved, rocking the Jag on its springs, rattling Skinny around inside. The guy's thin lips twisted in shock. Bony hands opened the console compartment and dug inside for what Gerald thought was a gun—every asshole on the road packed a cannon these days, Jesus, what were things coming to?—but what turned out to be a Vicks inhaler. The guy pumped with his thumb and sucked air. The window hummed partway down, the guy scared out of his wits but putting on a front. "Hey, yeah, whaddya want?" Tremor in the voice, effeminate tone. Likely a fag, Gerald thought.

Gerald bent close and grinned. "Listen, I need you to back up."

The man was confused now, peering over his shoulder at a green Buick Century whose bumper was two yards from the Jag's rear end.

"See, what I'm doing," Gerald said, "I'm going to pull in front of you, drive down the shoulder to get off on Normandie."

"Not enough room for you to do that," the guy said. The window slid up. End of conversation.

Gerald banged on the window. The guy put both hands on the wheel and looked straight ahead. Gerald rocked the boat once more, the guy now turning his head to mouth silently, "Leave me alone." Or maybe yelling it, the window cutting off the noise. Guy had no idea who he was fucking with. The woman in the Suburban stared openly, lips parted, all the little fuckers in the backseat with their noses pressed.

Gerald squinched his eyes closed. He couldn't take this, a goddam fruit acting like hot shit, making an ass out of Gerald in front of the woman and kids. He pointed just-a-minute, left old Skinny to wonder what was happening next, retreated to the back end of his Bronco and opened the tail door. He rummaged around inside and finally slammed the gate while holding a tire iron with a ninety-degree bend. He returned to the Jag, the guy now seeing what was coming, his lips moving, throwing his forearms up to cover his face as Gerald reared back and smashed in the window. The glass sagged, cracks spider-webbing as Gerald raised the iron to strike again. The second blow did the trick, shards scattering inside the Jag, cutting the guy's forearm, broken glass tinkling on leather seats.

Gerald reached in, bunched the vest up in his fist and yanked, the guy trying to fend Gerald off, smearing blood on the quilting at Gerald's shoulders. As the man struggled and squawked like a chicken, Gerald said, "Hold still. You hold still and listen, I'll break your fucking neck."

The man froze. His eyes moved from side to side in their sockets.

"I asked you nice to back up," Gerald said. "See what you did?"

The guy tried to pull away, clawing at Gerald's bunched-up fist.

"Now, you're going to back that fucking car up and out of my way, you hear me?" Gerald yelled. "You don't, I'll put something in your mouth you're not going to like. Or you might like it, you little fuck, I'm not too sure about you. You listening to me?"

The guy nodded in terror. Blood streamed down his forearm. Gerald released his hold and stood back, the guy panicked out of his skull, jamming the five-speed into reverse, the Jag leaping backward to slam the Buick's front bumper, the Buick recoiling and banging into a station wagon. Guy inside the Buick putting his own window down to yell, "You dumb cocksucker," all of which Gerald ignored.

Gerald now eye-measured the distance between the nose of the Jag and the car in front, and nodded in satisfaction. He walked around, climbed into the Bronco, and dropped the tire iron on the floorboard alongside two crumpled Silver Bullets. He backed up, cutting his wheels to the left, then whipped the steering wheel right as he inched by the nose of the Jag, Skinny watching as though hypnotized, the woman in the Suburban already in reverse, busting her ass to give Gerald room.

He reached the shoulder, twisting the wheel hard to the left, feeling the impact as the Bronco scraped the side rail, then straightened out and floored the accelerator, people in the traffic jam gaping at him as he transversed the hundred yards and lurched into the Normandie exit at fifty miles an hour. He bumped down the access, ran the red light, and squealed onto Normandie, adjusting the dial on the radio, switching the sound to the rear speakers, humming "I got friends in low places" along with Garth Brooks.

Gerald Hodge couldn't stand people ignoring him. Damn near made him lose control.

On the twelve-block jaunt from the freeway to the corner of Fifth and Normandie, Gerald snorted his second palmful of Mexican Brown of the day, popped another top and drank half of his third Coors' Light. Dead ahead were the high-rise office buildings along Wilshire Boulevard, the sun climbing above the horizon, the temperature a coolish mid-sixties. There was a fresh crack in the pavement between Sixth and Fifth but no other sign of earthquake damage, three- and four-story stucco apartments with palm trees growing along the curbs on both sides. He made a squealing left turn onto Fifth, fishtailed a quarter block before yanking the wheel hard left once more, and scooted into the covered parking beneath his own pale green apartment building. There was a lady in a cloth coat across the street, walking a giant white poodle, and as Gerald whipped into his numbered parking slot she gave him the evil eye. Gerald slid out of the Bronco, hefted what was left of the six-pack, and shot the woman the finger. She averted her gaze, interrupted the dog's pissing against a palm trunk, and hustled the animal away.

Gerald rode the clanking elevator up to the third level, pausing with his finger on the button, which would halt the car on two, then changing his mind. The second floor was where the manager lived, and Gerald's rent was eight days late. Old bastard had slipped a note in Gerald's mailbox, in fact, which pissed him off no end. The three hundred dollars he'd earned banging the woman plus the tips poked in the waistband of his briefs by panting females last night would cover the rent, no sweat, but Gerald wanted to teach the apartment manager a lesson. Nobody dunned Gerald Hodge, no way. Old fart didn't know who he was fucking with. Besides, if Gerald were to pony up the rent today he might not have enough left for heroin money. He exited the elevator, went down to stand outside his door, and fumbled in his pocket for his key. He froze.

The door was ajar. He snuffled through his nose, lifted his hat brim, and scratched his head. He'd never given anybody a key to his place, especially not broads. *Earthquake?* he thought, the vibrations knocking the latch from its slot. Could be. He nudged his way through the entry and stood in the foyer.

The TV was on in the living room, familiar theme music playing that Gerald had heard before but couldn't quite put his finger on. He got down into a half crouch, placed the six-pack carefully on the floor, and, lifting one leg at a time, quietly removed his boots. Then he crept down a short entry hall into the kitchen, ducked down behind the low counter, and slowly raised up to peer into the living room.

The drapes were drawn. Dancing light from the console TV illuminated a cloth divan and footstools, a cheap coffee table, one beanbag chair, photos hung on the wall of Gerald in costume: Boots, Badman, the Incredible Hump. A VCR with its red power light glowing sat on top of the TV. Bare feet with painted toenails were up on the coffee table, long legs bent at the knees.

Gerald rose. In the TV picture, Julia Roberts stood on a street corner wearing a leather mini and thigh-length boots, surrounded by women in curve-hugging pants or tiny skirts, all yelling and whistling at passing cars, Hey, baby, want a date, universal whore language. A gray sports car rounded the corner with Richard Gere in the driver's seat, the window sliding down as he pulled over. Julia Roberts approached the car in a hip-slinging gait and—as two soft clicks sounded within Gerald's living room—suddenly reversed her direction, retreating to join the other women once more, the car window rising to hide Richard Gere from view as the car backed around the corner and disappeared behind a building, hookers snapping their fingers and blowing kisses.

Two more clicks sounded. The sports car repeated its performance, coming forward with the window sliding down as Julia Roberts sashayed toward the curb.

Gerald went on into the living room and planted his rump on the arm of the sofa. "The one with her ass stuck out," he said.

Click. The car backed up. *Click.* The image froze, a tall hooker on Julia Roberts's left now center screen, bent from the waist, her hand extended toward the car, bottom thrust out in red skin-tight stretch pants and spike heels.

"Prime ass, huh?" a soft, cultured female voice said. "*Choice* ass." The woman bent forward to place the VCR remote on the table.

"Best ass I ever laid eyes on," Gerald said.

"Or ever will," the woman said.

"Ass I'd crawl a mile to let it sit on my face."

The woman pressed a button with a red-nailed index finger. The picture started in motion, the limo moving forward. "I was on my way. Had a speaking part I signed up for."

Gerald got up, went around the coffee table to switch off the VCR. The screen blanked into dancing snow. He turned on a standup lamp. "I didn't figure to see you again."

"Well, you were wrong. Everybody is sometime." The woman relaxed, stretched out her legs, crossed her ankles. She wore gray cuffed pants and a blue silk shirt. She picked up sunglasses with the L.A. Eyeworks emblem etched into the right lens and put them on. Auburn hair hung to her shoulders.

Gerald went into the hall for his beer and boots, dropped the boots on the living room floor and opened another Silver Bullet. "You really have a speaking part, or is that a lotta bullshit?"

"Supposed to start shooting two days after we got busted."

"*You* got busted."

"I took the dope, Gerald, told the DEA it was mine. Thanks to your lawyer."

"Our lawyer. You okayed the guy."

"He said you had a record. That I didn't, and that I'd get probation."

Gerald sat beside her on the sofa. "So I can help it he was wrong? How'd you get in?"

"A little tool a man gave me. Will open most anything."

"What man?"

"A guy. I'll tell you." She reached to the floor and picked up a small quirt with a woven handle. She dragged leather thongs lightly over her thigh.

Gerald watched her.

"I've been out over a year," she said.

"I heard. You haven't called or anything." He licked his lips, his gaze frozen on the quirt, thongs brushing gray cotton material stretched over thigh muscle. "I heard you had a thing for this guy you met in there."

"That might be just because you forgot to come to visit," she said. "Pleasanton's not that far."

"That's . . . the lawyer. Said it wouldn't look too good."

"The son of a bitch." She touched the whip's handle to his shoulder, then trailed the thongs down his chest.

He stiffened. "Guy said they might get suspicious, me visiting."

"They had contact visits. Lot of private places in the corners where people could—"

"Jesus." He closed his eyes.

"—do things the hacks didn't see. One girl I knew, gave her man head right there in the visiting room."

He humped his pelvis forward as the quirt touched his inner thigh. "Right-right there in prison?"

"Turned the guy on something else." She stood and stepped out of her slacks, tanned legs flashing in semi-light.

"Jesus." He left the sofa and got down on all fours, pulling at his belt, undoing his fly, yanking pants and briefs down to his knees. She straddled him from behind. He looked at her over his shoulder, baring his teeth. "Don't . . . don't cut my legs. Jesus, don't, I got to dance tonight. But, Jesus, hit me hard."

Gerald came out of the shower toweling himself and entered the bedroom. Darla was on the king-size, propped on pillows piled against the headboard, reading a *People* magazine. She wore pale blue French-cut panties along with her sunglasses. Her breasts were small with pointed nipples. He touched a welt on his rear and winced. "I told you, don't cut me."

She laid the magazine aside and watched him, removing her L.A. Eyeworks and sucking on an earpiece.

"I got to appear tonight." He held both ends of the towel and briskly dried his shoulder blades and upper back.

"You said, don't cut your legs."

"Part of my ass shows, these briefs I wear. Goddam earthquake . . ."

"Knocked me down," she said, "right in your entry hall."

"Four-thirty in the morning?"

"I thought I'd catch you in bed. I saw your pictures out there. When did you start stripping?"

"Come on, dancing. Eight months. I took a few lessons."

She adjusted her position, leaning on her elbow. "You ever see Marvin?"

"He calls. I don't do that shit anymore."

"It was good money, for getting established in acting. Let us get by."

He lifted one foot to a chair and toweled his thigh. "Too much AIDS going around. You hear about the guy, was John Holmes?"

"You ever work with him, Gerald?"

"Naw. Just knew who he was."

"I did once, this one movie," she said. "Never had him for a partner because of a script change, thank God. He was into gay."

"That's how it gets around, people going both ways. What turns them on is their business, but, hey. They need to tell whoever they're doing it with what they've been up to."

She rolled up the magazine and slid it up and down in a circle formed by her thumb and forefinger. "We came out lucky. You're pretty lucky your lights are on. What I heard on the radio, a lot of places don't even have power now."

"Fires, too. A lot of houses out in the Valley. Earthquakes scare the shit out of people."

"Not you?"

"Naw."

She smirked. "You don't get scared, Gerald?"

He lowered his foot and dried his scrotum, lifting his balls, squeezing with the towel. "Didn't bother me. Bothered this woman I was with."

She folded the earpieces over and laid the sunglasses on the bedside table. "I think you're bigger than I remember."

He looked down.

"Your shoulders and arms," she said.

"I'm bulking up, for this dancing. More bench-press weight."

"Taking steroids?"

"Certain kinds."

She raised one knee and crossed her legs, rocking her foot. "I've got something for us to do."

He paused with his foot on the chair. "I told you, I'm making no more pictures. Except the real thing, maybe someday."

"This has nothing to do with pictures. We'd have to leave town."

He rubbed down his thigh and calf with the towel. "Can't. I'm auditioning at Chippendale's, end of the month."

"We're talking a million dollars, Gerald. Maybe more."

"Yeah? Whose million?"

"Ours, eventually. There's a guy I met, Randolph Money."

"Bet they changed his name," Gerald said, "to Harold Thrust or something."

"Nobody in pictures. He was at Pleasanton. An older man."

"Oh. His million. He a drug guy?" Gerald finished drying his butt and sat on the end of the bed.

"His plan. He's done a lot of things, this guy. Has a law degree. Was into some banks, savings and loans. He's traveled a lot, knows people all over."

"What was he doing in prison?"

"I told you, savings and loans. Only Randolph was doing a lot of things, the S&L was an investment. Had to do with loans he got when he was on the board of directors. There were some other inmates that knew him on the street. Word was, you could get just about anything done knowing Randolph Money. Get someone murdered . . ."

Gerald stretched out on his side, facing her. The head of his penis dangled on his thigh. "I can't be messing with anything unless for a lot of money."

She lowered her gaze and scratched her forearm. "For this kind of money . . ."

"Chippendale's is big bucks," Gerald said.

"Not this big," Darla said. "And Chippendale's only pays if you get on there, at the audition."

"I will. I got this new act."

"But suppose you don't? Don't tell me, I've known strippers."

"Dancers. Jesus."

"One guy, built just like you. I met him doing pictures. Outside of Chippendale's, most of the places you starve to death. Have to hump old women to make ends meet."

"Or old men, like you did," Gerald said. "Those plays you used to try out for paid what?"

"I was advancing my career."

"I went one night, remember? You were running around onstage yelling at the top of your lungs. Front row, you'd bust people's eardrums."

"You have to be heard in back," Darla said, "or you're not effective."

"You do that in a movie they'll throw you off the set."

"You have to adjust," Darla said. "The motion-picture medium is more intimate."

"That's what Marvin thought. Liked to zoom in, get the real close come shots."

"Not that kind of intimate. That's one reason for this thing I'm talking about. Get some real money, you can relax and work on your acting technique until opportunity knocks. In those days I'd have an important audition, either I was too tired from filming all night or Marvin would have paid the rent on some motel. He wouldn't let me off to audition, said we only had a certain amount of time for shooting."

"Had to get it over with," Gerald said, "before the vice people zeroed in on his location. It's how I got to do the eighteen months. Marvin wouldn't let me off so I could go home and move the cocaine out of my apartment."

"What about the sentence for assault, Gerald?"

"That was a guy wouldn't keep his mouth shut. He had it coming." Gerald sat up, reached into a nightstand drawer for a small jar of flesh-colored cream. "It's good makeup, won't streak when I get to sweating. Put some on me, okay?" He handed Darla the jar, then scooted around on the bed so that his butt was facing her.

Darla leaned over to inspect his muscled ass. "They're not that noticeable."

"You'd be surprised what these women ringside will see. I had a little pimple once, this fat old broad kept yelling about it."

She made a face and uncapped the jar, then dipped her index finger into cream. She sniffed her finger, then spread some of the makeup over a blood-colored welt.

"Don't press too hard," he said. "Jesus, it stings."

"This thing we're talking about," Darla said. "There's some danger involved."

"Why don't you get your boyfriend from the joint? Chippendale's is the big time—no way will I miss out on that for anything that isn't sure."

Darla pressed his flesh with her fingers. As Gerald said, "Ow," she said, "Let's get it straight about this boyfriend. I had a little thing in there—that's all."

"The guy must have dumped on you then."

"Shut up, Gerald."

"You're forgetting I know you all this time. The only guys you act through with are the ones that dumped on you. All the others, you keep them on a string in case you need them for something."

"You mean, like you?"

"Difference is, I know what's happening," Gerald said. "We got no big romance, okay? You give me what I want, do pretty good at it, I do the same for you. Fuck you till you can't stand up no more, same as I do a lot of broads. Nothing to be ashamed of, the guy dumping on you. Happens all the time."

Darla sucked air in through her nose. "One last time. Nobody dumps on me, okay? If you've got to know, this thing we're planning, this guy is what Randolph Money calls the mooch?"

"What, the guy wants to borrow some money?"

"That's what I thought it meant at first. It's a con-game term, the mooch is the sucker. The one getting the shaft in the long run. This guy is in a position, we can use him. Only he won't know he's being used until it's too late." Darla dipped more cream, studying a smaller laceration. "On a scale of one to ten, say your chances of getting on at Chippendale's was a five. This thing I'm talking is probably an eight. We're not systems go until April, but we're supposed to go down early and get some things established."

Gerald bent his elbow and laid his cheek on his palm. "Go down where?"

"To Texas. Dallas. Get us a base of operations."

"Asshole of the world. I did a picture in Longview, Texas, one time, this girl had the worst fucking breath. Couple of hick deputy sheriffs ran Marvin out of town."

"Dallas is more cosmopolitan."

"Still a lot of rednecks," Gerald said.

"We'll have to work on our accents. You're from New Mexico and already have a start on the dialect. I'll really have to work on my diction."

"Yeah?" He raised his head. "With an acting coach, or . . . ?"

"I rented this video. Michelle Pfeiffer in *Love Field*, about a Texas woman and the effect the Kennedy assassination had on her. I'll work on my accent listening to Pfeiffer."

"I saw that," Gerald said. "She was playing some trailer-park trash."

"I'll have to upgrade it some, but there are some things all Texans say pretty much alike." She inspected her handiwork, screwed the cap back on the jar, and set it on the nightstand.

Suddenly the room shook, the floor vibrating, the jar toppling from the nightstand. In an instant, all was still.

"Aftershocks scare the Jesus out of me," Darla said.

"They're getting weaker. A couple earlier were damn near as strong as the main event. They'll go on for a year or more."

"Another argument for leaving town," Darla said.

"So, in Texas they got tornadoes. Good luck down there. If you stay long enough I might be through there with Chippendale's road show."

"Your audition is in February?"

He lowered his head to the pillow. "The first. Listen, I need some sleep."

"Gerald, let me proposition you."

"Make it fast, before I doze off."

"Say Chippendale's doesn't accept you. If we drive down the second week in February, that's still plenty of time for what Randolph wanted done. There's a man I'm going to contact down there."

"Sure. The guy you were screwing in prison."

"No, someone else. An actress friend of mine told me about, this guy that runs the Theater Center down there."

"This thing you're talking," Gerald said, "we have to kill somebody?"

Darla scooted up behind him and hooked her chin over his shoulder. "You're still a hunk, you know that?"

"Well, would we?"

She sighed. "We're talking a ton of money here, Gerald. Also talking a pile of time if we get caught. I'd have to say there's that possibility. On a scale of ten, call it an eight."

4

There were times when Frank White would imagine himself saying to Meg Carpenter, something like, "Well, I had some legal problems a while back," and then trying to laugh it off, as if twenty-eight months in federal custody wasn't any big deal. At other moments he'd consider getting really down-to-earth serious and saying to her, his voice deepening, "Meg, there's something about me it's time you knew." Neither scenario played out well in his mind. Whichever the manner in which he broke the news, the thought of losing her over his past scared him to death.

All of which he could have avoided, he thought, if he'd leveled with her the first time they'd met at the reading table in the Dallas Public Library, North Branch. But introducing himself as Frank White, currently on parole from the federal joint, would have sounded dumb as hell, and before he'd known Meg Carpenter for twenty-four hours they'd been to bed together. Then it had been too late, they were already involved.

He pondered the question of telling her as he munched on a cold turkey sandwich, Meg watching him over her shoulder from her seat at the picnic table. Her mouth puckered slightly, fine brown strands of hair waving in front of her face in the breeze as she said, "Penny."

He chased the turkey with Pepsi, deciding it was time to let her in on his secret, right now,

As she said, "Okay. Make it a dime."

And he lost his nerve, saying instead, "Hmmm?"

"Something's on your mind. Those girls flying kites aren't over fourteen, if that's it."

He looked down the slope toward the shore of White Rock Lake, three lithe bodies in shorts and halters, one girl holding a red and green triangular kite while another unraveled a ball of string and the third teenager stood by with hands on hips. "Nice day for it," Frank said. "Two weeks ago it was thirty degrees. Can you believe it? Another month and they'll be swimming."

She left the table and sat beside him on the quilt, drawing her legs up and hugging her bare knees. "It's always this way in February. Freezing your butt one week, warm the next. Beginning mid-March there'll be thunderstorms every other night. Talking about the weather's a good way to change the subject."

He shrugged and crossed his ankles. "Bet it's over eighty degrees."

"Bet it is. You're not going to tell me, huh?"

He laid his half-eaten sandwich on the paper plate and munched a Frito. "It's nothing. Just thinking about work. Thinking we need to add a couple of flavors."

"And that's why you've been staring off into space? Over ice-cream flavors."

He leaned back on his elbows, stretched out his legs and pointed his toes. "It's more serious than it sounds. Certain flavors attract adults, believe it or not. You have too much cookies 'n' cream or fudge brownie nut, you're going to wind up with a bunch of gang-bangers hanging around. Grown people go more for the vanilla, butter pecan. We learn that in training." He thought he'd improvised his answer pretty well, and added, "Was I staring off?"

"Like the Mad Bomber. If you don't want just the kids, do away with the whipped cream."

"We have to have that for sundaes. You need a mix of business. If you get nothing but teenagers acting tough, they'll scare all your other business off."

She half smiled, showing prominent dimples. "Why don't you just lay your gun up on the counter. That'll teach 'em."

He answered without thinking, "What gun?"

"The gun you were going to buy the day you picked me up at the library."

He tried to recover. "I didn't say I was *buying* a gun. I was just researching the different kinds." Actually he'd been looking up firearm laws, researching the procedure for regaining his gun rights as a convicted felon, when he'd noticed her frowning over magazine pictures of Llama .380s and Beretta .25s, both of which he could break down and reassemble in his sleep. "I like you in those shorts," he said.

Meg looked down at snow-white thigh-length shorts with pleats. "Thank you. That's not what you told me then."

"When?"

"At the library."

"Jesus, Meg, it must have been thirty-two degrees. I think you were wearing jeans. Long pants of some kind."

She showed an irritated smirk. "I'm not talking about shorts, dopey. I'm talking about guns. And you told me you were looking up to decide which one to buy, for protection. That's how you managed to strike up a conversation."

He dusted the leg of his khaki Dockers. "I thought it was you that struck up the conversation." Yellow-brown Bermuda blanketed the slope, with springtime weeds beginning to grow, creating minute swatches of green.

"I don't remember it that way." She turned her back.

"Yeah, you asked me, which one it'd be easiest for a woman to learn to shoot."

She looked at him, little laugh crinkles tightening at the corners of her eyes. "You sure you weren't just trolling, buster? Searching for a female alone, to put the story on?"

"No, I was . . ."

"I thought you came out from the shelves awfully fast for a guy thirsting for knowledge. You don't strike me as the library type. You did strike me as the gun type, though. The ice-cream type, I had to get used to that."

"I'm a management trainee."

"Nothing wrong with what you do," she said. "I just had you pegged as, maybe, a golf or tennis pro."

"I sunburn too easy for that. I told you a Beretta .25 doesn't have enough kick to throw off a lady's aim."

"And that's what I finally bought yesterday." Meg gestured behind them, up the grassy knoll where her Mazda was parked alongside his Jeep Cherokee in a grove of pecan trees with a couple of weeping willows mixed in. "It's in my glove compartment," she said.

He looked toward the car, wondering if the parole people could make something of it if he was with her during a routine traffic stop and the cop found the Beretta. He suspected that Ms. Marjorie Rapp would raise an issue, even if he proved the gun was Meg's. Being on parole, Frank was never certain what he could do and what he couldn't.

"I thought maybe this weekend," Meg said, "we could go somewhere and you could teach me to shoot."

He couldn't meet her gaze, looking instead down the slope to where one girl released the kite as another ran down the shoreline like a bat out of hell, dragging the string behind her. The kite became airborne, tail fluttering, then did a dipsy-doodle and crashed to earth. "I'm kind of rusty," Frank said.

"With all those trophies at your apartment," Meg said, "you shouldn't have any trouble getting into the swing."

"It's been a few years."

"You never practiced when you worked in California?"

A pang of guilt shot through him. *Liar, liar, pants on fire.* The

California job wasn't a complete falsehood, only a half-truth. He and four Bolivian cocaine dealers had built a little shack once with the hacks standing guard, and for a brief time he'd had a job in the prison sign factory. Forty-four cents an hour. "Never got the chance to shoot out there," he finally said.

"I still think you could teach me, if you really wanted to."

He rolled onto his side, pulling some grass and chewing on the blades. "Why do you need to shoot?"

"Don't you read the paper? Every day somebody's . . ."

"I mean, why not Mace or something?"

She seemed thoughtful. "I didn't really have a choice about buying the gun. It was Mrs. Dunn's idea."

"The principal at the school?"

She wrinkled her nose. "At Riverbend"—rolling the r, speaking through her nose hoity-toity fashion—"she's called the headmistress, Mr. Public Education. Yeah, Dunn the Hun. She's scared to death of kidnappers, she goes,"—Meg tucked her chin and deepened her voice—" 'Some of the wealthiest children in America are under our care here. We must be on guard.' God, everybody out there giggles behind her back."

"Why don't you move out of that place and into an apartment?" Frank said. "Make it easier for us to . . . you know, see more of each other."

She stuck out her tongue. "I know what it'd make it easier for you to do, bucko. Unless I get suddenly rich, though, you're going to have to content yourself with weekends. It's a good deal, free room and all, but I think this summer I'll be looking for another job. I've had about all of Mrs. Dunn I can stand."

"She must be something," Frank said. "She's the only one you've ever had a bad word to say about since I've known you."

Meg scootched around on the blanket and laid her head in his lap. "I should keep my mouth shut. Helen Dunn's only trying to do her job, but she's gotten paranoid about it. Now she's got me on patrol."

Frank stroked her hair. "You mean, like guard duty?"

She snickered. "All I'm lacking is the uniform. It started this semester when the Dalforth brats took up residence."

"The jeweler Dalforths?"

"None other. These are grandkids, Trina and Trisha, only they're not twins. Trina's a junior and the other little angel is in ninth grade. Talk about spoiled. God."

"They've got some bucks okay."

"You don't have to tell me," Meg said. "Mrs. Dunn reminds everybody on the staff, about a hundred times a day, that they're worth *millions*. That's just the way she says it, too, *millions*. She sounds like Tweety-bird. For someone that's not supposed to be materialistic, you know, a headmistress, Mrs. Dunn's more obsessed with people's wealth than anybody I ever saw."

"Their folks probably donate a lot to the school," Frank said.

"They'd have to, to keep me running around all night. Mrs. Dunn's got me setting my alarm every two hours. One, three, and five o'clock I go tramping around the dorm in my bathrobe making sure everybody's accounted for. Prayer number one is that no one snatches one of the Dalforth kids. Mrs. Dunn might not survive."

"A place like that does need some security," Frank said.

"I'll go along with you there, but why don't they hire some off-duty cops or something? I signed on to teach sophomore English. When they offered free room and board to be the dorm mother I jumped at it, but now I'm not so sure."

"Just cool it. Things'll get better."

"If they don't by the end of the term, it's adios, and I'm not kidding about it. Until then I'm gutting it out, but God—if something should happen, number one, I'm calling the police. Then I'm taking smelling salts over to Mrs. Dunn's house to break the news. I don't know which would be worse, a real kidnapping or having to tell her about it. A tossup, if you ask me."

Howard Molly, addicted to wintergreen Certs, popped one in his mouth, held it between capped front teeth, and smiled. "I'm enjoying our visit, don't get me wrong, but you really should have made an appointment with the casting director. My office only handles the business end."

"You've really got the credentials," Darla Bern said, running her finger inside her Bruno Magli sheenless spike-heeled pump and tugging back on the heel. "Hip Pocket Theater, that plaque says, that on the wall's an appreciation certificate from Little Chicago Theatrical . . . wow, that pen set, is that from . . . ?"

"Century Plaza Playhouse," Molly said, lovingly raising the fountain pen and then sliding it back into its holder. "Gave me that when I left to take this job, in fact."

"You like Dallas?"

Molly crunched on his Cert, the minty taste spreading throughout his mouth along with a slight stinging sensation. "Compared to what?"

"To wherever else you've lived. Which apparently is a lot of places." Darla wore a yellow silk sheath with leopard spots, the skirt halting six or eight inches above her knee, and her L.A. Eyeworks sunglasses. "I'd only want a small part."

"The city could stand more culture, which is what I've agreed to try and give it. Not much theatrical opportunity here, frankly."

Molly rubbed his temples with his forefingers. "Which part did you have in mind? There are several lesser roles." He had thick, jet-black hair, graying at the temples, and spent a lot of time in tanning salons. Visible through his office window were forty-foot elms and sycamores, the still waters of Turtle Creek, a chiseled stone sign reading "Dallas Theater Center," mounted on a block of granite.

"Which ones are open?"

Molly frowned, considering her, trying not to watch the shapely nyloned calf as the foot swung to and fro. "Have you read *Autumn Midnight*?"

"The play?"

"Yes. That is what you're here to talk about, right?"

"That, and to meet you in person. I've heard so much."

"You must know that I don't cast plays."

The corners of her mouth turned up. "The casting director works for you, doesn't he?"

"We give all our creative people full rein."

The smile broadened. "I know how that goes, Mr. Molly."

Molly leaned a bit sideways to look through the floor-to-ceiling window beside his closed door. In the reception area, a huge man with shoulder-length blond hair sat reading a magazine. Molly said to Darla, "Would your husband like some espresso, Mrs. Bern? Cafe mocha or something?"

"It's 'Miss.' "

"Oh? I thought he was with you."

"We traveled here together. There's no attachment."

"You came from . . . ?"

"L.A. I've brushed up on my Texas accent, in case the role requires it."

"I've got to say I find that strange, someone moving from the land of milk and honey to try to be an actress in Dallas. There isn't much work here." Molly swallowed his crunched Cert, quickly stripped another free of the package, and put it in between his lips. He made a sweeping gesture around his office.

"This you see here, this is more of a civic undertaking than any-thing else. If it wasn't for endowments we couldn't survive."

"I had other reasons to come to town," she said. "And I thought I had a connection here."

"Who is it?"

She removed her glasses and sucked on an earpiece. "Why, you."

Molly spread his hands. "But we've never even met."

"You know a friend of mine." Her lashes lowered. "Quite well."

Molly propped his shin against the edge of his desk and snugged up his tie.

"Lisa Reed," she said.

His pulse quickened. "She appeared in some things we did out on the Coast."

Darla let her shoe dangle from her toes. "She spent some time with you in Dallas a few months back. She says you were great to her."

"Was nothing. I only put in a word."

"Which is what I'm looking for." She gave him an airy wink.

"I'd, uh, seen her perform, Miss Bern."

"Darla. So I'm told."

He extended a hand toward the outer office. "But your friend out there."

"I told you. No attachments."

Christ, he thought, *she has the longest thighs.* "How long have you been in town?"

"Last night. Stayed in a motel by the airport."

"You came in on American?"

She wrinkled her nose. "We drove. The highway comes in by the airport."

"You know there are a couple of other theater groups here. There's Theater Three. . . . Do you have other appointments?"

Soft skin crinkled around ice-blue eyes. "I was hoping I wouldn't need any more."

He shot his snow-white cuff, checked his Piaget. "You're free for the afternoon, then."

She gave a little shrug. "As a bird . . . Howard."

He flipped through his calendar. "I don't seem to have anything going, either . . . Darla."

"How nice," she said. "What is there thrilling to do in this town?"

One hour, fourteen minutes, and twenty-seven seconds later, Howard Molly shrieked, "Christ," at the top of his lungs. He thrashed wildly about, kicking satin sheets into a jumble as Darla rose up on her haunches and finished him with her hand. Molly's pelvis rose, his body stiffening, hot semen pumping onto his belly. Finally he uttered a long sigh and relaxed, sinking slowly back down onto the mattress.

He softly closed his eyes. "Christ," he whispered.

She wiped her hands on purple satin. "You like it that way?"

"Christ."

"How else do you like it, Howard?"

He looked up, over the raised mound of his own belly, at a slim waist, pointed breasts, shoulders that were slumped as her hands rested on her thighs. Visible beyond her was his bedroom door, pictures of himself at social functions with Bette Midler, Tony Bennett, the mayors of Dallas and Baltimore. He felt poetic. "Let me count the ways . . ."

"You like threesomes? Lisa said you . . ."

"Christ."

"You'd like me to keep you happy, wouldn't you?"

"I'm a man of simple pleasures." He laughed.

She looked around the room. "I'm in a bit of a bind, Howard. I'd need a place to stay."

His mind drifted, spent, his body limp. "The man with you looks like a stud."

One corner of her mouth tightened. "He is. You'd want a

threesome with him? Maybe you'd like to watch, him and me."

"Oh no. Much more than that."

"We're waifs, Howard. Nowhere to call home."

He raised himself up on one elbow. "I couldn't do it here. My ex-wife comes by. Leaves the kids, every two weeks for the weekend. I've got appearances to keep up. I can have you over, often, I hope, but only when I'm sure we wouldn't be interrupted."

"Sure." Her look showed disappointment. "But we'd have to find someplace to live."

"Look, I have a lake house."

Her eyes widening. "You do?"

"It's where your friend Lisa stayed."

A softening of her mouth as she brought up one hand to touch her hair. "Seems like she said. I'd only need help until I can get a part."

"I'll set you up with our casting director."

"I'm a good actress. You won't—"

"Yes."

"—be disappointed."

"I'm sure I won't. Listen, I don't go to the lake house very often. It'll take some cleaning up."

"I've got no problem with housework, as long as it's not on a steady basis."

"Needs new drapes. Sheets on the bed. Just about everything."

She reached out and pinched his nipple. He gasped. "I'd have to go shopping, Howard," she said. "Listen, have you got a credit card or something I can . . . ?"

6

Twenty-six thousand feet above Denver, Colorado, Randolph Money mopped cold water from his face. He wadded and dropped the paper towel into the disposal slot. Seen in the mirror, his face was long and narrow with slightly drooping jowls. He wore a sky-blue blazer over a white-on-white shirt and tie combination, the aging exec on vacation, dressed for springtime. He flushed the toilet. Blued water swirled around before the vacuum sucked it below. He slid the latch to one side, opened the door, and excuse-me'd his way past a woman who'd been waiting to use the john. She shot Money a curious glance as she went inside. He moved up the aisle and passed the galley, flight attendants loading trays into slots with a series of flat, metallic clicks, and went up half the length of the Economy Class section to where Basil Gershwin sat.

He went up behind Gershwin and tapped him on the shoulder. Basil turned and grinned, indicating the two airline meals spread out before him, one baked chicken with green peas, the other slices of gristly beef with brown gravy. "I took yours," Basil said, "since you told the broad you weren't hungry." Which brought a scalding glare from a woman in an aisle seat, one row up.

Money crooked his finger. "Let's talk back here." He retreated toward the empty rows at the rear of the plane.

Basil frowned. "Soon as I eat."

"No, right now," Money said. "Now." He led the way, sinking into a window seat with four empty rows between him and the nearest passengers. Basil flopped down beside him, wearing a neon green sport shirt, yellow slacks, and black lace-up shoes. Money held up his flattened palm. "Hold your voice down, will you?"

Basil looked guardedly toward the front of the plane. "This ain't about your food, is it? You said—"

"No . . . food. Nothing about food. I've been thinking about what's going to happen when we land."

"We talked already. We got a rental car."

"We have a car arranged and paid for. I'm thinking we should part company."

Basil showed a hurt look, bushy brows tightening, mouth partway open. Like something from *Gorillas in the Mist*, Money thought. Or better yet, call this guy the misty gorilla. Basil wore a blue knit shirt and yellow slacks.

"Nothing against you," Money said, "but together we stand out too much, as I see it. Two men dressed so differently. People are less likely to remember us separately than if we're together."

Basil looked down and tugged at the front of his shirt.

Money reached in his inside breast pocket and brought out a tiny envelope. "This is the key Darla mailed me. It's to a lockbox at the Delta Terminal, DFW Airport. Now, when we land—"

"How we find these lockboxes?" Basil said.

"Listen. Just listen. Don't say anything else, okay?"

Basil closed his mouth and picked his nose with his thumb.

"As for the lockbox," Money said, "just go to the information desk. They'll tell you. Inside the lockbox are car keys and a Texas driver's license with your picture on it. Name of Daniel Hay. Also an American Express card under that name, but for God's sake don't try to charge anything on it. The credit card's for ID purposes only. You with me so far?"

Basil stared.

"Basil?" Money said.

"You told me not to say anything."

Money rolled his eyes. "You can answer in response to a direct question. Are you with me so far?"

"Yeah, I'm in the lockbox and I got the keys and the license. Also the credit card, which I ain't leaving home without. I wish you'd quit acting like I'm stupid."

Money sighed. "You're brilliant. It's just that a lot of you geniuses get preoccupied. Also in the lockbox, Darla's left an envelope. In it are a map, showing you how to get to the place where we'll be holding the . . . merchandise. Merchandise—remember that word. From now on that's the code. Don't call it the victim, the target, nothing like that. From now on it's the merchandise, okay?"

"Merchandise. Yeah, okay, the merchandise."

"Righto," Money said. "Also in the envelope are two more keys, one square-headed, the other flat with triangular teeth. Oh, also there's a note, telling you exactly where in the terminal she's parked the car. Now, the keys—"

"What about the parking fee?"

Money frowned. "The what?"

Basil propped a knee against the seat in front. "The parking fee. It paid, too?"

"Christ, how could I overlook something so critical? I don't know, Basil. I assume it isn't. If it's not, she'll have left a ticket and you can pay when you exit the airport."

"Just want to make sure we got things planned out."

"They are," Money said. "Trust me, they are. Now, the two keys. The square-headed one will let you in the lake cabin, the one on Darla's map. The other key, that's to the cage."

"This thing a cage, for real?" Basil said.

"That's my understanding. Came from a dog kennel. The physical description isn't that important, as long as it's secure and gives our . . . merchandise some room to move around. There are two bathrooms in the cabin, and the cage is set up in the larger of the two. It surrounds the toilet and provides access to the shower. There's a cot in there. The merchandise shouldn't have to leave the cage for any reason, as I see it."

"What about feeding it? Him. Her. What the fuck are we snatching, anyway?"

"You'll learn soon enough. For now, you simply don't know. No reason for you to get sympathetically involved at all. You'll know the identity when and if it's necessary."

" 'Cause I'm so fucking stupid, I guess."

"Intelligence has nothing to do with it. As far as you're concerned, the merchandise is a thing. An item. A means to an end, nothing more. Something I learned when I took control of Datatech."

"This ain't no company," Basil said.

"No, it isn't. But it's the same principle. I had to cut half the staff in that one, and the persons I laid off, every one of them, had a sob story. I distanced myself from all that. As far as I was concerned, those people were merely items. I had no feeling for them." Money paused to let his point sink home, then said, "And as for your original question, there is a food slot in the front of the cage. You've got provisions for a week, which should be plenty. A stove, refrigerator, the works."

"I ain't no fucking short-order cook."

"Your culinary skills won't be an issue, either. Most of the stuff is frozen dinners. I gave Darla a shopping list. I think there's some peanut butter and whatnot, but cooking won't be a problem. I'll be dropping in on you in a couple of days, to make sure everything is ready. We'll make our transaction, hopefully, on Sunday night. Three days from now, assuming we've got our ducks in a row."

"How'm I supposed to get it? The merchandise. Jesus, am I supposed to call it that when I'm with it? 'Hey, merchandise, you hungry?' " Basil grinned.

"I'll give you the transfer details when I drop by. For the next two days, concentrate on getting everything ready, making sure you have everything you need."

"And where you going to be while I'm doing this shit?" Basil said.

Money looked out the window. The eastbound jet had out-run the cloud cover, flatlands below now, farmland dotted here and there with planted fields and country towns. "I'll be making some arrangements," Money said.

"With who? Oh yeah, this fringe asshole. The guy we ain't supposed to know."

Money blinked. "Possibly."

"I don't like it, working with somebody I don't know who the fuck."

"It's the means to getting paid, Basil. We've been over this, and the only explanation I'm willing to give is, it's necessary." Money waved a hand. "Enough about that. Now, you're clear on this traveling with the parole people."

"Slicker'n owlshit." Basil touched his back pocket, leaning forward. "Got my authorization right here."

"And what did you tell them you were going to do?"

"Got a thirty-day permit to look for a job. Told the guy I was thinking about relocating."

Money's expression tightened. "Any conditions on your travel?"

"I got the name of a parole officer in Dallas. I'm supposed to check with this guy once a week while I'm in town."

Money leaned back and closed his eyes, grinning. "Christ, I love it. Brilliant, as I see it."

Basil cocked his head. "Who's brilliant?"

"The whole thing, you reporting to a parole officer. Last thing they'd suspect, you're involved in something like we're do-ing and all the time you're reporting." Money laughed aloud.

"I didn't figure," Basil said, "you'd give me credit for figuring out anything. I'm so fucking stupid."

Money studied the guy: bushy eyebrows on a wide, square face, the lower lip pooched out like a seven-year-old's. *Time to pump the bastard up,* Money thought. The secret to success, getting the maximum out of poor, dumb slobs. Money grinned. "I'll tell you something, Basil. In my estimation, aside from our fringe person, you're the most important cog in our entire operation."

Basil sank lower in his seat, dubious. "Don't give me that bullshit."

"It isn't bullshit. There's one thing you've got going for you none of the rest of us have."

Basil leaned forward and scratched his calf.

"What it is," Money said, "is that—face it—somewhere down the line it's possible we're going to have to dispose of the merchandise."

Basil did a double take. "You mean we could have to off somebody."

"Exactly. Not the most pleasant of prospects, but necessary for success. So maybe Darla could deal with that, maybe not. Her lover boy probably could, but he couldn't do it right. He'd have to give it some theatrical flair, but not you. You, my friend, I've got no doubt. If elimination becomes a factor, you'll do it without thinking twice. No remorse, no hesitation. And leave no evidence. Am I right?"

"Would I off somebody?"

"Right."

Basil looked up front toward the other passengers, people reading magazines, munching their dinners, businessmen rattling keyboards on laptop computers. Finally he said, "In a New York minute. Listen, okay I eat them dinners now? I'm so hungry I could eat the ass end out of a mule, if you understand what I'm telling you."

Joe Breen kept thinking, *Two more years, seven more years.* It was a big decision. Biggest he'd ever made. He glanced out the window, at one-way eastbound traffic far below on Commerce Street, at the stream of pedestrians crossing at the light in front of the Earle Cabell Federal Building, at the old red brick Dallas County Courthouse across the way. Lots of people out, must be noontime. *Damn*, Breen thought, *am I missing my lunch hour?* He checked his watch. Nope, still five till twelve. He relaxed, rattled the print-out to straighten the page, and scanned the figures for perhaps the hundredth time since he'd reported for duty at 8 A.M.

The more he thought about it, he had to opt for the seven years. Sure, retiring at fifty sounded good, but what was he going to do? FBI agents could always go the private security route, working for industrial firms, but there wasn't much demand out there for retired parole officers. Way Breen had it figured, his high three-year-average salary at fifty-five would give him three hundred dollars a month more than if he checked it to 'em at fifty. Even more if sometime in the next seven years he got the promotion to GS-13. He cleared his Texas Instruments pocket calculator, dug the salary chart out of his desk, and punched in the figures to determine his pension if he should make it to GS-13, eighth step. Damn, he thought, that'd be . . .

His phone rang. Breen looked in irritation at the cradled receiver, then checked his watch once more. Two minutes till, as if it were a conspiracy, everybody waiting until lunchtime to fuck with a person. He waited through three more rings, hoping the other party would give it up, then snatched up the receiver and said, "Breen," with an I-don't-have-time-for-you edge to his tone.

The voice on the line was a mellow tenor with a faint West Coast twang. "Joe?"

Breen frowned. "Yeah?"

"Joe Breen?"

Breen's teeth clicked together. Who the hell did the guy think it was? "Yeah?" he said again.

"Hagood Lawrence here. We met in Chicago."

Breen bit the end of his thumb. Chicago was last October, the nationwide conference over the proper filling out of Form DJ-21, the new probationer's report. He must have met a thousand guys in Chicago. "I'm thinking," Breen said.

"You know, from Los Angeles. We drank the yards of beer, down on the Loop."

Breen pictured the guy, tall and thin, with thick glasses magnifying owlish eyes. "Yeah, sure," Breen said. "How's everything out there since the earthquake?" His watch now showed one minute after. On my own time, Breen thought.

"A bit shook up."

Breen forced a laugh, stifling a yawn.

"Listen," Lawrence said, then coughed and said, "Jesus, it's your lunchtime in Texas, isn't it?"

"Getting close," Breen said.

"Well, I won't tie you up. But I've got one coming your way I think you need to know about."

Breen reached in his middle drawer and brought out a hand mirror, studying graying, slicked-back hair, a thin face, a dark mole on his chin. He picked up tiny scissors and trimmed his eyebrows as he said, "Somebody moving here, or . . . ?"

"No, this guy's on a thirty-day travel permit. Name's Gershwin, Basil Albert. Supposed to be in Dallas looking for a job."

Great, Breen thought, *as if I didn't already have enough of these assholes.* "Little unusual, isn't it?" he said. "Having someone report on a temporary basis. Usually we just let the guys go where they're going and call us when they get back."

Lawrence coughed. "I thought this boy needed watching."

"The regulations are, if the parolee's a problem he's not supposed to be traveling to begin with."

"I know all that." Lawrence's tone was suddenly brusque, the longtime government guy resenting someone's questioning his savvy to the regulations. *Tough,* Breen thought. *If they screw up, old Joe Breen's going to let them know about it.* "The trouble is," Lawrence said, "Mr. Gershwin's been a model guy. Reports like clockwork, last six months I've let him mail in his form every month without coming in in person. Straight from the manual."

"Well, if he doesn't have to report in his own district," Breen said, "how come you've got him reporting in mine? We've got plenty to do here."

"He doesn't have to report in this district," Lawrence said, "because the regs dictate he doesn't. You'll have to meet this guy to see what I'm talking about. Dumb-looking bastard, looks like the missing link. He's not real bright bookwise, but he's played the system, you know?"

"I can't say I'm indebted to you," Breen said. "Somebody like that's all I need right now."

"On paper this is a model person. Started out in Marion, Illinois, toughest joint in America, but graduated all the way up to the minimum security at Pleasanton, California. Made parole in the minimum possible, ten years on a thirty-year hit. Six years on parole he's never missed a meeting, not so much as a dirty urine sample. On paper he looks like Mr. Rehabilitation."

Breen held the receiver between his neck and shoulder, and angled the mirror to trim the hair from his nose. "If he's that clean, why do you want him watched? I've got guys selling dope every week, I've got no time to—"

"It's the notes in his file. The things that aren't in the official record."

Breen lowered the scissors.

"Our Mr. Gershwin is forty-eight years old," Lawrence said. "Nineteen seventy-eight, this guy and a couple of buddies did four banks in the Los Angeles area. At least that's the ones they owned up to in the plea bargain. The FBI report says they're the suspects in a half dozen more.

"The last one," Lawrence said, "was a Bank of America branch down in Oxnard, Orange County. Hit the place around two in the afternoon. The police were dumb lucky on that one, a patrolman happened to be inside cashing his paycheck at the time and managed to get out of the bank before the holdup men could get everybody down on the floor. Mr. Gershwin and his friends wound up pinned down themselves, held the employees and customers hostage for six hours. Finally surrendered, entered into a plea bargain with the U.S. Attorney, and took thirty years apiece. Part of the deal was that certain state charges were dropped, and some things about the holdup were expunged from the record at their sentencing. I'll say this for Mr. Gershwin, he had a bangup lawyer. What I know about the deal comes from informal notes an FBI agent made while he was investigating the case.

"According to these notes," Lawrence said, "Mr. Gershwin pistol-whipped the bank manager, broke the guy's jaw and a couple of ribs. Two women, one a bank employee and the other a customer, this guy's supposed to have raped in there. One of them he made go down on him."

Breen drummed his fingers. "Jesus Christ, a guy like that's got no business walking around on parole."

"Tell me about it. Problem was, neither of the women would sign a statement. Both of them married, you know how that goes. The FBI agent wrote all of it down and it's part of Gershwin's informal file, but there's nothing in the official record. Far as his record's concerned, he treated those hostages like royalty. And given his good prison conduct, the parole board had no choice under the guidelines but to turn him loose in the minimum time. Unofficially, there's a helluva lot more in his prison record, too."

Breen took a yellow pad and a ballpoint from his desk. "You say his name is Gershwin?"

"Basil Albert. You remember the riots at Marion in seventy-nine?"

Breen tapped the ballpoint on his blotter pad. "Read about it. Killed some guards, didn't they?"

"Six guards, to be exact. Worst way imaginable, castrated a couple of them. Marion's been solid lockdown ever since, only let those guys out once a day for an hour's exercise. One of the dead Bureau of Prisons people was right outside Gershwin's cell, shanked with a screwdriver. Our friend Gershwin's laying up in his bunk asleep and swore he never saw anything, of course, and nobody could prove otherwise. In fact his lack of involvement, involvement anybody could prove, won him a transfer down to Leavenworth when Marion went into lockdown. That was the rule, any prisoner with no recorded involvement in the riots got a transfer. People working at Marion at the time swear that Gershwin was among the baddest actors in the joint, and that he's the one that killed the guard. Nothing official, just like the rest of this stuff."

"Jesus, there's more?" Breen said.

"You bet," Lawrence said. "At Leavenworth, Mr. Gershwin's official rap sheet is once again spotless. A twenty-year-old kid turned in a complaint that Gershwin and two more guys pinned him down, held a screwdriver in his ear, and took turns buggering him. Once again, nothing in the record. Before they could complete the investigation, the boy turns up strangled in the shoe-factory bathroom, no witnesses, zero evidence. Just another lucky break for Mr. Gershwin. As far as official goes, he's as pure as the driven. Our model prisoner now moves on to minimum security at Pleasanton, where he's once again a pristine guy and receives his parole right on time. Five years on my caseload he's never one second late in reporting, gives me all his address changes up to snuff, holds a job a high percentage of the time. You know the rules as well as I do. Under the circumstances if I deny his request for a thirty-day travel permit, *I'm* in violation."

Breen shuddered. "This guy's not apt to attack me or anything, is he?"

"You? Not a chance. He'll come to see you right on schedule. Due to arrive in Dallas today, and I'll lay you odds he'll be on your doorstep no later than Friday afternoon. Dumb as he looks, you'll even like the guy. Has some pretty funny jokes. As his parole officer you'll get full cooperation, that's the way Mr. Gershwin plays the system. But private citizens are a different story. One of them he'd kill for a nickel, if you want my true opinion of the guy."

Frank White thought that Harold Willett looked as if he'd swallowed a hot pepper. "What's so important that you're calling me on Sunday?" Willett said.

"It's your instructions," Frank said, "that anytime I've got problems I'm supposed to call you. You're my district manager. If there's somebody else I should . . ."

"No. No, you did right, okay?" Willett had a wide mouth and sloping forehead, and was an import from the home office up in Minneapolis with the slightly nasal, fuck-you accent to prove it. He stood with his wrists against his waist, his palms reversed, facing out to the sides. "What, the freezers again?" He peered through the glass at rows of ice cream in two-gallon drums.

"No, I fixed that," Frank said, pointing. "It's . . . well, I need off for a while this afternoon."

Willett slowly raised his gaze from the row of ice-cream containers, until he seemed to be looking at Frank's Adam's apple. "It has to be today? April's our first really peak month."

Frank looked beyond the D.M. at a lobbyful of tourists, a couple of guys and their wives reading the display sign, considering the prices for one- and two-scoop cones, double- and triple-dip sundaes. On a stool down the way, a teenaged girl munched on a rocky-road sugar cone. "I know," Frank said. "And I've got to apologize for that. But something's come up."

Willett cleared his throat. "I promised my kid."

"If you can find somebody else to spell me," Frank said.

"Who? Who the hell at this time on Sunday?"

Frank lowered his chin. "Nobody, probably. Hey, I get four personal days a year. Two years on the job and I haven't taken any."

Willett raised a hand, palm out. "I can't argue with that. But you ought to give notice."

"This just came up a while ago. Maybe just three or four hours. Can you live with that?"

Willett narrowed his eyes. "Your parole officer called this week."

"She did? I sure hope you gave her a good report."

"I told her that your performance has been outstanding," Willett said. "So far."

"Well, I give you my word," Frank said, "that it'll continue to be. But, just today, I've got this business."

"What business is that?"

Frank leaned on the counter, looking down, then back up. "It's personal. How about if next week I do a double shift, with no overtime?"

Willett sighed, exasperated, a man planning a nice Sunday afternoon and having this convict guy screw up his day for him. He came around the counter and testily grabbed an apron. "You've got four hours, Mr. White," he said. "See that you don't abuse the privilege, okay?"

"Hey, great," Frank said, removing his paper cook's hat. "You know, Harold, it's working for guys like you that makes up for the lack of benefits around here."

Frank exited the mammoth hotel lobby and went out into seventy degrees, birds twitting in the hedges, a few puddles left over from last night's thunderstorm. He climbed into his Cherokee's backseat and, after looking right and left, wiggled out of his white pants and into a pair of Levi's. Then he removed his black bow tie, took off and carefully folded his white, short-sleeved dress shirt. The shirt had the "Sidewalk Humor" logo—the company name lettered on an ice cream cone—over one pocket, and "Frank" scripted in red thread over the other pocket. Frank twisted and shrugged into a pale green Tommy Hilfiger knit, and left the tails hanging out. He then eased in between the bucket seats, settled behind the wheel, and drove slowly out of the Loew's Anatole parking lot. Once clear of the hotel grounds, he shot the ramp and blended in with the Sunday drivers headed south on Stemmons Freeway.

Fifteen minutes later Frank parked nose-on to the curb in front of the Toledo Lounge, a sawdust joint in East Dallas on Samuell Boulevard. Across the street was Tenison Park, with fifty-foot elms and sycamores, azaleas coming into bloom, and Bermuda dotted here and there with Johnson grass and ragweed. Jukebox music drifted through the barroom's open entry, an old-timer, "Midnight Train to Georgia," Gladys Knight belting out the lyrics. Frank locked up the Cherokee and went inside.

He paused for a moment and waited for his pupils to dilate; first the revolving Schlitz sign above the bar came into view, then the bar itself, dim shapes of men and women hunched over longneck bottles and schooners of draft. There was a musty odor of stale tobacco and stale beer, blended in a cauldron of stale air. The Schlitz sign displayed a digital clock on one side, then revolved to show a grinning guy, a healthy girl, and a waterfall. The clock showed 1:52; Frank was a few minutes early. He approached the bar, edged in between a man in a suit and an elderly woman in slacks, and ordered two Miller Lites. The bartender, a black-haired woman with a gum-chewing, seen-it-all look about her, popped the tops and set the cans up alongside frosted glasses. Frank paid for the beers and carried cans and glasses to a back booth where he could watch the door. The Gladys Knight number ended, followed by "Love Potion Number Nine."

She came in at straight-up two wearing mid-thigh spandex shorts, hooked a thumb through the mesh in her see-through top, removed her L.A. Eyeworks, and peered into the dimness from just inside the door. She stood for a full thirty seconds in a backdrop of sunlight, then hesitantly stepped toward the bar. Frank raised a beer can over his head. She caught the gesture, showed a blink of recognition, came back, and sat across from him. She picked up the untouched Miller Lite and read the label on the can. "You remembered," she said.

"Who could forget? Hiding all those six-packs around the compound in the hedges, under the porch outside the chow hall." Frank turned sideways in the booth, leaned against the wall and watched her. In prison she used to braid her hair, one long queue down the back.

"Most of it for the hacks to drink, when they could find them." Beneath the mesh top she wore a spandex halter that matched her midnight blue shorts.

"It was only fair, the hacks bought the beer to begin with. Which one was it you had smuggling it in?"

She poured, beer gurgling, bubbles rising, foam building on top. "I don't remember."

"Easy to forget. The faces come to me, but I can't put a name with them."

She folded the earpieces and laid her sunglasses on the table. "I never forgot your name. You have any trouble finding this place?"

"I used to patrol right down the street when I was a rookie."

She watched him, a slight tiredness around her eyes. "It would be easier to find you if you hadn't changed your phone number, Frank."

"It's against the rules," he said. "Contacts with anybody you knew in there."

She scratched her forearm. "That's a copout. Sure, there's rules, but that's just one they use to bust you if there's something else they want you for but can't make a case on."

"I've been real careful," he said. "Trying to keep my nose to the grindstone."

She pursed her lips and gave two smacky kisses. "Poor baby. You must have a sore nose."

"You can knock it all you want to. But I'm serious, trying to get off Parole Commission paper and go on with life."

She reached testily for a shaker and salted her beer. "Why did you come today, then?"

He shrugged. "You said to. I'll be straight with you, Darla. I changed my home number because I wanted you to quit calling me. You were wasting your long-distance money. The only way you could have gotten the pay-phone number in the Anatole lobby was from Wilbur Dale, and I just figured out on the way over here that it was you that put him up to coming by and checking on me. When you called me at work today I was shocked that you were in town. Now I'm over the shock. The only reason I'm meeting you is to tell you to leave me alone."

She grimaced. "You tell your girlfriend you were coming?"

He tilted his chin. "Wilbur told you about her, too, huh? I shouldn't have given that guy the time of day."

"You didn't answer me."

"No, Darla. I didn't tell her. Didn't think it was important enough to tell her."

"Well, why not? If there's nothing between you and me, she shouldn't care."

"That's not what she'd care about. She doesn't know about my past, and I'm telling you now that if she suddenly finds out, you're in trouble with me."

She reached beneath the table and touched his knee. "I certainly wouldn't want to screw up your reputation, hon."

He firmly moved her hand away. "I don't think that's a good idea."

"You used to think it was a good idea. I'll bet you still do."

"Afraid you're wrong. Hey, you still look good, Darla."

She arched an eyebrow. "You bet your ass."

"You'll never have trouble getting guys. It's just, I'm spoke for."

She pouted. "You never really gave a damn about me. Did you?"

"I didn't know I was supposed to. There were a lot of other guys in there. We never had any understanding that I can remember."

"You sleep with somebody, there's an understanding. You don't have to say it in words."

"Yeah, but the other . . ."

"All in exchange for something, Frank. You, I never asked for a thing."

"We were just under different circumstances," Frank said. "In prison it's one world. This is another. Besides, I thought I made it clear while we were still there. Your territory was too crowded for me. It's why I cut us off when I did."

She swigged beer. "Jesus, Frank, you were one I'd never expect to turn into a boring asshole."

"Look around you. You can walk out that door and go anyplace you want. That's not boring. Prison, that was boring."

She folded her arms. "You know what I mean. Look, if you didn't want to make it, get your cock sucked or something, why didn't you just tell me? I'm taking a few chances myself, being here. There are people I'm with who would hit the ceiling if they knew. If I'm going out on a limb, don't you think you should be glad to see me?"

"I think you know that answer," Frank said, lifting his glass and drawing a circle in the frost with his thumb. "And whoever these people are you're talking about, I don't even want to know. I think you should take a long look before you get into something that's going to send you back, but that's your business."

"What, you want to reform me? Put me on the straight and narrow? That's what dear old daddy used to say, before I got old enough for him to fondle my tits."

Frank watched her, slim nose, high cheekbones, the classic

beauty look. She'd stand out in a crowd where Meg wouldn't, but once you got to know them both it'd be Meg all the way, hands down. In a few years Darla would fit right in with the crowd up there at the bar, older women swilling their beer and dreaming of how it used to be. "The only reason I came," Frank said, "is to tell you face to face to leave me alone."

She smirked at him.

"I mean it, Darla."

"You think it's really cute, trying to dump on me, don't you?"

"Jesus, I don't think it's anything. We don't have any relationship to dump and never have. Obviously you know about Meg."

She widened her eyes. "Meg who?"

Frank exhaled through his nose. "Trying to tell you nicely's a mistake. You just go away. I'll do whatever I have to to keep you from knowing where I live. My home phone's unlisted and you can't get the number. If you call me on the lobby pay phone again, I'll hang up in your face."

She screwed up her features. "Jesus, why does a hunk like you have to be such a prick?"

"You can call me that. Meg has a lot to do with making me think things out. Wasn't for her, believe me, I'd be sitting over there feeling you up right now."

She bunched up her lips and wrinkled her nose. "You're wanting a nice little house, I guess. Kids and shit. Join the fucking PTA."

He studied his glass. "Maybe. Whatever I do, it beats going to prison. You should think about that. Sorry to disappoint you, Darla. If you'd known I wasn't your kind of people anymore, you never would have asked me to meet you, right?"

"I might've." She swirled her glass around. "Yeah, I might've anyway, 'cause I would have had to see it for myself to make me believe it. I'd want to give you a chance to be a real person, not some character out of *Little House on the Prairie*."

One corner of his mouth tugged to one side. "Me is me, what can I tell you?"

She drained her glass. "Thanks for coming by, but I see we're not getting anywhere. I'd hoped maybe we could take up where we, you know. But now . . . oh hell. Just, fuck you, Frank, okay?"

He had a final sip, then stood up. "Believe it or not, I was hoping you'd say something like that. Soothes a guy's conscience, you know?"

Mrs. Helen Dunn, prim and properly hateful, folded her hands on her desk and peered down her nose. "I'm going to ask you to relieve me this afternoon, to take a group on tour."

Meg Carpenter crossed her legs, smoothed her gray business skirt, and let one black pump dangle away from her heel. "I'd planned to do something, ma'am. Friday afternoons are supposed to be my free time." She'd had problems with calling the headmistress Helen from the word go, particularly in view of the age difference, and had finally settled on *ma'am*. Mrs. Dunn had never come right out and said so, but the slight twitch in her eyelid told Meg that the headmistress would have preferred a more reverent title.

Mrs. Dunn thumbed through her desk calendar. "Weren't you off a day last week?" Steel-gray hair poked out over her forehead. She wore wire-framed bifocals.

Meg pretended to think. "You mean, when I was running a temperature?" Brought on by tramping around the halls at all hours of the night guarding the little darlings, she thought. "I think that was a half day, ma'am." Meg smiled sweetly.

"Whatever," the headmistress said. "I have a meeting and I can't be both places at once. These tour groups lead to donations. Donations are our lifeblood, pure and simple. The only one with the knowledge necessary to do the tour is you."

"What knowledge is it that I . . . ?"

"Security." Mrs. Dunn held up one wrinkled finger. "People in these financial brackets, that's the main thing they're interested in. That children will be safe here." Visible through the window behind her, a silver Chevy minivan sat in the drive against a backdrop of tall fir trees. Beyond the school's main entry were the shingled rooftops of the six-figure homes across the road, most of them two stories, some of them three.

"Is that this tour group's transportation?" Meg said.

Mrs. Dunn turned in her chair to look outside. "It is."

"Wow, some wagon," Meg said. A broad-shouldered young man in a chauffeur's uniform stood outside the minivan, polishing the fender. Blond shoulder-length hair hung below his billed cap. *Sort of a hunk for a hired hand,* Meg thought.

The headmistress's forehead wrinkled. "I certainly hope you'll be more formal than that."

Meg felt like biting her lip. "I can be, ma'am, of course. Is there something I should know about this bunch, before I show them around?"

"Such as?"

"Who they are. Social status, possibly. What it is that makes them preferred customers."

"Benefactors, Miss Carpenter. We don't have customers at Riverbend School." Mrs. Dunn touched the rosary on her desk, and for an instant Meg wondered if she'd upset the woman to the point of saying a few Hail Marys. On the western wall, beneath an antique hand-carved cuckoo clock, was an oil painting of the Savior on the cross between the two thieves. Mrs. Dunn squinted at a notepad. "It's a group from the Dallas Theater Center. One is Victoria Lee, in fact. *The* Victoria Lee. The actress."

Meg frowned. "What actress?"

The headmistress pursed her lips. "*The* actress."

"I'm sorry, ma'am," Meg said, "but I must be out of touch. I've never heard of her."

Mrs. Dunn blinked. "I agree. You are out of touch."

"What's she played in?"

"She's . . . oh, lots of things."

"Well, can you name just one of her roles? If I'm to meet the woman, I should comment on it."

Mrs. Dunn thumbed through her notepad, then let the pages flutter down. "Currently she's in *Autumn Midnight*, at the Center."

"I'm sure she's a good actress, ma'am. But Dallas Theater Center isn't exactly Broadway. Parts in these local productions don't pay diddly."

Mrs. Dunn's eyelids slitted. "Howard Molly wouldn't have referred her if she wasn't someone important. You should mind your p's and q's with these people, young lady."

God, Meg thought, *this woman redefines testy.* She opened her mouth to say something, but quickly zippered her lips. She had it now. Howard Molly, mucky-muck of the Theater Center, was one of the local bigwigs, and a call from him would cause Mrs. Dunn's glasses to fall off. Meg would bet a week's pay that the headmistress had never heard of this Victoria Whoever before Howard Molly had called, and would bet *two* weeks' pay that Mrs. Dunn was now pretending to have heard of the woman because she thought it was the thing to do. *Whether she's a legitimate actress or not*, Meg thought, *the setup with the chauffeured van requires some money.* The hunk/chauffeur now leaned against the fender with his arms folded, surveying the landscape with a bored look on his face.

Meg forced her lips to curve in a smile. "I'll roll out the red carpet, ma'am," she said.

The hair was a wig. A good one, but definitely a wig. Its color was a shade between black and brown, brushed out over the forehead in flippant bangs. The front of the do, in fact, was the giveaway; as Victoria Lee *awk*-ed and gawked around the dormitory, the bangs stayed rigidly in place. Less than a third of the way through the cook's tour, Meg was already thinking, God, when will this be over with?

"And what child's room is this, dear?" the actress said. She pronounced it, "deah," and while the Texas accent was pretty good it was as phony as the hair. Reminded Meg of Michelle Pfeiffer, playing the Kennedy assassination freak in the movie *Love Field*.

"I'd have to check the room chart," Meg said, which was a stall. Mrs. Dunn had a seemingly endless list of no-no's, most of which Meg considered idiotic, but the one with which she agreed the most was that nobody was to tell which child slept in which room. Meg glanced down the hallway, where a group of plump-ish, middle-aged women chatted patiently while the actress lagged behind. "Why do you ask?" Meg said.

"Just, just wondering." The actress batted mascaraed lashes. She's a bit much to stomach, Meg thought, sashaying here, twirling there, just loving everything about the place a little too enthusiastically for comfort. Victoria Lee wore a snow-white pantsuit and matching high heels, with a multicolored bandanna strung around her neck, and her skin was tanned the color of butter rum. Her sunglasses were L.A. Eyeworks with the emblem etched into the right lens, and she had an irritating habit of removing the glasses and sucking on an earpiece when she seemed in thought. "Do you attend the theater productions?" she asked.

"I go sometimes," Meg said. "My current, friend, I guess you'd say, isn't too interested in plays. But, yeah, I like to." She kept her tone light and airy. Something else about this Victoria Whatchamacallit, she seemed a bit too stereotyped, as if playing the *public perception* of an actress rather than being one for real. "What ages are your children?" Meg said.

"I don't have children." Victoria Lee was bent over, examining a row of clay vases molded, painted, and kilned in art class. The pantsuit hugged a fanny to die for. Meg thought her own bottom a little on the skimpy side—though she hadn't had any complaints, she reminded herself—and it occurred to her that this chick likely did a lot of working out. *About my age*, Meg thought, *a year or two either way, twenty-six to thirty, give or take.*

"How *darling*," Victoria Lee said.

"The kids worked hard on them." The short hairs at the nape of Meg's neck were suddenly standing on end. "What interested you in our school, Ms. Lee?"

There was the barest twitch in the actress's upper lip. "You should catch *Autumn Midnight*. I think you'd like it." She dug in her purse.

"I only have weekend evenings off. I live here in the dorm." Meg folded her arms. "Where did you hear of Riverbend?"

"Oh, perfect. Please take these for Saturday. It's our last performance, and you must come to the cast party afterward." She handed Meg two pasteboard tickets. "Bring your friend. Significant other's what they say these days."

Which Meg thought was tired jargon—significant other. She said, "I wouldn't want to crash someone's cast party, especially since I don't know—"

"Come on now, I insist." Victoria Lee looked closely at the fire extinguisher in the hallway case. "This is well maintained, isn't it?"

"Inspected every two months," Meg said.

"What about night patrols?"

"I check the girls through the night."

Victoria Lee arched an eyebrow. "Oh? How often?"

Meg's chin moved slightly to one side. "Occasionally."

The actress seemed irritated. "Come on. If I'm considering a donation, I want to know these kids are safe out here." She pointed down the hall, toward the back exit. "Does that door stay locked?"

Meg hesitated. Opening up to this woman would eliminate any complaints to Mrs. Dunn, which in turn would do away with more lectures from the old tyrant. But Meg stood her ground. "I don't have any problem with your knowing whatever, Mrs. Lee. But the rules here are, I'm not supposed to tell anyone certain things. If you want to talk it over with Mrs. Dunn, I'm sure she'd work something out. Answer all of your questions. Oh, and as for the tickets. I'm sure I'll be there, though I may have to drag my friend along by the ear."

Meg felt just the tiniest bit sorry for Frank, but wasn't about to let him off the hook. "Relax," she told him. "You might even enjoy it."

He sipped from a transparent plastic cup, which held just enough Scotch to color the water the shade of weak tea. "It's the suit. I wear one maybe twice a year, and this one's gotten too tight for me."

She rolled her program up and laid the cylinder affectionately on his forearm. "It doesn't look too tight. Be still, my heart."

"You're just saying that. Look, couldn't we just—"

"Am not. You look terrific in a suit." Which was the truth, she thought, wavy brown hair peaked over his forehead, a spray of winning freckles and sort of an Alfred E. Newman, what-me-worry grin. When she could get him to grin, which at the moment was quite a chore. Broad shoulders and a thick, muscular neck, like a jock dressed up for the Heisman Trophy ceremony, but an expression as if he'd be more at home doing some blocking and tackling.

"I don't feel terrific," Frank said. "Tell you the truth, I feel out of place."

Meg blinked. "I never would have guessed."

"It's these people." Frank looked around at a lobbyful of men in dark suits, a few tuxes in the crowd, women in drop-dead spring cocktail dresses and full-blown evening gowns, all creating a hubbub of conversation while sipping weak highballs from transparent plastic cups. The padded carpet was beige, four wide steps ascending to the exit, clear glass panels revealing stately elms and sycamores, moonlight reflecting from a still river and the mansion rooftops along Turtle Creek Boulevard. "A couple of guys over there, one of them saw this off-Broadway. Says he's dying to compare this cast with the one in New York. What do I do if somebody asks me something like that, offer them vanilla?" Frank ran his finger around inside his collar.

Meg showed what she hoped was an encouraging smile. "Just tell them you went to see *Guys and Dolls* instead, the last time you were on Broadway. Everybody's seen that one, so nobody's likely to ask you how it was."

"Jesus." Frank looked toward the auditorium entry, where a slim young woman collected tickets. She wore a floor-length pink gown. "How long's this going to take?" he said.

"There are two acts, the first is longer. Probably a couple of hours. Two and a half, at most."

One corner of his mouth bunched. "Can't we blow this off and go to a movie? Come on, Meg, let's go."

She blinked. "I've been invited, Frank, I can't just . . ."

"Oh hell, just read a review. Then tell this actress you saw the play if you ever run into her again. She won't know the difference."

"Somehow I think she will. And if Dunn the Hun finds out I took the tickets and then didn't show up, I'm never going to hear the end of it." Meg had worn her lone formal evening getup, a black straight dress with a lace jacket flared around her hips, and matching spike heels. The outfit had set her back two seventy-five the previous winter at Lord & Taylor's closeout sale, and she was reducing the balance at a snail's pace, twenty bucks a month on her revolving charge account. She was glad to finally have the chance to wear the damned thing, which made up some for the months of sneering at her closet every time the L & T statement arrived in the mail. "You'll probably enjoy the cast party more," Meg said.

"I'll bet."

Frank looked absolutely miserable, and Meg felt a twinge of guilt. She opened her program and ran a freshly manicured nail down the cast list. Victoria Lee was fourteenth in order of appearance, her part identified merely as "Woman in Station." Hardly a starring role, Meg thought. She examined the full-length program cover photo of the featured performer—Sarah Teas, an actress with Broadway credits—then thumbed through the pages to the bios. Not much on Victoria Lee, just a notation that she'd most recently appeared in *Garnet Acres* in Memphis, Tennessee, a play of which Meg had never heard. She closed her program, rolled it up, and shoved it under her arm.

Frank watched her like a man about to receive the death penalty.

"I'll level," Meg said. "I don't want to go through this any more than you do. But this woman seemed a little strange yesterday when she toured the school, and . . . let's just say I want to catch her act firsthand. Humor me, Frank." She threw him a saucy wink. "I might even make it worth your while."

Act II was ten minutes along before Victoria Lee made her appearance. By then Meg was every bit as bored as her escort, and probably more so. The play was a real yawner, action zero, a turn-of-the-century period piece about a young country girl falling in love in the big city.

The moment she'd been waiting for came in a train station scene, at a plot point where the heroine had decided to forsake unrequited love and head for home. If Meg hadn't been meticulously counting the actors' appearances, she never would have recognized Victoria Lee. The actress's hair was hidden by a different wig than she'd worn at the school, coal black this time, stuffed underneath a sunbonnet. She also wore a bustle and car-ried a parasol primly under her arm, and all of the phony Texas accent was gone as well. Victoria Lee's lone contribution was to shriek at the star, "There's a gentleman looking for you" so loudly that it was comical, then exit left. Some juicy part, Meg thought. She leaned over and whispered to Frank, "That's her," and then did a double take.

Frank's mouth was open in astonishment. His gaze was riv-eted to the spot on the stage where Victoria Lee had been.

Meg said softly, "What's wrong?"

Frank turned to her. "You mean, the one that just left?"

A woman with blued white hair, seated one row ahead, turned to stare daggers. Meg bent nearer to Frank and whis-pered, "Yeah. Why, something wrong?"

Frank relaxed and leaned back. "Aw, nothing. For a second there she looked like somebody I know."

Howard Molly had mint-sweet breath, a pointed chin, and a piercing, pin-you-down stare. "Since I've been single again," he said, "I've had trouble meeting people. The job takes up so much."

Which made about the tenth time he'd mentioned his divorce during a five-minute conversation. *Criminy*, Meg thought, *talk about backing a person into a corner.* She held her drink in both hands, keeping the glass in front of her in case she needed to fend the guy off. "Have you tried the singles clubs?" she said, glancing beyond him in search of Frank. She and Frank had gotten sepa-rated somewhere between the entrance and the hors d'oeuvres table, and Meg hadn't spotted him since Howard Molly had herded her off to one side.

"Those places are dangerous," Molly said. "So much disease going around." He wore a tux with blue satin lapels. He leered.

Meg continued her survey of the restaurant's interior, her gaze roaming the long, linen-covered table and falling in turn on cheese trays, shrimp on ice, crabmeat laid out with goblets of cocktail sauce, and a huge platter of smoked salmon. Arnold's-in-the-Quadrangle was the name of the place, and Meg had heard that the owner, a Lebanese guy, was quite a theater buff. He'd kept the restaurant open late for the cast party.

"You wouldn't have to worry about diseases," Meg said to Molly, "if you took your time getting to know people. Learn something about their background before you—"

"I believe in getting down to brass tacks," Molly said. "You attend our plays often?"

"Not much." Meg now looked to the standup bar, where a slender man in vest and bow tie mixed something in a cocktail shaker. Sarah Teas, the star with the Broadway credits, was holding court, surrounded by two older women and four men. Still no sign of Frank.

"Well, you should," Molly said, moving in closer. "I knew you weren't a regular, or I would have recognized you." He watched her as if trying to decide which part of her anatomy to grab.

"You make it a point to meet all the women," Meg said.

"Especially the attractive ones." Molly produced a business card. "I'm director of the Center."

"I know who you are."

"You do? Have we met?"

Meg moved in a half-circle around him so that her back was no longer against the wall, giving herself breathing room. "No, we haven't, but you know my boss."

Molly's chin tilted. "Who is . . . ?"

"Helen Dunn. I teach at Riverbend School. In fact I'm—"

"You do?" Molly stepped back as if she'd poked him with a cattle prod.

"—the one who showed Victoria Lee around the other day, after you referred her."

"You are?" Molly changed from Big Bad Wolf into Caspar Milquetoast in the wink of an eye. His thick hair was sprayed in

90

place and he was graying at the temples. An ample belly poked out against his coat.

"That's me. We had a nice visit. She seemed really interested, especially in our security."

Molly averted his gaze. "I don't seem to remember sending her."

"You must have. Mrs. Dunn doesn't forget those things."

Molly quickly had a sip from his highball. "I'm certainly glad you came. Can you excuse me? I see a . . ."

"Maybe we could have the two of you out. You and Ms. Lee."

Molly licked his lips. "I'm sorry, I do have to go." He left her flat, walking quickly away and mingling in the crowd.

God, Meg thought, is it my perfume? At that instant she spotted Frank. His shock of hair was visible near the bandstand, where a three-piece combo played. Frank balanced a plastic dish in one hand while shoving smoked salmon on a cracker into his mouth with the other, and Victoria Lee had all of his attention. She'd changed from her stage costume into a pale blue cocktail dress that looked painted on, and as she spoke to Frank her eyes twinkled in come-hither merriment. As Meg watched, Victoria Lee put her hand on Frank's shoulder, stood on tiptoes and whispered something in his ear.

Meg blinked. Dammit, this two-bit excuse for an actress was *hustling* Frank, no doubt about it. And Frank—the *slug*, Meg thought—acted as if he was enjoying the attention, grinning like a moron.

This chick had better go beat someone else's time, Meg thought. She made a beeline through the crowd, practically running over Howard Molly as he struck up a conversation with a thirtyish blonde. Molly didn't even glance at Meg. She walked up behind Frank and tapped him on the shoulder. "Hi," she said. Then, to the actress, she said, "Hello, Ms. Lee."

Victoria Lee smiled like Eve. "So glad to see you." She glanced quickly at Frank, then zeroed in on Meg.

I'll just bet you're glad to see me, sweetcakes, Meg thought.

"Frank mentioned during the play that you looked familiar," she said. "Do you two have something in common?"

They covered up pretty well, but Meg didn't miss the look that passed between the two. "Nothing at the moment," Victoria Lee said. "Must be one of those things, you know, where they say everyone has a double."

"Meg," Frank said quickly, "you want me to get you something?" He gestured toward the hors d'oeuvres and bar area.

Meg let her gaze roam back and forth between Frank and Victoria Lee. Finally she said, "I don't think so. I think we'd better leave, Frank. I feel a headache coming on. I can't imagine what's causing it."

10

During the ride to Frank's apartment, Meg made small talk. She absolutely *would not* ask him about Victoria Lee. Frank was her first real thing in a couple of years, and she was determined to give him plenty of room. The breathing-down-one's-neck approach had terminated her last relationship, with a corporate lawyer in a downtown firm, and the problems she'd had in breaking it off had given her the permanent willies. *God,* she recalled distastefully, *I couldn't even go to the supermarket without having to account to the guy.* So if Frank happened to know Victoria Lee from some other life, that was his business. No way was Margaret Ann Carpenter going to be anybody's clinging vine. . . .

Frank responded to Meg's small talk with a series of uh-huh's and uh-uh's, gripping his Jeep Cherokee's wheel with both hands, streetlamps casting moving shadows on his cheeks and nose. Aha, Meg thought, he's feeling guilty. I won't have to ask about Miss Footlights; before the night is over, good old Frank will spill the beans.

They bounced into the parking lot at his complex and nosed in between a Corvette and a Buick four-door. Frank cut the engine, then sat for a moment and toyed with his keys. Meg waited patiently. Finally he said, "I guess we'd better go on in."

The breath eased from her lungs. *He's on the verge,* she thought, *right there on the edge.* "All right," she said sweetly, then waited properly in place while he came around and opened the door. As she stepped down on the asphalt she kissed his cheek. He averted his gaze.

The breeze carried the scent of rain, and distant lightning illuminated a bank of thunderheads. Springtime in Texas was one raging storm after another. During the night a deluge would come; by morning the sun would shine. Meg climbed the metal steps, lightly touching the banister along the way, her gaze sweeping the parking lot and surrounding bushes in reflex. There'd been a recent string of driveway robberies in far North Dallas, but as yet the hijackers hadn't struck in Frank's eastside neighborhood. Nonetheless, coming in late gave Meg the creepy-crawlies. Once on the landing, she waited while he fumbled the key into the lock. Then he pushed the door ajar and stood aside. She showed him her best, not-the-slightest-bit-curious smile as she crossed the threshold.

He said, "Listen, do you . . ."

Meg waited.

". . . want a drink?" he finished.

Come on, Meg thought, *out with it. So you and old Victoria used to do the number. I can handle it*. She crossed the living room, switched on a lamp, and sat on the sofa. "Oh, I'll have a Coke," she said casually. The apartment was twenty or thirty years old, the carpet thinning. Frank's furniture was bought used; a couch, some end tables, a TV set on a rolling stand. The bare bones.

He went into the kitchen, set a two-liter bottle on the counter, produced two tumblers from the cabinet, and peered at her through the opening above the bar. "Ice?"

"Yes. Sure."

He opened the freezer compartment and fished in the ice-maker. "Mrs. Reed spelling you at the dorm this weekend?"

She is, Frank, Meg thought. *Just as Mrs. Reed stays at the dorm every Friday and Saturday night, as you damn well know.* "Yes," she said.

He dropped shards into the tumblers. "You're lucky you've got her. *We're* lucky."

Meg shrugged. "She's getting paid. It's a part-time job for her. She's retired, so . . ."

"I mean, it's good that the school could find somebody."

"I suppose it is." The suspense was killing her.

He poured Coke into both glasses and recapped the bottle, then carried the drinks over and set one beside her on an end table. "Listen, Meg."

She crossed her legs, smoothed her black skirt, and arched an eyebrow.

He took off his coat and yanked down his tie. "There was this situation one time."

His face is getting red, she thought. *Well, it ought to.*

He folded his coat and laid it across the back of the sofa. "I don't know how to begin." He sat down beside her.

She concentrated on the console stereo, somewhat of a relic, hand-carved Spanish-style wood. "You could try the beginning."

He leaned forward, forearms on thighs, and held his drink between his knees. "That actress?"

She sipped cold, fizzy Coke. "Oh? What actress is that?"

"You know. That Victoria Lee."

She looked at him. "Oh. *That* actress."

"Well, that's not her name."

Her lips parted.

He watched the floor. "I knew her in California."

"Before you met me."

"Well . . . yeah."

"I'd say that's your business, then," she said.

He ran his fingers through his hair. "Jesus, I don't know how to tell you this."

She tilted her chin. *You don't, huh? Let me guess, she's the best you ever had.* "I can handle it, Frank," she finally said.

"I was . . ."

"Sometimes if you blurt it out," she said, "that makes it easier. Look, if you had a thing with her, so what?"

"What the hell. I was in prison."

Her body sagged. "Frank, I . . ."

"I was a cop."

She felt relief. "You mean, you worked at a prison. What's so—?"

"You remember, six years ago, a cop shooting a black guy here in Dallas? Big federal trial, all in the papers."

She vaguely did. In those days she was more interested in the next Fiji party. Phi Delt, whatever. "I seem to," she said.

"Well, that was me. I did some time over it, in California."

She felt an odd emotion, somewhere between pity and anger. "That's the real reason you were out there? You weren't working in California, like you've told me."

"In the federal prison system they have a rule that law enforcement people get sent far away from home. For protection, to keep them from running into somebody they arrested."

Meg sat up straighter and returned her drink to the end table. "All this time, you've never told me. I'd be a better actress than Victoria Lee if I shrugged this off, Frank. Not that that's a primo accomplishment."

"Listen, I've wanted to."

She was suddenly calm. "Wanting to scores no points. What was she, some kind of prison groupie? She seems like a kook."

He fiddled with the ends of his tie. "She was an inmate. Darla Bern's her real name."

"Holy smoke, Frank . . ."

"We were at—"

". . . you two share the same rockpile, or—?"

"—Pleasanton, California, together. At the same time, not really together. It was coed."

She'd heard of federal boy-girl prisons and of what went on in there. "Were you two . . . ?"

He watched his knees. "Yeah. Yes." He looked at her. "Nothing emotional. I doubt if she's got any emotion in her body. Strictly a thing where she'd sneak into the men's dorm. Happened a lot in there, those women. Guys without any . . . you go a long time without . . . it affects you, you know?"

"God, spare me the details. Is she really even an actress? You couldn't tell by her performance."

He nodded. "She had bit parts. She showed me a picture once, of her and Julia Roberts on the set of *Pretty Woman*."

"I'll bet she was playing a whore."

Frank grinned. "How did you know?"

"Call me psychic." Meg tilted her head back, wheels turning. "Wonder why the pseudo. Darla Bern's a better stage name than what she's using."

"I guess it's 'cause she doesn't want anybody knowing she did time. A lot of ex-cons use aliases. I've even thought about it myself. Probably would, if I wasn't on parole."

"What's she want to tour a school for? She doesn't even have any kids."

"I don't even think she finished school herself," Frank said.

Meg had a sudden cold feeling in the pit of her stomach.

"In fact I remember," he said, "that she hates kids. Gave me a blow-by-blow description of this abortion she had when she was, about fifteen, I think."

"I've got to let Mrs. Dunn in on this," Meg said. "I hope the poor woman doesn't have a heart attack."

"I'm not sure I follow."

"Exclusive private school," Meg said. "Kids out there whose folks are worth millions." She drained her glass. "Your prison girlfriend taking a tour, that's a little on the fishy side."

"She's not my girlfriend. You are. Listen, Darla's not what you'd call a criminal mastermind. Strictly a dope fiend. It wasn't just me in the joint, she used to have some guards bring her grass, even some coke one time."

"How lovely. Whatever, she wasn't at the school to research a teacher's role she's going to play. God, that horny Howard Molly guy."

"Who?"

"The director of the Theater Center. He's the one that referred Miss Cellblock Poontang to the school. Probably took some in trade."

Frank got up. "You're guessing about that."

"Maybe. But better safe than, you know."

His forehead wrinkled. "Look, up front and with no dodging. Where does all this put us?"

Her features softened. "You mean, your prison term?"

"Sure. Hell, you wouldn't be the only one worried about hanging around with a jailbird. I've got experience in that."

She hesitated, then stood up and touched his cheek. "I'd be lying if I didn't tell you I'll have to think on it. Off the top of my head I'd say that it would depend on how much the convict beats himself up over his past. For now, let's just go to bed. I feel like being held, okay?" She took a couple of steps toward the bedroom and looked at him over her shoulder. "Want me to dress in stripes?" she said. "Maybe pretend I'm sneaking into your cell?"

Meg lay on her side, her cheek resting on her palm, watching the illuminated clock/radio digits change as if by magic to read 2:32. An easy-listening station was on low volume, old-time movie tunes, an orchestral version of the theme from *Picnic*. Bedsheets rustled behind her, weight impressing the mattress, moving up close, Frank's voice a near-whisper, practically in her ear. "You asleep?"

"Mmm."

"Me, neither. Tomorrow's going to be hell, with no sleep."

"Double mmm."

He raised up on his elbow. Stubble on his chin scratched her shoulder. "There's more I didn't tell you."

The song on the radio ended, the mellow violins now blending into the theme from *A Summer Place*. Meg hummed softly along.

"Do you want to hear it?" he said.

"Sure. Unless you're going to tell me you're an ax murderer. If you're going to bury a blade in my back, I'd rather be surprised."

"I wasn't telling the whole truth, about Darla not having any emotion."

She scooted onto her back, cast the sheet aside, flattened one foot on the mattress and rested her ankle on her knee. She watched him, the outline of his face and shock of hair, a dark shape against a background of ceiling tinted red by the light from the radio.

"After we'd been seeing each other awhile," he said.

"Is that what you call it? Seeing each other? Seeing up close, right?"

"I didn't know anything about her at first. I was the new guy in the compound."

"Sort of the rookie."

"It isn't funny, Meg."

"I agree with you."

He sat up, folded his legs yoga fashion, and hunched over. "She got a lot of favors from the guards in prison. Some of the other inmates."

"She wasn't your exclusive property."

"That's putting it mildly. What we had only lasted three or four months, while I was too much of a greenhorn to know what was going on with her. When I found out what she really was, I cut it off."

She raised her arms and interlocked her fingers behind her head. "How painful for you."

He lifted his chin. "You just make all the remarks you want to. I was in prison. Different world, you'd just have to be there. I gave up trying to tell people I didn't commit any crime a couple of years ago, because nobody believes you no matter what you tell them. The fact that the guy I killed was stoned on crack and doing his damnedest to cut my windpipe open doesn't matter anymore. What does matter to me, though, is what you think. And I'm telling you all this because I wouldn't want you finding it out from somebody else."

His bedroom window was open a fraction, and the breeze cooled her thighs. There was mist in her eyes and an odd pain in her throat. "I've got a problem with it, Frank. If she hadn't suddenly appeared, I'm not sure whether you'd have ever told me this. Maybe I'm supposed to say just, been there, done that, and go on, but I can't."

He looked at the ceiling, then back at Meg. "As soon as I quit having anything to do with her, she turned on me hard. Made a lot of scenes. I'd pass her on the compound and she'd scream out a lot of . . . I won't repeat some of the things she said."

He reached for her. She pulled away. "Not now, Frank. I want to hear all of this, but from a safe distance."

"I never would have believed she could be that vicious," Frank said. "Then sometimes she'd go the opposite, sidling up to me and trying to, you know, start things all over again. One time she got high on some wine a guy used to make, came up to my cubicle and tried to force her way in bed with me. I had to throw her out bodily."

"Why, anybody that's been through high school," Meg said, "could see right through that act. Might be it's more rustic in prison, but the same thing. The scorned-lover syndrome."

He scratched his bare shin. "She had all these other guys. Why me?"

"It doesn't matter who else she had. You were the one she couldn't have. Good-looking women who have a lot of men around them all the time are the worst losers in the world when something doesn't go their way." Meg wondered how anyone who'd been through what Frank had could possibly be this naive. Like a big, tough little boy.

"Whatever her motives," Frank said, "she almost drove me crazy. She got her release from prison about a year after I first went to Pleasanton. Doing time sure wasn't fun for me, but it was a whole lot more bearable after she was gone.

"Once she got out," Frank said, "I thought I'd never see or hear from her again. And I didn't, until about a year ago."

Meg took her ankle down from its resting place on her knee and straightened her legs. "I don't know if I want to hear this part, Frank. Before you met me, that's one thing. Please don't tell me you've been seeing this woman the whole time we've been . . ."

"Hell no, Meg. And much as I care about you, that's not the main reason I don't want to have anything to do with her. I wouldn't want to see Darla again if I never touched another female. She's downright scary.

"About a year ago," Frank said, "my phone rings one night about ten, ten-thirty, and it's her. Drunk as a skunk, I thought at first, but thinking on it she was probably high on drugs. She was calling from California, and starts in on this, how she missed me so much and wanted to hop on a plane for Dallas right then. I've never been able to get downright rude with anybody, and I talked to her longer than I probably should have. Told her, thanks for calling, but no thanks. Jesus, she went on and on.

"I should have been rude," Frank said, "because that started this series of calls, every day. If I wasn't home she'd leave messages on my machine, sometimes as many as ten in a two or three-hour period. Sometimes her messages were nasty as hell, calling me names for not getting back to her. She'd keep calling until I got home, even if it was four in the morning or something."

"It's obvious she needs help," Meg said. "What I'm wondering is, do *I* need more help than she does."

"She's not going to get any help from the people she hangs around. I finally moved, my lease was up anyway, changed my phone number, and had it unlisted. I thought, with her in California, that would be the end of it."

"Obviously it wasn't."

"Right on. Sometime back, I can't remember exactly when, a guy came by where I work. Wilbur Dale. He's the only person I did time with that lives in Dallas, that I know of. I really didn't think much of it at the time, sort of old home week, you know? Wilbur's still on parole, the same as me, and it was no trick at all for him to find out where I worked if he wanted to see me. All these parole officers, a guy's file's supposed to be confidential, but those people talk like the old ladies' bridge club.

"Anyway," Frank said, "I didn't mind because I always sort of liked Wilbur, and sometimes it helps to talk to somebody with the same problems you've got. Sort of like A.A., I guess. He wanted to know if I had any girlfriends. I didn't see anything un-usual about the question, and I told him all about you."

Meg sat up. Her lips parted.

"Hey, okay, I was wrong," Frank said. "But I was excited about you, what can I say? Wilbur had a sundae or something, we talked awhile and he left. No big deal, I thought at the time. Actu-ally, I don't think Wilbur Dale crossed my mind again until last week."

"He came by again?" Meg said.

"Nope. Darla called."

Meg stretched out on the bed and watched him. "I can for-give a lot. I don't know if things can be the same, but I can forgive. But, criminy, if you've put me in danger from this . . ."

"She somehow got the number of the pay phone across the lobby from the ice-cream place," Frank said, "which is what made me think of Wilbur Dale. He's the only connection, that knows both me and Darla, and the only way she could know where I'm working is through him. This time she was calling from here in Dallas. She wanted me to meet her, so I did."

"You shouldn't have done that," Meg said. "It's just egging her on."

"Obviously my life hasn't been free of screwups," Frank said, "so you can just add this one to the list. I talked to her in a bar on the East Side, by Tenison Park Golf Course. Told her to leave me alone and wound up with her in a screaming fit. She hasn't called me at home yet, so I don't guess she's found my number. Wilbur Dale doesn't have it, thank God. And then tonight, there she was onstage. She absolutely collared me at the cast party. Jesus, where were you?"

"Getting collared myself," Meg said, "by that Howard Molly."

"Anyway, that's the story," Frank said. "She's here, so she's here. I don't know for how long and don't care. I don't think Darla would try to do anything to you, but you need to keep your guard up."

"Her taking a tour of Riverbend wasn't a coincidence, Frank."

"I'd like to think that's what it was," Frank said. "But you're right, it wasn't. Jesus, Meg, I hate getting you mixed up in—"

"Hush." She put two fingers over his lips. "I've got to think this out. First of all, for precaution's sake, I need to let the school in on her past."

"I wouldn't think Darla's any kidnapper," Frank said. "All that she's ever been, other than crazy, is a dope fiend. She did mention that she's not in town alone. Said she could get in trouble with her friends if they knew she'd contacted me. With somebody to lead her, Darla might be mixed up in anything. And you're right to put the school on notice. You just never know."

"School on notice, check," Meg said. "They'll be grateful. Putting Daddy on notice, that's going to be different."

Frank rested his hand on her thigh. "Daddy who?"

"*My* daddy. My father. And my mother. Who you were going to have the pleasure of meeting next weekend."

"All I know about your folks," Frank said, "is that they live someplace in North Dallas."

"Well, I may be forward, but you were about to get invited home with me. I see them once a week, Tuesday afternoons. This week I was going to clear the decks, to get you invited to dinner next Saturday night. It was going to be a relief for them, since they've decided I've become a total hermit." Meg sat back up. "Now I just don't know, Frank."

He wiped his hand across his forehead.

"My parents don't dictate my life and don't want to. They're with me a hundred percent, whatever choice I make. You've hurt me with all this. I can deal with you being in prison. I can't deal with the fact that you've lied to me, and that you've seen this woman recently and kept it a secret from me."

He lowered his chin, hangdog. "I just didn't know how to tell you."

"I'm afraid I can't just grin and accept that." She turned away from him and faced the wall. "Let's just try and get some sleep, Frank. I'm afraid if I say anything else in the mood I'm in, it's going to be wrong."

He touched her shoulder. "Does that mean you're through with me?"

She shrugged him off. "I don't know just what it means. Whatever it means, I'm going to have to think on it. You haven't been open with me, Frank. Whether I can get over that . . . I'm afraid I'll just have to let you know."

11

The suitcase was brown alligator, inlaid with red-tinted cowhide. Each of its two gilt latches had an individual combination dial. Randolph Money worked first the left-hand dial, then the right, snapped the catches, and opened the suitcase on the bed like a silverware salesman. "Specially made, babes," he said. "Take a couple of weeks to duplicate. No way can they do that, as I see it."

"What's going to be in there," Darla Bern said, blinking, "they can deliver in a gunnysack. Cardboard box, for all I care." She was seated on a chair near the bureau, still in the pale blue backless minidress she'd worn to the cast party, exposing six to eight inches of taut stockinged thigh, bare shoulders, and breastbone. She'd removed her shoes and placed them side by side on the dresser. Her wig was draped over a Styrofoam head model, and she was brushing her hair.

"That's what makes me important in this," Money said. "The planning." He wore snow-white pants along with a robin's egg blue blazer. As he stroked the inner edges of the suitcase compartment, he said, "Take the dimensions. Twenty-four two-thousand-dollar wrappers of hundreds fit like a bug in a rug. They short us a stack, the money will rattle around. One wrapper too many, the lid won't close. Twenty-four two-thousand-dollar bundles. How much is that, my narcissistic friend?" He looked toward the window, crossed his legs and rocked one spotless white loafer up and down.

Gerald Hodge peered out between parted drapes at the LaQuinta Motel sign, at headlights moving back and forth along LBJ Freeway. He wore a black leotard and a ski mask. He turned to face the room. "Your what?"

"My narcis—... my *handsome* friend. That better?" Money winked at Darla, who smirked.

"I'm not as dumb as you think, using all those words," Gerald said. "Narcissus was the guy that fell in love with himself. I knew a dancer had that name, had a flower over his dick."

"Ah, experience replaces education once more," Money said. "Come on, how much? Twenty-four times two thou." His navy blue golf shirt was buttoned all the way up to his throat.

Gerald straightened his arm and stroked his triceps. His brows tightened in concentration. "Forty-eight grand."

"Exactly. Now, extend the equation. The stacks will fit twenty across, ten down. Not one cubic centimeter of wasted space and, more important, no room for any transmitting devices unless we can spot them. Two hundred stacks. How much money, total?" He snapped his fingers and pointed at Gerald. "Quick now, no pocket calculators allowed."

Gerald scratched his nose. "Two times forty-eight, that's . . . fuck, over nine million." Pale skin and mud-brown eyes were visible through the ski-mask openings.

Darla's chin tilted in interest. She laid her hairbrush down.

"Nine million six, Gerald," Money said. "I cheated on you a little, I already knew the answer. And yes, Miss Bern, before I arrived at the final figure I checked to find out what our merchandise might be worth to the interested parties. Took a couple of days." He closed the suitcase, sat on the bed and crossed his legs. He had a slight double chin. "Christ, I'd underestimated these people. I knew they had bread, but how much I hadn't imagined."

"I think they've got ways," Darla said, eyeing the suitcase, "to fit transmitters in the linings. I knew some kidnappers in Pleasanton."

"I remember," Money said. "A couple of them used to take turns on you. But trust me, babes. A microchip the size of a pin-head is all it takes. Let them. We don't care." He lovingly patted the suitcase.

Gerald sat down in a chair and propped his feet up on a table, listening.

"Cost me pretty good to cover all bases," Money said. "What the hell, we *hope* Mr. Fed hides one of his cute little transmitters in there. It'll give him something to do." He dug in his pocket and came up with what looked like a TV channel changer. "This thingy-bob," he said, "homes in on their transmitter. I click this baby, it tells me exactly where our prize is." He showed a toothy grin. "I'm worth more than my share, as I see it."

Darla reached to the nape of her neck and pulled the zipper a couple of inches down the back of her dress. "We've got the school layout down."

"That we do," Money said, folding his hands around his knee. "What about our old buddy Frank?"

"He came to the cast party with her."

Money grinned. "Goes without saying. You made yourself scarce, didn't you, babe?"

Darla stood, wiggling, pulling on the zipper. Her gaze averted slightly, she said, "Sure. The way she was hanging on to him I couldn't have gotten a word in anyway. I could show that bitch a few things." She gave up, walked over to the bed and turned her back. "Undo me, Randolph."

Money got up and tenderly brought the zipper down her spine. Gerald scooted his chair over for a better view. Money said, "They mingled, huh? Met some people."

"Even signed the guest register, names on the same line. Must have been seventy-five or a hundred there." Darla retreated to the bureau, pulled her dress off over her head, and tossed it on the floor. She shook her hair out.

Money looked her over, slim tanned legs, full hips, pale blue pushup bra. "What time's your date, babe?"

She checked her slim gold watch and stripped down her pantyhose. "Three-thirty. I've got an hour."

Money leaned back on his elbows. "We've got our ducks in a row what we're doing, huh?"

"My head hurts we've been over it so much," Gerald said. "Fuck."

"Well then, go over it till your head doesn't hurt anymore. Excellent therapy. Till you could do it in your sleep."

Gerald grunted and brought his feet down off the table, chewing on the lower edge of his ski mask's mouth opening.

"I understand everything," Darla said, "up to the point where they deposit the suitcase." She unsnapped and shrugged out of her bra. "What happens then?"

Money's gaze roamed her up and down. "Nice tits."

She tweaked her nipple. "How do we pick up the money, Randolph?" She raised one knee to step out of one side of her panties.

Money watched the ceiling. "We've talked about it before. It'll get done."

"Your mystery guy," Gerald said, running a finger underneath his mask and snapping the elastic. "This fucking outfit's hot, Darla. Get your ass in gear."

"Mystery man," Money said. "Mystery woman. Mystery dog, maybe."

Darla opened a drawer, picked up a box from Frederick's of Hollywood, lifted the lid and took out a pair of red bikini briefs with the crotch cut away. She put them on. "You know, Randolph, if it turns out we can't trust you, you're going to have both Gerald and Basil awfully pissed off at you. Me, too, if they don't get to you first." She smiled.

Money dusted his lapels. "This isn't about trust, babes. It's about, we need each other. I do my part, you do yours, everybody's happy in the end, as I see it."

"Best you make us happy, Randolph." Darla reached in the drawer for a short red dress and wriggled into it, then stepped into red spike heels. "You ready, Gerald?"

Gerald got up and, shoulders rotating slightly, followed her toward the door.

Money said, "Wait a minute."

Darla turned with her hand on the doorknob. "What is it?"

Money closed his eyes, his chin moving up and down. "Just thinking. You sure we're finished with this guy?"

"I can't imagine what else we'd need the asshole for," Darla said.

"You know the old saying," Money said. "You never know what you need something for until the day after you've gotten rid of it. Then it's too late. To put it another way, is there a good reason we can do without him?"

"He's the only one that knows we've got a key to his lake house. The official address they've got for me, at the Theater Center, is this motel. He wanted it that way, thinks he's having this really discreet affair. Minus him, there's no way for anybody to connect us to the house at the lake."

Money shrugged. "A point well taken."

Darla released the knob and rubbed a polished nail with her thumb. "Besides, if you think of something we need him for, tough shit. This guy's going. I can't stand one more time with him, the turd." She looked at Gerald and crooked a finger. "Come on, masked man."

They left. Money rolled onto his side and fiddled with the suitcase latches. He whistled a happy tune.

Howard Molly felt that the sessions were never long enough. Always too short. He wished they would go on and on. "Take your time with me," he pleaded.

Darla Bern finished tying Molly's ankle to the chairleg with a length of soft cotton sash material, and rose from her haunches.

"Is that too snug?" Both of his ankles were now secure and his arms were around the chair back, his wrists bound together.

"God, no." Molly struggled and strained. A strip of sash was tight around his chest. "I love them tight. Christ . . ." He wore flowered boxer shorts, his bare stomach hanging out over his lap, his fly gaped open, his erection sticking up.

Darla came around in front of him and brushed her nipple against his lips. "Who knows what you like, baby?"

"You. God, you." Molly poked his head forward, his lips straining for her breast. She backed away. Perspiration ran down his forehead. Visible beyond her were the hall tree just inside his bedroom door, a framed appreciation certificate to the Theater Center from the Dallas Junior League, photos of himself alongside the mayor and the governor of Texas. "Nobody but you," he panted.

She placed her hands behind her and thrust out her hips. "Since when, baby?"

His gaze riveted on red panties, elastic tight around the tops of her thighs, the crotch open to expose a patch of . . . *Christ.* "Since the first . . . *oh.*"

"Since the first time you laid eyes on me?" She sensuously ran her fingers up her sides to the tips of her breasts. "Remember how I sucked your cock?"

"Jesus. Oh, Jesus, do I . . . ?" Spittle ran down his chin and dripped onto his chest.

"And all the other times. Show me how much you like it, Howard." She bent from the waist, compressing her breasts with her upper arms.

He struggled even harder and made a choking sound.

"Am I a good actress, Howard?"

"Oh, God. Oh, God, yes."

She gritted her teeth. "And that's why you gave me the part, isn't it?"

He closed his eyes. "You're a great actress." He thought he might come, right now.

She grabbed his ears and yanked them outward. "Bullshit, Howard. Have you been good?"

"Oh yes. Done everything you . . ."

She bent near, nipples touching his cheeks, and put her lips close to his ear. "You have been good. And I have a surprise."

He opened his eyes, smiling. "A surprise?"

"Don't you like my surprises?"

"Yes. Yes, oh, God . . ."

She backed away. He looked down at his erection. Oh yes, a surprise, he thought, a surprise just for me. Oh . . .

She opened the door. A huge man came in wearing a ski mask. He was in a skintight black leotard, shoulders, biceps, and thighs bulging. He wore gloves and carried a short rope. He walked deliberately forward.

Molly's features sagged. "Who is . . . ?"

"Why, he's your surprise, Howard," Darla said. "Just wait, you'll like it."

Molly's eyes widened as the man approached and looped the rope around his neck. "You won't hurt me," Molly said.

Strong hands yanked. The rope bit into Molly's windpipe. He gagged. His cheeks were instantly bloated, filled with blood. He couldn't breathe. His lungs burned.

Darla came over and put her face just inches from his. "I want you to know something while you're dying, Howard. I hate you. Every time you've ever touched me, I wanted to puke. I think you're a sleazy little shit, do you understand me?"

Molly tried to speak, but the only sound he could make was a soft croak. The masked man pulled the rope even tighter, forearm muscles writhing under stretched black nylon.

"I hate your fucking guts, Howard," Darla hissed.

A red haze filtered over Molly's vision. He sagged in his chair. As he fell unconscious for the last time in his life, Darla Bern punched him in the ribs. The blow jarred him, but Howard Molly felt no pain.

12

Mrs. Helen Dunn's hand trembled as she held her teacup precariously in front of her lips, a puzzled look on her face as if she was having trouble finding her mouth. God, Meg thought, if she drops the whole mess in her lap I'm going to die laughing, right here.

Finally Mrs. Dunn sipped. She set the cup into its saucer with a soft glassy clink. "I'm going to give you the benefit of the doubt," she said, "and assume you're hallucinating."

Meg sat in an Early American chair with curved legs, her fanny barely making an indentation on the taut, springy cushion. "I'm not hallucinating, ma'am," she said. "And I'm not mistaken. The lady gave you a phony name."

Mrs. Dunn folded her hands in her lap. She was perched on the exact center of a sofa with a grape-leaf design, a matching piece to the chairs. The headmistress wore a long pleated blue velvet dress. Purplish veins and liver spots showed on the backs of her hands. "Before you throw out any more accusations," she said, "remember who referred her. Howard Molly wouldn't be a party to anything off-color."

"I met Mr. Molly," Meg said, "and got the impression that if you'd blow in his ear he'd be a party to anything." She mentally kicked herself. Tact, Meg thought, isn't my long suit. Frank had tried to kiss her that morning as she'd left his apartment. She'd averted her lips and offered her cheek. Meg's vision blurred. She lowered her gaze.

"Now that's uncalled for." Mrs. Dunn leaned back and testily folded her arms. "Howard has all the credentials." A six-foot grandfather clock towered against the wall to her left, its gilt pendulum swinging back and forth, ticking and tocking. Beside the clock was an Early American rolltop desk. The room smelled of rose sachet.

Meg took a shallow breath and forced herself to calm down. She was on a tear and knew it, so much so that she'd showed up in Mrs. Dunn's parlor wearing faded jeans, dirty white sneakers, and a blue T with "Hoo-hah" emblazoned across the front. Bearding the headmistress wasn't going to help the situation one bit. Meg assumed her best sympathetic tone. "I know you respect Mr. Molly, ma'am. But aside from your professional dealings, what do you really know about him?"

Mrs. Dunn sniffed the air as if detecting a pile of dog manure on the carpet. "The Dallas Theater Center wouldn't employ anyone without a thorough background check. You're dealing with the *crème de la crème* there."

If the Molly guy is the cream of the crop, Meg thought, then I'm Punjab. "Don't we emphasize security, ma'am?"

Mrs. Dunn added cream to her cup from a sterling pourer. "Security is one thing. Absurd conjecture is another."

Meg sat intently forward. "Please follow me, Mrs. Dunn. Victoria Lee. You mentioned her to me as if she's a famous actress, and I told you I'd never heard of her. Did you really know who she was, or did you rely on Mr. Molly's buildup?"

"Of *course* I'd . . ." Mrs. Dunn snapped, then seemed to think it over, and said, "I don't really keep up with that sort of thing."

"All the time I was giving her the tour, she asked about ten million questions about, let's see, which doors were locked when and how often I checked on the girls at night. She also wanted to know which child lived in which room. All of that information we hold confidential."

"Nothing suspicious about that, Miss Carpenter. Anyone leaving their children in our care would want to know those things."

"What does the room's individual occupants," Meg said, "have to do with whether her own kids would be safe?"

Mrs. Dunn closed her mouth, then said, "Just curiosity on her part."

"Quite a bit more than that, ma'am. I went to the performance on Saturday night, and to be kind, let's just say her part was somewhat less than the starring role. Plus, I later learned that Victoria Lee's not even her name."

"A lot of those people use pseudonyms." Mrs. Dunn's hostility had melted into a reserved curiosity.

At least I'm making progress, Meg thought. Mrs. Dunn stirred her tea.

"Certainly they use stage names, all the time," Meg said. She adjusted her position on the hard cushion. God, if she had to sit in this chair on a day-to-day basis, her rump would be terminally sore. "Her real name is Darla Bern, and she was sort of an actress out in California."

"See there?" Mrs. Dunn picked up her saucer. The teacup jiggled.

"Plus," Meg said, "she did some time in federal prison."

"My goodness." Tea mixed with cream sloshed around and dribbled over the edges of Mrs. Dunn's cup to puddle in the saucer.

"Also, for the clincher, she doesn't even have any children."

"That's ridiculous. Why would she be looking into a private school if she . . . ?"

"Exactly," Meg said. "I want to call the police, Mrs. Dunn."

The headmistress firmed her lips. "We can't go off half-cocked. What's the source of your information, Miss Carpenter?"

Meg opened, then closed her mouth. She's got me there, she thought. What do I tell her, that I found out from the ex-convict, my weekend shackup whose past has just now come up to slap me in the face? The old tyrant would really get some mileage out of that. "Please trust me, ma'am," Meg finally said.

"I have to have more than just your word," Mrs. Dunn said, "if I'm to tell the Board of Regents I'm calling the authorities in. I will do this, though. I'll call Howard Molly and discreetly inquire about the lady."

Discreetly inquire? Meg thought. *Discreetly inquire? We probably need around five thousand national guardsmen surrounding the place, and this woman's going to discreetly inquire. Great.* "I think it needs to be done immediately, ma'am," Meg said.

"This is Sunday, dear. People are otherwise occupied."

"I'm not sure we should chance another day. The kids will all be in the dorm tonight and I'll be alone with them. Excuse me if I won't be completely at ease."

"You're alone with them every night except weekends, Miss Carpenter, and this will be no different. Mrs. Reed hasn't reported anything out of the ordinary."

"It just takes one night, ma'am."

"No more melodrama, please. I've already said, I'll call Howard Molly. Tomorrow." Mrs. Dunn set her saucer down and folded her arms. Audience over.

Meg's jaws clenched. She looked at her lap and drew in breath. She sighed. "Thank you, ma'am," she finally said.

Meg pulled off Forest Lane into the Riverbend School grounds at five-fifteen, a quarter hour before she was to relieve Mrs. Reed, parked, and cut the engine. Tall trees surrounded the parking lot and perfectly mowed lawns showed on all sides through the trees. More stately elms and sycamores grew in front of the administration, classroom, and dormitory buildings. The weather was muggy, spring rain in the forecast, faraway thunderheads standing out against the horizon. *Likely a tornado coming,* Meg thought. *All I need.*

She left the car and went halfway to the dorm, then stopped

with her mouth working in thought. She retraced her steps, opened the Mazda's passenger door, and fished inside the glove compartment. Finally she stood holding her Beretta .25 and dropped the pistol into her handbag, then moved on to the dorm. Her footsteps echoed from the tan brick walls of the building, and the sound seemed to linger forever in the air.

As she ascended the steps and pushed open the door, she pictured Frank for perhaps the thousandth time that day. Twenty-four hours earlier she'd thought him the love of her life. *And what the hell,* she thought, *I'm still crazy about the guy.* Maybe in a few days the shock of knowing he'd lied to her would wear off. In the meanwhile, she'd take things one step at a time.

13

The Dalforth brats weren't about to turn their radio down, they told Meg, and they'd damn well listen to whatever station they wanted. "The Edge is rad," Trina said. She was a pretty blonde, tall and thin, wearing a shorty gown that barely covered the tops of spindly legs.

"It's awesome," Trisha said. She was a blonde as well, bigger-busted and wider-hipped than her sister, and wore blue satin pj's.

Meg forced a smile and hoped she didn't look as if she was in pain. "It may be rad, and it may be awesome. But it's not what we're going to broadcast up and down the hall. Other people want to sleep. Plus, I don't think the sexual innuendos are what teenage girls should be listening to."

The girls exchanged snickers, and then Trisha wrinkled her nose. "It's not Howard Stern, Miss Carpenter."

Meg folded her arms and leaned on the doorjamb. "Same stripe. Look, kids, when you're at home I don't control what you listen to. But we're accountable to everybody's parents, not just yours. I don't care for anyone to know I'm letting you play the freaking Edge on the radio after bedtime. Why don't you switch to ninety-eight point seven?" She glanced in turn at twin beds on either side, identical desks built into opposite walls, the entry to the bathroom the Dalforth girls shared with the students next door. Both desks were strewn with candy wrappers, lipstick, and wadded tissues. Shoes and clothes were scattered on the floor. "I don't think you'll pass inspection tomorrow unless you do some straightening up," Meg said.

Trisha picked up a brush and ran it through her hair. "Ooo, ninety-eight point seven, that's *oldies*."

"But goodies," Meg said. "Change the station or retrieve your radio from me in the morning." The boom box blared from the windowsill, in front of the lowered shade. The Dalforths' room was on the ground floor. The window was nailed shut from the outside, partially to protect the girls, but mainly to keep them from climbing out to snort dope with their friends. Earlier in the semester Meg had found nearly an ounce of cocaine in Trina's footlocker. After a conference with the girls' father (during which, Meg was sure, he'd opened his checkbook and made still another donation), Mrs. Dunn had swept the matter under the rug. A torrent of rain battered the window. The shade brightened, dimmed, then brightened again as lightning flashed.

Trisha adjusted the volume on the radio. The disc jockey bantered on about Madonna's appearance in Spain, where the Material Girl had rubbed the national flag up and down between her legs. According to the would-be radio comedian, after Madonna's performance the flagpole had disappeared. How utterly quaint, Meg thought. "Change the station," she said.

Trisha stuck out her tongue and made no move to touch the dial.

"That's it, Matilda." Meg stalked across the room, unplugged the radio, and stuffed it under her arm. "You can pick this up after breakfast. Oh, and it's ten-thirty, girls. Lights out. We're having lock-in tonight, by the way."

"You're locking us in our *room?*" Trisha shot her sister a glance of panic. "It's Sunday, Miss Carpenter. Hey, please."

"This isn't punishment, if it'll make you feel any better. I'm doing this for a reason." Call it overreaction, Meg thought, but I'll breathe a lot easier with the hatches battened down.

"Is *too* punishment," Trisha wailed. "And you'll be hearing about it."

Meg blinked. "Oh? From whom?"

"From Daddy." Trisha picked up an issue of *Vogue* and angrily riffled the pages. She looked at her sister, then back at the magazine.

"Well, I'll tell you, Miss Dalforth," Meg said, "you can tell Bill Clinton if you want. At this point I frankly don't care who you tell. Lights out."

Trisha sneered. "Tough titty, aren't you, Miss Carpenter."

One corner of Meg's mouth bunched. "No, I'm not tough . . . whatever. I'm responsible for you." How she kept from slapping both of these little trashmouths silly, she didn't know. With a nod for emphasis, Meg backed into the hall, tightened her hold on the radio, fished in her robe pocket for the key, closed the door, and locked the deadbolt.

From inside the room, her voice muffled, Trisha Dalforth said loudly, "Bitch." Meg gave the key an extra-angry twist for good measure.

With all eighty-six boarding students locked in their rooms, lightning flashing outside and thunderclaps shaking the windows, Meg prowled the corridors in her bathrobe. *Like some kind of freaking Anne Boleyn,* Meg thought, her head tucked underneath her arm, ta-taa. The Beretta bounced heavily around in her pocket. She rounded the corner into the east wing, went down the hallway and rattled the exit door. Securely locked, only one more to go. She retraced her steps, wrinkling her nose at the fire extinguisher, and made a left into the northern section. Thunder rolled. The lights went out for an instant, then flickered back on. Meg's heart pounded as if trying to tear its way through her rib cage. She took a deep breath and plodded ahead. The double door was ten steps away, the safety bar across, the panels tightly . . .

The left-hand portal was open a foot.

Frowning, a painful lump suddenly in her throat, she pushed the door further out and peered outside. The overhead floodlight glinted through rain like pellets. An inch-deep flood of water cascaded from the porch and splattered on fine white gravel in the flower bed. Meg forced a laugh; who the hell would be wandering around in a typhoon? She backed inside, yanked the door to, secured the safety bar. As she retreated down the hall she reached in her pocket to touch the Beretta's grip.

She entered her apartment, locked the door behind her, and gazed in disgust on ungraded themes stacked on her kitchen table. The thunderstorm, coupled with the run-in with the Dalforth brats, had Meg wired like ten gallons of coffee. She doubted she would sleep a wink, much less face a herd of boy-crazy sophomores in the morning with anything resembling a smile on her face. She picked up the papers and doggedly lugged them through the bathroom.

The apartment was a converted dormitory suite, with the bathroom in between the bedroom and kitchen/dining area. As she passed the shower, water dripped on tile. She'd had to buy a new twin bed when she'd moved in, because the king-size from her North Dallas apartment simply wouldn't fit. She sat on the mattress, scootched her fanny up to lean against the headboard, and steadied the pile of papers in her lap. She reached in her nightstand for her grade book, then looked in irritation toward the lit-up TV.

Jesus Christ, after eleven already. On the screen, the late news was wrapping up. She reached for the remote to turn the damned thing off. The remote wasn't in its usual place on the nightstand, so she slid the drawer open and felt inside. As she did, the television clicked off on its own.

Meg sat up straighter. Lightning flashed outside the window. Thunder shook the building.

A woman came out of the bathroom carrying the remote in one hand. In the other she held a revolver, which she pointed at Meg. "I can't stand TV, can you?" the woman said in a clear West Coast accent. She wore jean cutoffs and a man's shirt with the sleeves rolled up a couple of turns. A black ski mask covered her features, her eyes and mouth visible, outlined in white.

Meg couldn't move. Her throat constricted. The papers slid from her lap and fluttered to the floor.

A big man followed the woman in and stood beside her. Wet, shoulder-length blond hair hung below the bottom of his ski mask, which was identical to the woman's. He had a weightlifter's sloping shoulders and wore a muscle shirt along with black spandex shorts. *The chauffeur,* Meg thought. *Sure, drove the minivan. Why the ski masks?* she thought. *God, do they think I'm a retard?* A tight knot of fear growing in her chest, Meg giggled.

The woman raised the pistol in both hands, and aired back the hammer with two sharp clicks.

Meg said, "The," then her voice faltered. She cleared her throat and said, "The kids are all locked up. You can't get to them."

The woman and the muscle man exchanged a glance. He crossed in front of the woman and walked up to stand near the head of the bed. The woman said, "We can't?"

Meg firmed her lips. "No, you can't. So you might as well leave."

The woman tilted her head. "Well, maybe they can come out. You think?"

Meg raised her voice. "They can't get out. You can't get them." On her right, the big man laughed.

"Well, since they can't get out," the woman said, "then they won't see us carrying you down the hall, will they?"

Meg stared.

The woman nodded and waved the pistol. "Sure it's you, you dumb bitch. What, you think people can't find out who you are?"

The man grabbed Meg's wrist and brought a wad of cloth up

from behind him. She tried to pull back, but it was as if her arm were clamped in a vise. He pressed the cloth over her mouth and nose, and heady fumes wafted up her nostrils. The room tilted crazily. The woman's image blurred. Meg held her breath until her lungs ached, then gave it up and inhaled. Her senses left her. Just as she passed out cold, she remembered the Beretta in her pocket. *Useless*, Meg thought dreamily, *useless as hell.*

Part II

EXECUTION

〰〰〰

" 'Mr. Arrington, are you testifying today of your own volition?'

'Sure am.'

'You haven't made any deals, or received any offers of leniency?'

'Not a one.'

'And if you would, sir, please tell the jury. Why would you agree to do this?'

' 'Cause I want the record straight. I wanted the money, sure, but the rest was all him. Wasn't none o' me, wantin' to kill that woman.' "

—from trial transcript,
*State of Texas v. Gilbert Wayne Arrington
and Ronnie Louis Ward*

14

Frank was so dead to the world that the shotgun prodded his cheek three times before he came to.

He'd tossed and turned and stalked his apartment until three in the morning, picking up the phone to call Meg a half-dozen times before changing his mind. When he finally did sleep he had a series of nightmares, all with Darla Bern as the main performer. A couple of the dreams featured Darla in a Catwoman costume, scaling walls with feline grace and snatching sleeping kids from their beds. Twice Frank woke up in a cold sweat, got up, and plodded into the kitchen for a drink of ice water. Finally at six in the morning he snored off, only to dream of Darla once more. This time she was in bondage-game leather, snapping a lion tamer's whip at three teenagers who cowered in a corner. Just as she reared back to strike, something hard poked against Frank's cheek. He pushed the thing away and snuggled deeper under the covers. Darla had changed in the dream; now vampire fangs protruded from her mouth. The something hard nudged Frank a second time. He pushed it away again. He was in the dream room with Darla now, reaching out to grab her hand as she cracked the whip. He strained with all his might, trying to . . .

The hard thing prodded Frank again, with enough force to cut his cheek against his teeth. A husky male voice said, "You're not asleep, asshole." Frank opened his eyes. He tasted blood.

He was looking down the barrel of a sawed-off over-and-under. The slim young guy holding the shotgun squinted one eye. "Please try something, motherfuck," he said.

There was movement on Frank's left. He ran his tongue over the cut in his mouth as he shifted his gaze, getting a profile view of a second guy, this one husky with thick hair the color of dishwater, standing over the bureau with the top drawer open, rummaging around inside. Frank looked back at the shotgun. The slim guy grinned at him.

"The money's on top," Frank said, "in a clip, next to the wallet." His throat was dry. He was still too sleepy to be really scared, but the fear glands were beginning to flow.

The husky one paused, holding up one of Frank's three neckties. The tie was blue with white polka dots. "You got shitty taste, man," the guy said. "And I already found the money. You got thirty-eight bucks, Rockefeller, you think this is a heist?" He wore faded jeans along with a waist-length blue windbreaker. He turned his back to reveal "FBI" stitched between his shoulder blades in large gold letters. "We're the heat, Harold. Now you get up slow and get some britches on."

Frank expelled breath as anger welled. "Move the fucking shotgun," he said.

The thin guy sneered and prodded Frank's nose with the barrel.

Frank watched the guy. "I said move it. And show me a warrant or get the fuck out of my apartment."

The windbreaker wearer closed the drawer, turned to face the bed, leaned his rump against the bureau and folded his arms. "We got no warrant, Waldo. You used to be a cop, Chris, you'd know about all that. This is what we call emergency strategy. You don't like it, write your congressman." He looked toward the shotgun toter and said, "You can lower the weapon. You won't have to shoot this guy. Watch Mr. White put his pants on and then escort him out in the living room." He stepped toward the bedroom exit.

The guy backed off and lowered the over-and-under, barrels up. Frank threw the sheet back and swung his legs over the side of the bed. Mr. Windbreaker paused in the doorway and turned back. "The pants are optional, Oscar. But there's a lady waiting for you out here. You want to see her in your underwear, it's up to you."

There were two more men in FBI windbreakers searching the kitchen. As Frank came out of the bedroom followed closely by the shotgun, one agent toasted Frank with a coffee cup. "How you doing?" the agent said. They'd helped themselves, the Mr. Coffee pot half full on the counter alongside a pound tin of Folgers and a jar of powdered coffee creamer. The second agent was down on his haunches, peering up under the sink.

Frank made a right and led Mr. Shotgun into the living room. The shock had just about worn off, and Frank wasn't sure how he felt. Mad, yes. Afraid as well. The first year he'd been on parole, he'd felt like diving for cover every time a squad car drove by. As he entered the living room his emotions congealed into a lump that settled into the pit of his stomach like lead.

Ms. Marjorie Rapp wore the same outfit as the last time Frank had seen her, a plain brown dress with a shapeless skirt bunched around her calves, and brown flats. She clutched her plain brown shoulder bag in her lap, just as she had at the ice-cream counter, and regarded Frank with lifeless eyes beneath grainy lids. She was seated on the sofa alongside the husky FBI man. Frank coughed nervously and sat in an easy chair. Mr. Shotgun stood off to one side.

Ms. Rapp dug a legal-sized sheet of paper from her bag. "This is a parole commission warrant for your arrest, Mr. White. Unexecuted. Thus far."

Frank's gaze flicked at the paper, then back up. "I've made all my reports. Kept a job." He scratched his bare chest. He was barefoot, having slipped into loose-fitting jeans while Mr. Shotgun stood by.

"And have consorted with felons," Ms. Rapp said. "By your own admission. That's grounds, Mr. White."

Frank leaned forward and rested his forearms on his thighs. "One guy, I told you about. He came by work, I couldn't just—"

"You told me about, that's my point. It's grounds, technical though they may be." Ms. Rapp glanced at the FBI man as if seeking his approval. "You'll be entitled to a full hearing, Mr. White, after you've been in jail a couple of weeks."

Frank couldn't believe this. "I'd lose my job."

"And have to find another," Ms. Rapp said, "to comply with the conditions of your release on parole."

"Let's cut through," the agent said, then smiled at Ms. Rapp and said, "Excuse me, Ms. Rapp. I think we're confusing Mr. White." He sat back, crossed his legs, and rocked one gray running shoe up and down. "I'm Agent Turner, Mr. White. A while ago you said something about search warrants. I told you we've got none. But we do abide by the rules, one of which is that we're not supposed to contact guys on parole without first checking it out with their parole officer. And none of us want to violate any rules, am I right?"

Frank looked over his shoulder. The two guys in the kitchen had interrupted their search to come forward and lean on the counter. A draft from the air-conditioner vents raised goosebumps on Frank's neck and shoulders. He wished he'd put a shirt on.

"So here's the situation, Stanley," Agent Turner said. "You got every constitutional right in the book. No mistake about it, you want a lawyer you just say so. We'll even let you call one to meet you at the Mansfield jail, which is where we take federal prisoners these days. You can call this lawyer and refuse to talk to us and pull every stunt all you guys do to make things worse on yourselves. Personally, I think you could even beat the parole violation charge. After you have this hearing Ms. Rapp was talking about, which would take place after you've been in jail a week. Am I right about the procedure?" He looked at Marjorie Rapp.

"The rules say seven days," Ms. Rapp said, "*working* days, which is really nine, counting the weekend. Unless he executes a waiver of the time limit."

"Oh, I doubt he'd do that. Mr. White's way too savvy to be executing any waivers, huh?" Turner looked at Frank.

Frank intertwined his fingers and stared at the floor. "I'll bet there's an alternative," he said, "dealing with you guys."

Turner grinned and pointed a finger. "You're right, Snow White. Smart guy. Ms. Rapp here doesn't like to mess up anybody's life, picking the fly manure out of the pepper. She'd like to reserve parole revocations for times when there's something really serious."

Ms. Rapp smiled the first smile Frank had ever seen on her, and regarded Agent Turner with a pleasant expression. *Bet she'd like for him to get in her pants*, Frank thought.

"What we were thinking is," Agent Turner said, "that maybe you could go along with us without all the yelling for a lawyer and what-not. What we'd do is, just take a little ride and go visit some people. If you would, I think Ms. Rapp might tear up this arrest warrant she's got."

Frank sat up and shifted his weight from one buttock to the other.

Turner was suddenly serious. "We'd want it understood, from the outset, that you're not under arrest. Nobody's forcing you to do anything. Anytime you want to go, you're free to. Just you give the word." He spread his hands in an umpire's "safe" signal.

Frank couldn't resist a small grin. "Sure. That way I'm not entitled to a Miranda warning, and anything I say you can use against me."

Turner laughed. "Miranda . . . ?" He looked to the two guys

in the kitchen. "Who said these guys were dumb, huh?" He ze-roed in on Frank. "You got the picture, Paul, pretty well. Now. As long as we're going to be calling on people, I think you should finish getting dressed. Wouldn't want people to think we're haul-ing a half-naked Indian around, would you?"

Frank called Harold Willett to say that he'd be late for work, and that he wasn't sure what time he could come in. Willett said, "Second time in a week. This is getting sort of old."

"Nothing I planned," Frank said. "Personal business."

"That's one thing the parole people told us. If you changed your habits, started showing up late, we should let them know about it."

Frank glanced at Mr. Shotgun, who stood in the bathroom doorway, watching. Then he said to Willett, "Okay, Harold. Give them a call." He hung up, regretting his words and wondering if he'd still have a job tomorrow.

He put on a lime green Jack Nicklaus golf shirt, slipped his feet into off-white Nikes, and followed Mr. Shotgun out of the apartment, down the stairs, and into the parking lot. Puddles of rainwater glistened under a warm springtime sun. Agent Turner stood beside a dark blue Taurus four-door with the driver's door open, talking to Marjorie Rapp. As Frank approached, Ms. Rapp favored him with a final withering look, climbed into a red Geo Prism, and drove away. Mr. Shotgun stowed the over-and-under in the Taurus's trunk. Frank opened the rear door on the driver's side. Mr. Shotgun walked up to him and dug a pair of handcuffs from his pocket. The handcuff chain clinked faintly.

Agent Turner did a double take. "Jesus Christ, he's not under arrest."

Mr. Shotgun said, "Oh." He jammed one bracelet into his back pocket and let the other dangle, then went around and climbed into the front passenger seat. Frank got in back, and Agent Turner slid behind the wheel and started the engine. The upholstery was vinyl and smelled almost new. The air conditioner blew cool air on Frank's cheeks and nose.

Turner put the car in reverse, draped an arm over the seat, and looked through the rear window to back up. Frank said, "Where we going?"

Turner gave the Taurus a little gas and the car rolled backward. "You'll see."

Frank looked through the back window, up the stairs toward his apartment. "Those other two guys. They're still up there searching my place, huh?"

Turner spun the wheel and dropped the lever into the drive position. "Yeah. If they break anything we'll reimburse you, that fair enough?"

Frank leaned forward. "Hey, no reason you can't cut me some slack. I've been in law enforcement. What the hell you hassling me for?"

Turner braked at the driveway exit and turned around in the seat. "Once and for all, Allen. You just sit there. When we get where we're going you'll find out. Tell you what, though, I'll give you something to think about."

"Huh?" Frank said.

"Food for thought. You want to think while we're driving, don't you?"

"Well . . ."

"Sure you do. Now think, Thurman. You know somebody named Margaret Ann Carpenter?"

Frank was suddenly cold. "Meg?"

"Margaret Ann Carpenter. Now, while we're getting to where we're going, you try and remember where you know her from. Come up with a good one, okay?"

The last time Frank had taken a ride with the feds was the day of his indictment, and on that occasion he'd been handcuffed. They'd arrested him at main police headquarters downtown, just as he'd checked his squad car in at the end of the day shift. Frank would never forget the two guys, both wearing dark blue suits, one with a brush mustache and the other with a Band-Aid covering a cut underneath his eye. Just as he'd pulled up to the gas pumps they'd approached along with his shift captain, an overweight man named McFee. McFee had ordered Frank out of the car and had confiscated his .45 service revolver. Then the agents had flashed their IDs, manacled his wrists behind his back, and led him away. Frank had been too stunned to speak, and had been afraid that he might throw up.

Instead of the usual procedure—loading the prisoner into a vehicle in the police garage for transportation to the marshals' for booking—the agents had paraded him down the corridor and had taken him up to ground level on the elevator. Then they'd hustled him out through the main exit onto Commerce Street, where a gang of reporters and TV cameramen had been waiting, and Frank had turned his face away from the media people as he'd ducked into the backseat of a G.S.A. Motor Pool car. He'd seen himself on television as he went through in-processing at the county, and even standing in a group of prisoners he'd felt embarrassment. He remembered thinking about his mom and dad, who gathered around the TV every night at suppertime, and wondering how they felt when the image of their boy came on the screen. Since then he'd been imprisoned in the Dallas County jail, three more county holding facilities on his way to the pen, and two federal prisons. Every place where he'd done time, the other men had learned that Frank was a cop on the street. He suspected that the information had come from the guards, though his file was supposed to be strictly confidential. He'd had threats from some of the baddest inmates in the federal system, and even had broken his collarbone fighting off a bunch of prisoners as they'd lined up to do a gang rape on him. But he still considered the awful moment when the FBI agents had brought him into public view as the worst experience of his life.

Until now.

He sat in the backseat of the unmarked Taurus as Agent Turner drove north on Central Expressway, and worried about Meg. Jesus, he just had to know. As Turner exited the freeway just beyond Northpark Shopping Mall, and made a slow-moving left onto Walnut Hill Lane, Frank tried, "Look, has she been hurt or something?"

Mr. Shotgun draped an arm over the seatback and grinned at him. Turner watched Frank in the rearview mirror. Finally, Turner said, "Has who been hurt?"

Frank scooted his rump forward on the cushion. "Meg."

"Meg who?"

"Carpenter. You know who I . . ."

"Margaret Ann Carpenter?" Turner said.

"Sure, Meg."

"You tell me." Turner and Mr. Shotgun exchanged looks. "Has something happened to her?" Turner said.

All of which told Frank that talking to these guys was a waste of time. He leaned back. "I don't know," he said. "Has it?"

For the rest of the drive Frank watched the tree-shaded two-lane street on both sides, big homes getting even bigger as the Taurus proceeded to the west, two-story Gothic and rambling modern houses set behind yards the size of polo fields, creeks twisting through wooded properties. A few blocks beyond Inwood Road, Turner made a left on a curving blacktop, then wound his way even further left beside a three-story with its own moat in front, complete with draw-bridge. They left the main road and entered a gravel drive, lined on both sides with cedar bushes, and crunched over gravel for a hundred, hundred and fifty yards, to stop before a huge stone porch and a massive front door. Dead center in the door was a brass knocker. Frank blinked. Though he'd been raised in Dallas, and except for his time in prison had lived here all his life, he hadn't been in this neighborhood over three or four times. Once he recalled in connection with a burglary a couple of miles from here, when the chief had dispatched Frank's squad from South Dallas to help in the inves-

tigation because the owner of the burglarized home had political clout. Mr. Shotgun watched Frank with a strange, crooked grin.

Turner killed the engine. "This's it. You've been here before, huh?"

Frank frowned. "Me? Never."

Turner got out, opened Frank's door and stood aside. "Sure you haven't. Get a move on, Marvin, we got people waiting."

Frank stood up in the drive. Fifty feet away a bluebird hopped and twitted in the lower branches of a sycamore. The driveway up ahead widened into a turnaround, and Frank counted three more unmarked Tauruses in addition to a Porsche and a four-door Jag. The front door to the house opened and two men in dark blue suits came out. Turner climbed the steps up onto the porch and said something to the suits, who looked at Frank. Mr. Shotgun escorted Frank around the three men, past a statue of two cherubs, and on inside. Turner and the two blue suits followed. Turner closed the door with a solid, echoing thunk.

They were in a wide entry hall with a floor of marble tile. A thick oriental throw rug, around ten by twenty, covered the middle of the floor, and about twenty feet ahead a carpeted staircase ascended. Fifteen or twenty steps upward was a flat landing, after which the staircase bent to the left and went on up and out of sight behind the entry hall ceiling. Over to Frank's left was a teakwood breakfront; inside the breakfront were delicate china plates, cups, and saucers, and a gleaming sterling punchbowl. Photos in chrome frames decorated the walls; one featured a silver-haired man in slacks and a sweater with his arm around a beautiful woman with striking, graying hair. There were growing-up pictures of a little girl, one at around age three riding a tricycle, another a school picture with the front teeth missing. As Frank looked over the girl's graduation photo, complete with cap and gown, his eyes narrowed. The next picture in line, a full-length evening gown pose, confirmed it. The girl was Meg. Frank gaped at Turner, then moved in for a closer look at the photo.

The same silver-haired man who appeared in the picture came from the back of the house, around the base of the staircase. He wore a lightweight jogging suit, navy blue with red stripes down the arms and legs. The guy was trim and in shape. He looked at Frank and said to Turner, "This is him, huh?"

Turner didn't answer. Frank nervously cleared his throat and extended his hand. "Frank White." He grinned.

The guy said, "You cocksucker," knocked Frank's hand aside, and threw a haymaker.

The punch came in from left field and the guy didn't have his feet planted. Frank saw it coming and moved his head just enough so that the blow glanced off the side of his jaw. Nonetheless the punch stung, and for just an instant Frank's vision blurred. As the man wound up to swing again, Frank raised his hands in a defensive posture.

The two blue suits moved up, and Turner stepped in as well. "Now, Mr. Carpenter," Turner said, "you've got every right. But let's keep our purpose in mind, okay?"

Frank thought, Mr. Carpenter? He noted the family resemblance, the same slim nose and prominent dimples. Meg had told him she'd planned to get him together with her parents. Apparently her father didn't think that was a good idea.

The blue suits herded Carpenter back toward the rear of the house. As they did, Carpenter pointed a finger in Frank's direction. "You're dead meat, fella, you hear me? Dead fucking . . ." He was breathing hard, and showed a pained expression as the agents moved him out of sight behind the staircase banister.

Turner looked at Frank. "How's that affect you?" Turner said.

Frank bit his knuckle. "How does it . . . ?"

Turner sneered. "It doesn't. You guys, it never does." He crooked a finger. "Come on. Follow me."

The agent led Frank through double doors, through a den featuring a shiny black grand piano and a fifty-inch television screen, into a library which Frank figured to be forty feet long, minimum. The vaulted ceiling was two stories overhead. Book-cases extended floor to ceiling. There was a librarian's movable ladder attached to the cases, with rollers top and bottom. Frank caught a few of the titles as he passed: Dickens and Thoreau, modern works by Michener, Saul Bellow, and even some by Robert B. Parker, Elmore Leonard, and Stephen King. His feet sank into padded carpet. Ceiling fans *whup-whupped* overhead.

There were three sets of easy chairs in the room, each set surrounding a small reading table. In the center of one table, ivory pieces were aligned on a pewter chessboard. At the far end of the library was a huge mahogany desk, and behind the desk sat a pretty, fortyish woman in a black suit. Her hair was short and flippy, ice-skater fashion, and she wore tiny gold-framed reading glasses. Agent Turner escorted Frank over to stand in front of the desk. The woman was writing on a yellow legal pad, and now laid her pen aside and looked up. "Hello, Frank," she said.

Air escaped Frank's lungs in a long soft sigh. "How you, Miss Tate?" he finally said.

"It's Mrs. You have a short memory. My friends call me Felicia, but that doesn't include you at the moment." She pointed a forefinger in the direction of a straight-backed cushioned chair across the desk. Her nail displayed a clear lacquer polish. "Sit down, please."

Frank sat. Don't tell her anything, he thought. The last time he'd tried opening up to this lady, he was pretty sure the conversation had cost him an extra year or so in prison.

She reclined in a high-backed swivel chair and fiddled with her hair. "You know what I think about when I see old acquaintances like you?" Her voice was a husky alto, low-pitched.

Frank thought that one over. "No, I don't. Indictments. How much time you made us do, I don't . . ."

"Those thoughts come later. I mean, when I *first* see you. Like right now." Tate's manner was informal, her voice resonant. In closing arguments she'd take on an evangelistic dialect like

Sharon Falconer, something Frank had witnessed firsthand.

Frank rested his ankle on his opposite knee and folded his arms, not saying anything.

Tate put her elbows on the armrests and rested her chin on her intertwined fingers. "I think about my puppy." She glanced at the matching straightbacked cushioned chair alongside Frank's. "Sit down, Dave."

Agent Turner sprawled into the chair and regarded Frank through slitted lids.

"He's a cocker," Tate said. "Blond, cute, six months old. Everybody at our house adores him, including me. You know why he reminds me of you?"

Frank recalled that Tate wore a lilac scent. He had a quick whiff. "I don't have the slightest idea," Frank said.

"Because he does number two in the house, the naughty boy," Tate said. "Every day, three or four times we find a pile of physical evidence on the rug. The odor's enough, I don't even need the DNA testing to convict this dog."

"Maybe you should try rubbing his nose in it," Frank said. "Scolding him and putting him outside."

Tate looked upward as if in thought. "That's what I think when I see you, dear."

Frank and Turner exchanged a look. Turner shrugged.

"Now, what we've got here," Tate said, playing with the gold charm bracelet on her wrist, "is a kidnapping. This is a big enough deal, the girl's father and all, to where the U.S. Attorney assigned me to come out here and advise the FBI how to proceed, which, frankly, the FBI doesn't like one smidgen, interference from a federal prosecutor where they're investigating. Am I right, Dave?"

Agent Turner put on an earnest look. "You've got that wrong, Felicia. We're glad for the help."

"Which is what I'd expect you to say instead of something like, Fuck you." Tate looked back at Frank. "But no matter what they say to my face, they don't like it. But I'm out here. And the first thing I learn is, the missing girl has been going out with a man I prosecuted one time. You."

Frank sat forward. Sudden tears stung his eyes. "Meg's . . . ? Listen, she means a lot to me."

"I'll bet she does," Tate said. "What we're hoping is, she doesn't mean a lot of *money* to you. That's my original thought, then I say, Wait a minute. This is no kidnapper. This was a policeman who decided to blow some holes in a black guy."

"Who was trying to stab me," Frank said.

"That's something your lawyer should have established, at trial," Tate said. "But that was then. This is now. So I'm ready to dismiss the possibility that you're in on it, but then I remember the puppy. Then what I'm thinking is, Maybe Frank White is still doing number two, only he's doing it somewhere else. Maybe some time in custody has taught him not to go around shooting people, but maybe he's thought of another angle. You follow?"

Frank couldn't figure out what his answer should be. Meg being missing shook him up beyond words, and he was pretty sure he knew at least one of the people responsible, but he wasn't ready to tell Felicia Tate about Darla Bern. At least not until he'd heard a whole lot more. "Yeah, I suppose I follow," Frank said. "But you're way off base."

Tate looked at Turner. The FBI agent grinned. Tate fiddled with the earring on her right pierced lobe. "Fair is fair, Frank. Uncle Sam believes in fair. That's why we're going to give you a few minutes to convince us we should give you the benefit of the doubt and not arrest you right here and now."

Frank's hands trembled. He cleared his throat. "First of all I was a cop, remember? If you had anything but suspicion I'd be downtown at the marshals' instead of sitting here talking to you."

Tate's plucked eyebrows lifted. "Do you want to go to the marshals'? I can arrange that."

"Secondly," Frank said quickly, "I don't have a clue what's happened to Meg. Is she alive?"

Turner butted in. "That's what we're wanting you to tell us, Alphonse. Is she?"

"You're talking about kidnapping. Where from? At the school?"

Tate showed even white teeth in a smile. "Spare us, will you? You're dating this girl worth millions, you're with her about every Friday and Saturday night, but suddenly you haven't the vaguest idea where she was last night?"

"Oh, I know where she was," Frank said. "I just didn't know that's where they got her. And as for Meg being worth millions, you must have the wrong girl. She worries about making ends meet as much as I do. That's why she was living at the school. Free rent."

Tate picked up her pen and doodled on the legal pad. "Now you're going to tell us you never heard of Carpenter Truck Lines. And that elephants fly, and all that. My children enjoy *Dumbo*, Frank, but I've seen it so many times it's lost its fascination."

Frank was speechless for an instant. Carpenter Truck . . . ? He pictured the huge loading dock off Stemmons Freeway, a fleet of forty-foot rigs side by side, laborers moving around on the dock stacking freight like army ants. Morgan Carpenter, sure. Open shop, big time unpopular with the Teamsters. Meg's father? Jesus Christ, Frank thought. "Sure, I've heard of 'em," he finally said. "Who hasn't, that's lived around here for long? I just didn't know Meg was part of that family."

Turner shifted irritably and scratched his eyebrow. "Sure thing, Simon. You thought her old man was on a construction crew."

"I didn't think he was anything. All she ever told me was, he lived in North Dallas. Look, I'm interested in her, not who her folks are. She's . . . hey, corny as it sounds, Meg's turned my life around." Frank blinked, wondering why he was baring his feelings to the feds when he'd never expressed them to Meg. Wondering now if he was ever going to have the chance to tell her.

Frank rubbed his eyes, then finally looked up. Frank said,

"You're sure this is, that somebody's snatched her? Meg wasn't really happy with her job. It wouldn't be like her, but it's possible she just left on her own."

Tate leaned back and stroked her chin. She reached down to the floor and brought a plastic cigarette holder out of her purse, then sucked air through the holder. "Having to smoke outside is the pits," she said. She reached in a drawer and produced a hand-size tape recorder, then fitted a miniature cassette onto the spools.

Turner got up and leaned over the desk. "You want to think about that, playing it for this guy? If he's . . ." He looked over his shoulder at Frank.

"If he's in on it," Tate said, "then he already knows what it says. If he's as innocent as Dr. Kimball, he might catch something we wouldn't."

Turner drummed his fingers. "They say, no laws."

"Sure they do. All kidnappers do. Does it occur to you that if Frank's involved in the kidnapping, our cover's already blown just by picking him up?" Tate twirled the cigarette holder between her fingers, baton fashion, as she said, "It was in the Carpenters' mailbox. Not particularly original, this group, but I've got to admit pretty smart. The man's voice is . . . well, just listen to the love." She pressed the tape chamber down and pushed the PLAY button. Seen through clear plastic, tiny reels began to turn. Agent Turner sat down resignedly.

Frank rested his forehead on his lightly clenched fist, and listened to the silent noise of running tape punctuated by the airy thump of ceiling fans. After fifteen seconds the message began, a deep male voice distorted by tape speed, the words drawn out as if the recorder's battery was running down. The words were difficult to understand until Frank's ear got the hang of it. As he listened he raised his head.

The message was in short, terse sentences. "We have your daughter. In two days you will have instructions as to how to get her back. If you contact the FBI she will die. She will now speak briefly to you."

More running tape, followed by a clear, youthful female voice at normal speed, saying, "This isn't a play, Daddy. These people are serious. Don't do anything to set them off, okay? Remember, they aren't acting."

Frank's eyelids fluttered. The voice was Meg's, no doubt about it. Her tone was calm and matter-of-fact, and Frank felt a surge of admiration. In addition to the other things he liked about her, Meg was a pretty tough cookie. "Play" and "acting" were buzzwords, of course, intended to point toward Darla Bern, but were hints that he didn't really need. Just hang in there, babe, Frank thought.

There were a few more seconds of silence, then the distorted male voice came back on. "Remember, no FBI. As I see it, you have no choice. In two days you will hear more."

Frank looked at the ceiling. *As I see it*. Something about that. He'd have to think.

Tate clicked off the recorder, removed her glasses, and dangled them from a slim gold earpiece. Still sucking on the cigarette holder, she said, "So you'll know we haven't been sitting around enjoying the air-conditioning here, we've already speeded up the tape and listened to the guy. He's talking through a cloth of some kind, maybe just a handkerchief. Whatever it is, it muffles the vibrations enough so there's no traceable voice print for our lab folks to pick up on. It could be anybody talking."

"Including you, Yorick," Agent Turner said, looking at Frank.

Frank's forehead tightened. *As I see it* . . .

"One thing we think's significant," Tate said, "is the fact that he's instructing whoever not to call in the FBI. A yo-yo from Paducah would talk about just 'the police,' not knowing what falls under whose jurisdiction, but this man specifically says, 'FBI.' He says it twice. Makes me think the guy knows something about the system. Maybe he's even been our guest for some period."

"Which still doesn't eliminate you, Ishmael," Agent Turner said, looking at Frank.

Frank licked his lips. In the old days he would have cooperated in a heartbeat, but his own travels through the system had made him hesitant about giving the federal folks so much as his name. Finally he drew a shallow breath and said, "Look, there's this woman."

Tate put her glasses back on and picked up her pen. "There usually is. If we're getting a confession here, you need a lawyer first."

Frank waved a hand like, no, this isn't a confession, no way. "I hadn't seen her since Pleasanton, before last week. She was an actress. All that about, this isn't a play, and, these people aren't acting?"

Tate looked at Turner. "We wondered about that as well," Tate said. "We're astute wonderers, Frank."

"She took a tour of the school. Meg conducted it."

Tate dropped the holder back into her purse and now fiddled with her earring. "You're talking about Darla Bern?"

Frank inhaled, then exhaled. "You know about her."

"We haven't completely tuned out everything else just because we've got you, lover. Miss Carpenter talked to the school headmistress about Miss Bern."

"So you're already, you're going to talk to Darla."

"Even as we speak," Tate said, folding her arms. "And so we'll have everyone's story straight, let's you tell us why you think it's Darla Bern. She's a bit more than a passing acquaintance, or . . ."

"Pleasanton was a coed joint," Frank said. "I first knew her when we both worked in the sign factory."

"Odd you consider her a suspect," Tate said, "with a million and one other ex-cons running around."

Frank shifted his position and crossed his legs. "Several things. She shows up in town just before all this happens . . ."

"Not *just* before," Tate said. "She's been in Dallas a couple of months. Acted in two plays. So what? It could be strictly a coincidence that she's here, unless you know something that could eliminate the chance factor."

"That tour of the school," Frank said. "Meg said she wanted to know a lot of things about the security."

Agent Turner leaned in. "That all?"

Frank shot the agent a sidelong glance, suddenly on his guard. "Probably all that I think's suspicious."

Turner's expression tightened. "You're sure."

Frank tugged at the knee of his jeans. "Sure of what?"

"That those're the only reasons you've got to suspect this broad."

Frank's throat was suddenly dry. "What else could . . . ?"

Turner and Tate exchanged a look, then Turner leaned even closer to Frank and grinned. "That's funny," the agent said. "Some other people that were at Pleasanton say you used to fuck the young lady, Lawrence."

"Don't be crude, Dave," Tate said. "There's a lady present. It is sort of strange, though, that Frank would point the finger at someone he used to have a relationship with."

Frank wondered fleetingly who they'd been talking to. Could be any one of a number of people. The federal pen had been one place where keeping anything secret was impossible. One corner of Frank's mouth tightened. "Look, you have to understand about prison."

"I hope I never get the opportunity," Tate said. "But enlighten us. Share your firsthand knowledge."

"It wasn't like any ongoing thing. Only happened a few times. Before I knew some other things about her."

Turner sat forward in interest. "Those coed joints. I hear a lot of fucking went on in there."

Frank's chin tilted to one side. "Well, what would you expect? Isolate a bunch of men and women from society and put them together."

"I'll have to go along with Frank on that," Tate said. Coed institutions have to be one of the more lamebrained ideas our friends at the Bureau of Prisons have ever come up with. It's good they're no longer in existence, and why it took our lovely bureaucrats fifteen years to figure that out is a mystery to me. Which you should keep in mind, Frank, in case you might be headed for another little vacation. It will be all little boys, this time."

"I heard a lot of the guards used to get in on it," Turner said. Good-looking young druggie women."

Frank shrugged. "They had some, pretty nice-looking. Most of them, though, a guy would really have to be hard up."

Tate sat forward in irritation. "You know, Dave, you could tick me off if you tried hard. If you want I can find, maybe a copy of *Deep Throat* in the evidence room. You can watch it and masturbate if you want to, but for now let's stick to what's relevant. What I'm wondering is, why Frank thinks his prison relationship with this woman in California makes her a suspect in a kidnapping in Dallas, Texas."

"I'd been at Pleasanton maybe a week," Frank said, "after doing holdover at two county jails, La Tuna at El Paso and the federal pen at Phoenix. When you're a holdover they keep you in solitary, and you travel on a prison bus shackled up to a bunch of guys. Tell you the truth, when I got to Pleasanton I felt like they'd turned me loose, they got tennis courts and stuff. It's nice, as prisons go."

"Yeah," Tate said. "Too nice, a lot of people think."

"So I went to work in the sign factory, an assembly-line deal where everybody worked in teams, at various tables. One table attached the signposts, another table lettered, that kind of stuff. First day Darla was seated next to me. She's a fine-looking woman, that's something nobody can take away from her."

"So our sources tell us," Tate said.

Frank rubbed his forehead, remembering, then looked up. "It seemed to me like she was coming on, but I convinced myself I was imagining things. What she'd do, she'd put on a fatigue hat, stuff her hair up under it and walk right into the men's barracks like she was one of the guys."

"Where were the," Tate said, making a note, "where were the guards while all this was going on?"

Frank snorted. "Those guys were interested in two things, coffee break and payday. Darla did some disguising, but I think she could have walked in in her underwear and the hacks wouldn't have known the difference. She wasn't the only one, a lot of those girls used to do this stuff."

Agent Turner uncrossed and recrossed his legs, waving a hand around as he said, "Where you take her to do it?"

"She'd come, right up to my room," Frank said. "Hell, I'm single, and I'm telling you prison is just a different world."

Turner leaned over in a buddy-buddy attitude. "She blow you?"

"I'm throwing a party for our new pastor next week, Dave," Tate said. "Do you think you could come over and entertain?"

Frank ignored the agent and looked at the prosecutor. "The thing was, I hadn't been around long enough to know all the ropes about her. I found out, though.

"After a couple of weeks," Frank said, "Darla and I had been together twice, three times at the most, there was this other girl that came up to me at the sign factory and asked if I was Darla's private property. Said Darla'd threatened the other women if they came near me. I wasn't interested in this girl that was telling me, but it made me a little skittish, you know?

"I came to find out," Frank said, "that every female in there was scared to death of her. She could get things done. Half the guards, one captain I know of, she had them wrapped around her little finger. They brought her drugs, whatever she wanted, and just a word from her would get any of the other women she wanted thrown in solitary. Privileges suspended, things like that."

"She was what you might call Head Cunt," Turner said, grinning at Tate.

"Sort of," Frank said. "Anyway, the only thing I really wanted to do was do my time and get it over with, and fooling with women was something that could really get you in trouble. I knew guys that got their parole date canceled, some of them even moved to a higher-security prison over things like that. So I made the decision that fooling around with Darla wasn't in my game plan, and I cut things off with her. Made it tough on myself for quite a while.

"She used to come up to me," Frank went on, "at the chow hall, the sign factory, whatever, and say things like, 'So you think I'm not good enough for you?' She'd get this really bitchy look, and I'll tell you something. She's the downright meanest female I've ever come across, and that's saying a lot. Back when I was a cop I've dealt with street whores, you name it, but nobody that can be as vicious as she can. She got me locked in solitary once, just by giving the word to a guard, and when I got out she told me, 'You want to try for some more time in the hole, you just keep ignoring me.'"

"So we're supposed to believe," Turner said, "that this gorgeous woman was trying to force some pussy on you and you were resisting, right?"

Frank looked up and watched the ceiling fans turn, trying to calm down. He couldn't keep the anger from his tone as he said, "You can believe whatever you want to. Tell you the truth, I don't care what you believe."

Turner's lips relaxed in a shit-eating grin. "Temper, temper, Torrance."

Frank fought for control, realizing that he'd given just the reaction that Turner had been wanting, and mentally kicking himself. Finally, Frank said, "Yeah, I was out of line. Sorry. The end of the story is that Darla's sentence was over about a year before mine, and other than me getting out I couldn't think of another inmate I was gladder to see go. After the day she walked out of prison I never laid eyes on her again, until last week."

"So, other than the fact that she toured the school," Tate said, "you don't have anything really positive you can put your finger on, that might give us probable cause to haul the lady in."

Frank pretended to think while he made up his mind if he should tell about meeting Darla at the bar. He decided that would be just asking for trouble. "Nothing I can think of," he said, and then thought, *As I see it* . . . Jesus, somebody he knew used to say that all the time.

Tate fiddled with her ballpoint. "Anything else you want to ask, Dave? It's really your show, the FBI's show, and I'm just here to advise. Besides, I just love your quaint expressions." She smiled sweetly.

Turner shrugged and shook his head, his expression saying that he didn't like Tate's being here, and that if the U.S. Attorney's office hadn't horned in, Frank might be in for a session with the rubber hose.

"So you'll know, Frank," Tate said, "and since you're an ex-policeman I don't guess there's any point in beating around the bush. If we could hold you we would, but we have no probable cause. Ditto with the lady, though we're having a talk with her this morning."

"So *you'll* know," Frank said, "Meg is the most important person in my life right now. I wouldn't hurt her for all the money in the world, and if somebody else does, they're going to answer to me."

Tate gave a brief chuckle. "Well said. Well said, but that doesn't get you off the suspect list. We're going to be following you day and night till this is over. Oh yes. Up front, we're putting a tap on your phone. For that I do have probable cause. If you use the pay phone, someone's liable to be listening to that as well. No one but you knows the Carpenters have called us in on this, and if the bad people find out there's only one person who could have told them."

"What about Darla? You said you were talking to her."

"That's right, we are," Tate said. "Which makes two people we'll have to keep an eye on. Mind if I tell you how I see this?"

"See what?" Frank said.

"This whole matter. I think you're in on it. I think, just

maybe, Darla Bern is in on it, too. If she is, she's working with you. That's my intestinal reaction."

Frank sat up. "Well, you're wrong."

"I've been wrong before. But that doesn't keep me from speculating. We can't hold you, Frank, so until I think up some reason we can, you can go. You have a nice day. I'm not going to tell you not to worry, because I hope you do. If you worry enough you might make a mistake. If you do foul up, then we're going to get you. You'll think that last sentence you did was just staying after school by the time it's over, sweetie."

The two blue suits were waiting in the entry hall, talking to Mr. Shotgun. As Frank came out of the meeting with Agent Turner close on his heels, the blue suits moved aside to permit access to the front door. Instead of going in that direction, Frank did a sudden column-left and headed for the back of the house.

Turner quickened his pace. "What the hell you doing?"

Frank paused near the foot of the staircase and turned. "You invited me here. What, I don't get the tour?" He took off again, passing the banister and taking long, determined strides through a first-floor sitting room with a fireplace. Turner gave the blue suits a helpless look, then hustled in pursuit.

Frank found Morgan Carpenter in a kitchen with an island stove and wraparound overhead cabinets, drinking coffee with his wife. Meg had inherited the nose and dimples from her father, but her mannerisms came from the other side of the family. Same steady gaze, same inquisitive tilt to the chin. Mrs. Carpenter sat across from her husband at a tile-topped table. Her features had been flawless in the entry-hall photos, but seeing her in person Frank noted some lines around her eyes, and that the cords in her neck were beginning to sag. She wore a navy blue jogging suit with red stripes, identical to her husband's, and she drank what looked to be orange juice with a raw egg whipped in. On the counter sat a blender with more of the orangy liquid in the bottom, and citrus pulp clinging to the sides. Morgan Carpenter sat with his back to the entry. As Frank stormed in, Mrs. Carpenter looked up and said, "Yeah, well."

Carpenter turned with his cup to his lips, spit coffee back into the cup and started to rise. As he did, Agent Turner gently collided with Frank from behind. Turner stepped quickly in between Frank and Meg's father. "I apologize, sir," Turner said. "This guy just started wandering around."

Frank moved around the FBI man and faced Carpenter. "I wasn't wandering," Frank said. "I was looking for you."

Morgan Carpenter had a square forehead with deep creases. His complexion was light, like his daughter's, and now was slightly reddened from the sun. "I got ways to deal with you these guys don't have," he said to Frank while gesturing toward the FBI agent. "You don't believe it, go by the docks and check some of my guys out."

Turner stiffened. "I'm going to play like I didn't hear that, Mr. Carpenter."

Carpenter blinked. "Hear what? I didn't say I was going to do anything to the guy. I just said I've got ways."

Mrs. Carpenter watched Frank with a curious tilt to her mouth. If Meg aged as well as her mother, Frank thought, that would be nice.

"What I've got to say," Frank said, "is that, yeah, I've been seeing your daughter. A lot. Every chance I get. But I don't—"

"Seeing a jailbird," Carpenter said, hands now on hips. "About what I'd—"

"You're hurting my ears, Morgan," Mrs. Carpenter said. "Not to mention making an ass of yourself. You're not helping things, so why don't you put a sock in it." She looked at Frank. "Sis Carpenter, Mr. White. I've heard so much."

"What I was going to say is," Frank said, "is that I don't care what these guys have told you. I'm as worried about Meg as you are. Probably more."

"You can tell all that to the undertaker," Carpenter said. His eyes narrowed. "Now, you people want money, the money's there. That's all there is, money. You hurt my little girl, there's no place you can hide. The world's not big enough, you understand?"

"To the undertaker? God save us, I've married Wyatt Earp." Sis Carpenter got up and poured herself more juice-and-egg. "Sit down, Mr. White. If my husband continues to be an asshole I'll brain him for you." She had a drawl like Ann Richards's.

Turner shifted his gaze back and forth in confusion between Frank and the lady of the house. Morgan Carpenter had the look of a boxer whose manager had just thrown in the towel. Sis Carpenter made a beckoning gesture. "Come on, sit," she said.

Frank sat on the unoccupied straw-seated wooden chair beside Morgan Carpenter's coffee cup. Carpenter picked up the cup, went around the table, turned a chair around, and straddled it. He eyed Frank. "I've got people, bud," he said.

"What are you gonna do, Morgan?" Sis Carpenter said, sitting down. "Have him stuffed in the rear of a bobtail?" She smiled at Frank. "Give a man a few trucks and he thinks he's Al Capone. You're not exactly the man of the hour around here, Mr. White, but I tend to take my daughter's judgment as the gospel. If you were as bad as all these FBI people say, Meg wouldn't have fallen for you to begin with. I'll bet my boots on that."

Agent Turner retreated to stand by the counter, near the blender. Morgan Carpenter continued to scowl.

"Meg's a hardhead," Sis Carpenter said. "Always has been. She's got this off-the-wall idea that people are supposed to make it on their own. Gets the idea from her father, who's a pretty good dad when he's not snorting around at everybody."

"She could have anything she wants," Morgan Carpenter said, "and she takes up with a convict."

Sis Carpenter showed Frank a between-us wink. "Little girls tend to discuss their love life with their mamas, so I know more about you than Meg's daddy does. S'pect we would have had you as a dinner guest before long if all this hadn't happened. Don't think Meg knew you'd been in prison, though. That right, young man?" Her expression became serious.

Frank looked at his lap. "I told her this past weekend. I should have a long time ago."

Sis Carpenter's look was steady. "Yeah, you should. You kidnap my daughter, son?"

Frank raised his chin. "Before today, I didn't know Meg's family had a dime."

"S'pect that's the truth," Sis Carpenter said. "It's a rule Meg's always had with her men, and I've got to admit I gave her the idea. Romancin' for dollars never works out, in my experience. Love's a thing. If the thing's not there a pile o' money dudn change that. Me and old warhorse here"—she thumbed at her husband—"had Meg when we lived in a trailer home and he was drivin' long haul twenty-five days a month. That's love. Money ain't love."

Morgan Carpenter squeezed Sis's hand and sniffled, as if he had a cold.

"I'm actin' pretty brave here," Sis Carpenter said. "Truth is, if anything happens to my little girl I'll likely die myself. Can I call you Frank?"

Frank watched her, the perfect posture and regal bearing.

"Truth also is, Frank," she said, "that right now you look like the most likely candidate to do somethin' bad, if we believe what these FBI people are sayin'. I believe in lookin' at things head-on, and I'm preparin' myself that I may lose my daughter. If I do, I don't want to remember her as havin' faulty judgment. So you prove all these folks wrong, Frank, you hear me?"

Frank swallowed a lump.

Morgan Carpenter moved in close to his wife and put his arm around her. "And if they turn out to be right," he said, "there's no place you can hide. I'd be remembering that, too, if I was you."

15

The men in the FBI windbreakers had just finished their search of Frank's apartment and were trooping down the stairs into the parking lot as Turner pulled up with Mr. Shotgun alongside him and Frank hunched down in back. Last night's rain puddles had dried, leaving one rectangle of standing water the size of a hopscotch court. As the Taurus neared the foot of the steps, sunlight glinted from the water's surface. Turner managed to stop so that the puddle was directly outside the rear passenger door. Frank had to leap to dry pavement, using the Taurus's rocker panel as a launching pad. He stumbled and righted himself, then reached out to push the Taurus's door to. The driver's window hummed down and Turner grinned at him. "You keep Mr. Carpenter in mind, Frank," Turner said. "We don't want any tags winding up on your big toe, you hear?" He waved at the two denim-jacketed guys, raised the window, and drove away.

As Frank passed the two agents on his way to the steps, he said casually, "Find anything?"

The nearer of the two, a balding man with shaggy eyebrows, nodded but didn't answer. He and his partner got into still another Taurus, this one dark green, backed out of their parking space, drove into the shade of a tree near the lot's exit, and stopped.

Frank climbed halfway up the stairs and looked around. The

green Taurus hadn't moved. He went all the way up to the landing and looked again. Now the agents had their windows down, watching him. The balding guy dangled his car keys out the window. Visible through the windshield, the agent in the passenger seat raised a hand to ear level and waved. Frank sighed in disgust and went on inside. For just a crazy instant there he'd had an impulse to shoot the two guys the finger. As he entered his apartment, he wished that he had.

The agents were still in the parking lot an hour and a half later, having pulled the car forward enough to remain in the shade as the sun moved across the sky. They were drinking soda pop; as Frank watched through his window, the balding guy tilted a red-and-white can to his lips and swigged. Frank let go of the drape, which fell back in place with a ripple of cheesecloth. He went to the kitchen and squirted Palmolive lime on the scorched coffee in the bottom of the pot, then turned on the faucet and held his hand under the stream, waiting for the water to warm.

His bedroom had been a wreck—shirts, ties, socks, and underwear yanked from the drawers and scattered on the floor, the bed stripped, sheets, pillowcases, and bedspread piled in the corner. The clothes closet had been ransacked, shirts and pants twisted on hangers, pockets pulled inside out. Even the wastebasket had been turned upside down, with candy wrappers and used-up disposable ballpoints dumped on the floor along with wadded tissues. The two changes of clothes that Meg had left hung in his closet—a shirt-and-jeans combo and a pair of blue walking shorts with a white Dallas Cowboys T—were missing. Frank withdrew his fingers from the stream, half-filled the pot with hot, soapy water, and sloshed the pot around in a circular pattern. Suds rose inside the pot and the clear water became instantly murky gray. Frank glanced at the kitchen wall phone and curled his upper lip.

After he'd straightened his bedroom and closet as best he

could, he'd had no trouble in finding the bugs. The agents hadn't really attempted to hide the tiny transmitters; Frank had found them both just by unscrewing the phones' mouthpieces. S.O.P. in illegal phone taps—which, Frank knew, the FBI conducted a lot more often than the court-ordered kind—was a wire splice in the outside juncture box, and the agents' motive for leaving the bugs in the mouthpieces was pretty simple. They wanted Frank to blow his cool and remove the transmitters, then hire himself a lawyer and charge to the courthouse. Then the judge would give the FBI a verbal slap on the wrist, tell them to cut the bullshit, and within twenty-four hours Ms. Marjorie Rapp would have Frank's parole revoked and he would be in jail. Frank put on a padded rubber glove and scoured the bottom of the coffeepot with a Brillo pad, cussing the agents under his breath for going off and leaving the burner on. The mistake had been intentional, of course. The guys in the Taurus were probably still laughing about it.

With the scorched mess softened, Frank put the pot in the top basket inside the dishwasher. He'd already loaded the washer with the cups, saucers, plates, and glasses the agents had pulled from the cabinets and left on the counter. He filled the holder with Top Crest lemon powdered detergent, closed and secured the gate, and turned the handle. The dishwasher hummed and chugged. Frank took a Bud longneck from the refrigerator, retreated to the living room and sat on the couch. He had a sip and rolled the frosty bottle across his forehead.

I don't know how I'm going to help you, Frank thought. *But I am.* He leaned his head back against the cushions, crossed his ankles on the coffee table, and closed his eyes.

As I see it. Someone he'd known had used that expression a lot. Who in hell was it? Frank would think about it. Eventually the answer would come to him.

16

Earlier that morning Agent Turner had filled out Interagency Form 71, Request for Interview, directing that someone go talk to Darla Bern, and had sent the form via messenger to downtown FBI headquarters. He identified the suspect in the kidnapping as "White, Frank P.," and stated that the purpose of the interview was "to determine the extent of subject Bern's involvement if any, in the abduction of Margaret Ann Carpenter from Riverbend School sometime between 10 P.M. April 11 and 6 A.M. April 12." Justice Department files had coughed up mug shots of both Frank and Darla, taken on their respective releases from Pleasanton, and a GS-5 clerk had dutifully stapled wallet-sized prints of the photos to opposite corners of the form. Darla's name appeared in two fill-in-the-blanks, once as the subject of the interview, and again under the heading, "Additional Suspects." Turner designated the goal in talking to Darla as twofold: "To determine whether there is reason to believe that Darla Bern aka Victoria Lee assisted in the abduction," and "To determine whether the interviewee can provide the main suspect in the investigation with an alibi." Under, "Is Interviewee to be considered dangerous?" Agent Turner checked "No." Turner also provided information in the "Comments" blank, stating his belief that subject White, Frank P., had committed the kidnapping either alone or in consort with others, and further stating that

Mrs. Helen Dunn, the headmistress at Riverbend School, had furnished authorities Darla's name. Turner closed his brief dissertation by noting that Darla could be reached through Mr. Howard Molly, the director of the Dallas Theater Center.

A two-man team consisting of Agents Chad Wilson and Orville Sing drew the assignment, and were by no means grateful for same. Wilson was twenty-eight, Sing thirty-four. Wilson, a brown-haired, husky former football star at Chattanooga State University in Tennessee, was in his third year of service, having spent his first twenty-four months after graduation as a collector/repo man for Ford Motor Credit. He'd only recently transferred to the Dallas FBI office from Muskogee, Oklahoma, where his main duties had consisted of background checks on prospective federal employees, and the questioning of army deserters' lying relatives. As the new man on board, Wilson considered his forced teaming with Agent Sing as a form of rookie hazing.

Orville Sing was a third-generation descendant of Chinese immigrants, and in bearing, demeanor, and facial expression somewhat resembled Charlie Chan's Number One Son. Five years earlier his name had been listed as a co-plaintiff in a class-action lawsuit accusing the FBI of racial discrimination, and ever since had had his coworkers walking on eggs. The special agent-in-charge, in fact, had cautioned Agent Wilson to "Watch what you say around this guy," and had even suggested offhandedly that Wilson take notes of any discrepancies he observed in Sing's performance. Wilson saw the interest from the head man as a stepping-stone toward his own advancement with the Bureau. As a result he was a bit overzealous in watchdogging his partner, once causing Agent Sing to remark, "Look, if you want to ride around in my hip pocket just say so."

When the Request for Interview form landed in Agent Sing's in-basket, Sing was in the process of loading his attaché case with the materials he and Wilson needed for that day's foray into the field. He picked up the form, held it by one corner to look it over, and muttered, "As if we didn't have enough shit to do."

Which prompted Agent Wilson, who was lounging in a chair near the entrance to Sing's office, to observe mentally that Agent Sing's manner indicated a somewhat-less-than filial devotion to the job, and in the long run could cause Sing to become a security risk.

Sing then squinted long and hard at Darla's photo clipped to the page, and said in an interested tone, "Man, this is some babe we're going to see."

Which caused Agent Wilson to wonder if Sing's behavior could be considered sexist in nature, and to decide that the remark should be brought to the agent-in-charge's attention. He then rose to his feet and, hands in pockets, said noncommittally, "Guess we better be going," and kept his gaze on the floor as he followed Sing from the office.

The pair arrived at the Theater Center a few minutes before two, parked in the main lot, and stepped quickly across the asphalt under stately elms and sycamores to the entrance. A sign in the air-conditioned lobby directed them to the offices upstairs. On arriving at the theater office they encountered a comely brunette seated behind an oval desk. She wore a black sheath dress and blood-red nail polish. Agent Sing snapped open his wallet and exhibited his ID. The woman's eyes widened slightly, and she uttered a breathy, "Oh."

Sing closed the wallet, put it away, and squinted at the Request for Interview form. "We're here to see Mr. Howard Holly."

The woman, obviously relieved that the agents weren't there to see *her*, scooted back from her desk and crossed her legs, exposing six to eight inches of stockinged thigh. "Molly," she said.

Sing blinked and accepted the invitation to gaze at the brunette's leg. "Yeah, hi," he said. "I'm Orville."

Agent Wilson, who stood by with his arms folded, noted Sing's overfamiliarity while in the line of duty, and further observed that the brunette was more his own type than Sing's.

She appeared confused for an instant, then curved her lips in a smile. "No, I mean Howard *Molly*. That's his . . . name."

Now it was Sing's turn to appear confused. Wilson leaned over and, after making eye contact with the woman, pointed over Sing's shoulder at the form. "She means that the guy's name is Molly."

Sing looked closely at the handwriting on the form. "Doggone. It *is* an 'M.' " Then, to the woman, "Well, can we see him?"

She shook her head, now obviously enjoying herself. "He's not here."

Sing assumed a more official air. "And he's expected . . . ?"

"Good question," she said. "He hasn't been in today. Missed a couple of appointments, in fact."

Sing exchanged a glance with Wilson, then said, "Have you heard from him?"

"No, but that's not unusual. Howard sort of comes and goes. Listen, is there something I can help you with?" She scooted forward so that her desktop obscured the agents' view of her thigh.

Sing's expression showed disappointment. "Actually, we're looking for an actress."

The brunette pressed a polished nail between her thumb and forefinger. "I do some acting. This is just my day job."

Agent Wilson intervened, assuming his best Joe Friday posture. "We mean a particular actress, ma'am."

"That sounds pretty easy, detective. What actress?"

Wilson considered correcting her, that he was an agent and not a detective, while Sing rattled the form in irritation over Wilson's butting in. Sing read over the form. "Darla Bern," he finally said.

"Never heard of her."

Sing chewed the inside of his cheek. "Our information is, we can contact her through Howard Molly."

"You can contact a lot of actresses through Howard," the woman said. "But no Darla Bern."

Wilson raised on his tiptoes and read over Sing's shoulder. "How about," Wilson said, " 'aka Victoria Lee'?"

The brunette's nose wrinkled as if she'd just smelled something offensive. "You call *her* an actress?"

Wilson reverted to his *Dragnet* pose once again. "No, ma'am. We call her a suspect."

The woman placed her elbows on her desk and pyramided her fingers. "Oh? Of what?"

Which took some of the wind out of Wilson's sails, but did cause Sing to get snappily to the point. "Just her address, please. If you have it."

"Officially she's living in a motel," she said. "Between us girls, I suspect she's been staying at Howard's lake house."

"We'd want her official address first," said Sing, "and then take it from there."

"The Quality Inn LBJ," she said. "Which is where you probably can find her days. It's nighttime when they go to the lake." She widened her eyes. "I've heard."

Wilson and Sing exchanged a nod, after which Sing turned to lead the way out. He paused in the doorway and turned. "I'll need your name and phone number."

She lowered her lashes. "Detective."

"For records purposes."

Wilson, who'd already memorized the number by reading it upside down on the phone, decided that Sing's demeanor was pushy, and something that the agent-in-charge should know about. The woman toyed with a printed business card, turned the card over, and furnished her home number on the back before handing it over, and watched the agents leave with an impersonal smile.

Wilson and Sing wasted little time with the manager of the Quality Inn, a grossly overweight woman in her forties. She seemed as unimpressed by the FBI as the agents were with her, verified both men's credentials with a call downtown, then rattled her computer keys and squinted at her monitor. "Checked out," she said.

"Oh?" Sing said. "When was that?"

"Less than a half hour ago. You just missed her."

Which caused Agent Wilson to observe that if Sing had spent

less time ogling the brunette's leg, the two wouldn't have missed their interview. He said, "She give a home address?"

The manager continued to peer at the computer screen. "General Delivery, Los Angeles. Pretty large area."

"She pay by check, or . . . ?"

"Cash, in advance, day by day. She was with us about two months."

"Isn't that unusual?" Sing asked.

The manager folded chubby hands. "Very. So much so that ordinarily we wouldn't have booked her. Dallas Theater Center vouched for the lady. A Mr. . . ."

"Howard Molly," Wilson furnished.

She smiled. "You're way ahead of me."

Sing stood. "Mind if we have a look at her room?"

"You're in luck there. Housekeeping hasn't made it to the fifth floor." She reached in a drawer for a card-key blank, entered a room number into a smaller computer keypad, and ran the blank through a magnetizing slot. "I'm actually supposed to accompany you, gentlemen. But I have other things to do. Room five-seven-seven. I won't tell if you won't tell, all right?"

Less than five minutes later the agents stood outside Room 577 and looked up and down the corridor. An elevator opened fifty feet away, and a rosy-cheeked Hispanic woman pushed a cart holding sheets, pillowcases, and towels out into the hall. Wilson poked the card key into the slot, waited for the resulting click, and opened the door a foot. He reached inside, withdrew the pasteboard sign from within, and hung the sign from the handle with "Do Not Disturb" facing outward. With a final glance at the cleaning lady, the agents barged on in.

And stopped in their tracks, colliding in the entry, both staring open-mouthed at the young woman wriggling around on the bed. Bouncing, actually, her hands down as she tried to fasten the catches on the suitcase on which she sat, shapely legs flexed in red shorts, slender arms bare in a navy blue sleeveless pullover. Her auburn hair was disheveled and she wore dark sunglasses with an emblem etched into one lens. She ceased her contortions as the two men came in, said, "Oops," then grinned and said, "Listen, could you help me close this?"

Sing reached inside his coat, groping for his wallet. Wilson watched the woman's legs.

"I was about to call you guys," she said. "I don't have everything ready, so if you've got something else to do for a few minutes, well . . ."

Sing paused with his hand thrust inside his coat, like Napoleon. "Our information was, this room is vacant. That the—"

"Well, you can see that it isn't," she said.

"—occupant had checked out."

She climbed off of the suitcase and stood away from the bed. "I settled my bill. Checkout time isn't until three."

Wilson had the Request for Interview form out, studying the lower left mug shot, looking at the woman, back at the picture, and then at the woman again. "Darla Bern?"

She came over to stand beside him, raised on her tiptoes, and looked down at the form. Wilson caught a faint scent of Estée Lauder as she brushed against him. "It's not very good," she said. "They don't let you put on makeup." Her voice registered disappointment. "You guys aren't from the motel."

Sing had the wallet out, open. "FBI."

She sagged visibly. "Good for you. Listen, I'm off parole. Not required to register with anybody."

"Can we ask you some questions?" Sing said.

Wilson watched her from a scant foot away, a ray of light glinting from her soft lower lip. She reminded him of a girl he'd once known at Chattanooga State U.

She extended a hand toward the suitcase. "Go ahead and look. Have at it. I haven't touched so much as a joint in three years. The bathroom, too, I'll waive my right to a warrant. Gee, don't I ever get left alone?"

Sing let the wallet hang down beside his hip. "This isn't about drugs."

She walked around to the other side of the bed, gesturing with her hands. "And my taxes are filed. I haven't filled out any loan documents, false or otherwise."

Sing went over by the window, to a small table surrounded by three chairs. "Can we sit over here?"

She pulled back one of the chairs and sat, crossing her legs and folding her arms. "I can't afford a lawyer. I'm barely making ends meet."

Wilson pulled the cord, parting the drapes a foot, and took one of the other chairs. Sing remained standing, taking the form from Wilson and looking it over. "You know a Jack White?"

She remained deadpan. "No."

"Frank," Wilson said.

"Yeah, excuse me. *Frank* White." Sing towered over Darla, looking down on her. "You know a Frank White?"

Her mouth softened. "Is he in trouble again?"

"I didn't say that. I asked if you knew him." Sing showed his version of a slit-eyed, suspicious glare.

Wilson observed that Sing's manner was menacing, a far cry from the mild-mannered, let-them-do-the-talking approach taught in the Academy at Quantico. He watched the girl, noted her look of fear.

"Well . . . yes," Darla said. "Listen, that stuff about no contact with felons, I told you I'm off parole. We were friendly at Pleasanton, but you already know that or else you wouldn't be here."

"You've been in contact with him, then," Sing said.

She curled her fingers around her forehead, heavy drama style. "God, I told him to cool it."

Sing folded his arms and leaned his rump against the windowsill. "When did you last talk to Mr. White?"

Darla propped her feet against the edge of the table, turning her head and looking up. "I won't lie. No matter what, I learned my lesson. You guys were tailing him or something?"

Sing exchanged a look with Wilson and didn't answer, not telling an out-and-out lie but giving the impression that he al-

ready knew. Wilson noted that his partner's performance continued on the heavy-handed side.

Darla's lips twisted in anguish. "So I met him for a drink,
okay? But that's all. One drink. Then later I bumped into him at
our cast party. I didn't see any way out . . ."

"That's the play you just finished?" Sing said. "The cast party."

"Yeah, *Autumn Midnight*. He came with this schoolteacher.
When I saw him standing there I couldn't believe it."

"What schoolteacher is that?"

Darla gave Agent Wilson a helpless look, then said to Sing,
"You're scaring me to death. Couldn't you sort of relax?"

"What schoolteacher is that, Miss Bern?" Sing said.

"Oh, a Meg something. Margaret, I think."

"Margaret Carpenter? Margaret Ann Carpenter?"

"Meg Carpenter," Darla said. "Yeah, I think so."

Sing firmed up his mouth. "He came to the cast party with
her. Can that be verified?"

"I'm sure they signed the register," Darla said.

"Let's go to this earlier meeting you had with Mr. White."

"At the bar? It was sort of a sleazy place, I wouldn't want you
to think I make a habit of . . ."

"Sure, that one," Sing said.

"We had a drink. Said hello." Darla seemed suddenly on the
verge of tears. "Listen, what's he done? I told the dumb . . ."

Sing ran his tongue over his front teeth. "Told him what?"

Wilson pictured his report to the agent-in-charge. *Sing failed
to make the interviewee feel at ease.*

Darla fidgeted with her hands. "Look, I can't get in trouble
over this."

"If you haven't done anything," Sing said, "then you won't."

"And nobody's going to know you've talked to me?" Darla
said.

"If that's the way you want it." Sing nodded.

Wilson noted for the second time that day that Sing offered
relief not approved by the U.S. Attorney's office.

"He asked me," Darla began, then twisted her fingers in her lap and said, "God," her lashes down.

Sing watched her. Wilson shifted his weight in his chair.

"He didn't tell me exactly what," Darla said. "But he asked me if I'd help him with something he was doing."

Sing blinked. "That's it? He wanted you to help him with something, but he didn't say what?"

"Well, it wasn't exactly that way," Darla said. "He didn't say, Hey, help me, and then just quit talking. I'm not a total dork. I told him to stop, that I didn't want to hear any more."

"But you got the impression," Sing said, "that he was planning something."

"It's what he said. That he wanted me to help."

Sing softened his tone a bit. "Where were you last night, Miss Bern?"

"Well, I," Darla said, then looked away. "I wouldn't ask you something like that. It might be personal."

"This is an investigation, miss," Sing said. "Not a verbal window-peeping."

Wilson liked the phrase, verbal window-peeping, and immediately included it in his dictionary of FBI-isms, for future use.

Darla sighed in resignation. "I've been seeing this guy. If you have to know."

"It'll be better for you if we do know," Sing said. "What's his name?"

"I only met him this week. He's staying here."

"At this motel?"

"Listen, I don't usually," Darla said. "Sometimes you meet someone and, wow, you know?"

"Who is this man?" Sing said.

Wilson felt sorry for her, the pretty mouth twisted in anguish, Sing pouring it on. Like he enjoys making her squirm, Wilson thought.

"Listen," Darla said, "I don't want to get him involved. He could be married or something."

"You don't know if he's married?"

"A lot of these guys are, that you meet out of town."

"I thought you normally didn't take up with men you didn't know." Sing looked to Wilson as if for confirmation. "Isn't that what she just said?"

"I said *normally*," Darla replied. "Doesn't mean it's never happened."

"So, who is he?" Sing plodded ahead.

She lowered her head, resigned. "Two doors down the hall. Five eighty-one."

"And his name?"

"Harold," she said firmly, then, more hesitantly, "I think. Maybe Gerald. Look, this is embarrassing."

Sing rose and went to the door. "Let's hope it doesn't get even more so, miss. Agent Wilson will keep you company while I check this out, okay?"

The man in 581 wore shorts and a T and had a towel draped around his neck. There was a sheen of perspiration on his muscular forearms. Fifty-pound dumbbells rested on the floor near the foot of his bed. He reclined on one elbow, and tossed shoulder-length blond hair as he spelled out his name. "H-O-D-G-E. Listen, I got no truck with federal people."

Sing carefully wrote down the name. "I didn't say that you did, Mr. Hodge. I'm just trying to verify a story I've heard."

"Guys that do what I do get this kinda shit all the time. Well you're looking at one guy doesn't do any drugs."

"What is it that you do, Mr. Hodge?"

Gerald Hodge smirked in pride. "I'm a dancer."

"Yeah? Broadway, I guess. Bet you do those *West Side Story* numbers."

"Hey, don't laugh. I might some day." Gerald's posture sagged. "I had an audition at Chippendale's, out in L.A. Got to do that kind of crap until your career gets kicked off good."

"An exotic dancer in women-only places," Sing said, his lids at half-mast.

"Yeah. That illegal or something?"

"What brings you to Texas, Mr. Hodge?"

"I had some time in between jobs. Thought I'd see some country. If you're writing a book, there's some chapters I'd want you to leave out."

"Are you acquainted," Sing said, "with a Darla Bern? You could know her as Victoria Lee."

"What, some broad said I did something?" Gerald testily tucked his chin. "I don't force none of these women."

"The lady's been occupying the room down the hall—five-seven-seven," Sing said.

Gerald slightly averted his gaze. "Oh yeah, her."

"She says she was with you last night."

Gerald frowned. "I need a lawyer?"

Sing raised his eyebrows. "You don't right now. You're not a suspect at present."

"A suspect of what?"

"A . . . suspect. All I'm trying to do, Mr. Hodge, is check out the lady's alibi."

"Yeah? Well, who's going to give *me* a fucking alibi?"

"I don't know that you need one. Do you think you need an alibi?"

Gerald sat up, grabbed one of the dumbbells, braced his elbow against his inner knee, and began a series of one-arm curls. His biceps bunched like a cantaloupe. His forearm muscles writhed. "What did this broad say we were doing?"

Sing blinked. "What *were* you doing, Mr. Hodge?"

Gerald expelled three hard breaths, his lips compressed, and slowly lowered the dumbbell. He looked up. "So I fucked her brains out. What brains she's got. That a crime?" There was an angry red welt on his thigh, inflamed from exertion.

"It's not a crime that I know of," Sing said. "Mmm, where did you meet this woman?"

"By the pool. I need to keep tan. Women come up to me all the time."

"With regard to last night," Sing said, "how long were you with her?"

"She come down here about seven."

Sing wrote something down. "Seven in the evening?"

"Yeah, you know, begging for it. I run her ass off, oh, about five in the morning. Broads are tough to get rid of sometimes. Want to hang around and shoot the shit."

"That must be difficult," Sing said. "So she was with you from seven last night until five in the morning?"

"Give or take."

"Constantly. She never left."

Gerald shrugged. "If you were a broad, would you?" He launched into another curl.

"That's something I couldn't answer," Sing said. "But you're sure she was with you the entire time."

Gerald lowered the dumbbell. "Yeah, I'm sure. Listen, you're not going to give the broad my name, are you? I got enough women bugging me as it is."

Both Darla Bern and Gerald Hodge furnished Los Angeles addresses, which Wilson thought quite a coincidence, two L.A. people getting acquainted in a motel in Dallas, Texas. Sing pointed out that, since there were twenty million people living in the Los Angeles basin, the odds of two strangers being from that area were only a little better than ten to one, the U.S. population being 250 mil or so. Each of the interviewees asked if they were free to travel home, Hodge to take a dancing gig, Bern because she had a chance to audition for a speaking part in a movie. The agents made a show of thinking that one over; the truth was, since neither Darla nor Gerald were charged with anything, they could go wherever the hell they pleased. Both provided L.A. phone numbers, Gerald balking until the agents assured him they wouldn't give the number to the broad. Then the agents left the motel, returning to the office a little before four.

The pair then collaborated on a report which they attached to the Request for Interview form. They pointed out that Darla Bern had an ironclad alibi for her whereabouts on the night in question, and that the man furnishing the alibi was barely acquainted with Darla and therefore had no reason to lie. Furthermore, Interviewee Bern had indicated that not only was she not involved in the kidnapping, she wasn't even aware it had taken place. Suspect Frank White, in fact, had attempted to recruit Miss Bern for an operation which she suspected to be illegal, and she had turned him down flat before he could give her the details. The agents omitted any mention of Howard Molly in the report because they considered the Theater Center Director's absence insignificant. Los Angeles addresses and phone numbers for the interviewees were included as a footnote.

Sing signed off on the form as lead investigator, and gave the form to Wilson for transmission to Agent Turner at the kidnap victim's family home, via courier. Wilson carried the form and attached report to his own cubbyhole, stared for a few moments at his view of the alley behind the West End Marketplace Cinema 10, and pictured Agent Sing's view of the shiny ball atop Reunion Tower with Dallas's majestic skyline stretching out to the east. Then he sat at his scarred government-issue desk and set the form aside as he prepared his report to the agent-in-charge. He pointed out each shortcoming he'd noted in Sing's behavior during the day, carefully omitting the expense-account lunch which the agents had shared in the West End. When he'd completed the report, Wilson checked his watch, then picked up the phone and punched in a number he'd committed to memory only that day. In the middle of the third ring a click sounded, and a soft female voice said, "Dallas Theater Center."

Wilson cleared his throat. "Yes, Agent Wilson, FBI." He paused. "You remember me?"

"You're the other one. Not the oriental guy."

"Right, the other one."

There was a pause, after which the brunette said, "Sure. Can I help you?"

Wilson softly closed his eyes. Nothing ventured, nothing gained. "I just wondered what you were doing."

"In twenty minutes I'll be going home. At the moment, twiddling my thumbs."

Wilson felt a tightness in his chest, then blurted out, "I was wondering, I thought you might be free for dinner."

There was a sharp intake of breath, then, "What is this, a joke?"

"I didn't mean it as a joke."

"The other guy's sitting there, right? You two have a bet? Come on."

"I'm not sure I—"

"Well, you can tell him," the woman said, "that the answer was the same to you as it was to him. As in, 'No, thanks.'"

"Are you saying that Agent Sing's already called you?"

"Not five minutes ago, as if you didn't already know. And five minutes ago I told him I already had a boyfriend. Now, five minutes later, I've still got one. Goodbye." There was a click as she disconnected.

Wilson stared in shock at the receiver, then replaced it in its cradle. His neck was red. He slid his daily report back in front of him and added the following sentence: "Agent Sing further displayed familiarity with the receptionist at the Dallas Theater Center, and I later learned that he had asked her for a date." He signed his name and hustled down the corridor to place the report in the agent-in-charge's confidential file. So intent was he in snitching on Agent Sing that he completely forgot about forwarding the Request for Interview form to Agent Turner. That document, along with the attached report, was to remain on Wilson's desk for two more days.

17

Meg felt naked in spite of the pale blue cotton boxer shorts and matching T she wore. No panties, no bra. Just the gym outfit which, freshly laundered, had been placed in the cage's food slot about an hour ago. There'd been a note folded in with the clothes, typewritten on plain white twenty-pound bond. She curled her legs up under her and blinked away tears as she read the note for perhaps the fiftieth time.

```
You will receive clean clothes each morn-
ing, along with one fresh towel to re-
place the one hanging on the rack. The
shower is stocked with gentle liquid soap
and hazelnut shampoo, for normal hair.
The shampoo contains a conditioner. If
either the soap or shampoo are not satis-
factory, or if you require some other
form of conditioner, you need merely
speak out. Someone will be listening to
you at all times. After you bathe you
should lay the spent towel in the food
slot, where it will be replaced at the
same time your daily allotment of cloth-
```

ing arrives. We apologize that you will have to air-dry your hair, but you will not be furnished any electrical appliances with which you could harm yourself or others.

Meals will be furnished twice daily. They will be microwaved frozen dinners, and let us apologize as well for the cuisine, as we were unable to find a chef who met our other requirements for employment. Hopefully your ordeal will not continue for long, and it is our intent to make you as comfortable as possible. If you desire privacy while changing you should step inside the shower and close the curtain or retreat to the toilet area. As long as your behavior is acceptable the portable partition and curtain will remain around the toilet and over the shower opening respectively. If you do not behave, these privacy items will be removed and you will have to bathe and use the toilet in plain sight. Remember, someone will always be watching you.

Meg let the note flutter down to the mattress and peered through the heavy wire mesh and out the door. Someone watching. In the outer room, the bathroom entry cast a parallelogram of light on worn brown carpet. Beyond the doorway outline, Meg's world ended in blackness.

She sat on the edge of an iron cot. The mattress was thin plastic stuffed with rags, supported by metal slats that were welded to the bed frame. Around each individual leg of the cot the tile was chipped from the floor, and the metal legs were sunk several inches into freshly poured cement. So she couldn't move the bed and she couldn't slide one of the slats from under the mattress to use as a weapon. They seemed to have thought of everything. She wondered if indeed they had.

Her hair was still damp from the first bath she'd had in her prison, and the bath itself had been an eye-opener. They'd done a makeshift plumbing job on the shower, removing the hot- and cold-water handles, and in their place installing spring-loaded buttons. It had taken her a few minutes to get the hang of it; in order to keep the water running she had to hold the button in with her thumb. She'd been worried about scalding herself, but apparently they'd thought of that as well; the hot water was diluted with cold, and never was more than lukewarm. The removal of the handles made it impossible for her to leave the water on and flood the place.

Someone watching. She shivered and hugged herself, then stretched out full-length on the bed.

A chest-high cloth hospital partition blocked the commode from outside view, the toilet itself a scant six inches from the far side of the cage. Lysol bowl cleaner sat on top of the tank along with a nylon toilet brush. So great. Meg could threaten her captors with the brush while forcing them to drink the bowl cleaner. If she drank the cleaner herself, thus committing suicide, she doubted if they'd care.

The cage was made of cyclone fence wire, flexible but unbreakable. The supporting frame was steel, riveted to the walls. One corner of the cage was arranged so that it half blocked the bathroom door, and so that someone could wedge through to stand in the two-foot corridor between the cage and the window. That's where the hooded man had stood and held the recorder while she'd spoken her message to Mom and Dad.

The chloroform jolt in her bedroom had zonked her pretty well, but she did have one foggy memory of the trip from the school to wherever the hell she was now. She recalled the sack-of-flour sensation as the big blond man had carried her from the backseat of a minivan and had transferred her into a second man's arms. The second guy had worn a ski mask as well. He was short, squatty, and strong as a bull. As he'd deposited her in the trunk of a second vehicle, she'd caught a whiff of cheapo aftershave. Within seconds after he'd slammed the trunk lid, she'd been off in dreamland once more. When she'd come to she'd been inside the cage, lying on the bed.

Her gaze rested wearily on the ten-foot wooden pole propped in one corner of the bathroom, outside the cage. They'd shoved the pole in through the mesh and prodded her awake to make the recording. The squatty guy and an older man, both wearing ski masks, had stood side-by-side in front of the window and held the recorder up for her to talk into the mike. The older man had worn shorts and a flowered shirt with the tail out, and had had skinny white legs and a middle-aged paunch. His speech had been clipped and precise, with a faint New York accent and he'd talked in a grating falsetto to disguise his voice. She supposed the older man had written the note she'd just read, but only because he'd sounded educated. As yet she hadn't heard the squatty guy say a word. After she'd said her little ditty to Dad, they'd handed her her first set of gym clothes and ordered her to change. She'd slipped into the shower stall and done so.

Frightened and disoriented as she'd been, the thought of worrying her parents had practically made the words she'd spoken stick in her throat. The folks would do anything they could to get her out of this mess, Meg had no doubt about that, but her independence had been a bone of contention between her and her family—especially her father—for quite some time. She had a standing lunch date with Daddy, Casa Dominguez Mexican restaurant every Tuesday, eleven-thirty on the dot, and only last week they'd gotten into it.

"You ashamed to be a Carpenter or something?" he'd said, dipping a corn chip into *chili con queso*.

"Don't be silly," she'd said, mashing guacamole with her fork, "if it was that I'd change my name. I'm getting a kick out of supporting myself, Daddy, watching budgets and all that, so let me play if I want to."

"Supporting yourself, that's one thing. I just don't want people knowing a daughter of mine's eating beans to get by."

She'd laid down her fork and looked at him. "You did."

"That was different. We had to. Now you've got people thinking I've cut you off."

"They don't think any such thing, those that have any sense. Most people I know don't know we're related. I like it that way. Makes for real relationships."

He'd frowned at her then. "Don't think anybody that wants to can't find out who your family is, Meg. It's not just you supportin' yourself. There's people out there could be dangerous."

Right again, Daddy, Meg thought as she looked around at her prison. Being rich sure does have its advantages.

She'd slipped in the references to "plays" and "acting" as a hidden message while making the recording, but didn't have much hope that her cutesy idea would alert anyone that the chick in the ski mask was none other than that Victoria Lee/Darla Bern person. *God*, Meg thought, *why did the silly woman bother to disguise herself?* Frank and Mrs. Helen Dunn were the only ones likely to make the connection, but Meg doubted Frank would ever hear the recording, and thought that Mrs. Dunn was too dense to get the hint if it walked up and pulled her hair.

Mom and Dad would come across with the money, Meg knew, so at least she wasn't going to die. That was one comfort, that she was going to live to see another day.

Or was she?

Basil Gershwin tried to remember where he'd ever seen such a succulent fucking broad. Maybe on a movie screen, never in person. If Randolph Money thought a guy could spend time with this broad twenty-four hours a day and never try to strike up a conversation, Money was crazy as hell.

Basil sat unmoving in the dark, where he'd been for going on eighteen hours. He'd gotten up twice, once to stand by while Money did the recording, and once to put clean clothes in the food slot. He was mesmerized, wide awake. Basil hated sleep, had hated it in the joint, and hated it even more since he'd been a free-world guy. Anytime you snooze, Basil thought, you're likely to miss something important. Such as this absolutely luscious fucking broad.

It was the overall view, something about her. Darla had better wheels and a better ass, but to Basil's way of thinking Darla couldn't hold a candle to this woman. Basil thought he could spend the rest of his life hiding here in the dark just watching her. He'd like it even better if he could do something to her, of course, but Basil thought for a guy like him, getting next to this broad was out of the question. Basil Gershwin was one guy who knew his place, and his place definitely wasn't with a woman had any class.

He was sprawled out in an easy chair, facing the bathroom and the cage within. His ski mask lay in his lap, and he wore surgical gloves. The thick black curtains he'd hung over the windows worked perfectly; from within the room it was impossible to tell if it was day or night outside. It was four in the afternoon. In another two hours he'd get the broad her dinner, which tonight would be Salisbury steak, peas, and mashed potatoes.

Something people would never understand about Basil—he wasn't any wild man. He'd raped four women in his life, two of the broads he'd held hostage in the bank and two before that, but those were certain kinds of women. One bank teller he remembered really good, a pouty teenager with a big ass and short, tight skirt, and that broad had definitely been asking for it. The woman inside the cage wasn't like that, she was something special. Something which a guy would like to take to dinner, be seen in public with.

Basil was proud of the changes he'd made to the cage. Jesus, the dumb Gerald guy, Darla's guy, he'd just hauled the collapsible kennel pen into the bathroom and unfolded it. During the time since he'd left Money at the airport and come to the hiding place, Basil had done some remodeling. He'd riveted the cage to the bathroom walls, anchored the bed to the floor, and installed the shower buttons. Guy who'd spent as much time in jail as Basil knew how to keep a prisoner. Wasn't nobody in the group could fix up a cell the way that Basil could.

Inside the cage, the woman turned onto her side and drew up her legs. Her eyes were closed. Christ, Basil thought, in them shorts you can see the cheeks of her ass, then felt like slapping himself, having thoughts like that about a woman with the class this one had. Christ, though, he was getting a bulge on. He reached inside his pants and touched himself, then quickly withdrew his hand. Basil couldn't stand guys who couldn't control themselves. Guys out of control made Basil sick to his stomach.

Basil wondered if he'd have to kill this woman, the way he and Money had talked on the airplane. If it came down to it he'd have to. The thought saddened Basil, and a tear formed in one corner of his eye.

18

Agent David Turner didn't like sleeping in the Carpenters' guest house, but he supposed it was part of the job. The bed was too short for him, and his feet hung over the end. He woke up stiff and sore, showered and shaved, microwaved a ham, egg, and cheese Border Breakfast he found in the freezer, and wolfed down the concoction. He didn't feel much better but decided he'd live.

Turner came out of the guest house in clean jeans and a short-sleeved yellow shirt, wearing his FBI jacket. He ducked underneath ferns in hanging baskets as he approached the pool, stroking his freshly shaved cheek. The scent of Brut was on his hands. A cool spring breeze sent ripples over the surface of the water. He walked on rough stone tile, skirting wooden chaise longues and round tables on his way to the back door. A Mexican in overalls was pruning roses near the porch; Turner nodded as he went by. Early on in the investigation—within an hour of the time he'd responded to Morgan Carpenter's call and come to the house, in fact—Turner had questioned the gardener. The gardener had spread his hands and said, "*No sé*. No English, *señor*." Turner didn't know whether to believe the guy.

He went inside and through the kitchen, and entered the library. AUSDA Felicia Tate was seated behind the oversized desk, wearing a navy blue suit along with a white silk blouse buttoned up to her throat. She had company, Morgan Carpenter in the flesh, along with a couple of lab guys from downtown whom Turner recognized. The forensics guys were off to one side, hovering over a suitcase. One man dusted for prints while the other poked around inside the case, feeling the linings. The suitcase was brown alligator with red leather inlays. High-priced item if the 'gator hide's real, Turner thought. He hello'd the lab guys and went over to the desk.

Morgan Carpenter wore slacks and a golf shirt, and was slumped down in one of the easy chairs. As Turner approached, Carpenter said, "Christ, I'll have to borrow it." He looked about to throw up. Turner sank into the other chair and crossed his legs.

Tate acknowledged the FBI man with a nod, and used a pair of tweezers to lift a sheet of typing paper from the desk. "We've got our note here, Dave."

Turner bent closer for a better look. The note was the standard kidnap message, words clipped from magazines and glued to the page. The forensics guys would dust the paper and do DNA tests on the glue. Their tests wouldn't reveal a fucking thing, which was always the case with perps who knew what they were doing. "Came with the suitcase, huh?" Turner said.

"FedEx." Tate dropped the note, took off her glasses, and rubbed the bridge of her nose. "Delivered by hand to the Fort Worth office, paid for in cash. Phony name in the sender blank on the airbill. The FedEx clerks see a lot of people, you know how that goes. One seems to think it was a big guy. Really precise description."

Morgan Carpenter ran his fingers through silver hair and muttered, "Christ," again.

"These people have rather high aspirations," Tate said. "They're asking for nine million six hundred thousand dollars."

Turner's jaw slacked. He muttered, "Christ," along with Morgan Carpenter.

"Brand-new hundred-dollar bills," Tate said, "twenty to a

wrapper, all out of numerical sequence. They claim the money will just fit into the suitcase. From what we've seen of these folks so far, it will."

Turner studied Morgan Carpenter, the good-looking, fiftyish man worried, now mopping his face with a handkerchief. "Your call, Mr. Carpenter," Turner said. "Your money."

"I'm not even sure I can raise that kind of . . ." Carpenter said. "The bank, I'll have to talk to this guy."

"Does that mean," Tate said, replacing her glasses on her nose, "that if you can, we're going ahead with this?"

Carpenter shrugged. "It's my daughter. I'll have to."

"If it was my little girl," Turner said, "I guess I'd do the same thing." Turner didn't have a little girl, and wondered if he'd pony up nine million six if he did. What a fucking fortune, Turner thought.

"Not much I can see unusual about this," Tate said, "except that they've provided their own carrier. I'm wondering about that."

"Something about the bug we use?" Turner said.

Tate ran her little finger across her upper lip. "That's the first thing that crossed my mind. But no. In all cases we've got to assume they'll know there's a tracer. Anyone who watches television. It's something else. That suitcase is too distinctive. We're scouting the stores right now, but I'll bet a month's pay we can't find a duplicate."

"Christ," Carpenter said.

I wish he'd stop saying that, Turner thought. He said, "I think we'd better withdraw our guys following Frank White, at least where he knows they're there. Now they've made their move, he's going to have to get in touch with somebody. My way of thinking is, we want him to. We'll have to start watching him from afar."

Tate looked at Carpenter, then said to Turner, "That won't be necessary."

"I can't go along with that, Felicia," Turner said. "The Frank White guy, he has to be the key. Lose sight of him and we're liable to blow the whole deal."

"Oh, I agree with you. It's just that keeping up with Mr. White isn't going to require all that cloak and dagger."

Turner frowned. His chin moved slightly to one side.

Tate used the tweezers to pluck the note up from the table. "The instructions say that Mr. Frank White's the one that's going to deliver the money. No one else. Seems as if your man Frank has got a starring role."

Part III

REWARD

« « « «

" 'You testified earlier that you hadn't received any offers of leniency from the prose-
cution, is that right?'

'It's what I said. I didn't get any, either.'

'Is it possible, sir, that your views could be
tainted by the fact, that you didn't get your
share of the booty?'

'Objection.'

'I'll rephrase, your honor. Your share of the
loot, or whatever you want to call it.'

'That's nothin' to do with what I'm sayin',
sir. But it's true Ronnie never gave me my
part. He never had no intention of splittin'
that money, not the way he was s'posed
to.' "

—from trial transcript,
*State of Texas v. Gilbert Wayne Arrington
and Ronnie Louis Ward*

19

There were three pairs of FBI agents working Frank in eight-hour shifts; he'd nicknamed the eight-to-four couple Jack and Jill, the four-to-eight duo Frick and Frack, and the night-shift guys Two Live Crew. At the moment Jack and Jill were on the job, sitting across the lobby and trying to stay awake, watching through half-lidded eyes as their subject scraped the residue from a drum of cherry vanilla, mashed the residue down into a full container, and rolled the new drum into line alongside the rest. Frank wiped his hands, then held up a scoop and cone in the agents' direction, questioningly raising his eyebrows. *You want some?* Jack looked away. Jill licked her lips. Frank dropped the scoop into milky water.

It was ten-fifteen, a quarter hour since Frank had opened up, and the Loew's Anatole lobby was practically deserted. Except for the FBI, there were only two groups the entire width and breadth of the mammoth enclosure: four women window-shopping across the way and what looked to be a grammar school field trip, a harried-looking lady and twenty or so giggly kids down at the far end, looking at the fountain. As Jack watched, the fountain spewed a cone of mist thirty feet into the air. One of the kids moved forward and seemed about to dive in. The teacher grabbed the kid's arm and pulled her back. A second kid headed for the fountain. Jack supposed that the field trip's next stop would be the ice-cream stand and added extra drums of rocky road and fudge ripple.

Over where Jack and Jill lounged, an irritating *beep-beep* sounded. Frank shifted his gaze in that direction. Jill fumbled in her handbag and switched the beeper off, then produced a cellular phone and punched in a number. She listened intently, said a few words, then listened some more. She shoved the antenna down with her palm, motioned to her partner, and the two agents headed across the lobby in Frank's direction.

This must be it, he thought, his throat suddenly dry. His arrest in the police station basement had been a total surprise, but even though he'd halfway expected this one, the helpless feeling now was even worse than the first time. For a fleeting instant he considered making a run for it. Jill led the way, walked up and leaned her elbows on the counter.

She was around twenty-five, with straight brown hair clipped in a line at her collar, a not-unpleasant young lady who would have been pretty good-looking with a little makeup on. She said deadpan, "We're going to have to ask a favor of you, Mr. White."

Frank did a double take. Her words hadn't sounded like making-the-collar talk, and neither agent had the handcuffs out. He choked out, "Well, sure."

She wore a gray business suit and medium heels. "We'd like you to go with us now. Some people want to see you." Her partner stood alongside her, maybe even younger than she was, a just-out-of-college type, still with the frat-rat look and a suit off the rack from JCPenney.

"I'm not under arrest?" Frank said.

"We don't have any instruction to do that. Just to bring you to a certain location."

Frank's anxiety subsided, in its place a dogged mad-on. "Well, then," he said, "I can't."

The agents frowned at each other.

"Hey, I want to help all I can," Frank said, gesturing around.

"But I can't just walk off. What about my job?"

The agents' look said they hadn't thought of that one.

"Course," Frank said, "if one of you could spell me."

Jill's expression said she thought that might be a good idea. Jack squinched his nose up like a man who'd just realized he'd stepped in dog manure. "That's not in my job description," Jack said. Frank couldn't tell if the guy was pissed off over the prospect of serving ice cream, or over having to take orders from a female. Could be either one.

"Not that much to it," Frank said, undoing his bow tie, unbuttoning his Sidewalk Humor uniform shirt. "You want to watch those kids when they get here, and go easy on the Reddi Wip. They'll have you squirting all your profits off, if you aren't careful."

Ever since his incarceration Frank had made it a point to steer clear of banks. Just over two years in the joint had ruined his credit, and it had been less than a year since he'd been able to pay off his prejail pile of bills. Even though his record was clean now, his computerized credit report still reflected some slow pay, and the idea of a bank turning him down for a loan made him cringe. He'd rather do without than ask and be refused, so since he'd been a free man he'd made a practice of paying cash for things.

Yet here he sat, just before noon on a Wednesday morning, in a plush-carpeted office at the downtown main branch of Lone Star Bank & Trust. Directly in front of him, an entire wall was tinted safety glass. A mile or so in the distance, the glistening ball atop Reunion Tower was at eye level, surrounded by a halo of springtime smog. To the right of the tower were the somber roofs of Frank Crowley Courts Building and the Lew Sterrett Justice Center. Frank recalled the months he'd spent in the justice center awaiting trial, and a slight quiver traveled the length of his backbone.

The banker seated behind the half-moon desk was named

Davis Boyle; Frank had met the guy just moments ago. Boyle's sandy hair was conservatively short, whitening at the sideburns, and his suit was charcoal gray with a Kiwanis pin attached to the lapel. His handshake had been limp and dry, his disapproving glance at Frank's knit sportshirt appropriately fleeting. His lips were thin and pliable, ready to twist into a panicked expression, which they probably did if anyone mentioned a sum over five thousand dollars. After his brief ackowledgment, Boyle had pointedly ignored Frank and concentrated on the other men in the room.

Boyle now said, "Sure it's feasible, Morg. The collateral, the trucks and the building, those are primo. You've been with us a long time. Financial statements up to date and up to snuff. It's the conditions the board's going to worry about. Cash, for Christ's sake, plus turning the money over to an ex-con."

Morgan Carpenter, seated across the banker's desk in a conservative gray suit of his own, regarded Frank with an open sneer, then returned his attention to the banker. "Once you make the loan, what difference it make what I do with it? Flush it down the toilet, piss it off at the racetrack, what's it matter?"

"We have a right to know," Boyle said, "what's going to happen to the money."

FBI Agent Turner, seated on a couch underneath a desert landscape print, pointed in Frank's direction. "Mr. Boyle, if you're worried about this guy," Turner said, "then don't. We'll be watching him so close he'll have a telescope up his ass, excuse the expression."

"The choice of words may be bad," Assistant USDA Felicia Tate said, "but the sentiment is right on line. Where our friend Frank goes, we go with him." She was alongside Turner on the sofa. Light from the window wall reflected from Tate's reading glasses.

Frank started to say, "Hey, you guys called me," but thought it over and closed his mouth. He and Jill sat close together on a leather love seat, a matching piece to the couch. The picture above them was another desert scene, this one a jackrabbit with rugged mountains in the background. Jill glanced in Frank's direction, batted mascara-free lashes once, then looked away.

Morgan Carpenter said, "If a deal this size requires a meeting of the board, when's that supposed to happen? Look, I got to have an answer today."

Boyle rubbed his palms together. "You're in luck there, we've already got one scheduled for two o'clock. What I've got to do is, between now and then, is have a feasible presentation. My assistant's on that, putting together your info. Not that it'll take a lot, the board for the most part is familiar with your transactions here."

"Well, they fucking well ought to be," Carpenter said, crossing his legs.

"I can see a problem," Tate said, "with how much to tell these board members."

Boyle's lips twisted in a fleeting look of panic. "It goes without saying, I have to make full disclosure."

"That's up to you," Tate said. "Here's what's up to me, the U.S. Attorney's office. To protect the victim, none of this can be leaked out to the newspapers. The cheese will get really binding if that happens."

"These are businessmen," Boyle said. "Discretion is all a part of it."

Tate exchanged a look with Turner, then said, "Well, just to be certain, let's make these gentlemen aware that anyone talking, anything coming out on the newscasts, that's going to be obstruction of justice. It's a broad statute, and we can make it stick." In addition to her suit and blouse, she wore navy blue spike heels, and now hooked the toe of one shoe around behind her shin, her calves bunched as she crossed her legs.

"You're threatening the board of directors of Lone Star Bank & Trust," Boyle said, "with a criminal indictment?"

"We indicted the Attorney General of the United States once," Tate said. "Why would we worry about someone's board of directors?"

Boyle stared at the prosecutor, who stared back. Boyle nervously cleared his throat. "Once we lay the groundwork and fund the deal, what are the nuts and bolts of getting the money to this guy?" The banker pointed at Frank without looking at him. Agent Turner did look at Frank, the FBI man's eyes narrowing. Frank stared at the floor. Jill flattened her hands on either side of her hips, raised up and scooted forward on the love seat.

Tate reached down to the floor and moved a suitcase around to sit before her shins. Frank looked over the suitcase, alligator inlaid with red leather. Tate said, "The cash goes in here. And here's a copy of"—reaching inside her briefcase for a piece of paper, laying the paper up on the banker's desk—"the packaging instructions. Twenty bills to a bundle. No two bills in numerical sequence."

Boyle held the paper up and leaned back against his credenza. "Christ, this is a tall order. It'll take some overtime, these tellers."

Carpenter yanked on his lapel in irritation. "That's not our problem."

"I'm not too sure about that, Morg," Boyle said, laying the paper aside. "I've got to do something to justify the expense factor to the board."

"Tell 'em if they don't," Carpenter said, "there's other banks."

"I don't know if that'll swing it, by itself. What I'm thinking is, maybe an increase in the loan origination fee." He raised his hand in what looked like the "V for Victory" sign. "Two. Two points."

Carpenter scowled. "Two points?"

"Point and a half, then."

Carpenter's upper lip curled. "You fucking bloodsuckers."

Boyle spread his hands in apology. "Hey, Morg, I don't make the rules. I'm not the manager, I just play in the infield."

"All that," Tate interrupted, "is between you and your customer, Mr. Boyle. All we're interested in, once the money is packaged we'll meet down here and our Mr. White will take possession."

Boyle's chin moved slightly to one side. "Not in this bank, young lady."

Both Tate and Turner stared at the banker. Jill's eyes widened slightly with interest. Frank continued to watch the floor.

"We'll package your money for you," Boyle said, "and you can check the contents however you please. But the suitcase is leaving these premises via our security service. No way is Lone Star Bank & Trust accepting responsibility for any transfer of money to this man."

Tate thoughtfully expelled a breath. "I suppose Agent Turner can wait with Mr. White outside the building. I'll check the contents in Mr. Boyle's office, then your, what, Brink's men, can bring it out. You see any problem with that, Agent?" She swiveled her head to look at Turner.

Turner scratched his cheek. He looked at the banker, then at Tate, then over at Frank. "I don't suppose I do," Turner said. "Me and old Frank here will be waiting for you. You don't be wearing no track shoes, Frank, you hear me? Anything happens to this money, you can't run fast enough to get away."

20

At twenty-three minutes after two by the reception area clock, Davis Boyle came out of the board meeting on the fifty-second floor of Lone Star Tower. His mouth was set in a rigid line, and he carried two thick file folders. He dropped one in front of the receptionist, set the other off to one side, and fiddled with the Kiwanis pin on his lapel. "That one's approved," he said, "and ready for processing."

The receptionist, a matronly, thick-set woman, opened one folder and glanced at the other. "That one's declined, or . . . ?" She had perm-curled strawberry-blond hair.

Boyle quickly scooped up the remaining file. "No, it's been okayed. Requires personal attention." He hustled out into the hall like a man on a mission from God. The receptionist wrinkled her nose at Boyle's back and went on about her business.

Boyle shared the elevator down to the twenty-sixth floor with two young women from the personnel section. One lady remarked, "You look awfully sad, Mr. Boyle. You should brighten up, it's a beautiful day."

To which Boyle testily replied, shifting the folder from one arm to the other, "I don't have time for beautiful days. Pressing matters. So damned pressing." The elevator halted abruptly, sinking the passengers' feet deeper into plush carpet. The doors hissed open. Boyle goose-stepped out of the car. After he'd gone the young woman rocked her head from side to side, hoity-toity fashion, and stuck out her tongue.

Serita Mayes was a former Dallas homicide detective now in charge of bank security. She was flaxen-haired, salty-tongued, and a high finisher each winter in the White Rock Marathon. An executive VP had once remarked in the lunchroom that he thought Serita might be a butch; when she'd heard about the off-the-cuff statement, she'd climbed fourteen flights of stairs and barged into the exec's suite in the middle of a staff meeting. In front of fourteen astonished loan officers she'd told the guy that for his information she was currently fucking one of his male superiors, and that if he ever said anything like that again she'd sue his ass. Boyle breezed past Serita's assistant and walked into her office unannounced. She was eating a chicken salad sandwich, which she pushed aside. "You're maybe wanting some dental work," she said, "blowing in here like you're the potentate."

Boyle didn't answer. He sat down across from her, fished inside the folder and handed her a typewritten sheet of paper.

Serita read over the instructions. Her green-flecked brown eyes widened. "Great fuck. How long have we got to do all this?"

"It's going to take an armored car trip over to the federal reserve," Boyle said, "to come up with these denominations. While you're doing that, I'll have my girls type up the collateral documents."

Her plucked eyebrow arched. "Your what?"

"My . . . people. The young women in my office."

"That's better."

"Here's the order to the fed." Boyle whipped out a federal form and floated the page over to land in front of her. "As quick as you can. Top priority. We'll use the vault to package the money, the long table."

"How many people is it going to take?"

"Fourteen girls, I don't think there's any room downstairs for more than that. Your pick, Serita, tell them there's overtime in it for them."

"Fourteen what?"

"Fourteen young women, okay? Fourteen bodies is what we need."

She testily put the papers away. "Well, if you're going to help me supervise this," she said, "then I'll bring along a few prissy little boys. They'll be more your type, Davis."

After the Brink's men stacked the money in the center of the vault's long counting table, the group Serita Mayes had put together went to work assembly-line fashion. There were seven female and seven male workers, including two recent-graduate management trainees. The Joe Colleges were both men, and neither seemed thrilled. They situated themselves at the head of the table and tried to look as important as possible, middle-management moguls helping out the secretarial staff in a pinch. Serita Mayes, however, had other ideas. She pointedly stripped open the first bundle of hundred-dollar bills and handed them to one of the trainees, and pointed to the far end of the table. "Down there, Junior," she said. "You, too, Andrew Carnegie. We'll do our best to have you two big shots out of here before sundown, okay?" With the downcast trainees muttering about their job descriptions, the assembly line then got into gear.

The lead worker broke open the bundles, one at a time, and handed them to the next person down. The money was then divided into four equal stacks, the next bundle split into fours as well, and each person at the table grabbed a pair of stacks from different bundles and shuffled them card-deck fashion. On down the line, more young men and women divided the piles even further, while others shuffled three and four more times. The next-to-last people on opposite sides of the table—a Hispanic woman from personnel and a Filipino girl from the Trust Department—made the final checks, thumbing through the piles to be certain there were no two serial numbers in sequence, and finally handing the stacks to the two Joe College trainees for rebundling.

Davis Boyle hovered over the workers like a man at a crap game with money on the line, while Serita Mayes stood in the corner, arms folded, and kept a watchful eye on Boyle. Once during the packaging process he walked up behind the Filipino girl, bent over her shoulder, and said, "Utmost care. Life or death here, utmost care."

The young woman exchanged a what-a-prick glance with Serita Mayes, then offered a stack of money to Boyle. "Tell you what, Mr. Boyle," she said, "you want to do this, be my guest." Boyle *harrumphed* and retreated, while Serita Mayes laughed aloud.

At fifteen minutes after five, Boyle huffed and puffed into his office reception area lugging the suitcase. He was mopping his forehead with a handkerchief. His secretary had her pens, pencils, and spiral pads in perfect alignment on her blotter, and as Boyle came in she picked up her purse and pushed back her chair. "Good night, Mr. Boyle," she said.

"No, hold it." Boyle reached inside his coat and produced a wrinkled slip of paper. "Get this lady on the phone for me. Mrs. Tate, U.S. Attorney's office."

The secretary's smile seemed frozen in place. "It's after five."

Boyle testily shook his head. "Just get her, will you?" He carried the case through the entry into his office and closed the door. The secretary watched Boyle's door for a moment through slitted eyelids, then picked up the phone and punched in the number as if she might break a nail.

When his intercom buzzed, Boyle had opened the suitcase and was staring at its contents as if in a hypnotic trance. His mouth twisted as he eyed the neatly stacked bundles of hundreds. His

197

eyes bugged. He gulped in air. The intercom buzzed again. Boyle picked up the receiver and averted his gaze from the money. "Mrs. Tate?"

"I'm here." There was a slight crackling over the line. The prosecutor's tone was all business.

"It took some doing," Boyle said, "but I've gotten it done. Handled it personally to avoid the possibility of a screwup."

"Okay, I'll buy that. What's the drill for us getting our hands on . . . ?"

"At straight-up six," Boyle said, "I'm coming out the alley exit, ground level. I'll have two security guards in tow, and another will be parked nearby in an armored truck. He'll be holding a rifle on us, just in case. I'll have the suitcase in my possession. I want you to check out its contents."

"We don't have time to count all that."

"It's not the count I'm worried about," Boyle said. "The money's there, the exact sum, our people have counted four times. It's up to you if you want to trust us on that."

"We'll have to," Tate said. "We all trust each other, don't we?" The edge in her voice said she didn't trust Boyle as far as she could throw him, and knew the feeling was mutual.

"I just want you to be sure," Boyle said, "what's in the suitcase."

"You don't have to worry about that, Mr. Boyle. We will be."

"Oh, by the way, Morg's going to have to be with you."

"Who?"

"Morgan Carpenter. To sign the loan documents and receipt for the cash. Once Morg signs and the suitcase is gone from our premises, what you do with the money is your problem. I'm bearing no responsibility for transfer to your convict person. That's between the FBI and the Lord on High, as far as Lone Star Bank & Trust is concerned."

• • •

Frank stood in the alley behind the bank in straight-up six o'clock cool spring air, a big green dimpster-dumpster directly behind him and federal people on both sides, Agent Turner and Assistant USDA Tate lounging alongside Turner's Taurus with both left-hand doors open. It was an hour before sundown, blue sky over-head, thunderheads on the horizon headed in from the west. A dirty white Brink's armored truck was parked twenty feet away; the driver squinted through the bulletproof windshield from un-der his billed cap. An over-and-under riot gun lay across the dash. It occurred to Frank that if any shit were to start, the guy might open fire, hit the windshield, and die from the ricochet.

Frank had showered, shaved, and changed into dark clothes: a black cotton crewneck, dark blue Levi's, and black high-top Nikes. He'd stood before his closet for a few minutes, making up his mind what a guy delivering a ransom was supposed to wear, and had finally decided he might need to blend in with some shadows or something. Now he felt a little bit silly, like a guy in a movie playing Murf the Surf, some character like that. He briefly wondered if he should've put soot on his face. He decided that would be carrying things too far.

The same four-door gray Jag Frank had seen in the Carpen-ters' driveway was parked at the far end of the alley. In it sat Mr. and Mrs. Morgan Carpenter, Sis Carpenter with her hair fluffed out around her head like the Liberty Bell, a slim bare arm over the seatback, her eyes hidden behind Kool-ray shades. Morgan Carpenter was hunched down over the wheel. The steel bank door groaned open. Frank and the federal people turned as one.

A tall, thin Brink's man with pimples on his neck led the way, fingering his holstered automatic Gary Cooper fashion. Davis Boyle followed close behind, canted slightly from the weight of the suitcase, carrying papers on a clipboard in his free hand. A second guard followed Boyle. The three men stopped halfway to the Taurus, and Boyle motioned in the direction of the Jag.

Morgan Carpenter came out of the Jag wearing baggy shorts

and an oversize blue knit shirt. He went up to Boyle, read over the papers on the clipboard, said gruffly, "Point and a fucking half," and signed his name three different times. Boyle then came the rest of the way to the Taurus and handed the suitcase over to Felicia Tate. Tate had changed into a jogging suit and white canvas Keds. Her hair was tied up with a white strip of cloth whose ends hung below her shoulders.

Carpenter took a step toward the Taurus and pointed a finger. "Just so it's clear, I'm holding you responsible for that money, Mrs. Tate. If this guy"—jabbing his finger now in Frank's direction—"loses it, that's the federal government's problem."

Tate exchanged a glance with Agent Turner, who now stepped forward. "No need to worry about old Frank here. He's not making a move we don't have monitored."

Frank bit his lower lip. He closed his eyes, then opened them. Keep your mouth shut, he thought, then couldn't help himself and spoke up anyway. "I'll tell all you people something," he said. "Every one of you. All I've heard is, this convict and, that convict, and who's responsible for the convict if he loses the money, and I'm sick of it. I didn't volunteer for this."

Tate stared open-mouthed. Turner watched Frank like a man seeing a horror movie. Carpenter and Boyle seemed paralyzed. Frank went on.

"I'm the only one here, and I mean the only one, that seems to care about what all this is supposed to be for. The kidnap victim, remember? And I care one helluva lot about that part of it. The money, I don't care about the money, understand? Now give me the suitcase." He walked over and yanked the suitcase out of Tate's hand, then returned to the Taurus. "Now let's get going, okay? First thing you know the vice squad's going to show up, thinking we're having a dice game back here."

As Frank reached out for the door, Sis Carpenter blocked his path. She'd alighted unnoticed from the Jag and now removed her sunglasses to look Frank squarely in the eye. She smiled sadly. "You're just almost right, about who cares. You left out me and Meg's daddy, but I think you're right about these other folks. I'm still countin' on my daughter's instincts, Frank. You just prove them all wrong and get my little girl home. I'm dependin' on you, you hear?" A sudden tear rolled down her cheek.

Frank watched her for a minute, then lowered his gaze. He gave Sis Carpenter's arm an affectionate squeeze, then lifted the suitcase into the Taurus's backseat and climbed on in.

21

At five minutes after four West Coast time—at almost the exact instant, in fact, when Frank White delivered a piece of his mind in a Dallas, Texas, alleyway at 6:05 by Big D clocks—a Delta Boeing 737 Stretchliner floated in on smoggy currents, bounced once, twice, and then laid stripes of rubber on Los Angeles International Airport's tar-veined runway. The pilot braked, braked again, made a sweeping left turn, rolled the plane past tractor-pulled baggage cart trains and single- and twin-engined private aircraft, and finally halted alongside the terminal. The accordion walkway extended and clamped onto the airliner.

Passengers inside the cabin stretched, yawned away the popping sensations in their ears, stood up in the aisle and opened overhead baggage compartments, and formed a line in front of the gangway. The young lady in Seat 14C took her sweet time. She scratched her leg through the stylish rip in her jeans, dangled L.A. Eyeworks sunglasses from one corner of her mouth, and smiled at the gentleman on her left. "Hope you're not in a hurry," she said. "I don't understand people, breaking their necks to get in line and wait. I'm more laid back than that, aren't you?"

The man beside her, thirty-fiveish with curly hair, wearing a suit with his shirt collar unbuttoned and his tie pulled down, agreed with her. "I don't have any fires to put out," he said. "When'd you say your next audition was?"

There was a quick, getting-interested tightening in one corner of her eye. "I don't think I did. It's next Tuesday, though. You going to be in L.A. that long?"

The lady in the window seat, slender and wearing a gray business dress, twisted her mouth into an irritated smirk. "Do you mind?" she said. "I've got someone waiting."

The man ignored the woman on his left and continued to smile at the girl in the ripped-look jeans. "Afraid I won't be. I've got to hustle back to Houston, darlin', Saturday mornin'. Actin', that must be, hey, one great way to make a livin'."

She examined her L.A. Eyeworks, huffed fog onto one lens, and poked the glasses inside her shirt, polishing the lens with the shirt fabric held between her thumb and forefinger. "Just like any other job. The work's not as steady. Get to meet interesting people, like you. This is a flight to remember, right?"

His grin broadened, became wolf-hungry. "Gotcha there, darlin'. Look, you got a number I can . . . ?"

The other passengers moved up the aisle. The window-seat woman twisted in her chair. "Excuse me, but my husband's—"

"Oh, why don't I call you?" Miss Ripped-jeans-look said. She reached inside her purse, and came up with a pad and pen. "Charley, right?"

"Reasor, yeah, Charley Reasor. I'll be at the Century Plaza."

"Ooo, uptown, I like that. Listen, if I did call, you probably wouldn't even remember me." Her lips circled into a Monroe pout.

He winked at her. "You kiddin'?"

"Well, just so you don't forget," she said, "I'll write it down. Darla, that's me, and this is Flight"—she checked her ticket—"three forty-two, Wednesday afternoon." She bent her classic neck and began to write.

The window-seat woman fidgeted even more. As the passengers cleared out, a man with blond, shoulder-length hair paused beside Row 14 and touched Darla on the shoulder. She glanced up as he nodded to her. He wore slacks and a skin-tight knit shirt and had bulging pectorals. She said, "Oh, hi," and went on with her writing as he moved on up the aisle.

Charley Reasor showed a hurtful look as his gaze followed the big blond man. "Somebody you know, darlin'?"

She wrinkled her nose. "Oh, just this guy that stayed in the same motel with me, back in Dallas. Thinks he's Mr. God." She tore off a page and handed it over. "You won't forget me now. And if something happens, I can't get in touch with you the next couple of days, can I find you in Houston?"

He showed some panic. "Reasor Oil, that's easy. It's in the book. But listen, you wouldn't call me at home . . ."

She teasingly placed her forefinger over his lips. "I'm smarter than that, Charley. Give me some credit, okay? Just don't forget where you met me."

He looked relieved. "You can count on it, darlin'."

The window-seat woman leaned forward to glare at Darla. "Couldn't you two continue this in the terminal? My goodness."

Darla's brows lifted in surprise. "Oh, you want out? Sure." She stood, reached under the seat in front of her, and pulled a cosmetics case on rollers out into the aisle. She said to the woman, "You'll have to excuse me," then winked at Charley and said, "I've got this nasty habit of tying people up sometimes."

She strolled through the terminal, dragging her case by the strap, men halting and doing double takes as she went by, her L.A. Eyeworks jauntily on top of her head. There was an escalator leading to the lower level, with a gift and magazine shop to the right. Darla went into the shop. She looked through the shelves, selected a teddy bear, and waited in line at the register. When it was Darla's turn, the clerk scanned the price tag and watched as the register lit up. "It's six-eighteen," the clerk said.

Darla fished in her purse and pulled out a ten. "It's for my friend's little boy. I'll need a cash receipt."

The clerk said, "Sure thing," tore off the register tape, and dropped it in the bag along with the teddy bear.

Darla fished the receipt out and squinted at the figures. "The date and time are on here, right?"

The clerk pointed at some numbers on the lower portion. "Sure, right there."

Darla smiled in apology as she handed the receipt back over the counter. "Gee, I hate to ask this," she said, "but my friend's a real chinch about reimbursements sometimes. Just sign your name to verify that I paid you in cash, okay?"

22

Joe Breen kept a fancy pen set on his desk. There was a gilt cylinder mounted on the base, and a glowing digital clock set into the cylinder above the inscription, "Joseph Breen, U.S. Probation Officer, June 12, 1988, Twenty Years." It was common knowledge among his co-workers that the government would never spring for such an expensive trinket, so Breen's story for office consumption was that his wife had presented him with the gift on his twentieth anniversary of service with Uncle Sam. Which wasn't true. Breen, in fact, had told his wife that the office pool had ponied up the money in appreciation for the sterling job Breen had done. Which was an even bigger bunch of bullshit than the story he'd told his co-workers, since none of the people in the probation department liked each other very much, and none of them would dream of buying a fellow employee so much as a cup of coffee. The truth was that Breen had ordered and paid for the pen set out of his own pocket, and ever since had taken pains to make sure that his wife and his co-workers didn't get together and compare notes. That would be embarrassing as hell.

Normally Breen gazed on his trophy with a sense of pride. But now he scowled. "Seven minutes after six already. I've got to be getting out of here."

Basil Gershwin sank deeper into the visitor's chair and

twisted his features like a scolded puppy. "Hey, I'm keeping you? I got this list of job interviews I've been having." He unfolded a square of yellow paper. The sheet was legal-sized, and covered with handwriting in blue ballpoint.

"I stay late Wednesdays, every week," Breen said. "Four to six, that's for my people that have job conflicts or something, so they can make their report dates. But six o'clock is the limit. If you can't get your business done by then, you've got to make other arrangements, to get off work or something."

"How I'm supposed to know that?" Gershwin said. "I never reported to you before."

Breen frowned, raising the corner of a stack of folders and thumbing through them. "What'd you say your name was?"

"Gershwin. Basil Albert."

"I got no Gershwin. You sure you're reporting to the right guy?"

"I'm reporting temporary. My man in California, Mr. Lawrence, he said he was sending my file. Gave me your name."

Breen had a closer look at the guy, wide forehead and flaring nostrils, tufts of hair poking out from underneath a blue baseball cap. The hat's crown displayed a replica of the Shock Wave roller coaster underneath the heading, "Six Flags Over Texas." *Christ*, Breen thought, *this is the guy I got the call about. Raped some women while he was robbing a bank. His parole officer thinks he killed some Bureau of Prisons employees. Christ, how they let these guys walk around.* Breen felt a twinge of fear as he reached in his lower drawer to extract the notes he'd made during the phone call. "I remember now," Breen said. "Your file hasn't caught up with you yet. Why do you want to move to Dallas, Mr. Gershwin?"

The toothy grin seemed friendly enough. "I'll tell you about that. I been in and around L.A. all my life. It's where my troubles began, you know? I thought maybe a new location, a different climate. Guys I knew in prison are always calling me in L.A. I don't need those kind of associations."

"You're wanting a fresh start," Breen said. *Maybe a new spot to rob some banks,* he thought.

"Yeah, in fact I got me a game plan. Goes deeper than just relocating. It's the times I work, too."

"You feel that there are certain times of day when you're more apt to slip up," Breen said, "if you aren't on a job."

"Sure, nights, that's when all the whiskey drinking goes on. I get a few pops in me, you know?"

"Makes you act irrationally."

"This bank I did. Long time ago, but it was me, I was drunker'n Cooter Brown. Walked up to the teller's window, I could barely see the lady in there."

The guy seemed earnest, Breen had to admit. "I guess this means you're looking for night work."

"Ten until six A.M., if I can get it. Ten o'clock's early enough— I won't get started drinking before. Six in the morning's late enough, almost all the shit's over with by then."

"I don't see anything wrong with your reasoning." Breen looked at his pen-set clock. "Look, it is getting pretty late." *Especially,* he thought, *when I'm probably alone in the building with this guy.*

"What I was thinking," Gershwin said, offering the piece of yellow paper once more, "I think you're supposed to fill out a report to my officer in L.A."

"It's part of the procedure." Breen took the paper and looked down the list, fast-food restaurants, a couple of 7-Elevens, one freight loading dock. "You have to interview these people at night?"

"Most of 'em. Sometimes I got to talk to the manager and he works days only, but usually there's a night guy in charge. I've listed everybody I'm seeing on there, so you can let Mr. Lawrence know I'm not down here in Texas screwing around."

"No one said, no one's accusing you," Breen said. "Thing is, you've got these dates written down. The last one's today. You already talked to all these people you got down here?"

"No, now, one thing I won't do, I won't lie to you. The last three I'm seeing tonight. But I was hoping you could help me out with this problem I've got."

"If I can," Breen said. "And as long as it doesn't violate rules."

"Actually, according to what I told California, I should be reporting to you tomorrow. But I'm going to be up nearly all night, interviewing people, and I got another interview way the hell out in Garland tomorrow at two. I thought maybe I could include those I'm going to see tonight, so your report on my week would have everything in it I did."

"The ones you've already talked to, yeah. But ones you haven't seen yet . . ."

"The report's got to include the interviews I do tonight," Basil Gershwin said. "That's Mr. Lawrence, that's what he insisted, that he know everything I've done up to date. If you don't include tonight's stuff he's going to call up wanting to know what's going on."

Breen didn't care to talk to the guy from California, Hagood Lawrence, again; he might tie Breen up on the phone forever. "How do I know you're really going to see these people?" Breen tapped the yellow paper.

Gershwin spread his hands, his eyes wide. "Hey, if you'd like to ride along with me."

Breen mentally winced. Christ, riding around after dark with this guy. He pictured the scene, the guy pretending to be going to an interview, driving up an alley, pulling a gun, and saying, Down on your knees, motherfucker, something like that. "That won't be necessary," Breen said. "I've got your word you're going to see these folks tonight?"

Gershwin raised two fingers. "Scout's honor, Mr. Breen. I just can't do all this and report tomorrow, too. If you don't have a form into Mr. Lawrence by tomorrow I'm going to be hurting."

Breen pretended to study the list. The rules were the rules, but—Christ!—if he followed the rules to the letter, Breen was supposed to verify every job interview the guy had had, and wasn't supposed to list anything he couldn't verify. But Christ, with everything else Joe Breen had to do. And if he didn't include tonight's interviews, Breen would have to spend time with this ugly bastard tomorrow as well.

Breen laid the yellow page aside. "I'm going to cut you some slack, Mr. Gershwin. Yeah, I'm going to include tonight's stuff in my report. I'm depending on you to see that nothing comes back on me, okay? You help me, I'll be glad to help you. Now, can I count on you?"

Gershwin's grin was ear to ear. "Like death and taxes, Mr. Breen," he said.

Basil arrived at the house by the lake at a quarter past seven, leaving the blacktop road, crunching over the gravel drive for a hundred yards or so, parking the rented Avis Honda in front of the carport alongside the Ford Randolph Money was using. Basil liked the view, sundown rays glinting from the water, faraway bluish thunderheads low on the horizon. On the lake's northwest shore, maybe two hundred yards away, pointed condo roofs stood up. The roofs marked a cluster of two-story zero-lot-line homes with a community swimming pool and private dock. At the moment two boats swung from moorings at the dock, both with topside cabins, one with *Sassy Seaman* painted on its hull and the other named *Li'l Sis*. Basil didn't know shit from Shinola about boats, but liked the names pretty well, picturing himself in a captain's hat and deck outfit, lounging around while this fine-looking woman brought him a beer. In Basil's fantasy the woman was always the broad now caged inside the house. She'd be wearing a bikini, or maybe these cute jean shorts, white canvas shoes and a mesh top, and after she'd served him the beer she'd massage his neck for him.

Basil had spent part of his daylight hours keeping an eye on the condo subdivision across the way. He'd seen a few people coming and going, no one paying any mind to the house where, unbeknownst to the condo squarejohns, some pretty smart guys from California were about to make a killing in the kidnap business. Which made things just perfect, to Basil's way of thinking. He still thought that Randolph Money was somebody who needed watching, but had to admit the guy had figured things out pretty well.

He went up on the redwood porch and used the secret knock, *rap, rap, rap-rap-rap*, which Basil thought was unnecessary. Who the fuck else would come knocking? After a few seconds the peephole opened, then closed, and Randolph Money clicked the latch and pulled the door inward. Money was dressed in a maroon shirt and white pants, and a ski mask was rolled up into a cap on top of his head. Behind him, the house's interior was dark. "You report?" Money said. "How'd it go?" He came out tugging off surgical gloves.

"Just like you said. The guy's sending in a form says I'm out doing interviews tonight. I don't know why I need no alibi, tell you the truth."

"You need an alibi," Money said, "because you never know when one will be necessary. Cover every base you can, then hold on to your ass. Trust me, I've seen it work."

"How did it work," Basil said, "the time they sent you to the joint, huh?" He was carrying a paper shopping bag by its handles, and now shifted the bag around slightly behind him.

Money looked at the bag. "What's in there?"

"Nothing. Stuff I got."

"Personal things? It's none of my business what you buy, but what we can't do is leave any of our effects lying around here when this is over. No paper bags, nothing floating in the johns, nothing."

Basil raised the shopping bag and hugged it protectively to his chest. "I won't leave nothing here. Just some stuff I got."

"See that you don't." Money pulled the ski mask off and handed it to Basil. "No masks, nothing," Money said. "In something like this the smallest detail is what's going to ruin you, as I see it." Tendrils of gray hair waved in the breeze.

"As you see it. As you fucking see it."

"And the way I see it," Money said, "is the way things have to be. No residue."

Basil set the bag down, removed his Six Flags cap, and put the rolled-up ski mask on top of his head. He retreated to the Honda and dropped the Six Flags hat and the shopping bag in the front seat. "That better?" He started to roll down the mask to cover his face.

"You crazy?" Money said. "You're going to stand out in the yard looking like a hijacker, I suppose."

Basil paused, then rolled the mask up on top of his head. "Ain't nobody watching." He began to snug up his gloves, wiggling his fingers as he did.

"Don't ever forget those," Money said. "Just when you think they aren't watching is when they are." He walked over to his car. "No more rehearsals. By the numbers, now, what's the plan?"

"I'm going in to baby-sit the broad."

"The merchandise. With your gloves and mask on. And then?"

"Four o'clock tomorrow I'm driving in to this pay phone."

"Which is where?" Money intensely cocked his head.

"Corner of Ross and Fitzhugh, across from a washateria. Jesus, we just drove down there this afternoon."

"Which means you shouldn't have any trouble remembering. I'm calling you there, right?"

"That's what you said. And telling me what?"

Money opened his car door. "Depends on whether I've got the money in hand. If I don't I'll tell you we have to arrange a meeting."

"Jesus Christ, you telling me you might not have the money? I thought you and your fringe asshole had that covered. Whoever the fuck he is."

"Oh, it's covered. It's just, you have to prepare for every possibility. Chances of me having the money by then are, say, ninety-nine to one in favor of."

"So if you got the money you're going to tell me where to take the broad."

Money sat down in the front seat and grabbed the door handle. "Afraid that's not in the program, Basil."

"You mean I'm going to off her?"

"Yeah, it's a pity. We can do everything to see she doesn't recognize any of us, but those chances aren't a hundred percent. Same with our friend from the Theater Center. Elimination of prospective witnesses, that's the only way to be sure. Listen, you got a problem with that, say so now."

Basil hesitated, wondering. "Naw, I got no problem. Listen, are there any of them lasagnas left in the freezer? I can't stand that Mexican food."

Meg had never thought she'd yearn for the sound of dripping water. Noise, any kind of noise, anything to break the silence. She reached inside the shower stall and pressed the button. The water cascaded against the curtain, then, as she released the button, receded to a steady *plop-plop* on tile. Meg sat down on the cot. In approximately two minutes the water would stop dripping, then she'd have the choice between pressing the button once more or flushing the toilet. Anything to create sound.

She wondered if she'd lost her mind. She didn't think so, but nutsos never realized it when they went off their rockers. Flushing toilets and pressing shower buttons like a wild woman, were those the early signs? Or did she need the noise, any kind of activity, to keep her senses? At this point she wasn't sure. She raised her bare feet, curled up her legs, and sat on her ankles.

What was she thinking about? She wasn't going crazy, no way. Not the original Rational Rhoda, feet on the ground and all that. Why just that morning she'd done a hundred situps, whistled during her bath, and recited the first six verses of "The Midnight Ride of Paul Revere" from memory. *Nothing nutty about you, kiddo,* she thought. *I'll just sit here and make a joyful noise unto my-*

self, and wait them out. *Before you know it Daddy will pay the ransom and I'll be free as a bird. Free as a freaking . . .*

You know the woman, a hollow voice inside Meg's subconscious said. *You can identify her, so what do you think's going to happen whether they get their money or not?*

Meg firmed up her mouth. That's nonsense, she thought, they wouldn't . . .

Oh yes they would, and you damn well know it.

Meg swallowed a lump from her throat and forced the death thoughts from her mind. *Think positive. Think freaking positive. What do I know that will help them nail these bastards, once this is over?*

Absolutely nothing, really. She'd seen the older man and the squatty guy, both wearing ski masks, but wouldn't know either one of them if he walked up to her on the street and pinched her bottom. Other than the flushing toilet and the dripping shower she'd heard one sound, the faraway whining of a motor. Sounded like a boat, which could mean they were holding her close to a lake. Which narrowed her location to about five thousand bodies of water in the Dallas area. Margaret Ann Carpenter had never felt so helpless in her life.

There was movement outside the bathroom door. Meg stiffened. The squatty man came into view, complete with ski mask, set a tray in the food slot, and retreated into darkness. A plastic hospital serving cover hid the food from view, but a spicy odor wafted up her nostrils. Spaghetti, or maybe lasagna.

She was suddenly ravenous and tried to remember when she'd last eaten. Had she been here two days? Three? However long, she hadn't touched the microwaved frozen dinners they'd left her. She'd had tea and one of those horrendous little crumpets with Mrs. Dunn on Sunday, was that her last food? No, wait. She'd stopped off at a McDonald's on her way to the school Sunday afternoon. *Great gadzooks,* Meg thought, *is that to be my legacy? That the condemned woman went to meet her Maker with nothing but a Big Mac with cheese in her stomach, and that two days old?*

She went over and picked up the tray, lugged it back over to the bed and removed the cover.

It was lasagna, deliciously runny, served on a paper plate and accompanied by a Styrofoam cup of red Kool-Aid. A white plastic spoon lay alongside the plate—no weapon that, Meg instantly thought—and beside the spoon was a . . .

She blinked.

Beside the spoon was a perfectly formed miniature pink rose, its petals curled up in the shape of a candle flame. Meg lifted up the flower by its stem and sniffed its freshness. Recently picked. Her eyes widened in surprise.

A rose for my nose, she thought, *how absolutely freaking quaint. Me Esmeralda, him Quasimodo. Next he'll be swinging back and forth on the church bell.*

All fear left Meg in a rush. She was suddenly furious, as absolutely goddam *mad* as she'd ever been in her life. She poked the rose, stem and all, through the wire and dropped it on the floor outside the cage. "You go right straight to hell," she screamed. The sound reverberated through the house, and then dissolved in total silence.

As Meg's angry words reached his ears, Basil Gershwin winced in the darkness as if he'd been slapped. And he felt as if he *had* been slapped, a broad kicking him in the teeth one more time. All his life, always the same. Jesus, he'd sneaked the flowers in past Randolph Money just for her, and had planned to give her a rose with every meal. Make things nicer for her.

Basil slumped down in the chair. His eyes narrowed to slits. He must have been crazy, liking this broad. Broads weren't nothing, none of them.

His chin moved up and down in a brief nod. If that's the way she wanted it, good. Made things a lot easier that way.

23

Frank didn't think the federal surveillance man had done a good job of hiding the transmitter and said so. The guy winked in turn at Tate, at Turner, and then said to Frank, "What, you don't like my sewing?"

"I think I'd spot it," Frank said.

The federal man was named Weir, and at the moment was closing a rip in the suitcase lining with a needle and thread. The repair wasn't that obvious, but on close inspection would stand out, the seam crooked where two pieces of satin material joined inside the lid. He said, "It occur to you that I might want you to find it?" and went on about his business.

"He means," Turner said, "that he'd want you to find it if you were one of the bad guys. Which we all know you're not, right?" The FBI agent smirked at Tate, who smiled and tugged at the cloth that hung loosely at the nape of her neck.

Weir was bald, with a fringe of hair around the back and over his ears and one tuft dead center above his forehead. "The trick is to make it look like I'm trying to hide it, when really I want it found. We don't want to be too obvious here."

The four were in the study at Morgan Carpenter's house, ceiling fans whirling overhead, reading tables placed around the room. Tate was behind the mahogany desk with Turner and Frank seated across from her, craning their necks to watch the bugging job. Weir did his work with the suitcase open on one of the tables, bundles of hundred-dollar bills stacked in rows inside. The surveillance man was slightly red-faced, his complexion darkening each time he glanced at the money.

"The second transmitter," Tate said, leaning back, "is the one you darlings probably wouldn't find. Excuse me, Frank, I mean *those* darlings. This is a Braunflas, a German make. Let's don't hear any 'Buy American' chants, okay? It's transparent, flexible as a contact lens, and fits down in between two of the stacks. Would you like to know how I'm going to make a case on you, Frank?"

"Let's talk about what I'm supposed to do," Frank said. "I'm tired of hearing how you're going to shaft me."

"You'll be really weary of it, before I'm through. We know you're going to expect a transmitter, so we'll give you one. Let the boys have some fun over, Look how stupid these authorities are, they don't even know how to sew up a seam, right? So while they find the one transmitter, the other's going to be ticking away. You know a little about evidence, don't you? Sure, you were on the police force."

Frank yawned, doing his best to look bored, his stomach churning, scared to death he'd mess up somehow and cause harm to Meg. He doubted if he'd get another night's sleep the rest of his life, if that happened. "What time are they supposed to call?" he said.

Agent Turner leaned forward. "Come on, Frank, you don't need no fucking phone call. Bet you got it memorized, every phone booth you're going to, and exactly where you're dropping the money within six inches either way. Give us a break." He wore his FBI windbreaker with khaki Dockers, and cowboy boots with scarred toes.

"Evidence is something that builds," Felicia Tate said. "And if you think good-boy alley speeches are going to fool anyone, you're terribly mistaken. You people have obviously got some on-the-job training in legal matters, and you're smart enough to know I can do nothing with the fact that these kidnappers you never heard of have suddenly specified Mr. Frank White as their deliveryman. Just a coincidence—perhaps they picked your name out of the phone book, right? So we're assuming our bad boys would find the dummy transmitter anyway, since they're going to be expecting one. But if they come up with the main bug, someone's giving them information. That's going to be a problem for you, because your people can't go around with a beep-beeping suitcase, right? But if you tell them about the second transmitter, that's evidence you're involved. Four people know it exists; you, me, Dave here, and the surveillance man. If the second transmitter suddenly winds up stuck to the fender of a southbound city bus, you have problems. Sticky wicket, Frank. How are you going to handle that? How are you going to tip your friends off without giving me some courtroom ammunition?"

"You've been wrong all along," Frank said. "Now you're even wronger."

Turner and Tate exchanged a look. Weir stood still with the second transmitter, inside a tiny plastic case, grasped between a thumb and forefinger.

"Sure we're wrong, Frank," Turner finally said. "So let's just sit here in suspense and wait for this fucking phone call. Bet you're on pins and needles wondering what the guy's going to tell us, huh?"

Sundown came early, as Old Sol ducked behind the boiling thunder-heads that filled the horizon. The approaching storm had already wreaked havoc in Abilene, Mineral Wells, Weatherford, and points west, and six o'clock weathermen warned Dallas to batten down the hatches and prepare for a big one.

The phone in the study rang at seven-thirty on the dot. Morgan Carpenter now sat behind the desk, his wife bolt upright in an armchair, her face creased in worry lines. Turner was perched on the edge of the desk, his shins dangling, his ankles crossed.

Felicia Tate sat in an attentive posture beside Sis Carpenter. Frank and Weir sat at one of the reading tables with the suitcase, now closed and latched, in between them on its side. The surveillance man regarded Frank with a bland smile.

Morgan Carpenter picked up the phone and said, "Yeah?" Then he listened and said, "Yeah?" again, listened some more and said, "Shoot," while reaching for a ballpoint and writing pad.

Frank hunched nearer the table, watching the silver-haired man write furiously, listening to him say, "Slow down, I'm having trouble following," and watching him write some more. Finally Carpenter said, "I gotcha," hung up the phone and looked at Frank. "This is bullshit," Carpenter said.

Sis Carpenter stood up to read what her husband had written. Felicia Tate spun the writing pad around so it was right side up to her. Sis Carpenter said, "It's at the Hillcrest intersection, on LBJ Freeway."

"I know where the hell it is," Carpenter said. "It's still bullshit."

"On the phone," Tate said. "That was . . . ?"

"Probably the same guy as on the tape," Carpenter said. "Sounded like he had a mouthful of spaghetti. It could be my brother and I wouldn't know the difference." He continued to watch Frank and speak to the room at large. "He's supposed to lock the money up in the tail section of his car until they tell him to take it out. He drives to the Doubletree Inn, asks the desk clerk for any messages for Harold Classen. There's supposed to be a reservation under that name, but after he gets the message he's supposed to tell them there's been a mistake, that he's staying downtown someplace."

"They made the reservation," Tate said, "because they knew the hotel wouldn't take messages for somebody that wasn't about to check in. So far their thinking's not so bad."

Carpenter squinted over Frank's head, at the clock on the wall above the library entry. "Guy says he's got twenty minutes to show at the Doubletree."

Turner spoke up. "How're they going to know what time he gets there, to pick up a written message, unless they've got somebody hanging around? Maybe we should get a couple of guys to watch the lobby."

"I don't think that would help," Tate said. "They're holding all the cards right now, and they know we can't afford to be late. Also they may have a lot of confidence in Frank. Know he's going to be prompt." She smiled at Frank.

Frank scratched his chest. The wire with which Weir had fitted him moments earlier was uncomfortable against his skin. "It's a good twelve-, fifteen-minute drive from here," Frank said. "I think I'd better get going."

"That wire," Tate pointed at the tiny mike clipped to Frank's collar. "In case you're thinking of getting cutesy and putting it out of commission, don't. We'll never be more than eight blocks away, and we can pick you up on the beeper even if we can't hear you."

Frank gave Tate a sideways glance, then climbed to his feet and hefted the suitcase off of the reading table. One corner of Agent Turner's mouth pulled to one side. "Just a second, Stanley. Mr. Carpenter, the guy said he's supposed to lock the money in the tail section? Not the trunk."

Carpenter checked his writing pad. "That's the way I wrote it down."

Turner grinned. "Lot of coincidence here, Frank. You're driving a Jeep. Funny the guy'd know you don't have a trunk. Ain't it, Alphonse?"

As Frank carried the suitcase out the front door, Sis Carpenter squeezed his arm and smiled at him. He paused and said softly, "Thanks," then went outside.

He didn't speak to any of the federal people as he descended the two steps onto the drive, and loaded the suitcase into the back end of his Cherokee. The air was warm, beginning to cool as the front lumbered in. Nine million dollars didn't weigh nearly as much as he'd expected; the suitcase was light and easy to handle. He closed the tail door with a thunk, inserted his key, and clicked the lock into place. Turner, Tate, and Weir climbed into the back of a white panel truck with "Doran Cleaners" painted on its side, underneath a logo showing four shirts on hangers. As Turner closed the door from within, he formed a pistol with his hand and shot Frank with an imaginary bullet. Frank ignored him.

He climbed into the Jeep, sat with the key poised near the ignition while he drew a deep breath, then started the engine and turned on his lights. The headlamp beams reflected from the bumper of the panel truck. Frank drove a hundred feet forward, made the turnaround, and headed up the drive toward the street. The panel truck followed two car lengths behind. Frank made a left and kept his gaze on the rearview. The truck hesitated at the end of the driveway, and then turned in the opposite direction. Frank watched the FBI vehicle's taillights recede, then concentrated on the road ahead. A clipped-nail moon, surrounded by four bravely twinkling stars, rode in the upper left portion of his windshield. As Frank made the turn onto Walnut Hill Lane, a gash of lightning illuminated the approaching thunderheads.

A pebble had lodged in the Cherokee's tire tread, the rapid *click-click* slowing in tempo as Frank pulled in underneath the awning at the Doubletree Inn. The cloud bank had now obliterated the moon, and drops of rain splattered against the hood and windshield. Frank parked at the curb and got out, jamming his hands into his pockets and hunching his shoulders. The cool front had blown in in earnest, a strong fifty-degree wind whipping his hair and molding his pants against his legs. A spread-out double newspaper page fluttered in from the street and plastered itself against the Cherokee's fender. Frank peeled off and wadded the newspaper, and reached for the electronic door locks to thunk the plungers down. He slammed the door, then, head down, jogged up to the entry and pushed his way through the revolving door.

The lobby was practically deserted, with three check-ins—a man in a houndstooth jacket and two women in slacks—occupying one desk clerk's time while the other clerk stood off to one side with folded arms. Frank approached the counter, his feet sinking down into richly padded carpet, and motioned. The idle clerk unfolded his arms and came over, regarding Frank through thick bifocals. Frank said, "You have a message for Harold Classen?"

The clerk wore a navy blue blazer with the green hotel emblem—twin trees with their mushroom-shaped top branches interlocked—on the breast pocket. He retreated, pulled a stack of folded papers from a slot, thumbed through them, and handed one to Frank. The clerk then punched up Harold Classen's reservation on his computer screen. "You'll be with us how long, Mr. Classen?"

"Won't be," Frank said. "My plans have changed. Just picking up the message."

The clerk's lips puckered in irritation as he rattled the keys and punched the ENTER button. The screen went blank. Frank retreated to stand near a pillar in the middle of the lobby and look around. A man and a woman lounged near the exit, sharing a newspaper, and a group of uniformed bellmen stood before the concierge's desk, shooting the bull. From within the cocktail lounge, trumpet music rose to a crescendo and then died away to a smattering of applause.

Frank unfolded the note. It was typewritten in bold pica characters, the spelling and punctuation letter-perfect. Frank tucked his chin and read in a soft voice into his collar mike.

"If you are on time, and we assume you are, you have about a half hour to reach the intersection of Southwestern Boulevard and Greenville Avenue. Humperdinck's is a bar/restaurant on Greenville, two hundred yards north of the intersection, and that's where the scavenger hunt begins."

Frank paused. "Scavenger hunt" would be for the benefit of

nosy hotel people. He cleared his throat and went on.

"Go into Humperdinck's and sit at the bar. You'll be paged for a call at exactly eight thirty-five. If you don't answer, the game will be over, she's pregnant, the rabbit dies. We're depending on you, Frank. If you have any elves following you, suggest you apply the quirt to the reindeer and ditch them. Signed, Santa Claus."

Frank glanced toward the check-in desk, where both clerks now stood and chewed the fat. Neither looked in his direction. He said into the mike, "There's no signature. The 'Signed, Santa Claus,' that's typewritten just the way I read it to you." He started to fold the note, then paused. "Oh," he said. "The part about ditching the elves. That's written in the note, too, I didn't make it up. Wouldn't want you guys to think I'm getting ideas or anything." He folded and put the note away, went out the revolving door, and then halted in consternation. Beyond the protection of the entrance canopy was a billowing, windblown curtain of rain.

Less than five minutes after Frank left the Doubletree Inn, two men wearing suits came into the lobby. Their padded shoulders were drenched and their hair was soaking wet. They approached the desk at a fast walk, flashed federal shields, and demanded to know who had made the reservation for Harold Classen and who'd delivered the message. As the clerk gazed at the snapped-open wallets, sweat broke out on his forehead and his glasses fogged.

He made the drive from the Doubletree Inn in under twenty minutes with his wipers thunking monotonously, and sheets of rain rippling the windshield. The gutters were swollen streams, torrents of water rushing over the curbs and covering the sidewalks. The green digital clock in the Cherokee read 8:23 as he whipped into Humperdinck's parking lot, sending sheets of water out from under his wheels. He parked in between a supercab pickup and a Mazda, got out, ducked his head, and made a run for the entrance, and reached the air-conditioned foyer with his drenched T-shirt clinging to his body. The sudden damp coldness on his chest and shoulders made him sneeze.

There was quite a crowd for a weeknight, four or five couples in the back shooting pool, men and women in twos and threes at the tables drinking beer, wine in stemmed glasses, or highballs mixed in brandy snifters. Frank ducked around a row of tables and made a beeline for the bar. Two young women in thigh-length shorts moved out of his path, then grinned at him as he went by. He lowered his gaze and kept on walking.

Over half of the barstools were occupied; Frank sat at the end with two seats between him and the nearest customer. The bartender, a young guy in a flowered shirt, approached, drying his hands on a towel. Frank considered a Scotch and water, changed his mind, ordered plain soda with a twist, then said, "Look, I'm expecting a call in here. Frank White, that's me." The young man nodded, squirted soda from a liquor gun and added a rind of lime, served the drink, and went on about his business.

Frank fiddled with his glass, vaguely conscious of Garth Brooks's voice on the sound system, and squinted at the clock above the cash register. He swallowed hard as he scanned the numbers reading 8:42. Jesus, was the clock in the Cherokee slow or something? Had he missed his call? *The rabbit dies*, the note had said. Then all at once he relaxed; Alcoholic Beverage Commission watchdogs came down hard on bars caught serving booze after two in the morning, so nearly all Dallas gin mills turned the time forward a quarter hour or so. Frank motioned to the bartender and pointed at the clock, saying, "How fast is that?"

The young guy followed Frank's direction, nodded slightly and said, "Thirteen minutes." Frank expelled a relieved breath and fooled with his glass some more.

The back bar phone rang at 8:45 by the register clock, and Frank straightened on his stool. The bartender answered, looked directly at Frank, then laid the receiver up between two half-full Jack Daniel's bottles and called out, "Louise." Frank slumped.

Louise was a floor waitress wearing tight jeans and a loose mesh top, and set her tip tray up on the bar before grabbing up the phone. Then she leaned a hip against the counter and told someone named Jack that she was working double shift, and that she wouldn't be off until around three in the morning. Apparently, Jack didn't like those arrangements. Louise's features twisted as she told Jack that if he didn't like it, he should get off his ass and get a job. Apparently Jack said that he couldn't find a job, because Louise further opined that Jack might have better luck if he'd quit sitting around watching Oprah and all that other shit.

Frank ran his fingers through wet hair and had a sip of soda. The register clock changed to 8:47. He nervously scratched a knuckle.

Louise was saying, "Here's the picture, Jack. I don't leave here with any men 'cause I'm so tired I couldn't even give a good hand job. And if you don't believe it you can kiss my ay-yass."

Frank went around behind the bar and tapped Louise on the shoulder. From down the way, the bartender said loudly, "Excuse me, sir, you can't . . ."

Louise turned to face Frank, her dark eyes rolling up to look at him. Frank said, "Look, I'm expecting a call any minute."

Louise showed a quick smile. "You are? Well, you can keep on expecting, then. I've already got a call." Then, into the receiver she said, "Just some guy, Jack. No, not some guy I'm screwing, just this guy in here." She turned her back and lowered her head.

Frank's temper boiled. He reached to the phone base and pressed the disconnect button. Louise looked stunned, stared arm's length at the receiver. Then her gaze fell on Frank's finger, still with the button held down. "Listen, mister," she said.

"What the hell you think you're doing?" the bartender said, hustling down the runway like a man on fire.

Frank looked at the bartender, then at Louise, then at the bartender again. The phone rang. Frank released the cutoff button, grabbed the receiver from Louise and placed it to his ear. Louise said, eyes flashing fire and hands on hips, "You goddam bastard." Frank said into the mouthpiece, "Hello?"

The voice was deep and muffled, like that of a man talking with something in his mouth. "I'm calling for Frank White."

The bartender made a move as if to grab for the phone and then apparently changed his mind. "This is Frank," Frank said.

"Congratulations, you're right on time. Doing good. You getting wet?"

"I've had better days." Frank turned his back on Louise and the bartender, and stuck his finger in his unoccupied ear to shut out the sounds of "Lookin' for Love" on the sound system.

"So far this has been a drill. Now we're getting serious. You ready?"

Frank softly closed his eyes. Something about the accent. "Yeah, I'm listening," he said.

"Go back to the pisser, middle stall, there's three of them. Reach up inside the toilet-paper dispenser and you'll find an envelope taped to the metal. There are instructions and a map in there. You with me?"

"Note inside the toilet paper dispenser, gotcha."

"This is all very simple. You're still under a limit. Forty minutes this time. Plenty if you take the shortest route from A to B, but no leeway for a lot of fucking around. You're doing fine, Frank. You make this one last leg on your trip, you're okay, we're okay, she's okay. Easy as eggs over, as I see it."

Frank sagged against the counter. Jesus. *As I see it.* The picture came to him, wavy gray hair parted on the right, wide-gapped teeth with silver-filled molars. Jesus. A table in the prison chow hall, ham salad oozing with too much mayonnaise. *We need a new chef, men, as I see it.* A bench under a tree just outside the prison library, Darla Bern walking away, hips undulating. The gray-haired guy on the bench next to Frank, watching Darla go, saying, *Best arse in the camp, Frank, as I see it.*

"You listening, Frank?" the muffled voice said.

Frank gritted his teeth. "You better take good care of her, Randolph. If I find so much as a scratch on her body, you're dead."

The pause lasted a full ten seconds. Then, his voice no longer muffled, the New York accent clear as a bell, Randolph Money said, "Just bring us the money, Frank. Not one tiny bit of fucking around, you understand?"

The middle stall was locked, and a pair of cowboy boots crossed at the ankles were visible underneath the door. Frank stood back and looked both ways, at tiny white tiles on the floor, porcelain sinks and a hot-air hand dryer on the wall. A young guy with a skater cut was washing his hands. Frank stepped up and knocked on the stall. "Listen, I need to get in there."

There was a startled gasp from within, then a gruff voice said, "The fuck, man, just a minute." Skater cut swiveled his head to look, rubbing his hands together under the faucet. His jaw slacked.

"It's an emergency," Frank said.

"Jesus Christ," the voice inside the stall said. "Ain't one of the others open?"

"No, I mean," Frank said, "there's something in there I need."

"Look, I ain't gay, if that's what you're . . ."

"No, no, I . . ." Frank tugged at the hem of his T-shirt. Skater cut was now grinning. "I don't have to come in," Frank said, "if you could do something for me."

"Listen, buddy," the voice inside the stall said.

"Reach up inside the toilet-paper dispenser," Frank said. "There should be an envelope taped in there."

There was a rustling noise, a faint *clink* of metal. A big hand appeared beside the boots holding an envelope with a strip of tape stuck to its edge. Frank reached down, took the envelope, and stepped back. "Hey, thanks."

"You guys running around leaving each other messages in the toilet," the voice inside the stall said. "Just don't include me in no daisy chain, okay?"

The federal people were six blocks to the south, crammed like sardines in the back of the white Doran Cleaners panel truck, which sat in the storm-drenched parking lot of a Tom Thumb Supermarket. The camouflaged surveillance vehicle was directly behind a row of cars nosed in to the curb, blocking their exit route. Twice during the past ten minutes the truck had had to move to let autos back out, the most recent of which was a pickup driven by a cigar-smoking, red-faced man who'd shot the feds the finger. The panel truck's driver, a rookie FBI agent named Marks, had briefly considered arresting the guy. The rain had subsided some, tiny drops spattering the puddles like pepper grains. Lightning continued to flash and thunder continued to roll.

In the rear of the truck, the blinking cursor shifted its position on the monitor. "He's moving," Weir said.

The surveillance expert was hunched over the computer and audio receiver, Tate and Turner side by side on a built-in padded bench, Turner's knees splayed out, Tate's legs crossed finishing school style. "Let's have some audio," Turner said.

As if on cue, Frank White's voice cut into the speaker static. "I'm southbound on Greenville, planning to cut over and head south on I-45. The instructions are I'm supposed to take I-30 east out to Lake Ray Hubbard, cut across the dam to the north side of the lake, and find a pier in front of a bunch of condos. I'll be giving you the exact location once I get off of the interstate. Listen, I know the guy on the phone."

Tate and Turner exchanged a look. Tate murmured, "I'll just bet you do, sweetie." Frank's voice went on.

"Check out Randolph Money, guy was at Pleasanton until late eighty-eight or early eighty-nine, I'm not sure exactly. Some kind of white-collar fraud conviction. I've turned west now, and I'm about to enter southbound I-45 at the University Boulevard on-ramp. I'll be back in touch when I get to the lake."

The speaker continued to crackle. The cursor moved slowly toward the lower portion of the screen. Weir pressed some buttons on the keyboard and the cursor was once again centered in the picture. Turner scratched his ankle as he said, "Mr. Money wants the money, huh? Well, ain't that cute."

Tate leaned forward, removed her petite glasses, and rubbed her eyes. "What do you think?"

"Same thing I've always thought," Turner said. "I think our boy Frank's full of it."

"We've got to check this Randolph Money out."

"Sure we do. Just like we checked out the broad, that Darla Bern. I got the report back on her today."

Tate swiveled her head, light from the computer screen coloring her features an eerie green and adding sparkling highlights to her hair. "That's the first I've heard of it."

"Guys were a couple of days late getting it to us," Turner said. "The night they snatched the girl, the Bern woman was shacked up in her motel with a guy staying down the hall. Our people interviewed him, he verified. This afternoon she flew back to California, we also verified the flight number and the fact that her cute little fanny was in one of the seats. Also, according to Darla Bern, our man Frank tried to recruit her to help in the kidnapping."

"She'll testify to that?" Tate extracted a notepad and wrote something down.

"Not specifically the kidnapping. What she said was, Frank White met her in some honky-tonk and asked her to help him out with something. According to our report, she turned him down before he could tell her exactly what it was he was up to."

"We know how to get in touch with this woman if we need her?"

"Got her address and phone number in L.A. Big point is, if she's in on it she's doing it long distance at the moment. Like I said, I think our boy Frank's full of shit."

Tate chewed on the end of her ballpoint. "Him just talking to her, that's grounds to revoke his parole. Consorting with a felon."

"Yep," Turner said. "Asshole's in on it, take it from me." He leaned up behind Weir and tapped him on the shoulder. "That gizmo of yours got the capacity to call us up a map?"

Weir swiveled his head. "Sure, I just give her the command and it comes out on the printer over there. I can even get you recipes if you want 'em."

"Good," Turner said. "I want a detailed layout of the area around Lake Ray Hubbard, kabish?" He knocked on the partition separating the rear of the truck from the cab. "Hey up there," Turner called out.

The partition slid to one side and the driver stuck his head through. "Guy gave me the finger a minute ago."

"Yeah?" Turner said. "Well, just you find I-forty-five, head south, then take us east on Interstate Thirty. You start bouncing us around back here and I'll give you more than the finger, you listening to me?"

24

Frank steered down a twisty wet gravel road in the dark, with barely enough room ahead for two autos to pass abreast. Gnarly mesquite trees grew on both sides, and overhanging branches slid over the Cherokee's roof like car-wash brushes. Darts of rain reflected in the headlamp beams. The deluge slackened for an instant, then beat steadily down, the wipers swishing back and forth, back and forth across the windshield. The defroster was blowing and the window was partway down, the odor of soaked vegetation drifting up his nostrils.

As he inched along at ten miles per, Frank switched on the interior lights and checked the map. Five minutes earlier he'd read the dropoff instructions into his collar mike, assuming the federal people were hearing him but never sure. All at once he was clear of the mesquites, the path in front of him dipping down and to his left, the *lap-lap* of wavelets providing background to the whisper of rain. Visible through the right rear window, condo roofs towered in the darkness.

Frank's breathing quickened as the dock came into view, solid gray planks stretching forth, two cabin boats rocking up and down, up and down, tied to the end of the pier. He stopped, read over the instructions one final time, extinguished the interiors, and fished in the glove compartment for his flashlight. He thumbed the switch and a sudden beam stabbed the interior of the Cherokee. After turning off his headlights, he killed the engine and pocketed his car keys, then shouldered the door open and stepped outside. Rain soaked his hair, ran down his face, and dripped from his chin. On the way to the rear of the car, his foot slipped. He staggered, righted himself, and continued on.

He opened the tailgate and hefted out the suitcase, then stood in the downpour and directed the flashlight beam down to the dock. The beam spotlighted the words *Sassy Seaman* painted aft on one of the cabin boats, then zeroed in on the end of the pier. The anvil-shaped piece of iron was right where the instructions had said it would be. Frank's jaws clenched as he lugged the suitcase down the incline and out onto the dock.

He knelt and touched lukewarm metal and grunted slightly as he hefted the anvil to test its weight. A chain encircled the iron and looped inside itself, and a hook dangled from the chain's slack end. Frank fastened the hook to the suitcase handle, squatted down, placed his hands on the anvil, and, with a heavy sigh of exertion, shoved. The iron slug teetered, then toppled from the dock, dragging its load behind. The suitcase bounced once, then vanished over the side, the splash barely audible over the deluge and the lapping tide. Frank stood and shone the flashlight on inky-black, rain-pocked waves for a moment, then trudged up the dock in the direction of the Cherokee.

Chester Rankin's secretary sat bolt upright and said breathlessly, "Oh, it's her. I know it is." Then she pulled the sheet up to cover her bare breasts, lay back down, and buried her head underneath the pillow. The loud pounding downstairs continued.

Rankin raised up on one elbow, his hard-on wilting. "No way, I put her on the plane."

"Some private detective, then." The pillow muffled her words. "Someone taking pictures."

The knocking ceased for a count of three, then resumed,

echoing up the staircase and reverberating through the bedroom like jungle drums.

Rankin scratched his head through thinning hair, peering through the darkness at shapes, his robe laid over a vanity chair, her dress, panties and bra strewn about on the floor. He threw the sheet back and sat naked on the side of the bed. On the nightstand, a roach glowed in an ashtray. He ground out the stub, then dug in the drawer for his Beretta. Pistol in hand, he went over and put on his robe. The hardwood was cool underfoot.

His secretary raised up, curls askew in the semi-light. "You're not going to *shoot somebody*."

"Protection," Rankin said. He leaned over her to peer out the window. Two hundred yards away and a story below, someone came off the dock carrying a flashlight. Visible through a film of rain, the beam swiveled left and right as it approached a shit-kicker vehicle of some kind parked on the incline. A Bronco, maybe, or could be a Jeep or an Isuzu, Rankin didn't know one of these goat-roper cars from the other. Somebody was out there fucking around in a downpour, while somebody else pounded on the condo door in the middle of the fucking night. Rankin didn't know what the fuck was going on. Some fucking hideaway, huh? Next time he wanted to bang his secretary he'd do it downtown in the middle of Main Street, less of a fucking audience.

The knocking quickened its pace, *bang-bang-bang, bang-bang-bang, bang-bang-bang.*

Rankin sucked in his gut as he went down the steps. Then he thought, *To hell with it,* and relaxed, letting it all hang out, figuring the loose-fitting robe for plenty of camouflage. He reached the door and looked out through the peephole, at huddled shapes on the porch, heads bent down in the rain. "The fuck you want?" Rankin yelled.

A brisk male voice spoke out. "FBI, sir. I'm Agent Weir. We need your help."

Rankin nearly gagged. He switched on the outside light, the

two figures in full view now, men wearing yellow slickers, rain-drops plummeting through the yellow glow all around them. "You better show some ID," Rankin said. "I got a gun in here."

One man reached up inside his coat, snapped open a wallet, and exhibited the shield to the peephole. Rankin opened the door a foot. "You need a warrant." It was more of a question than a statement; Rankin didn't know if the FBI needed fucking *any-thing* to hassle somebody.

A smallish figure stepped around the guy holding the wallet, and said in a businesslike female alto, "I'm not FBI, sir, he is. I'm Felicia Tate, Assistant United States Attorney, and we've got a critical stakeout going. Your condo backs up to the lake, and we need to set up shop where we can watch from your upstairs win-dow. The government will reimburse you for—"

"Not without a warrant," Rankin said.

"—any inconvenience. I beg your pardon?" She held a ciga-rette in a holder clamped between her teeth, the hot end glowing, smoke rising, trapped underneath her rain hat, drifting up around the edges of the brim.

"I know my rights. No tickee, no laundry." Rankin trembled slightly. The truth was that he didn't know his rights from Adam's ass, but he'd seen a lot of TV.

The glow under the rain hat illuminated glasses with tiny lenses. Felicia Tate held the cigarette off to one side as she sniffed the air through the partially open door. She smiled. "You have a right to ask for a court order, sir. But I'll make you a proposition. You give us some slack on the procedures and I'll forget about that strange-smelling tobacco you've been smoking in there. You help us, we'll help you, is the way it's done. The guys on *Law and Order* aren't telling it like it is, in case you're wondering."

25

Frank squinted over the hood through the rain as he drove away from the lakeshore. His clothes were soaking wet, rivulets of water running over the seats and dripping on the floorboard. Two hundred yards from the lake, where the mesquite forest opened into a clearing, the gravel road became blacktop and forked in opposite directions. The interstate highway was to his right, the pathway leading behind the condos to his left. Frank turned the wheel toward I-30; as he did, a figure loomed in the headlamp beams, arms waving. Frank reached instinctively under the seat, then remembered that he hadn't carried a pistol since his conviction, something like nine years ago. He straightened and put on the brakes.

The figure wore a yellow slicker and a floppy hat and sprinted around to the passenger door to knock on the window. Frank hesitated, then flicked the doorlock switch. The door opened, and Agent Turner stuck his head inside. "You're going the wrong way," he said. As he turned to sit down inside the car, the blue letters "FBI" showed on the back of his raingear. "Over there, Thurman, toward them condos." Turner gestured with his head. Drops of water flew from his hatbrim.

Frank made a U-turn and inched his way toward the cluster of rooftops, winding down the lane until rows of zero lot-line houses were on both sides. Recognition flooded over him as the white Doran Cleaners panel truck came into view on his left. Parked in front of the truck was a dark four-door Ford Taurus, interior lights on, two people in the front seat. Frank halted as the Taurus's left front window slid down, then nodded in acknowledgment as Jill smiled at him. Falling drops spattered the shoulder of her raincoat. Jack sat beside her. He formed a pistol with his thumb and forefinger, and grinned as he shot Frank with an imaginary bullet. Turner said, "You know those two, huh?"

Frank sighed and hung his wrists over the steering wheel. "Seen 'em before."

"Yeah? I think they look heavier, must have been tanking up on that ice cream you sell." Turner rose on his knees, produced a penlight, and shone the beam into the Cherokee's backseat. "Where you got the frogman costume, Frank? You doing the diving, or somebody else?"

Frank kept his wrists draped over the wheel, stared ahead, and didn't say anything.

Turner picked up the drop instructions and slid them into a plastic evidence bag. "That soaked-down money's going to be heavy, Harold. Ruined a pretty good-looking suitcase dumping it in the lake. I was planning on buying that fucker myself, once we used it for evidence to help convict your ass. Why you want to fuck up my suitcase, Frank?"

Frank said, "Look, Turner."

Turner twisted around and sat. "Look at what? You were in a helluva hurry back there, you think we're going to let you dump nine million dollars in a lake someplace and then drive the fuck away? You got no frogman suit in here, so I guess you do have help. Tell you the truth, I've been thinking along maybe it was just you, until the phone calls tonight. Who's your buddy? I guess you're going to tell me it's the Money guy you were telling us about."

"The guy on the phone is named Randolph Money. I recognized this expression he uses a lot."

"Yeah, what expression is that? 'One for you, one for me,' when you assholes are splitting the money? I already got a sheet on the guy, Frank, we got this cute little printer in the truck. Lives in Newport Beach, California. Come on, this guy's no kidnapper. He was doing time for some pissant false statement on a loan application. First you talk the broad, now another guy. You got a hard-on for California people, you keep pointing the finger?"

"Randolph Money's been into a helluva lot more than bank fraud," Frank said. "And Darla's in on it, too."

"Sure she is. From Los Angeles"—Turner pronounced it, Los Angle-eez—"fucking California, which is where she landed this afternoon around four o'clock. You're going to have trouble convincing people, these folks two thousand miles from here are doing all this. Come on, you mad at this woman 'cause she quit giving you any pussy when you were in the joint?"

"Randolph Money's not in California," Frank said, "unless he was calling long distance. The guy on the phone was him."

"I'll give you this much credit, you're forcing us to check the guy out. Which I think is a bullshit waste of time."

Frank turned his head to the left. Jill continued to watch him from the Taurus. Frank looked straight ahead.

"So here's the drill, Donald Duck," Turner said. "You drive straight to your place, and your friends over there are going to follow. Then you're going to be a good boy and go to bed, or whatever you do at home. We're going to stay here and wait for your buddies to haul the money off."

Sudden tears stung Frank's eyes. He said, "Do me one favor."

"Sure," Turner said. "I'll tell them to let you keep a couple of extra people on your visiting list. Maybe even get visits twice a week, you like that?"

"I just want to know," Frank said, "the minute there's any word on Meg. Whether she's . . ." His grip on the wheel tightened.

Turner looked at him. He took off his hat, then put it back on as he opened the door. "You know what, Frank?" Turner said. "I think you already know the answer to that one. I'll bet you could tell us right where her body's buried, if you weren't so busy fucking us around."

26

The storm had petered out by two in the morning, leaving fresh, rain-washed air, stars twinkling at intervals in a blue-black sky, and a mirror-still lake bathed in the light of the moon. In the condo's upstairs bedroom, Special Agent Weir watched the computer terminal as if hypnotized, the stationary cursor blinking, blinking, blinking, in abject monotony. "Froggy-man, Froggy-man, where you be?" Weir said. "I got to tell you, this doesn't make any sense."

Felicia Tate stood up from a rocking chair, removed her coat, folded and dropped the coat on the bed, and sat back down. "My husband suspects me of screwing around, being out all night. This case is ruining my happy home. Really getting after it, weren't they?" The bed looked like a cyclone survivor, the fitted bottom sheet yanked down to expose the mattress, pillows wadded and jammed against the headboard. "You can tell they're not married, my husband and I barely wrinkle the covers. A couple of times a week when I'm lucky."

"Even if they've got a plan to get it out of the lake," Weir said, "they've got problems. They'd have to spread that money out to dry, and that many bills'd take some major space. They can't go around spending wet money, especially where it smells like lake water."

"You notice the fanny on her?" Tate said. "Twenty-four,

twenty-five maybe. What wouldn't I give. I could tell her, Give it a few years, hon, but she wouldn't believe me. I had one like that at her age, though you'd never know it. You ever notice I allow plenty of room in the rear, when I wear pants?"

"You know what I think?" Weir said.

"Same thing I do. That he's not the only one she's doing it with. A man his age . . ."

"I'm thinking," Weir said, "that the suitcase may be empty already. That we may be sitting up here expecting somebody in a submarine, and all the while the guys are a thousand miles away, counting their loot and laughing their asses off."

"Turner inspected the Jeep before our man Frank went home. We watched him lock the money in the back, it's got to be either there or in the lake. It's not in the Jeep, so . . ."

"Whole thing's just too corny, Felicia. All these kidnappings, I never heard of having the ransom money sunk in a lake before."

Tate wistfully patted the bed, looking at the rumpled sheets. "So maybe they're breaking new ground, okay?"

Weir rested his chin on his intertwined fingers and watched the dock, the cabin boats still as painted pictures. "I'm betting the money's gone, Felicia. Five bucks, that's as high as I'm going. How 'bout it, you taking me on?"

In the downstairs sitting room, Chester Rankin's secretary asked Agent Turner, "You think he did it? I don't." She adjusted her position on the sofa, curling up her legs, six to eight inches of milky thigh showing beneath a skirt made of shiny black stretch material.

Turner stood, walked over and adjusted the color knob on the television, Sally Jessy Raphael's dress changing instantly from pink to cardinal red, Sally Jessy walking among a sea of raised hands in the audience, people just dying to say something on national television. "Sure, he was buying all that poison," Turner said. "Look, the guy gets home at five in the afternoon, seven-thirty his wife's got cramps and diarrhea, the next morning she's like, adios. He's just going on TV, trying to get sympathy." Turner went back and sat beside the secretary. Chester Rankin was seated on her other side, Rankin still in his robe, rolling his eyes and looking nervous. The scene on television switched to the stage, an earnest young brown-haired man explaining to the studio audience that the indictment was full of shit, that he didn't do it, no way.

"He looks so sincere," the secretary said, chewing gum.

"All these guys do," Turner said. "You should see some of 'em I talk to." He'd shed his rain slicker.

"Listen," Rankin said, standing up and pacing back and forth, "we've got to get going from here, pretty soon."

"I wish I could let you," Turner said. "But what we're doing up there, it's pretty top secret. If word gets out what we've got going, a life could be in danger. Under the circumstances we've got to keep you-all here."

"So? We won't tell anybody." Rankin tightened the belt on his robe.

"Too critical for that, sir," Turner said. "If this operation should blow up, then somebody finds out we let two people walk out of here with knowledge . . ."

"Christ," Rankin said. "My business . . ."

"*Shh.*" The secretary uncurled her legs and leaned forward. "They've got an outside caller. They usually ask the best questions, people that've been following the case."

"I'm afraid your business'll have to wait, sir," Turner said. "But really, it's a long time before your office opens."

"What he's worried about," the secretary said, "is that his wife's due home in the morning. She's shopping down in Houston." She squinted at the TV, then said to Turner, "You get what the caller was asking? Something about arsenic being easy to get."

"Naw, I missed it," Turner said. "You want me to turn up the volume?"

Rankin rubbed his eyes. "Christ, you people are going to ruin me."

"I can't let you leave," Turner said. "But if you should have wife problems, maybe we can cover for you. We don't want to cause trouble."

"My God, man, you've already . . ."

"You may be right," the secretary said. "That time, when he said he bought the poison to kill fire ants, you see him? Looks like he's hiding something, you catch that?" She nudged Turner with her elbow.

Rankin spread his hands to Turner in supplication. "Christ, can't you be human?"

"That could be a nervous twitch," Turner said to the secretary. "Some people have 'em, the main thing you want to watch for is, does his story stay the same? If he tells it exactly the same every time, he's memorized it. Everybody, if they're on the square, their story changes some."

Rankin sank down on the couch, pushing his robe down between his knees. "Jesus . . . oh Christ, I'm . . ."

The secretary touched Turner on the shoulder. "Can I ask you something?"

"Sure," Turner said. "It's what I'm here for, to help."

She lowered her lashes. "Look, are you married?" she said.

At nine in the morning, Felicia Tate finally said, "I don't know what's blown up in our faces, but something has." Overnight her makeup had faded, her eyes slightly red as she looked down from the second-story window. The wind had picked up during the morning, the boats now rocking in little wavelets, a row of tall grass rippling over near the mesquite grove. The sun was twenty degrees above the horizon and climbing.

Weir rose painfully from his seat before the computer screen, yawned, and stretched. "It went wrong last night, like I said. That has to be it. The suitcase hasn't moved, just drifted some on the bottom."

"Well, order us up a couple of divers," Tate said. "I suppose we have to bring it up."

Weir sat down, rattled the keys, and brought his menu up on the monitor. "The money's gone, Felicia. I can't help it, I've just got that feeling."

As Weir loaded his monitor, disk drive, and software into the panel truck, a cab pulled up to the curb in front of the condo. The driver went around and held the door for a plumpish woman who stepped down and headed up the walk, high heels clicking. The driver opened the trunk and hauled out two big suitcases, then huffed and puffed his way in pursuit of the woman.

The woman stepped up on the porch just as Chester Rankin came out, followed by Agent Turner and Assistant USDA Felicia Tate. Rankin was still in his robe, and bent to kiss the woman on the cheek. "Hello, dear," he said. "Nice trip?"

The woman had bleached blond hair and wore rings on four fingers of each hand. Her eyes widened as she looked from Tate to Turner, and back again. "Who are these people?" she said.

"They're federal agents," Rankin said. "Been using our place to conduct a stakeout. I'll tell you all—"

"Your husband," Turner said, "has been a tremendous help to us, ma'am. Something we won't forget."

The woman's mouth opened in astonishment. She gaped at Rankin.

Tate said to Turner, "I suppose we're ready to move along."

"Sure are," Turner said. He went back to the door and said to someone inside, "Come on, agent, we're going now."

A small figure came through the entry, wearing an FBI rain slicker and a yellow hat pulled low over the eyes. As the figure went down the step in a rapid, hip-slinging gait, the raingear dragged the ground.

Mrs. Chester Rankin regained her composure, saying to

Turner, "Someone should tell that person it's not raining any-more."

Turner grinned. "You just have to know us federal gumshoes, ma'am. Some of us are crazy as loons."

Felicia Tate stood on the dock, weaving in place, halfway afraid she'd fall asleep and tumble headlong into the water. All night, sitting up in that bedroom watching the godforsaken cursor blink, she'd be seeing it, *blink-blink-blink,* in the back of her mind for days. Her pink jogging suit hung limply from her body, her hair a stringy mess, the white bandanna's ends drooping around her shoulders. A film of dust covered her glasses, but she was too tired to so much as clean the damn things.

There was a splashing noise as a head broke the surface five yards from the dock, smooth rubber covering the head, the face obscured behind a diving mask with water running down the lens. The diver paddled over to grip the edge of the pier, then raised his mask up on top of his head. His skin was pasty white. "I've separated 'em," he said loudly. "Which you want first, the suitcase or the iron? That hunk of iron's going to be a problem, heavy as it is."

Tate bent from the waist and rested her palms on her knees. She was suddenly dizzy, and stood to keep from toppling over on her face. Oh God but she needed sleep. "The money. We've got to have the money."

Ten minutes later Tate stood beside Turner as the FBI agent turned the crank to raise the grappling chain. The links clanked and straightened, coming up from the depths in slow, steady progression. The suitcase followed, swinging from the hook, filthy water dripping from its side and pouring from its interior through the crack. Turner reached out from the end of the pier and drew the cargo in, flopping the suitcase soggily onto its side. Beads of water flowed on the planks.

"Get the damned thing open," Tate said, picturing toilet paper stuffed inside, picturing herself explaining to the Big Man himself what she'd done with nine million dollars. She swallowed.

Turner squatted down and clicked the latches. There was an odor of wet moss, accompanied by the stink of dead fish. Bile rose in Tate's throat. Turner raised the lid and stood, and the two looked down on rows of sopping wet hundred-dollar bills, bundled in wrappers. Tate breathed a loud sigh. "Get Mr. Carpenter," she said, then cleared her throat and said, "Get Carpenter on the phone and tell him to meet us at the bank. Tell him we don't have his daughter but we've still got his money. Ought to make him half happy, anyway."

Turner inflated one cheek in thought, then expelled air between his lips. "Something blew our cover, Felicia. Our boy Frank, I thought we had him covered pretty good, but . . ."

"Someone knew we were watching, all right," Tate said. "Nothing we can do about what's happened. It's what they're going to do next that I'm wondering about."

Turner lugged the suitcase into Lone Star Bank at five minutes before ten, with Felicia Tate on his heels like a woman walking in ankle-deep mud. The agent still wore his T-shirt, Dockers, and boots. Tate had fixed her makeup as best she could and brushed out her hair, but her jogging suit and white bandanna were grimy and limp. Turner sported a heavy overnight beard. They rode the elevator up to the twenty-third floor, and trudged down the hall to enter Davis Boyle's reception area. Boyle's assistant eyed the suitcase, sniffed the air, and wrinkled her nose.

Morgan Carpenter rose from the couch, wearing an off-white summerweight suit, yellow tie, and two-tone shoes. He said, "If I find out calling you people in was a screwup . . ."

"We followed security procedures to the letter," Tate said,

raising a hand. "There's nothing to say we won't get another chance. What I think, I think our messenger found a way to tip off his friends."

Carpenter stared, hands on hips. Tate dropped her gaze. The receptionist came around to usher the three into Davis Boyle's inner chamber, with Turner bringing up the rear.

Boyle was behind his desk in a dark blue suit, his Kiwanis pin neatly in place on his lapel. Across from him was a muscular, flaxen-haired woman of around forty, wearing slacks and a pullover. As Turner closed the door behind him, the woman eyed the suitcase with open interest. She reminded Turner of a character in a James Bond movie, a tough-looking broad who'd snapped poisoned blades out from the tips of her shoes and tried to kick 007 in the shins.

Boyle stood and looked at Carpenter in sympathy. "Condolences, Morg."

"Those aren't in order," Tate said quickly, "until the cards are all played. We're returning the money and we'll need a receipt. I'd suggest you don't unpack the suitcase, 'cause we'll likely be needing it again. I'll confess it could stand some drying out."

"You don't get any receipt," the muscular woman said, "until it's all counted. Every dollar." Her voice was gravelly, like Ma Barker's.

"Serita Mayes, gentlemen," Boyle said, extending a hand toward the woman. "She's our main security person. With this much cash I thought I needed . . ."

Turner lifted the suitcase and set it on Boyle's desk. "We've been up all night. How long's the counting going to take?"

Serita Mayes favored the FBI agent with a bored blink. "Until it's done," she said.

Turner snapped open the catches and lifted the lid. "Well get after it, then. If you can stand the wait, so can we."

"We've got a lounge downstairs, with coffee and whatnot," Boyle said. "Maybe we'd be more comfortable . . ."

"We're staying with the money," Tate said, "until we get the receipt."

Morgan Carpenter sat down and folded his arms, watching Boyle. "I'm not paying any interest as long as the bank's got the money. Let's get that clear."

Boyle spread his hands, palms up. "That'd take paying off the loan, Morg. Along with the interest it's already earned, and returning the money to our asset account. Then if you need it again there'll be another board meeting, new collateral documents . . . you sure you want to go through all that?"

"What I want to go through," Morgan Carpenter said, "is not paying you bloodsuckers any more interest than I have to."

"Well, if you insist," Boyle said, "then we'll—"

"You're not expecting a receipt for *this* shit, are you?" Serita Mayes said. She was standing, holding one of the damp packets of hundreds out in Turner's direction.

Carpenter sat forward, his lips parted. Turner cocked his head. Boyle bent over his desk and looked closer at the money. Tate gave a nervous laugh and said, "I know it's a little wet, but . . ."

"Wet," Serita Mayes said, riffling the money with her thumb, "and phony as hell. I don't know who's trying to pull what, but, you know."

Carpenter stiffened as if poked from behind. Tate said weakly, "You're joking, right?"

"If I am, the joke's on somebody else. Not me." Serita held the packet up and ran her thumbnail over the top bill's surface. A gray streak appeared above the serial number. "It's not even good counterfeit." She dropped the bundle back into the suitcase. "We send out the real stuff and you bring us back funny money, guys. What, they don't teach you federal people how to spot it?"

27

After the confrontation with Agent Turner outside the condos, Frank decided that he had to do something even if the something was wrong. He'd seen these investigations before, where one guy was "it," and was pretty sure that nothing he could say was going to change his situation with the feds. He could give them Darla Bern and Randolph Money until the cows came home, but he was wasting his breath. Even if the FBI bothered to check those people out, the agents would only be going through the motions.

Getting rid of Jack and Jill was fairly easy. Halfway to his apartment, Frank steered the Cherokee off of I-20 and under the awning in front of a convenience store, and stopped beside the self-service super-unleaded gas pump. Right on cue the unmarked Taurus cruised in out of the rain and halted behind him, leaving two wet tire tracks on the pavement. Frank got out, shivering in his soaked clothing, went back and told Jill, "You got to pay inside first." He pointed at a sign on the pump. She nodded. Frank jogged across the neon-lit driveway and entered the store.

Once inside he went down aisles of shelves exhibiting Kraft's Macaroni & Cheese Dinners, liquid Tide, and every brand of candy bar known to man. He selected a toothbrush, toothpaste, a bar of Dial soap, Gillette lime shave cream along with a pack of Bic disposable razors, and approached the counter. A Hispanic woman in a red uniform smock rang up his purchase, gave him change, and sacked his order. Frank then said, "Listen, you have a restroom?" She nodded and pointed to the rear of the store. Frank followed her directions, carrying the items he'd bought in a small paper bag.

The men's room was down a ten-foot corridor that opened up beside the beer coolers, and halfway down the hall was a door on Frank's left leading to the storage area. Frank tried the door and gently pushed it open, then looked for a second at stacked card-board boxes holding Snickers and Mars bars. He glanced quickly toward the register; the clerk was nowhere in sight. Frank went into the storage room, skirted the boxes and a broken Slurpee dispenser, and went out through the back exit into the rain. The deluge beat down on a metal dimpster-dumpster and four large garbage cans. Frank wiped water from his eyes, stuffed the sack underneath his shirt, and sprinted around to the east side of the store.

There were more gas pumps on that side, and a six-foot hedge separating the driveway from the street beyond. Frank's breath came in gasps as he passed the pumps, skirted and then ducked down behind the hedge, and squinted through the leaves and tiny branches. On the north driveway, the Taurus was still parked behind the Cherokee, both cars blocking the super-unleaded pump. The Hispanic woman was visible through the store's side window, piling something on an overhead shelf above the regis-ter. Frank blew water from his nose and mouth and waited.

In a couple of minutes the Taurus's passenger door opened and Jack got out. He walked three quarters of the way across the drive, stood on tiptoes, and peered inside the store through the window. Then he went in, approached the counter, and talked to the clerk. The clerk gestured toward the restrooms, and Jack took off in that direction. He returned within seconds and said some-thing else to the clerk, who gestured some more with chubby hands. Jack charged out into the drive, yelling at Jill and waving his arms. Jill hit the pavement at a trot, her heels clicking and her tan raincoat swirling around her calves. Both agents hustled into the store, where Jack dashed off in the direction of the restrooms while Jill showed her shield to the clerk and began to speak a mile a minute. Frank rose into a crouch, ran ducked down to the far end of the hedge, sprinted across the drive and dived behind the wheel of the Cherokee. As he started the engine and drove away he glanced to his left. The clerk was now talking while Jill took notes on a pad. Neither woman looked in Frank's direction.

Frank stopped off in a twenty-four-hour Tom Thumb Supermarket, prowled the sporting goods section until he found a pair of shorts that fit, then checked into a motel in South Dallas whose sign read, "Nite-Nite Courts," in flickering, about-to-burn-out neon. He accepted one towel and one washcloth from the desk clerk, then made his way around to the back and found his room. There was barely enough space in the room for a double bed and a small table, and the wallpaper sagged. A window air conditioner blew frigid air. Frank shivered and switched the unit off.

He stripped to the buff, put on the shorts he'd bought, then drove out and found the nearest laundromat. Midnight found him watching dull-eyed through a round window as his pants, shirt, socks and underwear tumbled dry. Finally he managed four hours' sleep on a mattress whose innersprings creaked, faintly listening to giggles and squeals from a couple of hookers who'd set up shop in the room next door. Around five o'clock he switched on the light, groped in the nightstand for his wallet, and fished out a small photo. The picture was of Meg, seated on the bank of the pool at his apartment, a pose he'd shot less than a month ago. He stared at the photo until dawn.

He showered in water the temperature of day-old coffee, shaved, brushed his teeth, then dumped all of the items from the convenience store into the wastebasket. He dropped the key off in the motel office, dawdled over coffee in a Denny's Restaurant until around eight-thirty, then drove a couple of blocks until he located a pay phone in front of a grocery store. After first dialing

Information to get the number, he placed a call. As he listened to a series of rings over the line, a couple of black guys with their hair in dreadlocks stopped to peer inside the Cherokee, then moseyed on. A pregnant black woman came out of the grocery store carrying a sack, climbed into a fifteen-year-old Buick, and chugged away. There was a click in Frank's ear, then a bored female voice said, "U.S. Probation Office."

"Yeah, this is Patrolman Willis, Dallas Police Department. I need to speak to whatever probation officer handles a parolee named Wilbur Dale."

The operator told him to hold. For a full minute he listened to a recording of Bill Clinton talking about health care. Then there was a final click, and Marjorie Rapp's husky voice said, "Rapp."

Frank's throat constricted. Jesus, of all the . . . He very nearly hung up, then forced his tone to be calm and matter-of-fact as he said, "Patrolman Willis, Ms. Rapp, Dallas Police. I need a current address for one of your parolees. A Wilbur Dale."

"You're law enforcement? We don't give out that information to just . . ."

"Yes, ma'am, Dallas Police." Frank pictured Marjorie Rapp, her mouth puckered with authority, likely hoping one of her coworkers was listening as she told the Dallas Police Department how the cow ate the cabbage.

"I'll need your badge number, Officer, and your supervisor's telephone number."

Frank gave his old badge number, from back when he'd been on the force, and the number and extension for his former shift captain, which he hoped hadn't changed in the past few years. If Marjorie Rapp put him on hold to check his story out, he was going to hang up and make a run for it. Instead she said merely, "Who's the parolee, sir?"

"Wilbur Dale."

"Wilbur? He's one of our better ones. Does this involve some sort of crime he's . . ."

"No. No, ma'am." Frank swallowed, giving himself time to

think. Jesus, Wilbur Dale a model parolee. The idea made Frank sick. Frank said, "This is just an investigation where we think Mr. Dale might have some information on one of his former associates. Has nothing to do with anything he's done."

"I'm really not supposed to give this out over the phone, unless I've checked you out, Officer," Ms. Rapp said.

Frank held his breath, started to hang up.

"But I've got a lot going myself," she said. "A parolee ex-cop I'm handling, seems he's really gone off the deep end, and that fine gentleman's taking up all my time right now. So I'm willing to bend procedures if you're willing to promise you didn't get this information from me."

Frank blinked. He was now a few rungs lower on Marjorie Rapp's list than Wilbur Dale. He almost laughed aloud. "I'll give you my word, ma'am," he said.

She gave the address and phone number, which Frank scribbled hastily on the back of one of his Sidewalk Humor business cards. "Thanks, Ms. Rapp," Frank said officially. "And good luck with your ex-cop. Anything I hate to see it's a fellow officer doing something wrong. Makes us all look bad, you know?"

The address was in Garland, in northeast Dallas County, and on the drive out Frank was suddenly nervous. He was on Central Expressway, stuck in crawling traffic due to the construction barriers, when it occurred to him that by now he was probably wanted. Would definitely be the subject of a warrant if he wasn't already, and here he was driving a sore-thumb Jeep Cherokee whose license plate might be on a hot sheet. He spent the rest of the trip with one eye on his rearview mirror.

He found the house, a wood frame job on a block of unkempt yards with pickups and campers parked in the driveways. The house needed painting in the worst way, but so did the other homes up and down the street, so Wilbur Dale's place blended right in. Frank left the Cherokee at the curb, crossed a lawn strewn with crumpled cans and little piles of dog shit, stepped up on the porch, and knocked. He stood first on one foot and then the other, then knocked again. He put his ear to the doorcrack. From inside the house came the *whup-whup* of running machinery.

Frank checked both ways up and down the block, making certain that no one was watching, then double-timed it to the back of the house. He vaulted a hip-high cyclone fence into a backyard with patches of dirt showing through a blanket of weeds. A doghouse was against the western fence, and a fox terrier came out and yapped at him. Frank went to the back door and opened the screen. The *whup-whup* sound was louder.

The door was locked; Frank slid his library card into the crack and pried the plunger out and slipped on into the kitchen. There were dirty plates and saucers in the sink, part submerged in soapy water. A buzzing came from the refrigerator, and an odor of grease-cooked meat hung in the air. Frank walked over yellowed linoleum toward the *whup-whup* sound.

He inched open a swinging door, and looked into what was once a formal dining room. A cracked chandelier hung from the ceiling. On a scarred long table a printing press chugged, spitting big sheets of paper out into a stack. A man with hunched shoulders and a bowed back was making an adjustment at the top of the press. Frank tiptoed on in and used a stiffened forefinger to poke the guy's shoulder. A screwdriver clattered on the table. The man turned; Frank looked at a hooked nose, shaggy gray brows over narrowed eyes, and a thin mouth twisted in fear. Recognition showed in the eyes, and the mouth relaxed. The man reached up and flicked a switch. The press turned over a couple of times, spitting two more sheets onto the stack, then was still.

"Hi, Wilbur," Frank said.

Irritation replaced the frightened expression. "Scare the shit out of a man."

"That's good," Frank said. "I was trying to." He rested a hip on the edge of the table and folded his arms.

"You could get shot." Wilbur Dale had a cracked sixty-year-old voice with a heavy East Texas drawl.

"You don't come by for ice cream anymore." Frank picked the top sheet from the stack, looked over rows of twenty-dollar bills, ten across, twenty down. The brand name "A.B. Dick" was on the press's engine cover. "Jesus, Wilbur, what if your probation officer comes by?"

Dale wiped his hands on his apron. His fingers were stained with printer's ink. "That don't happen except end of the month. The fuck, you back to being a cop?"

Frank patted the press, and gestured toward a photographic plate maker in the corner. "You rent this stuff, right? Make up a batch, then take the machinery back. Need some more money you just rent it again."

Frank watched Dale's face, remembering the expressions he'd learned doing time with the guy, the slight shift in the gaze as Wilbur Dale got ready to lie. "I was just, you know, doing a little practicing," Dale said.

"You can do better than that. I'm not going to snitch you off, Wilbur, I'm just trying to find out what you're up to. In addition to helping some people screw me."

Dale sagged into his broken-old-man routine, which impressed Frank about as much as the about-to-lie expression. In the penitentiary, Dale had become a broken old man each time the hack had tried to hand out yard-mowing duty. "I had a square job," Dale said. "I lost it is all."

"Or quit it." Frank tossed the fresh-printed counterfeit money back on the table. "I don't give a shit about all this, Wilbur. I'm just interested in why you told Randolph Money all about my private life. Or Darla Bern—one's the same as the other."

Dale's wrinkled forehead wrinkled even more. He had stiff brown hair, showing a few gray streaks, and a round bald spot at the crown of his head. "Seems like I remember a Randolph Money," he said.

Frank expelled a long sigh, went over to the window and pulled the drape aside. Next door a woman in Bermuda shorts was mowing her weeds, heavy legs pumping along behind a Briggs & Stratton hand-propelled. Frank let the curtain fall back into place, whirled, and grabbed Wilbur Dale by the shirtfront. He yanked, the older man wheezing as Frank held him nose to nose.

"I don't have any time to screw around," Frank said. "And if you think acting hurt's going to stop me from beating the shit out of you, you're wrong. You came by my place. You talked to me, I was dumb enough to tell you this girl's name I'm dating. You told all this stuff to either Darla or Money. I want to know which, why, and for how much."

Tiny drops of saliva fell on Frank's cheeks as Dale struggled to get away. "The fuck you talking?" Dale said. "I don't tell anybody's business to nobody."

Frank bunched Dale's shirtfront up and drew back a balled fist.

Dale squawked, "Goddammit, it was Bern called me."

Frank's arm relaxed and dropped to his side. He released Dale's shirtfront. "She what?" Frank said.

"I swear to God." Dale raised a hand as if he was about to take the witness stand. "Mindin' my own business, she calls up one day. It was her idea for me to drop by and check on you. So I give her the girl's name. Meg, right?"

Frank relaxed against the table. "Carpenter, yeah."

"That's her. Darla told me to find out where you worked, and I knew we was reporting to the same probation office and wouldn't have no trouble finding out. I was a little short, so Darla mailed me some cash. So what?"

"So now you give her Meg's name." It was a statement, not a question, Frank's brain in a whirl as he tried to sort things out. "What next? The only way you'll get hurt is to lie to me."

"No use to hurt me, I done nothing to you. She told me to investigate your woman, is all."

"And she paid you for that, too?"

"Shit, Frank, I don't do nothing for free."

Frank watched him.

"I followed you a couple of days, seen you and the girl going to the movies. Then I followed her. Couple of days later she goes to lunch with this older guy. At first I thought she might be screwing around on you, Frank."

"I'm surprised you didn't come back and try to sell *me* that information," Frank said.

Dale grinned, the crafty con eyes relaxing now, a man in his element, wanting to brag a little. "I thought about that, but I didn't have to. Darla paid me more, sent it express. She wanted to know about the older guy, so then I checked him out."

"Darla's father, right? Morgan Carpenter."

Withered lips turned up at the corners. "How'd you know them rich people, Frank? I could get me a rich woman like that, I'd never hit another lick."

"I don't suppose you would. Okay. What about Randolph Money? When's he enter the picture?"

"He come later, just a few weeks ago. There some connection between him and Darla Bern?"

Frank's chin tilted. Dale's eyes were widened slightly and his lips were relaxed. Frank decided the guy was telling the truth. "You don't know the connection?" Frank said.

"Naw, just, Randolph come around wanting to buy some-thing. He never mentioned no Darla Bern. I 'as surprised he come to town, tell you the truth."

Frank's mouth tightened in thought. "Wanting to buy what?"

Dale lifted skinny fingers. "I don't tell no—"

"Wanting to buy what, Wilbur?" Frank stood away from the table and took a menacing step forward.

"Now hold," Dale said, then dropped his hand and looked at the floor. "Some, you know, some money."

Frank tapped the stack of fresh-printed twenties still in sheets. "Some of this?"

"Different denominations. Hey, Frank, anybody finds out I'm telling this shit . . ."

Frank studied the skinny man, understanding the code, knowing that the Wilbur Dales of the world would say anything if they thought they were in a crack. For these people, there were no friendships. Only survival. "Bigger bills?" Frank said.

Dale reached up and adjusted his collar. "Hundreds."

"A lot?"

Dale shrugged. "A bunch. Gimme a penny on the dollar. Smaller shipments I wouldn't fuck with at that price. It wasn't even good stuff, tell you the truth. It'll fool the shopping-mall clerks, but nobody that knows their ass from a hole in the ground."

"So that I've got this," Frank said. "Darla called you and told you to find out if I was seeing anybody, which you did. That makes sense, because Darla'd been bugging me and I'd been ducking her. Later she had you follow Meg, and that's how you found out who her father is. Then later, a lot later, you hear from Randolph."

"You got it, bro," Dale said.

Frank stepped back and relaxed against the edge of the table. Jesus, the whole thing had started because he'd tuned Darla out when she'd made all those long-distance phone calls. Miffed, she'd had Wilbur Dale check up on him, then check up on Meg. When Darla had discovered that Meg's family was wealthy, she'd run straight to Randolph Money, who'd taken it from there. Any way Frank sliced it, Meg was now in danger because Frank White couldn't keep his fly buttoned while he was in prison. "What did Randolph want the counterfeit money for? Don't bullshit me, Wilbur. I got too much in this."

The corners of Dale's mouth bunched. "Shit, look around you, Frank. You see where I'm living. If somebody wants to buy something from me, I ask no questions. I need the cash too bad."

Frank's gaze softened as he looked around. Out in the front room was a cloth sofa with cotton stuffing poking out. "I guess you do. You're probably pretty flush now, with what you just sold Randolph."

Dale looked down. "I still got the habit. No amount, it's never enough. Why you think I'm in here, printing this?"

"Your probation officer doesn't have you giving urine tests?"

"Sure. They're easy to beat, you know how. Poke a little Comet cleanser up the end of your dick, it neutralizes the test."

Frank thought of something. "There's more I want from you."

"Jesus Christ, Frank, I already told you too much."

"This is different," Frank said. "You got a gun, don't you? Sure, more than one."

"I ain't supposed to. I'm a felon."

"I want a gun, Wilbur. I think I'm going to need one."

Dale squinched one eye closed. "You're a felon, too, Frank. You don't need to be getting mixed up in that kind of shit."

Frank reached for his wallet. "I'll buy it, Wilbur."

Dale's mouth relaxed. His eyebrows lifted. "Well, sure, Frank, you know that. Anything I got's for sale."

28

Randolph Money ate calamari for lunch in a seafood restaurant next door to the Ballpark in Arlington. The squid was flown in frozen from the coast and made him long for California. He shared a table with a woman from Big Spring, Texas, who, Money figured, baked about four thousand cakes each year for the Big Spring charity bazaar, knew everybody in the whole jerkwater town, and looked down her nose at the guys who hung out down at the domino hall. Came to the big city once a year, saw the sights, and hoped to run into somebody would fuck her silly. Which most times, Money thought, would likely be me, but not today, I got business. Focus, Money thought, focus, focus, focus. He bade the woman a friendly goodbye, paid his tab, and strolled into the parking lot.

He stood underneath the huge overhead sign reading, "Pappadeaux," with "Cajun Seafood" underneath in smaller letters, giving the impression that he wasn't in a hurry, no way. He wore a pale blue blazer, navy blue Dockers, and a white knit golf shirt open at the neck. He glanced up at the window to make certain the woman wasn't watching him from the table they'd shared. Wasn't likely she would be, a woman like that would run across someone else tonight, and tomorrow wouldn't remember Randolph Money from Ned in the First.

Money relaxed and gazed over toward the Ballpark. The stadium was the ultimate state-of-the-art, tall brick arches around its outer perimeter, 450 in the power alleys to left- and right-center fields, and an inning-by-inning scoreboard operated by a real live guy in a booth, just like the old days at Ebbets Field or Yankee Stadium. Showplace of the American League, a wonder-of-the-world spot for the Texas Rangers to get their butts kicked night after night. The springtime temperature was in the seventies, cars already parking over at the Ballpark, people coming out early to watch batting practice, the pitchers warming up, the manager standing around seeing if the left-hander or the right-hander had the most stuff on the ball, and whether the opposition's lineup was batting a lot of southpaws. He withdrew one hand from his pocket and inserted a toothpick in his mouth, thinking it safe to pick his teeth with nobody watching him. As he did, a dark green four-door Buick left the interstate and cruised into the parking lot. Money put the toothpick away and stepped further from the sign pole; he'd say this for the guy, he was right on time.

The Buick cruised up slowly, the driver invisible behind tinted windows, brake lights flashing to accompany a faint hydraulic hiss, the passenger window sliding down, a panicky male voice saying, "Get in, Randy. Dammit, hurry."

Which Money couldn't stand, anyone calling him Randy, which no one had in his entire life except this one particular guy. Money opened the door and slid in, doing a double take as his gaze rested on the suitcase, alligator with red leather inserts, on its side in the middle of the backseat. "Jesus fucking Christ," Money said. "That ought to be in the trunk. Come on, let's get someplace." He studied the guy, short sandy hair with more gray in the sideburns than Money remembered, mouth ready to twist into a panicked expression, wearing a dark blue banker's suit with a pin stuck to the lapel. Money squinted. "They let you in the Kiwanis, huh? Lot of wasted time, eating lunches and listening to speeches."

"You're sure nobody followed you?" Davis Boyle said. "What about that guy?"

Money followed the banker's direction, watched a portly man in a jogging suit exit from a Mercedes and stroll toward the restaurant. "No, I missed that guy," Money said. "Looks suspicious, doesn't he? Come on, Davis, get this fucker in gear."

Boyle slipped the lever into drive and headed out of the lot, his thin lips twisting in fear, shooting anxious looks both ways, adjusting the rearview mirror, winding around onto a bridge over I-30, the sign pointing to Highway 360 North and Six Flags over Texas. "Christ, I thought I'd never get away from the office. My secretary, even my secretary, for Christ's sake, she's giving me these looks."

"Maybe she just wants you to fuck her," Money said.

"And the board of directors," Boyle said. "Jesus, every time I run into one of those guys . . ."

"I took off some gut while I was at Pleasanton," Money said. "You can do a lot of walking. I've kept it off, watch my diet. What do you think?" He patted his midsection, which was still over-hanging some but not near as much as before, before he went to the joint, Money trying to say anything to keep this jumpy ass-hole from having a wreck or a heart attack.

"Those FBI people," Boyle said, "when our security gal spot-ted the counterfeit. Jesus, I was just waiting for one of them to re-member it was me that delivered the suitcase out in that alley." He steered onto a three-lane expressway, hugging the stripe be-tween lanes, a pickup truck careening to its left and honking like, fuck you, as they passed underneath a sign reading, "Six Flags Drive, Exit 3/4 mile."

"Davis," Money said. "Davis, listen to me. I'm going to knock the shit out of you and take the wheel, if you don't straighten up."

Boyle's lips continued to twist like those of a man watching a horror movie, but he did slow down and move the car over be-tween the stripes.

"What goes down comes around," Money said. "Anything I ever told you failed to happen? Anything?"

"Well, no. But . . ."

"But nothing. Ten years ago I told you, you get me the loans, the money, if it all blows up in our face I'm taking the heat. Did I tell you that or not?"

"Christ, I got those loans approved without any credit reports."

"They'd never have traced it to you, the money coming from your correspondent bank in California. Only way was for me to finger you, and I wasn't about to do that. That kind of shit comes back to haunt you. I did time I could have transferred to you, Davis, you and some other guys still in the banking business. Suppose I'd done that. Then when this Carpenter thing became a real possibility, you think I could have called you? Hell no, you would've blown the whistle on me in a minute, if you weren't sure you could trust me. I told you then and I'm telling you now. Things happen the way I say they're going to." Money reached over the seat and patted the suitcase. "You have any problems?"

"Not with the loan, with Morg's credit. The switch, either, those two suitcases you had made, I wasn't sure which was which myself. Had to check the contents before we delivered to the federal guys in the alley."

"It's how I had 'em made," Money said. "Fucking identical."

"I spent the night holding my breath," Boyle said, "worrying about those federal people checking that money out. It's shitty counterfeit, Randy."

Money grimaced at the name, Randy, and looked to his left as they passed the Six Flags amusement park, the Texas Chute-Out and the Shock Wave roller coaster with its loop-de-loops. "Where we going?"

"Golf course up here. Private club, closed on Wednesdays. Nobody around there now."

"Way I had it figured," Money said, "it didn't make any difference if it was good counterfeit or bad. If the feds were expecting phony money, they'd spot it if it was the best stuff made. Thing was, counterfeit money in the suitcase was the last thing they'd look for, coming from Lone Star Bank & Trust. I was right, wasn't I?"

"You should have seen those guys when our security gal spotted the counterfeit." Boyle relaxing some now, showing the barest hint of a smile.

"What I'd really like to have seen," Money said, "was those assholes staking out that sunken suitcase, waiting for somebody in a diving suit. Stupid fuckers."

"It was soaked to the bone. Left a puddle on my desk," Boyle said in admiring, you're-the-greatest fashion, always the flatterer, another thing that Randolph Money didn't particularly like about the guy. A man had confidence in himself, Money thought, he didn't need any pumping up. Boyle left the freeway, turned right beside some redstone apartments, cruised alongside a golf course on the left, a grassy fairway rolling off into the distance, a water hazard maybe fifty yards in front of a green. On the green a man in sleeveless overalls operated a gang mower. A half block further down was a brick clubhouse, a sign on the front reading, "Great Southwest Golf Club—Members Only." Across the street was a driving range, four or five golfers limbering up, making jerky passes at the ball, scratching their heads as they hit big slices or screaming duckhooks. "Looks like a convention," Money said. "You sure we're going to have some privacy?"

"The members can practice even when the course is closed. Far end of the parking lot, take my word. If we see anybody down there, they've gotten lost." Boyle turned the wheel to the left, the Buick passing through a slot in the median and bouncing into an asphalt parking lot, not a car in sight, new yellow stripes for slant-in parking. Boyle cruised to the far end, nosed in and cut the engine, the Buick facing a grove of trees, wide open spaces in the distance, more workmen on mowers cutting greens or rolling fairways. Boyle's grin faded, replaced by the look of mouthtwisting panic once more. "My sweet Christ, if anybody should find out I'm doing this . . ."

Money rolled his eyes. "Goddammit, Davis, how often do I have to tell you? If you do things right, you don't have to worry."

"But the other people with you . . ."

"Don't even know your name, Davis. Don't even know your fucking name. All they know you as, they think you're just the . . . fringe guy, okay? The only one taking any heat right now is poor Frank White, who you don't even know. I sort of hate that. Believe it or not, I always liked that guy. I really did, for an ex-cop he was more than all right. It's just business, though—he's the best available decoy. I'm even pulling for him, you know? I'm hoping the feds figure out they've got the wrong man, as long as they don't catch on before I'm the hell out of this part of the country." Money reached into the back, tugging the handle, hauling the suitcase into the front seat as Davis Boyle bent sideways to keep from getting conked. "Let's have a look at this now," Money said.

Boyle glanced fearfully over his shoulder as Money snapped the catches, then drew an admiring breath as both men gazed at nine million-plus dollars against a background of cushioned velour, all encased in red-tinted leather and alligator hide. Money whistled under his breath. "Where you want to put yours, Davis? In the trunk?"

"Probably be best," Boyle said, staring at the money like an Israelite before the Ark of the Covenant.

"How far is it," Money said, looking up the twisty road in the direction from which they'd just come, "back to that freeway? Not over a half mile, right?"

Boyle followed Money's gaze, looking confused.

"We've got to part company, Davis. For life, not that that's going to bother you. I'm going to put your share in your trunk, then I'm taking the suitcase and walking to the highway, finding a phone where I can call a cab. Never darken your door again. Makes sense, doesn't it?"

"I could give you a ride."

"The less time we're together, the better." Money opened his door and stood outside the car, bending from the waist to pick up four packets of money, bending even further to look past Boyle through the driver's window, Money's eyes widening in surprise as he said, "Who the fuck is that coming, Davis?"

Boyle's eyes bugged, his head snapping around to look, his jaw dropping, then his mouth closing as he gazed on an empty parking lot. He turned back to Money as if to say, What is this, a joke?

Money extended the palm-sized .22 automatic pistol he'd drawn from inside his coat, extended the pistol, and pulled the trigger once with a noise like a muffled firecracker, his hand jumping slightly from the recoil as the bullet entered Davis Boyle's cheek and exited from the back of his head; the window suddenly covered in red ooze as Boyle's chin slumped down to his chest, his eyes wide and staring, likely dead before he even realized what the fuck was going on. Money put the gun away, dropped the cash back into the suitcase and closed the lid, lifted the suitcase out by the handle. Then he closed the door and walked away whistling, looking left and right, headed for the street, his right shoulder lowered under his load like Willie Loman in *Death of a Salesman.*

Less than a half hour later a cab pulled off of I-30 into the parking lot of Pappadeaux Cajun Seafood, a blue-and-white Plymouth with a sign across the trunk advertising all-day oldies on 98.7, KLUV. Money exited carrying the suitcase, paid the fare—leaving just the right-sized tip so that the driver wouldn't be resentful, but at the same time wouldn't be thinking, Hey, the big spender from the East—and hefted more than nine million dollars over to his rented Ford and locked the money in the trunk. As he entered the eastbound interstate, headed for downtown

Dallas, he remembered the taxicab sign and punched up 98.7 on the radio. The Monotones were doo-wopping "Book of Love." *Christ,* Money thought, *from back when I was in high school, Buffalo, New York, freezing my cods off.* He flattened his palm and beat time to the music on the dashboard. *One down,* he thought, *three more to go.* Just business, absolutely nothing personal about it. *Too many cooks fuck up the broth,* Randolph Money thought.

29

The intersection of Ross Avenue and Fitzhugh Street was in East Dallas, just a mile from the state fairgrounds, and Basil Gershwin found the corner without any trouble. Without *much* trouble, to be exact, driving up and down narrow two-way streets, homes with sagging porches and roofs on both sides, the city map that Randolph Money had given him draped across the steering wheel. Money had marked the intersection with a big red "X," as if Basil was too stupid to find the shithouse without somebody pointing the way. Basil was sick of the guy's attitude. Money acted as if he was the only one in the world with a hint of fucking brains. Once this deal was history Basil was going back to Los Angeles, to his friends in the Eighth Street gin mills, people who looked up to him and thought Basil Gershwin was a special guy. Basil thought that if he ever saw Randolph Money again, it wasn't going to be soon enough. Or maybe it was going to be *too* soon. Basil wasn't so good at remembering what the fuck the saying was supposed to be.

He parked in a slant-in space in front of a Domino's Pizza, walked the half block to the corner of Ross and Fitzhugh, and then just hung around being inconspicuous. He wore pressed Bermuda shorts, a sleeveless mesh shirt, and a blue Dallas Cowboys Super Bowl XXVIII baseball cap, tufts of unruly hair sticking out around his ears. He'd bought the cap at DFW Airport, thinking that the Cowboy logo would make him blend in with the locals. It hurt Basil's feelings, Randolph Money's remark that the hat was ridiculous. There Basil stood, hands in his pockets, first on one foot and then the other, watching two women—a chubby Hispanic, eighteen or so, and a gray-haired black lady in her sixties or seventies—wash their clothes in the laundromat across the street. He whistled a silent tune as old Chevys and Dodges paraded up and down Ross Avenue, some of them pulling into the beer bar a block away. Basil checked his watch over and over. At four on the dot, the pay phone jangled.

He moseyed over and picked up the receiver. "Yeah, Basil."

"Yeah, Money," Randolph Money's damnyankee accent said. "The eagle's flown, my friend."

Basil's forehead wrinkled in anger. "Shit. You didn't get it."

"I *did* get it. The eagle's flown. Landed. I've got the money, Basil."

"Why didn't you say so? All that eagle shit, that's confusing."

Money's tone became serious. "Well, maybe this won't confuse you. You know what to do now? I'll have your ticket at the gate. Shouldn't take you over a couple of hours."

"What we talked about?" Basil said.

"Yes, what we talked about. For you to go and get it over with."

"You want me to off the broad."

"It's what we discussed. You having a problem with that?"

"Naw, she did something that pissed me off, anyway. What you want me to do with all that food?"

"All that . . . ?"

"There ain't that much. Think there's maybe still some lasagna, but most of it's that Birdseye shit. Guess I ought to throw it all away, huh?"

There were fifteen seconds of silence. "Basil, you," Money began, then cleared his throat and said, "you're the eighth wonder of the world, Mr. Gershwin. You know that?"

• • •

Randolph Money shook his head in bewilderment, and even in some admiration, as he replaced the receiver in its cradle and strolled out of the diner at the corner of Ross and Haskell avenues, eight blocks southwest of the spot where Basil Gershwin simultaneously hung up the pay phone and lumbered away toward his rental car. There were two customers in the diner, teenaged black kids in No Fear T's, dawdling over greasy cheeseburgers and scratching their noses.

Money kicked a pebble into the gutter as he shook his head some more, thinking, Christ, the ultimate killing machine. Rates doing the woman in the same category with cleaning out the refrigerator—no conscience, no hesitation, no remorse. Will no doubt achieve sexual gratification in the process, but will never lose sight of the goal line. The perfect chess piece for the perfect move, choreographed by the ultimate planner, Randolph Money, Esquire.

Money felt uncomfortable in his blazer and Dockers as black guys with mottled beards, their eyes hidden in the shadow of greasy baseball caps, shuffled past eyeing his clothes. So he hustled down to the end of the block, got in his Ford, and thunked the door locks into place. Then he pressed the stem on his digital watch until the lap timer appeared, activated the timer, and sat mesmerized as the seconds flashed by. In exactly four minutes and thirty seconds he pressed the stem once more. The glowing red numbers froze in place. Money looked to the northeast, up Ross Avenue, and grinned. Right on time, Basil Gershwin's Honda rolled by, Basil hunched over the wheel, his gaze straight ahead, his Neanderthal features impassive beneath the brim of the silly Dallas Cowboys hat.

Christ, Money thought, better than Robocop. He started his engine, checked his clearance, and backed slowly out into the southwest-bound lane to follow the Honda. Since Money knew the Honda's destination, keeping the other vehicle in sight wasn't that important. Nonetheless he gave his Ford a little extra gas,

269

speeding up so as not to lose his view of the back of Basil Gershwin's head. Christ, Money loved it just watching the guy.

Meg was certain that she was alone in the house for the first time in . . . God—three days? Four? She'd lost track.

She was absolutely sure that no one else was in the house, though she couldn't have explained *how* that she knew in a thousand years. She'd been caged in the bathroom ever since she'd been a captive, and—except for the time when she'd made the recording, and the times when the disgusting, squatty man had brought her meals—she'd never actually *seen* anyone or anything beyond the doorway. But always there had been a *presence*, someone out there in the darkness watching her, and whatever sixth sense it was that caused her to be aware of the presence now told her that the presence was no longer there. Poof. Gone.

She'd been alone, in fact, for quite some time and had spent the past half hour or so wondering what in God's name she was going to do about it. Probably nothing, she realized, but rational thought was the only thing that kept her from going into screaming fits and tearing her hair. *Rational Rhoda to the rescue*, Meg thought.

The rose, its petals now a wilted brown, lay where it had fallen when she'd poked it through the wire. Since then she hadn't received a bite of food—she could only assume that the Quasimodo character was miffed because she'd rejected his present; and she hoped that he *was* miffed, the freaking suck—and the grumblings in the pit of her stomach told her that the rose had been on the floor for at least twelve hours, maybe more. In her current circumstance, hunger didn't come knocking very often.

She wondered why the kidnappers had disappeared all of a sudden. *It's possible*, she thought, *that Daddy—God bless him, God, God bless him—has forked over the ransom, and that the bad guys have called up the good guys to tell them where I am, and that any minute the*

U.S. Cavalry will come charging in. The idea gave Meg a rush of adrenaline. Sure, that was it, she was . . .

Locked inside a cage somewhere in East Jesus, Meg thought, and until she saw the cavalry in person she had to assume they weren't coming. Not ever. Until freedom was a reality, she must direct every effort toward survival. Such as survival was.

She got up and moved around, the tiles cool to her bare feet, the cotton shorts soft against her outer thighs. From within the stall came the steady *drip-drip* from the shower, the sound that had been soothing during her early time in the cage, but that now was merely familiar background. She went over and stood inside the partition surrounding the toilet. Her gaze fell on the toilet brush, resting on its bristled end with its plastic handle leaned against the wall. She picked up the brush and looked it over.

Her commode was clean, all right. She'd brushed it spotless, it seemed to Meg, about twenty times a day to fight the boredom, the result being that she'd created the absolute pristine crapper to beat all. *The modern flushing toilet was invented by Thomas Crapper.* Ho, ho, ho, big joke in college, until Meg had looked it up in the encyclopedia to learn that the guy who'd invented the toilet *really was* named Thomas Crapper, which at the time had made the joke even funnier. *Old Thomas has sure sent* his *name down in history,* Meg thought. *Maybe his competition was someone named Bernard Shitter, you think?* Meg giggled. Where was old man Crapper when a girl needed him?

She had an idea. She put the bristle end of the brush inside the toilet bowl, closed the lid, sat down, and pried the handle upward with all her might. Her wiry biceps stood out and her neck corded from exertion. Her cheeks and throat turned a bright red as blood coursed through her veins. *Kidnap* me, *will you?* Meg thought. *Lock* me *up, eh? Well, I'll show you, you freaking jerks, I'll sit right here on Thomas Crapper's old crapper and I'll break your freaking toilet brush, cost you another buck twenty-nine to replace the freaking thing. Break, damn you,* Meg thought. *Break in two. Break in two, you freaking . . .*

The handle snapped an inch from the edge of the toilet seat. The sudden cessation of pressure sent Meg lurching backward. She painfully banged her shoulders on the tank. The back of her head slammed into the wall. For an instant she saw stars.

She shook it off, touching the back of her head and gingerly massaging the brand-new lump. *Now, what did I go and do that for?* Meg thought. She held up the broken handle and looked at it in a daze. The snapped-off end had a jagged edge, slanted into a crude point.

Reeling, more than a little bit dizzy, Meg carried the handle over to the bed and hid it under the mattress. It was certainly no billy club, but it was the only weapon she had.

Basil Gershwin parked behind the lake house, put his gloves on, and trudged inside. He didn't glance at the shining water, the condo roofs, or the boats anchored to the dock across the way. He had two things to do, and paused just inside the darkened entry to make up his mind which came first. Clean the kitchen or kill the woman. The thought of killing the woman didn't bother him, but the idea of cleaning the kitchen made him wrinkle his nose. Basil Albert Gershwin didn't sign up to be no fucking custodian. In offing the broad he was going to take his time, teach her a lesson or two about screaming at guys and throwing presents away, the guy just trying to do something nice for her. Basil made his decision. First he'd do the dirty work, then get on to the good stuff.

He turned to his right just past a short entry corridor, and muscled open the kitchen door to step in on plastic tile. He flicked the switch, sudden artificial light illuminating the sink, the gas stove, the microwave oven on the counter, and the small standup refrigerator. The light flooded through the doorway and made a parallelogram on the worn carpet outside. In the past Basil had been careful to close the door before turning the light on, and to be as quiet as possible while moving around in the kitchen. Some kind of psychological bullshit, Randolph Money's idea, keeping the broad in the dark as to what was going on in the house while she sat back in the cage. Basil thought that a little noise now and then might scare the pants off the woman, which was exactly what he had in mind.

He yanked a plastic garbage bag from a box on the counter and opened the refrigerator, first thudding a half-full bottle of milk and a carton of eggs into the bottom of the bag, then rummaging around in the freezer. One box of Stouffer's lasagna and three cartons of vegetables—one broccoli, one box of green beans, one peas mixed with carrots—remained. He dumped the lasagna on top of the milk and eggs, dropped the broccoli and the veggie mix in as well, then held the green beans at arm's length. A puzzled look crossed his face.

Basil was suddenly filled with rage. He bashed the frozen box against the counter once, then twice, then looked at it again. Jesus, what's wrong with me? he thought, then sheepishly dropped the carton into the bag. For just a second there, he'd imagined that the box of beans was the woman's head. Funny what came over a guy sometimes.

When the outside door opened and then closed, Meg had her first glimpse of daylight since she'd been imprisoned. It was the briefest of flashes, a sudden illumination of the sitting room—an easy chair and one end of a sofa with curved arms—and the light vanished so quickly that it took a few seconds for it to register on her exactly what she'd seen. She was rooted in her tracks near the food slot in the cage. Three heavy footfalls vibrated the floor, then there was silence. Meg strained to listen. Out there in the darkness, someone breathed. Then the footfalls resumed, retreating away from her. There was a creak of hinges, then a banging noise, and suddenly more light. The illumination was fainter than before, and Meg expected total darkness any second, but the weak light continued to shine somewhere in the far reaches of the house. There was a muted rustling and a series of sloughing, rattly noises, like someone loading a plastic bag.

Meg peered into the outer room. Once again there was the easy chair, the entire sofa now visible to her, and an arched doorway leading out into a hall. Out in the hall to her right was a closed door. *Thank God for small favors,* Meg thought; she felt some comfort in seeing something—any freaking thing—outside her prison. As she retreated, sat on the bed and hugged herself, there were two violent, faraway thuds. Meg gasped. Any comfort she'd felt was immediately replaced by throat-clutching fear.

Basil looked around the kitchen to be certain he wasn't leaving anything. The box of garbage bags went into the sack, followed by the knives and forks from the drawer beside the sink. He paused while dropping the utensils in and studied a ten-inch carving knife with a serrated blade. He tested the blade with his latex-covered thumb, then jammed the knife, handle first, into his back pocket. Finally he twirled the bag around to cinch up the neck, and secured the entire mess with a twist-tie. He glanced toward the doorway, his features tightening in anticipation. On the way out of the kitchen, he turned off the light.

His pulse quickening, Basil strode through the entry hall, pulled open the door, and went out in springtime sunshine. Wavelets lapped the shore, and somewhere nearby a crappie jumped and splashed. He opened the Honda's trunk, stuffed the bag inside, and slammed the lid. He lifted the knife partway out of his pocket, then snuggled the handle back down. As he looked around to check out the landscape, Basil drew a short breath in through his nose. He could wait no longer. Without another second's hesitation, he went back in to kill the woman.

Meg's eyelids twitched as the outside door opened, bathing the sitting room in muted light, but otherwise she didn't move. The heavy footfalls sounded out in the hallway, drawing nearer and nearer. *Please, God*, she thought, *let them just be bringing me another meal. Let it be the police, someone coming to . . .*

The squatty man came around the doorjamb and stopped outside the cage. All hope that Meg had held faded instantly away.

He wasn't wearing his mask. God, she thought, he doesn't care if I see him. They've decided to . . . She searched his face, his thick shaggy brows, the broad forehead, the wide humped nose, tufts of unruly hair sprouting over his ears. No pity in his look, nothing. Eyes like dead gray coals.

He raised the padlock with one gloved hand, fished in his pocket, inserted and twisted a key. The lock sprang open with a deafening click. He rattled the wire, pulled open the swinging door. His nostrils flared. He looked at her.

Meg jumped to her feet and, her heart sinking into the pit of her stomach, tried to dodge around him and run. He grabbed her hair. She clutched and clawed at his wrist. He took a long, powerful stride, yanked so hard that she thought her hair would come out by the roots, and threw her bodily across the mattress.

Now he straddled her, thick legs on either side, hot garlic breath rushing up her nose. She lay unmoving. He grinned at her, and from his pocket pulled the biggest knife that Meg had ever seen. He gently inserted the blade under the neck of her T-shirt and began to cut downward with a sawing motion.

Meg moved more by reaction than by will, her hand going up over her head and groping beneath the mattress. Her fingers closed around slick plastic. With the last ounce of strength left in her, she brought the broken brush handle up and stabbed at his face.

She got lucky. The pointed end of the handle gouged his eye, sliced into the lid. A quick red stream flowed down his cheek. Her second thrust missed the eye and cut his forehead. He screamed and covered his face, the knife bouncing from the mattress and clattering to the floor.

Meg wiggled and squirmed, grabbing at his buttocks, pushing herself downward, the rough crotch of his trousers pinching first her chin, then her nose, and then her forehead. All at once she was free, rising, stumbling, righting herself. Then she was running for all she was worth, her bare feet slapping tile, then thudding on carpet as she left the cage and sprinted through the sitting room. The open front door was in sight, just a few more strides, the outside light flooding the hallway like the near-death experience. She would make it. She would *will herself* to make it. Just a few more . . .

She stubbed her toe on a leg of the sofa. Blinding pain shot through her foot and halfway up her calf as she sprawled headlong and rolled onto her side, looking fearfully over her shoulder. Inside the cage, the squatty man stood upright, then bent down and picked up the knife. Blood dripped from the end of his nose onto the tiles. Meg choked back a sob and scrambled behind the couch, grabbing at her injured foot and biting her lip to hold back screams of agony.

Basil thought that he'd lost his eye. He screamed, dropped the knife, and brought up his hands to shield his face. Jesus fucking Christ, she'd blinded him. The goddam vicious broad had *attacked him*. Oh, Jesus, oh, Jesus, it hurt, it hurt.

He barely felt the woman as she squirmed down between his legs and fought her way free, barely heard the sound of her bare feet as she sprinted from the cage. Christ, he was blind, was going to be a fucking beggar poking around on Eighth Street with a cane and a tin cup. He lurched backward, fell from the bed onto the floor, and uttered a series of moans as he struggled to his feet. The goddam heartless woman had ruined his life. Had ruined his goddam life, goddam her, she had . . .

He wiped blood from his eye with his fingers, and suddenly he could see. More blood flowed down to block his vision. Dumbly, he wiped again. He wasn't blind. Oh, thank sweet

Christ, he *wasn't blind*. He stared at his reddened fingers as relief flooded over him.

He peered around inside the cage. Jesus, the broad was gone. Where the hell did she . . . ? Basil bent over, picked up the knife, looked at the open cage door. She wasn't going to escape, no way would he let her do that. Jesus, a mile and a half minimum to the highway, he'd run her down before she was out of the house's shadow. Goddam broad had tried to blind him.

Roaring in anger, swabbing the blood from his eye with one hand and brandishing the knife in the other, Basil charged from the cage and out through the sitting room.

Meg was certain that her right little toe was broken, but barely noticed the pain. She curled up into a ball behind the couch and tried to squirm underneath. He was coming. She had hurt him with the brush handle, and now she was going to die. It was all over, everything was over. God, she was going to . . .

He ran right past her. She blinked in astonishment as the squatty man thundered by, his foot landing heavily less than a yard from the end of her nose. He kept on going, snarling, the floor shaking with his every step. As he charged through the entry hall and, his frame outlined in sunlight pouring through the doorway, ran outside, Meg drew her knees up to her chest and hugged them. Her entire body shook. The pain shooting through her toe and up her ankle was a godsend, a blessed reminder that she wasn't dead.

Basil Gershwin blinked his one good eye against the glare of sunlight and paused for an instant on the porch. A gentle wind rustled tall grass on his left. His Honda sat where he'd parked it, nose on to the porch. He shook his head in confusion. His vision blurred by blood and perspiration, he looked up the path leading toward the blacktop road. At the top of the rise, a figure stood.

The fucking broad. Jesus Christ, the fucking woman up there, getting away. She'd run a helluva lot faster than he'd thought she could, Jesus, a hundred yards or more. No matter, he'd run her down. Run her down and then haul her kicking and screaming back into the house, and then he'd teach her a fucking lesson. Teach her to try and put out old Basil's eye. Damn right he would. He yelled at the top of his lungs, jumped from the porch, and charged up the hill.

He'd gone four or five steps when he heard the *pop*, a tiny explosion from up where the figure stood. The noise puzzled him. His vision cleared for the barest instant, and the figure on the hill sharpened into focus. Jesus Christ, that wasn't no broad up there, it was . . .

The bullet tore into Basil's forehead just above his eye, disintegrated bone and brain matter in its path, and then sizzled on to finally lodge in the dirt at the foot of the porch. Basil stood still as a painting for an instant, the top of his head missing, ripped arteries spraying a high-pressure geyser of blood. A final thought remained frozen in the half second of consciousness left to him. *That ain't no broad up there.* Then the lights went out forever. Basil Gershwin fell forward onto his face and died.

Randolph Money lowered the rifle, unscrewed the silencer from its barrel, and shook his head in admiration. Christ, there'd never be another guy like that, never in a million years. No need to go inside and check on the girl. The absolute killing machine had done its work, and then had lusted for more, charging straight up the hill in the face of a loaded gun aimed at his head, no fear, absolute concentration. Randolph Money should pen an ode to the guy. Give Money a holding company, say a movie or publishing outfit, staffed with killing machines like Basil Gershwin, no conscience, absolute concentration on the goal, and Randolph Money would own the fucking world.

He returned to his rented Ford, dropped the rifle in the trunk along with the pistol, and left the scene with twin dust clouds billowing out behind. Halfway to DFW Airport he pulled off Highway 183, drove a mile to the north, and finally stopped beside a creek which wound through a forest of mesquite trees. After weighting the rifle and pistol down with good-sized rocks, he tossed them into the stream.

He arrived at the Delta counter three quarters of an hour ahead of his L.A. flight's departure time. When the gate attendant asked, Money told her that he wasn't checking his luggage, that the alligator-and-leather suitcase was light as a feather, just the right size for carry-on. Then he took the suitcase with him into the gift shop and looked over the rack of paperback books. One was a movie tie-in, *Robocop,* and as he studied the half robot, half man pictured on the cover, Money showed wide-gapped teeth in a grin. Christ, as if they'd had the guy in mind, Randolph Money thought. Jesus, but he was going to miss that Basil Gershwin guy.

Meg lay curled up behind the sofa for more than an hour. The pain in her foot settled gradually down to a throb. Two or three times she touched her swollen toe, but otherwise she didn't move. Each outside noise, each rustling of the wind through the open doorway, brought instant terror. She finally decided that maybe, just maybe, she was going to go on living.

She struggled up, tested her weight on her right foot, then yelped in anguish. Her mouth worked in concentration for a moment, then she gritted her teeth. Walking on her heel with her toes pointed up, she limped through the front door and out onto the porch. She gulped coolish, fresh air. She didn't have the slightest idea where she was, might even be in Oklahoma. There was a lake nearby, water lapping a shoreline, the odor of wet moss wafting up her nostrils. She looked up the slope, caught sight of the sprawled body, averted her gaze from the bloody head.

There was a Honda parked at the end of the porch. She moved in the auto's direction and, hopping on one foot and using the fender for support, peered in the driver's window. No keys in the ignition. She wondered if it was the squatty man's car, and if so, if the keys were in his pocket. She limped over and stood over the body. Flies swarmed around the head. She bent from the waist and retched.

She summoned up her willpower, stooped down, and felt in the corpse's pocket while keeping her head turned away. On the opposite shore of the lake were condo roofs, a dock, two cabin boats swinging from moorings. Her hand inside the pocket contacted pieces of metal. She pulled out two keys, connected by a chain from which also dangled a plastic Avis tag.

She hobbled over to the car, got in and turned the key, halfway expecting a bomb under the hood to blow her to kingdom come. The engine caught and raced, then smoothed out and purred. Meg inhaled through her nose, put the lever in reverse, backed out, then drove slowly up the incline. Halfway to the crest of the hill she stopped, the squatty man's near-decapitated form visible in the rearview mirror. *God*, Meg thought, *someone killed him. Someone that's likely still nearby.* Her hands trembling, her heart coming up in her throat, Meg gave the Honda some gas and proceeded on.

30

Felicia Tate stood with one drape pulled back, looking out the den window in Morgan Carpenter's home. "Who called those people?" Tate said. Visible through the pane, a white Channel 8 News truck sat in the drive behind the Porsche, the Jag, and two unmarked federal Tauruses. A young man in shirtsleeves emerged from the driver's door of the mobile news unit. He was beefy, sweating profusely, and toted a Minicam. From the passenger side came a beautiful, willowy black woman of around thirty, wearing high heels and a beige dress. Tate recognized the woman, Janet-Wheeler-reporting-from-the-scene, articulate and with the camera presence of a Kathleen Turner. From the rear of the truck came two more men, one of whom began to assemble a tripod. "Who yanked their chain, Dave?" Tate said. She let the drape fall back into place and turned to face the room.

Agent Turner was seated on the bench in front of the grand piano. He watched the far corner of the room. "Yanked whose chain?" He lifted his ankle to rest on his knee and pinched the scarred toe of his boot.

"*Who?*" Tate said. "Those television people out there." She'd borrowed the Carpenters' servants' quarters to shower and freshen up, but still wore the wilted jogging suit in which she'd stayed the night at the lakeside condo. She went over and sat on the front edge of a straight-backed chair, folded her arms, and gave Turner the evil eye. At that instant the doorbell *bong-bong*ed.

Turner pulled on the front of his T-shirt.

"Have you got any idea what this can cause?" Tate said.

Turner used one finger to play a note on the piano, bonking the key four times.

"Who called these people?" she said.

Turner cleared his throat. "I think they assumed the deal would be over by now. That the—"

"They who, Dave?"

"—money'd be delivered, and we'd have the girl back."

"*They who?*" Tate said.

Turner looked at the ceiling. "Suits downtown. Look, I got no say-so."

An FBI agent in a brown suit came in from the entry hall. "There's some media people out here," he said, leaning on the piano's coal-black lacquered wood.

"Tell them . . ." Tate rubbed her eyes, muttered, "God help us," then said, "tell them just a minute."

The FBI agent went back into the foyer.

"So I'll understand all this," Tate said to Turner, "the FBI alerted the media without discussing it with the U.S. Attorney's office. When did this happen?"

One corner of Turner's mouth tugged to the side. He got up and stood facing the fireplace, picked up a gilt poker, placed the poker back into the rack. "Last night, I think. Look, they thought that even if we didn't have the girl, by now it'd be too late to do anything."

Tate blinked. "They, hell, Dave. You."

"Now hold . . ." Turner retreated from the fireplace and now sat in a chair in front of the piano. "We just wanted to be the ones doing the announcing. Since it's our case."

"Sweet Jesus. You're sacrificing the victim just so the FBI can make the announcement. Sweet Jesus. So now, what do you think you're going to tell them?"

"They should have been called and told the deal was off," Turner said.

"So why weren't they?"

"I forgot. Hauling that suitcase down to the bank and all that."

"Just superior," Tate said. "So what do you tell them?"

"I don't tell them shit. The agent-in-charge is due out here."

Tate pointed a finger with a dully polished nail. "Your agency's going to have hell to pay." She raised her voice and shouted out into the foyer, "Someone get Mr. Carpenter in here. Seems we've got a problem to solve."

Morgan Carpenter said dully, "You people called the television."

"We acknowledge it's a little glitch," Turner said. "It's not a mountain. More of a molehill."

"You people called the television," Carpenter said. He was seated in one of the easy chairs with Turner on the piano bench. Sis Carpenter, wearing a pale blue parachute silk jogging suit, leaned on the piano. Her gaze moved incredulously from Tate to Turner to Carpenter, and back to Tate.

"The FBI called them," Tate said.

"It's a federal error," Turner said. "The agency making it really doesn't matter."

Tate moved the drape aside and peered out the window. "For the record, don't be involving our office in this."

"Why not?" Turner said. "It was you people that caused it, butting in on the investigation."

"You people called the television," Carpenter said.

Tate spread her fingers, then her hands, palms down. "It's your daughter, Mr. Carpenter. But I've been in on a few of these things, and I hope we'll benefit from experience. I think, here's what we should do."

Carpenter leaned back and studied the ceiling like a man who'd just learned that he had terminal cancer.

"These reporters," Tate said, "aren't going to listen to law enforcement. An appeal from the victim's family, asking that they put the lid on it, might do the trick. I think you should go out there and face them along with us. Appeal to their sense that, releasing the story now puts your daughter in jeopardy."

"You people called the television," Carpenter said.

The agent in the brown suit came in from the foyer. "Mr. Brickman's out here."

Tate snapped her chin to one side. "Who is he?"

"The agent . . ." Turner said. "The agent-in-charge of the Dallas office. He's the one that has to give any statement to the media."

"What happened to the other guy Percell?" Tate asked.

"Took an appointment in Washington."

"He wasn't here six months."

Turner shrugged. "They change guys pretty often."

"You people called the television," Carpenter said.

Tate walked up nearer Carpenter's chair. "I think we have to go out there, Mr. Carpenter. It's the best chance we've got." She showed a sympathetic smile and extended her hand.

"You people called the television," Morgan Carpenter said.

Wilson Brickman had iron-gray hair, a square jut-jawed face, and a neck like a retired linebacker's. He wore a charcoal gray suit, and stood near the stone cherubs on the porch with Assistant USDA Tate and FBI Agent Turner behind him. Morgan Carpenter, blinking in the glare from the handheld light, slumped alongside. Brickman said in a Pat Summerall baritone, "You're taping this, right?"

Janet Wheeler smiled an *Entertainment Tonight* lead-in smile, at the same time checking the sound meter on her handheld microphone. "No interviews are live anymore," she said. "Just action scenes. Mostly ball games, the sports. Maybe we should wire you with a clip-on."

"There's been a . . . listen, can we be off the record here?"

Brickman said. Behind him, Turner and Tate exchanged a look. Morgan Carpenter stared off into space.

"Douse it, John," Janet Wheeler said loudly. The light went off. The beefy mobile unit driver lowered his Minicam.

"We're trying to prevent a tragedy here," Brickman said.

"We've got to make the public aware. Sometimes it's painful to some, but we feel—"

"There's been a big mistake. This shouldn't have been released as yet."

"It can be a major story," Wheeler said. "National import. I assume the victim's indisposed, following her ordeal."

"I've got to level," Brickman said. "We don't have the victim as yet. To release the story might put her life in—"

"Over nine million dollars, is that right?" Wheeler said.

"This man could lose his daughter," Brickman said, indicating Carpenter. "None of us want the responsibility for that."

"How about," Wheeler said, "an interview where we agree not to release it until the victim's accounted for?" Then, over her shoulder, "John? John. Do you think we need some powder, on Mr. Carpenter's forehead?"

"What we're wanting to do," Brickman said, "is withhold all comment until the thing's over, and ask your cooperation in keeping the lid on."

"It's a big expense," Wheeler said, "bringing all these people out, where the release came from your office to begin with."

"Maybe we can . . ." Brickman looked beyond the media people, toward the street. "What's this?" he said.

A brown four-door Buick Roadmaster pulled in and parked in the drive, followed by a red panel truck with "Channel 4 News" painted on its side. A man in a suit emerged from the Buick, a square-shouldered guy of around forty with razored hair and polished shoes. He fast-stepped across the drive toward the porch. A thin man in shirtsleeves came from behind the wheel of the mobile news unit, lugging a Minicam, as a black woman with an hourglass figure came from the passenger door carrying a microphone. Two guys climbed out of the back of the truck, and one of them set about assembling a tripod.

As the square-shouldered man came up on the porch, Brickman said, "What's this?" a second time.

The newcomer extended his hand. "Wilson? George Patman. It's high time we met, though these circumstances are a bit out of the ordinary."

Standing behind the pair, FBI Agent Turner nudged Assistant USDA Felicia Tate. "Who the hell is George Patman?"

"New," Tate said, lowering her lashes, "United States Attorney for the Northern District."

"What happened to the other guy? Brown," Turner said.

"Too close to Whitewater," Tate said. "The guy resigned."

"Jesus, he wasn't there a year," Turner said.

"We change quite often," Tate said.

Janet Wheeler lowered her microphone and made a sour face toward the red panel truck. "I thought we had an exclusive on this. Who called that bitch?" Her mike had a Channel 8 logo on the handle.

AUSDA Tate murmured apologetically to FBI Agent Turner, "They were supposed to be called off if we didn't get the girl back."

Morgan Carpenter looked at Tate and Turner over his shoulder. "You people called another television."

Tate studied her white canvas Keds and yanked on the fabric of her jogging suit.

The Channel 4 crew lugged their paraphernalia up and gathered around the Channel 8 crew. The second female newsperson smiled an identical *Entertainment Tonight* lead-in smile to the one that Janet Wheeler had smiled just moments ago. "Barbara Reed, gentlemen," she said. "Channel Four. Is the victim going to be available for an interview?"

"Listen," Brickman said, "there's been a problem, since our office inadvertently alerted the media."

"Your office didn't call us," Barbara Reed said. "It was the

United States Attorney, Mr. Patman, over there."

Turner stared daggers at Tate. Tate continued to watch her shoes.

"Whoever called you," Brickman said, "these Channel Eight folks have agreed to keep the lid on the story until we can get the victim back. This was premature."

Janet Wheeler slapped her microphone against her well-formed thigh. "We didn't agree to shit," she said, "unless they're going to keep their mouths shut, too." She pointed at Barbara Reed.

Brickman looked past the knot of media people. "What's this?" he said.

A Honda pulled in to park behind the red Channel 4 mobile unit. A pretty young woman got slowly out, barefoot, wearing gym shorts and a T ripped at the neck. Her face was smudged and her auburn hair was messy. She limped on her right foot as she made her painful way up toward the porch.

Felicia Tate stepped to the front and called out urgently, "Young woman, I don't know what your business is, but this is private."

Morgan Carpenter was looking at the newcomer with his mouth agape. "Meg," he said, choking.

Meg Carpenter came around the reporters and faced her father. "I hope I've saved you the ransom, Daddy." She held up a set of keys. "You think you could spring for the Avis car? I can't afford it, to tell you the truth."

United States Attorney George Patman stepped quickly in front of FBI Agent-in-Charge Wilson Brickman, and faced the television people. "We're glad to announce," he said loudly, "that we have a suspect. An ex-convict, name of Frank White."

Meg's face relaxed in shock. "Frank?"

Brickman grabbed the collar of Patman's suit and yanked the United States Attorney backward. "Hold it. This is *our* fucking investigation," Brickman said.

• • •

Because of the size of the ransom, the networks selected the kidnapping as an item on the coast-to-coast 6 P.M. newscasts. Both Janet Wheeler and Barbara Reed received national exposure, causing CBS execs to add Barbara's name to the short list of anchor candidates for an *Entertainment Tonight* clone in development, and ABC honchos to discuss Janet as possible competition for Sally Jessy Raphael.

Frank White watched the broadcast in a diner on the outskirts of Deming, New Mexico, fifty miles west of Las Cruces on the I-10 access road. He was seated at the counter, hunched over a plate holding a scorched cheese omelet and half-raw hash browns. On his left sat a grizzled man with burly forearms, munching a cheeseburger. On his right was a woman who weighed at least three hundred pounds, and who was eating a wilted salad. The TV sat on a shelf over the register. The rabbit-ears antenna was adequate, but occasional static sizzled across the face of the picture tube. Frank's Jeep Cherokee, its windshield peppered with bug spots, sat in the parking lot among the forty-foot trailer rigs and wheezy old pickups.

The image of Meg, limping badly as she entered the Carpenter home in between Assistant USDA Tate and FBI Agent Turner, brought tears of relief to Frank's eyes, and he dropped his fork and lowered his head to regain his composure. When he looked up, there he was, Frank White in living color, the mug shot taken on his release from Pleasanton, his hair in an inch-long burr, his expression menacing. Frank tucked his chin and risked two glances, left and right. The grizzled man laid his burger down to chase a bite with milk, and the overweight lady morosely studied a piece of brown-edged lettuce. Neither looked at Frank. He picked the check up from under the edge of his plate, slid from the stool, and backed away from the counter. The girl at the register, wearing a soiled white uniform, was chewing gum and barely glanced at his face as she rang up the sale.

Frank took the access road away from the diner, dusty expanses of cactus and sage on both sides, and bore to his right on the business route into Deming. Once in town he cruised streets lined with adobe, flat-roofed houses, and located a battered Buick station wagon parked near the entrance to an alleyway. He left his engine running, rummaged in his tool box for a screwdriver, then relieved the Buick of its New Mexico tags. Less than fifteen minutes later, the stolen license plates now attached to the front and rear of the Cherokee, Frank gunned onto I-10 headed west. He set the cruise control on 65, leaned back, and draped his wrist over the steering wheel.

The road map told him that Interstate 10 would do a dipsy-doodle just south of Phoenix, skirt the northern edge of Phoenix proper, and then make a beeline across the desert into Los Angeles. His dashboard clock read 6:38 but was an hour fast because he'd crossed over into Rocky Mountain Standard Time at El Paso. He figured to make the Arizona/California line around three in the morning, and tried to remember the last time he'd driven all night. Probably twelve years ago, when he'd come home from the army after his mustering out in Kentucky. He felt inside the glove compartment, and touched the grip on the .38 police special he'd bought from Wilbur Dale. Frank stretched, yawned, slapped his cheeks, and concentrated on the highway ahead.

31

When Howard Molly hadn't appeared in his office at Dallas Theater Center by Thursday morning, his brunette secretary began to fidget. Her concern wasn't for Howard Molly's safety. Friday was payday, and it was up to Molly to pick up the checks from the board of governors and pass them around.

When Molly hadn't called in by one in the afternoon, the brunette secretary rang his apartment and left a message on his answering machine. Three o'clock rolled around and she hadn't heard back from him, so she tried again, with the same results. No Howard, only his recorded voice cooing that he was anxious to speak to all callers, and that if they'd leave their number he'd get back to them lickety-split. She hung up, drummed her fingers, then called her boyfriend at the collection agency where he worked.

She told her guy of the moment, in her softest it-just-kills-me-to-do-this voice, that she was leaving the office to audition for a part in a play, and that their five o'clock meeting for drinks and discussion of wedding plans would have to wait until tomorrow. Then she flicked on her own answering machine, gathered up her purse and car keys, left the office with her spike heels beating rhythm, and drove to Howard Molly's apartment in far North Dallas.

Once there, she pressed the doorbell until her thumb was

sore. Then she stood on one tiptoe, with the other leg fetchingly bent at the knee, as she brought down a key from the overhanging ledge. After hasty glances in all directions, she went on in. No sign of Howard Molly in the living or dining rooms. She opened a hall closet, took two dresses from hangers and tossed them over her arm, then entered the bedroom. She stopped and blinked in consternation.

Howard Molly, dead as a doornail, was bound to a straightbacked chair. A rope was tied around his neck so tightly that his windpipe was crushed in. He was naked save for boxer trunks. His protruding belly was the color of ripe plums. The secretary wrinkled her nose. Howard was beginning to smell.

She walked over to the bureau and went through the drawers, draping four pairs of panties and two brassieres over her arm to go along with the dresses, then carried all of the articles of clothing outside and locked them in the trunk of her car. Back inside the apartment, she picked up the phone in the living room and called the Theater Center's board of governors. She notified the secretary there that she, and not Howard Molly, would be picking up the checks in the morning. That chore accomplished, she punched 911 into the dial, left the receiver dangling from its cord, and gently pulled the door to behind her as she left. She stretched up to replace the key on the ledge, looked all around her once again, then made her way toward the parking lot.

Homer Knighton thought that Ralston Tagg needed some work on hitting his woods. Holy Jesus, the guy lying two on the second hole, to hell and gone over in number one fairway directly in front of the tee, in the path of guys ready to play their shots, who in turn were yelling and shooting the finger. Ralston Tagg ignored the insults as he peered through the trees toward the second green like Nick Faldo, one of those guys. As if after two wild slices in a row he was now ready to pull one out of his ass and save the day. All of which, Homer Knighton thought, explained the reason that the noon Thursday foursome here at Great Southwest Golf Club wouldn't tee off without the guy, figuring to make cart fees and a whole bunch more gambling with Ralston Tagg. Which suited Homer just fine as long as Tagg had enough left at the end of the day to pay Homer's caddy fee.

Tagg stood with folded arms, a skinny, fortyish man with a knit polo draped around his hips. "What do you think, caddy?" Tagg said.

Get the hell out of the way before one of those guys up there tees off and brains you with a Maxfli balata, Homer thought. He shifted the bag of clubs from one shoulder to the other. Visible far in the distance, the other three men in Tagg's foursome sat around the second green, scratching their asses and waiting for Ralston Tagg to hit. Homer said hopefully, "Pitch out? Maybe try to get back in the right fairway?"

Tagg firmly shook his head. "Too late, I'm laying two. I've got to go for it. Gimme the five wood."

Holy Jesus, Homer thought, *another wood he's going to hit.* Up on number one tee, one of the foursome waiting to play yelled, "Hit and get the hell out of our way."

Homer studied the trajectory Tagg had in mind, a thirty-degree hook up and over the trees, hopefully clearing the parking lot, a shot which, say, Paul Azinger might pull off once in a bucket of practice balls. Ralston Tagg, never in a lifetime. Not to mention the dark green four-door Buick with the guy inside, parked directly in Tagg's line of flight, the guy slumped against the driver's window like he was asleep, the odds-on favorite to wind up beaned by Ralston Tagg's golf ball. What the hell, Homer Knighton was nothing but the caddy. He drew the five wood from the bag, removed the headcover, and handed the club to Ralston Tagg.

Tagg took a couple of lazy practice swings as one of the men on the tee yelled, "Hit, goddammit." Tagg ignored the guy and shaded his eyes, gazing toward the parking lot. "Guy's parked in my line of flight," Tagg said.

What a news flash, Homer thought. He leaned on the bag and didn't say anything.

"Guy's in my way," Tagg said.

And you're in those *guys' way, the guys on the tee,* Homer thought.

Tagg tapped Homer on the elbow with the toe of the five wood. "Aren't you listening, caddy? Guy's in my way. Go up there and tell the guy, move his fuckin' car."

Holy Jesus, Homer thought. Muttering under his breath, considering walking off and leaving Tagg to carry his own clubs, Homer Knighton shouldered the bag and trudged off toward the parking lot. Thinking about it, Homer had to admit that it was kind of a funny place to park and go to sleep. Guy must have gotten drunk or something.

Felicia Tate withdrew a spotless white folded handkerchief from her handbag, shook the hanky out, and took off her glasses. She huffed fog onto one lens and began her cleaning job, squinting occasionally through the lens at the desk lamp as she did. "This case is taking on some interesting wrinkles," she said. "Three dead men, telling no tales." There were red marks where the nosepieces normally rested.

Agent Turner scooted his rump forward in the armchair, propping his elbows up and holding a computer printout by the corners, between a thumb and forefinger of each hand. "This Mr. Gershwin was a badass."

The pair were in Tate's office in the Earle Cabell Federal Building, fourth floor, All-Right Parking across the street, the old red Dallas County Courthouse and the Records Building, all visible through the window. Her desk and credenza were matching blond wood. On the wall were Tate's bachelor's and law degrees, both from Texas Tech, and a blown-up photo of Tate arguing a case before the Fifth Circuit Court of Appeals in New Orleans, her figure svelte in a tailored, short-skirted business suit. Tate had lost her argument with the jurists, but had had quite a night down on Bourbon Street.

"Gershwin did time with our man Frank, didn't he?" Tate said.

"Two years. We got evidence zero that either one has seen the other since they got out. A lot of pieces missing, Felicia."

"There are always pieces missing. What does the deed record say, on the lake house?"

"Howard Molly owned it," Turner said. "Also rented the car, his American Express. The guy rented two cars, in fact, one of which got turned in at DFW, at the Avis counter, just about an hour after the M.E.'s report lists as the time of death for our banker friend. Jesus, I'll bet that caddy jumped through his asshole."

"Could you temper that to, 'Did a double take' or something? Someone had to sign for the car."

"Sure did," Turner said. "Peter Smith, ain't that cute? They might as well have signed, Donald fucking Duck."

Tate spun around in her swivel chair, faced the window, put her glasses on. "I'm considering contact lenses. Our man Frank turned in the car?"

"Could be Frank. Could be Ronald Reagan. The counter girl sees a thousand people a day, you know? Typical shit, she looks at Frank's picture and goes, 'Gee, I don't remember.'"

"No sign of Frank at the Theater Center director's apartment? Fingerprints . . . ?"

Turner lowered the printout. "Come on, Felicia, Frank White's only got two hands. He didn't do all these people. Plus, Frank ain't no queer."

Tate frowned. "Isn't any what?"

"All right then, gay. Happy as hell. This guy stripped down to his underwear, this is some sexual murder."

"That's easy. Darla Bern, Frank's old jailhouse girlfriend."

"Who had an alibi for that night, screwing the guy down the hall in the motel, and who caught her plane to California like a good little girl. We've been in contact with her. She's home in L.A. and accounted for."

"And identified by the victim as one of the pair that snatched her," Tate said.

"Well," Turner said, "not exactly."

Tate turned her chair back around.

"It looked like a Darla Bern," Turner said. "It acted like a Darla Bern. So it must be a Darla Bern, it looks and acts like one. Broad had on a ski mask."

"So in the courtroom the woman was bare-faced," Tate said.

"Not with this victim. Miss Margaret Ann Carpenter won't testify black is gray, much less white. Fucking Girl Scout we're dealing with here."

"Creates a problem," Tate said.

"Whole thing is a problem, Peppermint Patty. We've got our own kidnap victim saying we're full of shit, that our man Frank couldn't have done this on account of they're all so fucking much in love. Jesus, guy must have one"—Turner held up his hands, two feet apart—"yay long."

Tate pursed her lips. "Having one yay long isn't necessarily the answer, Dave. Sometimes it's big bat, weak hitter. Can't we have her father talk some sense . . .?"

Turner snorted. "Guy doesn't wear the pants in that family. The girl and her mother have got him buffaloed."

Tate's chin moved slightly to one side. "Oh? Who wears the pants at your house, Dave? With three ex-wives, it looks like you might've been better off delegating some authority yourself."

Turner propped his knee against the corner of her desk and slumped down even further, his gaze on the corner of the room, not saying anything.

Tate played with a Rubik's Cube on her desk, twisting the multicolored squares around. "So what we've got is, the kidnap victim in love with who we think is the kidnapper. Rather touching, actually. It's going to be tough making a case under the circumstances, Dave. Do we have surveillance on the girl's phone?"

"That we do."

"Any results?"

"Some. Frank called her this morning."

Tate dropped the Rubik's Cube. "Get a location on him?"

"So far as," Turner said, "he's in the L.A. area code. You want to hear?" He reached in the pocket of his FBI windbreaker and produced a tape cassette.

Tate's nose twitched. She produced a hand-sized recorder from her middle drawer, took the cassette from Turner and opened the recorder's tape carriage.

As Felicia Tate fitted the cassette onto the spools, Turner said thoughtfully, "We haven't checked out the other guy Frank was talking about."

Tate pressed the tape holder back down into the machine. "Who's that?"

"The Randolph Money guy. The one Frank said was the caller."

"Frank's the only one who's mentioned Randolph Money. Not too much credibility there." Tate pressed the PLAY button, leaned back, and examined her makeup in a compact mirror. From her purse she produced a tube of pale pink lipstick.

Turner leaned forward and rested his forearms on his thighs, cocking one ear. Seen through clear plastic, tiny reels turned. "This came in at ten-oh-two," Turner said.

The tape ran silently for a few seconds, then a click sounded and Meg Carpenter's soft, cultured voice said, "Hello?"

Followed by a cautious, "Can you talk?" This in Frank White's baritone.

Tate dabbed lipstick on, then leaned forward with the tube in one hand and her compact in the other.

On the tape, Meg said, "Frank? God, Frank, I . . ."

"I can't talk long," Frank said. "Less than a minute, they might be tracing me."

Turner's look said, Aha, more guilty shit on old Frank, afraid of somebody tracking him down.

Frank's voice went on. "I saw you on television. Made me cry, to know you're all right."

"Where are you, Frank?"

"Not now. I've just got a couple of seconds. I just had to hear your voice. Listen . . ."

"I'm listening, sweetheart," Meg said.

Frank's tone took on a saddened edge. "You know it's not me, don't you? I didn't have anything to do with . . . hey, you believe that, huh?"

There were five beats of silence. Then Meg said, "You betchum I do, Red Ryder."

"I have to go," Frank said.

"Frank, I . . ."

"They may be listening, Meg. I'll call you later. I love you, babe."

"Say that again?"

"I said, 'I love you,' "

"Yeah, me too, buster."

There was a click, then more blank tape running. Tate switched off the machine.

Turner scratched his own shin. "Well, what do you think?"

Tate leaned back and looked at the ceiling. "I think we've got the wrong guy."

Turner looked at her.

"What's his motive for making the call, Dave? They've already got the money and made their escape. The victim's the last person in the world he should be wanting to talk to."

"Maybe he figures, keep her on the string, she might not testify against him."

"Didn't you hear him?"

"Yeah, the tape's clearer than most."

"Not *what* he said, Dave. The way he said it. What I wouldn't give for my husband to talk to me that way."

"Lot of hearts-and-flowers bullshit," Turner said.

"If you'd sent more flowers yourself," Tate said, "then you

297

might not be cooking your own beans for dinner. Have we alerted our West Coast office?"

"An APB, the guy's description, license number, all that."

Tate capped her lipstick, flopped a legal pad onto her desk, and began to write. "We need more. Twenty-four-hour watch on Darla Bern, as of fifteen seconds from now. A thirty-day history on this Randolph Money, where his sweet self has been and what he's up to at the moment." She tore the page from the pad and extended it in Turner's direction. Her gaze softened. "Frank didn't do it, Dave, and I'm afraid he's in danger now." There was a hesitant rolling of her eyes, then she licked her lips and went on. "We've all got jobs to do, but I'll tell you something I've never told anybody. The first time I prosecuted Frank White, on the police shooting? Frank had every right to kill the guy, and if it had been you, you would have pulled the trigger a whole lot quicker than he did. I won, hooray for me, but I wasn't really enthusiastic. In fifteen years it's the only case I've had where I was secretly pulling for the other side, and if I hear you've repeated that, you're the biggest liar in the history of the Justice Department."

Turner sat up, his jaw slack.

"Put the watch on Darla Bern, Dave," Tate said. "And quit looking at me that way. We heard the same tape, only you're just hearing words. I'm hearing feelings. If you want to know what I'm talking about, you should try really falling in love sometime."

32

Frank hung up, stood back from the pay phone, and looked to the north. The tree-covered San Gabriel Mountains were surrounded by a bluish haze; the Griffith Park Observatory, miniature in the distance, stood out against a backdrop of green. On a mountain-side to the west of the observatory, giant white letters spelled out "Hollywood," visible over the flat roofs of apartments and low-slung office buildings. The air was cool and smelled faintly of soot.

Frank rubbed the back of his neck, Jesus, stiff and sore from two hours of sleep in the rear of the Cherokee, parked on a side road north of I-10 near Indio. Later he'd paid a night's rent at a run-down motel, only to shower and shave and be on his way. His eyelids felt as if they weighed a hundred pounds apiece. He checked the street signs at the corner, Western Avenue at Olympic Boulevard, watched two women in short cotton skirts enter a building through a glass-paneled door. The light changed; westbound traffic on Olympic came to a halt as cars and trucks on Western proceeded north and south.

He pictured the night, Jesus, six years ago he supposed, Darla Bern naked on his bunk in a Pleasanton cell, shafts of moonlight highlighting her hair with tints of red, one bare leg draped over his thighs as she told him, "There'll always be a way, a way for you to get in touch. Always." The words had meant a lot to him then, a single guy doing time. Hadn't signified a thing to Darla, of course, and he'd often wondered since then how many men in prison she'd told that, that there'd always be a way for them to find her.

"You can get me through the Guild," she'd said, as if any fool would know what the Guild was, and in case the fool *didn't* happen to know, an important actress like Darla Bern didn't have the time to explain. And Frank had to admit he'd been impressed at the time, never having met an actress before, but after thinking on the subject he'd realized that a really important actress wouldn't have been turning tricks for favors from prison guards. The Guild it was, however, and it was the Guild he was going to try. He stepped back up to the phone. As he punched in the number for information, a smog warning siren wailed in the distance.

Frank really didn't expect the Screen Actors Guild to list Darla Bern at all, but the hip-talking young woman on the phone surprised him. She knew Darla personally, in fact, but also told him that it was outside Guild policy to give out addresses or numbers for the members. She did supply him with Darla's agent's name, which made Frank think, *Are you kidding me?* But then he supposed that just about everybody in Los Angeles had an agent, and his surprise drifted quickly away. He flattened a business card on the phone shelf and scribbled like crazy to write the number down; Vickie Warren, with an address on Avenue of the Stars in Century City. Frank wondered if Century City was really the name of a town or was just a section of Los Angeles where all the actors hung out. He spun a quarter into the slot, punched in the first three digits of Vickie Warren's number, then replaced the receiver in its cradle and stepped back once again.

He touched the hem of his wilted black crewneck shirt, the same one he'd worn along with dark blue Levi's and black high-top Nikes for the past two days, the clothes he'd washed night before last at the laundromat near his Dallas motel. His outfit could stand another washing, but he supposed that people in grimy clothes showed up in agents' offices all the time, looking for hobo parts. He trudged over to the curb where he'd left the Cherokee running, drove two blocks and located a convenience store. There he bought a Los Angeles area map on which he sketched out his route in ballpoint, then, peering occasionally at the map, proceeded north on Western Avenue.

Frank didn't see any celebrities walking around on the Avenue of the Stars, at least none he recognized. There were a lot of people who were *trying* to pass themselves off as stars, young women in spike heels and form-fitting slacks, Jesus, walking poodles, and guys hustling down the street in yellow or electric blue suits or sport coats, wearing sunglasses, guys who couldn't possibly be in as much of a hurry as they were letting on. Frank decided that he'd rather be just a regular guy.

The avenue was lined with trendy shops, upscale mirror-walled office buildings, big hotels with valet parking. Frank very nearly rear-ended two different cars—one BMW and one Range Rover—as he craned his neck looking for the address, and he finally parked in a pay lot and set off on foot.

Vickie Warren's office was in an old two-story building wedged in between two skyscrapers, as if the building's owner had bowed his neck and said, I'm not moving no matter how much I'm offered. Through a door with glass inserts was a stairway leading up. Frank climbed the steps to the second floor, found the office, then went in and sat down on a couch beside a black girl who was reading a *People* magazine. There were audition notices thumbtacked to a bulletin board, and on the far wall were black-and-white photos of Michelle Pfeiffer, Demi Moore, and Dustin Hoffman. Frank wondered if Vickie Warren represented any of those people. He doubted it. He crossed his legs and waited.

The receptionist wore big round, rose-tinted glasses. She was a puffy-cheeked woman, middle thirties, and was saying into the phone, "You bet, Stan. Of course. The one I have in mind is just the type. David Caruso personified, what's the . . . ?" She slid a pad over in front of her and wrote something down. "Four-thirty, right. Right. He'll be there." She hung up, said to the black girl, "Just a minute, Sandy, be right with you," then said to Frank, "You ever done a cop?"

Frank looked around, thinking someone he hadn't noticed must be in the room. "I'm not an actor," he finally said.

"Too bad. Would you like to *audition* for a cop?"

"Actually, what I'd like to do is see Vickie Warren," Frank said, feeling uncomfortable.

The receptionist stood. She wore a pale green skirt and a dark green jacket with padded shoulders. "Don't move," she said, then went quickly into the inner office.

The black girl nudged Frank and laid her magazine aside. "They always think they've got you pegged," she said, "in a certain slot."

Frank looked at her.

"I can get work if I want," she said. "I need to know two lines, they fit in any part I'm offered. 'Hey, baby, you want a date?' and 'I'd do anything for some of those drugs, sugar.' You need to learn, 'I don't like the way this is coming down,' and, 'You okay with that?' You're going to need both of them. Also, if you really want some consideration, put on the audition form that you're willing to show your dick. It's the latest thing." She picked up and thumbed through the magazine.

The receptionist returned and sat on her ankle behind her desk. "Okay, I'm Vickie," she said.

Frank blinked.

"I get a live one like that," she said, "maybe once a month. And once a month I don't have anybody."

"I won't take up your time. I'm looking for one of your clients."

"For what kind of part? Obviously, cops I don't have right now."

"Darla Bern," Frank said.

Vickie Warren crossed her forearms and leaned on them. "Hookers I've got by the hatful."

The black girl testily rattled magazine pages.

"I'm not looking to cast anything," Frank said.

"I suppose you're a stalker, then," Vickie Warren said. "I've got 'em that would love to be stalked. Get their names in the newspapers."

"No, I'm . . . she's a friend."

Vickie Warren opened a bottom drawer, thumbed through files, drew out one folder and laid it in front of her. "You on her list?"

"I'm not sure. Good list, or bad list?" Frank looked at the black girl, hoping for a smile, received none, and decided that comedy wasn't his thing.

"The list my clients give me," Vickie Warren said, "that tells me who I can give information to. If you're not on it, you couldn't sweat anything out of me." She took a sheet of paper from the folder. "What's your name?"

Frank licked his lips. He wasn't ready for this. He said quickly, "Randolph Money," and prepared to bolt from the office in case Money was someone Vickie Warren happened to know.

She smirked as she ran a red-nailed index finger down the page. "You have any money, Mr. Money?" She bent closer to squint through her glasses at the list. "Yeah, okay," she said, then flipped to a fresh sheet on her notepad and began to write. Finished, she tore off the sheet and offered it to Frank. "You sure you couldn't at least *read* for a cop? I need a warm body, don't you know?"

Frank called Darla's number from a pay station across from the Century Plaza Hotel, and got her machine. He listened to the message for long enough to identify her voice, then hung up, walked up the street, and paid his parking. Then he steered the Cherokee a few blocks north, made a left, and followed his map west on Santa Monica Boulevard.

He took the boulevard in stop-and-go traffic all the way to Santa Monica, and found Darla's place around four in the afternoon. It was a small wooden house on the beach, with a screened-in porch and scraggly front yard, in a block of almost identical houses all facing a narrow asphalt street and backing up to the Pacific Ocean. Surf rolled two hundred yards to the west, foamy crests that broke at sea and battered the flotsam-strewn beach in an endless parade. Frank parked in front and made his way up the sidewalk, skirted a flower bed overgrown with weeds, and trotted around to the back. With the ocean behind him he peered in three different windows. He saw a bedroom featuring a king-size water bed and mirrored ceiling, a dining room with a breakfront cabinet, and a kitchen with a microwave and standup freezer. No one was home, all the lights off. He went around the south side of the house, past a vacant carport, and jogged up the driveway to the street. Then he backed the Cherokee up and stopped three houses away. The street was a cul-de-sac; he faced the lone entrance to the block. He killed the engine, rolled down the window, and listened to the ocean swish and hiss. Cool, salty wind blew on his cheek. His eyelids drooped—Jesus, two hours' sleep in the past forty-eight. His chin lowered down to his chest. In seconds, he accompanied the ocean noises with a series of snores.

A brilliant headlamp beam stabbed the interior of the Cherokee, touched Frank's face for an instant, and then moved on. He started and opened his eyes. It was night; pinpoint stars twinkled in a blue-black sky, encircling a rind of moon. Lights shone in windows up and down the block. The surf continued to pound; somewhere a wailing guitar twanged, Willie Nelson singing the blues. In the driveways sat small cars and minivans, none of which had been there when he'd fallen asleep. The dashboard clock showed 10:42 Texas time, two hours earlier in California. Frank sat up and squinted toward Darla's house. A light-colored convertible, likely a Chrysler LeBaron, was nestled in under the carport. On the screened-in porch, a desk lamp glowed. Frank reached for the door handle, then froze.

The headlights which had awakened him drifted to the curb in front of Darla's house, then went out. The vehicle was either black or dark blue, a goat-roper car of some kind, likely a Bronco. The driver's door opened and a man got out, a big, square-shouldered form in the moonlight, and crossed the yard to knock on the screen. The light filtering out from the desk lamp showed a slightly jutted jaw, and shoulder-length straight blond hair. Frank couldn't see too well in the semi-light but was pretty sure that he'd never laid eyes on the guy. The man wore western boots, jeans, a shirt with quilting at the shoulders, and he carried a Stetson in his hands. The screen door opened. As he stepped across the threshold, the man placed the hat on top of his head.

Frank now dug the .38 police special he'd bought from Wilbur Dale from the glove compartment. He climbed cautiously out of the Cherokee and made his way up the grassy corridor in between two houses toward the ocean. Suddenly he halted in his tracks as light from a side window on his left flooded over him, and held his breath as a woman inside the house—middle-aged, graying, wearing a lounging robe—turned a page in the book she was reading. She never looked up. Frank moved on as if walking on eggs, cleared the space between the houses, and tiptoed out onto the beach.

He ran in heavy sand, his soles sinking a full three inches with every step, and crossed the distance to the back of Darla's place in a count of five. Now he was in the walkway between her house and the one next door. Sand burrs pricked his ankles through his socks; he raised first one foot and then the other, pulled the burrs out, and tossed them away. He waited for his breathing to slow, then got down in a crouch and crept toward the street, halting at the corner where the screened porch connected on to the front of the house. He looked to his right. The Cherokee, ghost pale in the moonlight, sat at the curb fifty yards away. He'd been right about the car now parked directly in front; it was a Bronco, the big spare tire jutting out from the rear. Slowly, his pulse racing, Frank peered around the corner through the screen. About ten feet from his nose was Darla's suntanned naked butt.

Actually, only part of one cheek was visible. She wore ripped-look jean shorts, cut off an inch below her ass with a stitched opening halfway up the back, displaying a rectangle of flesh the color of butter rum. She was bent over in front of the big blond man, handing him a glass filled with ice and amber liquid. He was seated in a wicker chair. As he sipped, she backed up and sank down on a matching love seat. A round wicker hassock was directly in front of her. She extended perfectly formed legs, propped up her feet, and crossed her ankles.

The blond guy said, "I don't like it for shit."

To which Darla replied, "He said he'd be here, Gerald." In addition to the cutoffs she wore a white tank top. She draped a slim arm over the back of the love seat.

"It was on the news," Gerald said. "You see it, about Basil?"

"Does it make you sad?" Darla reached to the floor and picked up a can of diet Coke.

"They know his name."

"So what? He's not going to tell anybody anything unless his ghost returns."

"The girl said somebody shot him. The girl we . . ."

"Doesn't mean anything," Darla said. "Those federal guys may have done it. They lie all the time."

Gerald took a large swig from his glass and made a face. "It makes me nervous is all. You having any auditions?"

"One today, with about thirty other people. French maid. If you're so worried, I'll take your part of the money."

"I'm just afraid it was Randolph took Basil's share."

"What if he did? It'll make more for us, Gerald."

"I just don't trust the guy."

"Come on. You don't even know him."

"Yeah, but all that about a fringe guy, keeping it a secret."

"If you've got a complaint," Darla said, "tell it to him. Here he comes." She gestured toward the street with the Coke can, then took a swallow.

A long dark car, a Caddy, had now parked behind the Bronco. Frank inched further back from the street and crouched even lower, the barrel of the .38 resting against his inner thigh. A slightly round figure crossed the yard. The figure emerged from the darkness into the light. Randolph Money, of course, with the alligator-and-leather suitcase swinging by its handle, bumping his hip. He wore a pale yellow sport coat along with a royal blue knit shirt, high open collar standing up on both sides of his throat, dark blue slacks, and two-tone blue-and-white loafers with a tassel.

Money grinned, his nose casting a shadow on his cheek, dark spaces between his wide-gapped teeth. "As I see it, you're expecting someone."

Gerald looked, his gaze roaming Money head to toe, and didn't say anything. Darla crossed over and undid the latch, opened the door with a protesting creak from the spring, and stood aside. Money walked onto the porch and sat in the love seat. Darla remained near the entrance, one arm akimbo, one hip thrust slightly out. Money laid the suitcase flat on the ottoman.

Frank's leg suddenly itched like blazes. Mosquitoes. He gritted his teeth and resisted the urge to scratch.

Visible through the screen, Gerald used a forefinger to tilt his hat back. "You kill the guy? The TV said Basil Gershwin . . ."

Money brushed chubby hands together. "Of course. You think it was some amateur?"

"Helluva way, the guy doing all that."

"He was a weak link. Too subject to suspicion, his record. What, you don't like getting more of a share? I told you I'd take care of you."

"The Molly guy was a pussy, that's one thing. Basil was one of us."

Money put a hand over his heart. "You're breaking me up, you know? Come on, let's do it and part company. You want to pay for the guy's funeral, hey. I told you, your share." Money snapped the catches, spun the suitcase around and opened the lid. "*Voilà*, babes."

Gerald murmured, "Jesus," and leaned forward, his jaw slack. Darla left the door and came nearer. She bent over and placed her hands on her knees, staring.

Money's arm was draped over the back of the love seat, hand down, hidden from the two on the porch, visible to Frank. Money's fingers wiggled. His coat sleeve billowed slightly. A pearl-handled derringer dropped into his palm, Money still grinning, his posture relaxed. "We can count it out," he said, "one for you, one for you, all that."

Frank tensed and rose to his feet, watching through the screen as Darla said in a half-whisper, "How much is there?" Gerald leaned even nearer the suitcase, his gaze riveted on the bundles of cash, as Money brought the pistol up over the back of the love seat. Frank opened his mouth to yell a warning, too late, as Money shot Gerald in the center of the forehead, Gerald's head rolling back on his neck, a sigh escaping from his lungs as he fell backward to sprawl into the wicker chair, his arms flapping like a scarecrow's.

Frank gritted his teeth, raised his leg and kicked at the screen. The wire came loose from the molding with a metallic rip. Money's head snapped around, the derringer aimed at Darla's chest, Randolph Money's fat lips parting, wide-gapped teeth showing in an expression that was part surprise and part snarling anger.

Frank wedged in through the tear and jammed the barrel of

the .38 in Money's ear. Hard. Money's head lurched to one side, but otherwise he didn't move, keeping the derringer leveled on Darla's midsection. The three froze in place for a full five seconds, Darla not breathing, Frank watching Money's index finger, thinking, *The slightest pressure on the trigger, the bastard's dead.*

Finally, Money grinned. "I don't suppose there's any point, telling you I'll trade you her life for mine, is there?"

"You've got to be kidding," Frank said.

"I just thought, sometimes a man gets pussy-whipped. Remembers how good a woman gave it to him." Money laughed, relaxed his hand, let the derringer dangle upside down by the trigger guard. "You travel far and wide, Tex," Money said. "I told a man just the other day, I always liked that Frank White guy."

Frank reached down and took the derringer, slipped the little pistol in his pocket, risked a glance over at Gerald. Gerald's Stetson was down over his eyes, his head flopped to his right, his mouth slack, a red stain spreading on the cushion behind him. Frank took the .38 out of Money's ear and stepped back.

Darla leaned over and patted the money in the suitcase. "Take me somewhere on this, Frank. We can . . ." She looked up at him, batted long lashes.

"Now *you've* got to be kidding," Frank said.

Darla's mouth circled into a pout.

Money half-turned to face Frank, and spread his hands, palms up. "Christ, I should have known. She got in touch with you, didn't she?"

Frank watched him. Darla's breathing quickened.

"Of course she did," Money said. His chin moved up and down in a wistful nod. "Only way you could have known me on the telephone, Frank, only way you could ever guess it was somebody you knew when you were down." He laughed out loud, tightly closing his eyes. "Christ, I had it figured perfect. As far as you knew, the whole bunch of us were in California and you'd never see any of us again. I counted on everything except the woman-scorned factor. The goddam woman was more interested in getting even with you than in getting the money, now isn't that a kick in the head?"

"I recognized that expression you use all the time," Frank said. " 'As I see it . . .' "

"You did? Bullshit, Frank. You may think that's what it was, but it was seeing Darla. If she'd kept out of your sight like she was supposed to, we'd be home free. My own fucking fault. Christ, my own fault. Shame on me, huh?" Money sadly shook his head.

Darla took a step in Frank's direction. "Frank, I . . ."

Frank pointed the .38 at her. "Don't dare, Darla. That's far enough. You tried to hurt somebody close to me. Don't think I wouldn't shoot you."

Darla halted in her tracks. Her lips parted.

Money flopped down on the love seat. "Waste of breath, babe. It's a new one on you, a man you can't control. What we have here, Darla, is a man gone straight." He regarded Frank through slitted eyes. "What now, old Frank? You going to shoot me down like the dirty dog I am, save the day or something? At least steal the money, will you? I've got to have *some* fucking thing to feel good about. Honest people I cannot stand."

"Oh, I'm taking the money," Frank said, gesturing with the pistol. "Up. Come on, up now." He closed the suitcase, snapped the catches with one hand, hoisted the load up by the handle.

Money rose, looked at Darla, and shrugged. "At least the guy's making a little sense," Money said.

Frank herded the pair through the door, off the porch, and across the yard, directing them with the pistol, Darla moving in hesitant baby steps, watching over her shoulder, Money shuffling along shaking his head and laughing out loud. Frank set the suitcase down behind the Cherokee, fumbled for his keys, opened the tailgate, hefted the suitcase inside, and slammed the door. Halfway down the block a man came out in his bathrobe, yelled, "Let's have some quiet, huh?" and went back inside.

Frank now said, "Okay, come over here, Darla," and gestured

again with the pistol. "Stay where you are, Randolph, just her."

Darla tilted her chin as she walked nearer to Frank. Money kept his distance, his expression resigned, knowing what was coming, but also knowing there was nothing he could do about it.

Frank kept the pistol trained on Money as he said to Darla, "You're the one with the parachute. You know that, don't you?"

She made a noise that was near a sob. "You'll let me go, won't you, Frank? Won't you?"

"Christ, I'm not believing this," Money said.

"Not a chance," Frank said. "You're a been-around girl. Think. The guy was going to kill you. Talk about him to the feds. You can save yourself some time in the joint, doing that, will probably get out in time to act again. Might be a *Driving Miss Daisy* role by then, but at least you'll get to see the world. Randolph won't."

She seemed to brighten. "I am a good actress."

Frank felt the barest twinge of pity. "I'm sure you are. Tell me, you think you can work yourself up to tell about this guy?" He jerked his head in Money's direction.

Darla looked at Money as if she'd never seen him before. Money met her gaze for an instant, then looked at his feet. Darla turned to Frank, her features setting in a hopeful look. "Till I'm so hoarse I can't say any more, Frank," she said.

When the black-and-white Santa Monica P.D. squad car pulled up behind the Cadillac, Frank had Darla and Money in the front yard, lying on their faces. Frank leaned over Darla and said, "Remember, now, just like you said. You can't talk your way all the way out, but you can do yourself a lot of good. Believe it or not, Darla, I'm sort of pulling for you." Knots of people stood around in the adjacent yards, gawking, some of them still in their pajamas.

Money turned his head to one side. "You be nice to my fucking money, Frank."

Two uniformed patrolmen left the squad vehicle at a sprint, revolvers drawn. Frank lowered his .38 to his side and said loudly to the cops, "Good work. Dead guy inside, on that screened porch." He started to walk away, toward the Bronco.

One of the policemen, a young guy with a mustache, stood guard over Money and Darla while the other man ran toward the porch. The guy with the mustache yelled to Frank, "You get statements from these people?" He waved his pistol at Darla. "Keep your head down, miss." He watched the exposed cheek of her ass.

"Tell them at the precinct," Frank said loudly, over his shoulder, "that they'll be hearing from a Dallas federal prosecutor named Felicia Tate. Also, possibly an FBI agent named Turner. I'm not sure which one's going to call." He increased his pace, walking at a fast clip past the nose of the Cherokee.

The cop looked toward Frank, then at his prisoners, unsure of himself now, not understanding exactly what was going on. He shouted, "Hey. What station you say you were from? L.A.P.D., right?"

Frank now had the Cherokee's door open, and called out to the cop, "You'll find the murder weapon on the porch, with the guy's prints. Good work, you hear?" He dropped the .38 inside on the seat, fell in behind the wheel, started the engine, and pulled away from the curb.

The cop yelled as Frank rolled past. "What precinct you say you were . . . ?"

Money lifted his head. "You owe me money, asshole," Randolph Money shouted, loudly enough for Frank to hear him over the hiss of the ocean and the Cherokee's churning engine.

Darla raised up and batted her eyes at the policeman. "Can I stand up now?" she said. "These mosquitoes are eating me alive."

When the unmarked Plymouth four-door pulled to the curb in front of Darla's house, the Santa Monica P.D.'s crime scene unit had things in high gear. The house and grounds were cordoned off with yellow tape, and uniformed officers guarded the perimeters. Forensics and crime lab people moved around on the lighted screened porch, dusting for prints, taking blood samples. As two men in dark suits alighted from the Plymouth, assistant medical examiners lifted Gerald Hodge from the wicker chair and dumped him into a body bag.

The suits hustled across the lawn and approached one of the officers, a squinty-eyed young man who seemed to be suffering from hay fever. One of the suits exhibited his shield. "FBI," he said. "What's going on here?"

The policeman looked closely at the ID while snuffling through his nose. "This is a murder scene," he said. "What's it look like?"

"We've got instructions from our Dallas office," the FBI agent said, "to set up surveillance on the occupant of this house. A . . ." He checked his notes. "Darla Bern," he finally said.

The cop peered up the sidewalk, to where the M.E.s now lugged what was left of Gerald Hodge out the screen door and toward the waiting meat wagon. "Darla Bern's downtown in jail," the cop said. "And there's nobody else inside for you to survey. The dead guy's headed for the morgue. If you want to follow him, I suppose that's up to you."

33

Agent Turner said over the phone, "Trouble with you guys is, you keep everybody up all night. Give it up, Gertrude. Long as you keep this shit up you're not going to sleep a wink, and neither am I."

Frank stepped away from the pay station and looked toward the LAX boarding gate, only four or five passengers left in line, the gate agent tearing boarding passes as people went by toting carry-on luggage. Visible through the plate glass window, a 747 sat ready with its rudder lights winking on and off, on and off. "I don't have time for bullshit," Frank said to Turner.

"Makes two of us, Thomas. I'm not real crazy about you calling me at home. I got a right to sit on my ass once in a while."

"Call the Santa Monica, California, police department," Frank said. "They've got Randolph Money and Darla Bern in custody. Probably they'll hook you up with Darla. She's got some things to tell you."

"We're already putting a surveillance team on her. You ask me, I think you got Felicia Tate snowed along with everybody else. Where you calling from, Frank?"

"You don't have time to pinpoint me, Turner. Give it up. Look, I've got to catch my plane." Frank kicked the suitcase on the floor beside him. "I'm bringing the money with me. Delta

Flight seven-eight-one, lands DFW around four in the morning."

"Look, we'll have some guys meet you. Nice guys. You can relax, have a cup of coffee . . ."

"Call the Santa Monica P.D. All it'll cost you is a phone call. Oh, and listen. I've spent some of the money."

"Why am I not surprised at that?" Turner said. "What is it, you got a gambling problem?"

"I had to pay for my plane ticket, plus I've taken some to pay parking at this airport four or five days."

Static crackled on the line for a count of four. Then Turner said, "You get receipts, you hear me? If you think I'm taking responsibility for that, you've got your head up your ass is all I can tell you."

Frank hung up, took two steps in the direction of the boarding gate, then stopped in his tracks. He returned to the phone, called Meg's home number using his credit card, waited through five rings, and got her machine. Frank softly closed his eyes. She slept like a rock, and calling her after 10 P.M. was useless. He waited through the message, listened for the beep, and cleared his throat. He gave his flight number and estimated time of arrival, started to hang up, then placed the receiver to his ear once again.

"I'm coming home," Frank said. "Reserve a life for me, okay?"

The bump-and-screech of the wheels hitting the runway jarred Frank into wakefulness. He was in a double aisle seat with the armrest folded down, his head reclining on a pincushion-sized white pillow. He rubbed his sore neck and watched through the porthole as the landing lights flashed by, a billboard in the distance showing a full-length shot of the Loew's Anatole. Frank thought fleetingly of the ice-cream stand. All up and down the length of the cabin, people stretched, yawned, and tossed little white pillows away. The aircraft braked, made a sweeping right turn, and taxied up to the unfolding accordion walkway. The engines shut down and whined to a standstill. The eastern horizon was beginning to gray.

A flight attendant approached. "Mr. White?"

Frank watched her—pretty face, wide brown eyes, uncertainty in her look as if she wondered whether he was about to attack. "Yes?" he said.

"They've asked, some *people* have asked, if you'd remain on board until the other passengers have . . ." Visible beyond her, a girl in jeans rose on tiptoes to drag a folded coat down from the overhead compartment.

Frank leaned back and touched his fingertips together, pressing his shin against the seatback in front of him. "They're FBI," he said.

Her lips parted. She uttered a little gasp.

"And, yes, I'll wait," Frank said. "Relax, miss. I'm way too tired to pull a hijacking, okay?"

Turner, Felicia Tate, and two stone-faced FBIs in suits waited for him as he stepped clear of the skyway. Frank raised the suitcase to shoulder level, and one of the suits yanked it from his grasp. Tate and Turner hustled him across the terminal, past the baggage claim and restroom signs, through double doors into the VIP Lounge. The carpeted lounge was deserted, booths and cushioned seats, a horseshoe bar in the center. Frank sat down in a half-moon booth with Tate on his left, Turner on the other side. He rubbed his eyes. "You bother calling the Santa Monica P.D.? Or was I wasting my breath?"

Turner wore his windbreaker with the bureau letters in gold across the back, and jeans. "This Randolph Money. Guy's done a lot of shit."

Tate wore loose-fitting jeans and a man's white shirt with the sleeves rolled up to her elbows. Her makeup was all in place, and Frank thought she looked nicer than he'd ever seen her. "You're familiar enough with his voice," she said, "that you can testify it was him on the phone, telling you where to take the money?"

Frank relaxed. He was so tired. "I'll bet if I'm not," he said, "you'll see that I am before I take any witness stand. How much did Darla tell you?"

"Jesus," Turner said, "who'd have thought the banker switched the suitcases? We'd have figured it out eventually."

"I'll just bet you would have," Frank said. "All these financial, these swindler guys, there's a network."

"The board of directors at the bank never even saw the loan AP," Tate said, leaning forward. "Boyle faked all that, carried the AP into the meeting with another couple of loans, then told everybody he'd gotten the loan approved. Faked the board's signatures."

"Boyle and Randolph Money go way back, to when the savings and loans were riding high," Turner said. "Before Money went to the pen the first time. He'd kept Boyle's chestnuts out of the fire once by keeping his mouth shut, so when he called with a new deal, Boyle couldn't wait to get in on it."

"Randolph didn't plan to leave any witnesses," Frank said. "The rifle he used on Basil Gershwin and the pistol he did the banker with, I doubt Darla can tell you where he dumped them. I suspect Money also had plans to kill Wilbur Dale, eventually, the guy who supplied the counterfeit money. When Wilbur finds that out, you'll have yourself another witness. Wilbur loves to talk, I'll warn you about him." He bent his head to rub his eyes. "What about the warrant for me? I've got to get some sleep, and I'm so beat I don't particularly care if I have to sleep in jail. I stole some New Mexico license plates, by the way."

Tate and Turner exchanged a look. Turner said, "Sounds like a major felony to me. Get the fuck out of here, Frank, I've gotten tired of looking at you." He rose to let Frank out of the booth, and Frank started to slide around.

Turner reached over and stopped him. "Hey, you get those receipts I was talking about?"

Frank stood up and grinned. "Naw. Guess I'm going to have to owe you, okay?"

She waited in the walkway halfway to the baggage claim, leaning on crutches, her right foot in a metal splint and suspended off the floor. As he approached she hobbled forward, threw her arms around his neck, and let the crutches fall. They kissed, their tongues meeting, held the kiss for a good ten seconds, held the embrace for even longer. Fine brown hair tickled his cheek. She smelled of lilac.

He grasped her shoulders and held her away. "You're hurt."

She showed an impish grin. "My toe. No mo'."

He was suddenly sad. "I got you in trouble, not telling you about my past from the beginning. I deserve whatever I get for that."

Her gaze was level. "I don't suppose I was up front either, Frank. Should we start over with introductions?"

He felt a smile spreading his mouth. "Sure, I guess so. How about this?" He deepened his voice. "Hello, I'm Frank White, fresh from the pen and currently on parole. How's that?"

She hugged his arm, and winked up at him. "And I'm Meg Carpenter, rich as all getout. I think that starts us off on the right foot, don't you?"